Jeanne Winer

The Furthest
City Light

Bella
BOOKS

2012

Bella Books, Inc.
P.O. Box 10543
Tallahassee, FL 32302

Printed in the United States of America on acid-free paper
First published 2012

Editor: Katherine V. Forrest
Cover Designer: Kiaro Creative

ISBN 13: 978-1-59493-325-7

PUBLISHER'S NOTE

Dedication

For Leslie, *el amor de mi vida loca*

And for Public Defenders everywhere

About the Author

Jeanne Winer was a criminal defense attorney in Colorado for thirty-five years. During that time, she represented thousands of people accused of murder, kidnapping, rape, assault, robbery, theft, etcetera. Now, she's a full-time writer. During the eighties, she visited Nicaragua twice—in 1985 and again in 1987—in support of the Sandinista revolution. The trips radically altered her life: the way she saw the world, her health and her commitment to human rights. Like her heroine, she is a rock climber, a hiker and a skier. She's also a third-degree black belt in karate. Mostly she lives in Boulder, Colorado with her partner, and periodically in Taos, New Mexico where she wrote the bulk of this novel.

Please visit Jeanne at *www.jeannewiner.com*

PROLOGUE

Zihuatanejo, Mexico

Edith Piaf famously sang, "*Je ne regrette rien.*" Lucky her. Although it's hard to believe anyone could sail into middle age without regretting something. Perhaps when she sang it was true, but later when she was alone again without an audience, without her makeup, it was only partly true and partly defiant wishful thinking. Which I applaud. Nothing wrong with defiant wishful thinking. Criminal defense lawyers, like myself, have won many difficult cases by engaging in exactly that kind of thinking. It's what gives us confidence when the facts are lined up against us, drives our rhetoric across the finish line when, without it, we'd sputter to a stop halfway through the trial at the time an acquittal seems hopelessly far away, a moth-sized beacon in a raging storm. No, nothing wrong with defiant wishful thinking unless it begins to dominate more than just your career.

Now that I've landed here in Mexico where I intend to rest and recover, I'm alone again, without an audience, without my makeup. There's no one to sing to here, except myself. I'm standing on a bright pink balcony overlooking the water. I've managed to find the same studio apartment that my partner Vickie and I rented a few years ago. Back when we were a stable twosome, the American dream, a doctor and a lawyer. At the time, though, just a pair of grateful snowbirds from Colorado looking to land on a warm sandy beach and take a couple of breaths before returning to our busy lives. Our friends, of course, thought we had it all. Actually, so did we. Had it all: what a ridiculous sounding cliché. Makes you want to grab a nice sharp pin, stick it in, and hear that satisfying pop. Which I suppose is what I did, in retrospect a terrible mistake. And not even the only one.

How could I have been so careless, stepping out like that without looking to see what was coming? A year ago, I was cohabiting with my partner and just about to meet a new client, someone who would become my friend, an innocent woman accused of murder. It's a burden and a privilege to defend an innocent person. It's every defense lawyer's dream. Makes you go all out, and then it would make sense to stop and rest but you can't remember how, and besides, where's the thrill in that? Might as well keep on going until you finally run out of gas. So I headed south, bypassing Mexico, and went to Nicaragua, a small car accident of a country, mired in a bloody civil war. And, in a convoluted way, the perfect destination, the trip I may never stop paying for. Vickie warned me, but I didn't listen. Vickie was always warning me.

Vickie Ferraro. Who told me love was the last refuge we have against the world and all its sorrows. Who I may have lost along the route, the only belonging that mattered.

But it's late now. Time to go inside, unpack my duffel, turn on the ceiling fan, and make myself at home. Catch my breath. Sleep. As I start to turn away, though, the view begins to change. I can't move. I'd forgotten the spectacular sunsets here, the beauty that is sometimes possible. I feel mesmerized. No, I feel awe. Suddenly, I realize there was no way I could have gotten here except the way I came. Maybe that's what Edith meant. If so, *je ne regrette rien.*

PART I:
THE KIND OF CASE EVERY PUBLIC DEFENDER WAS BORN FOR

CHAPTER ONE

Boulder, Colorado ten months earlier

"*I have walked out in rain—and back in rain. I have outwalked the furthest city light.*"

Those were the first words Emily Watkins said to me when I met her at the Boulder County Jail.

Not, "Are you my public defender?" Or, "Hey lady, you gotta get me off. I didn't do it." Not even, "What the hell took you so long?" I'd been in a two-day pre-trial motions hearing on a kidnapping case and

Ray Martinelli, another lawyer in our office, had been holding her hand until I could get over there.

Ray, of course, had briefed me about the case. My new client had apparently stabbed her husband in the stomach and then barricaded herself in the bathroom. For more than an hour, according to her statement, she'd listened to him wandering around the apartment, slamming doors and turning on the television and radio.

The next morning, she'd ventured out and found his body lying in a pool of blood in front of the television set. Afterward, she'd sat down on the couch and watched a Jane Fonda wannabe in a silver leotard demonstrate to a group of middle-aged housewives how to firm up their thighs and buttocks. As soon as the show was over, she'd called the police and confessed to the murder. Her motive—if she had one—was unknown. The last woman I'd defended for killing someone had shot her pimp in the chest because he'd refused to share his bag of Cheetos with her.

Based on past experience, I'd been expecting a teary, panic-stricken lady with furtive eyes, alternately defensive and apologetic. Someone who would collapse into hysterics as soon as I mentioned the possibility of prison. Instead, I met an intelligent, dignified woman in her mid-thirties, physically fit with an enviable tan. A gardener, perhaps, like my girlfriend Vickie. The woman looked solemn, but relieved to see me, as if she'd been waiting too long outside a restaurant or a movie theater and was beginning to wonder if she'd penciled the wrong date into her calendar. Oh good, you made it. I have so much to tell you. I stabbed my husband with a pair of scissors and the police have charged me with murder.

I have walked out in rain—and back in rain. I have outwalked the furthest city light. I'd always loved those lines. I hadn't read the poem since college, but I still remembered it. "They're from 'Acquainted with the Night' by Robert Frost," I said.

"Oh my God." She looked stunned, then smiled delightedly. "I've never met anyone who knew I was quoting Frost. A public defender who reads poetry! Oh my goodness, Hal must have killed me after all and I've died and gone to heaven."

"In which case, you wouldn't need me," I said, offering her my hand. "My name is Rachel Stein."

"Emily Watkins. Pleased to meet you."

We shook hands, and then sat down on a pair of green plastic chairs. The room was small and windowless, about three times the size of a telephone booth. Someone had recently doused the floor and walls with undiluted Pine-Sol. Ah, nothing like the smell of an extremely clean bathroom. I pulled out my legal pad and set it on my lap.

"So, would you like to talk about your case?"

Emily made a face. "Oh, do we have to? I'd much rather talk about poetry. Almost no one reads it nowadays. Your colleague—what's his name?"

"Ray."

"Ray," she repeated. "He was very nice, but clueless. I mentioned 'The Love Song of J. Alfred Prufrock' and he just looked at me. Finally, he asked if it was a new play on Broadway."

"A rock opera?"

She smiled and waited. I was being tested again: tell me you know this poem, too, and maybe then we'll talk. I studied her face, which looked older now that I was paying close attention. Her eyes were sky-blue, but completely opaque; looking at them was like looking at someone wearing mirrored sunglasses. Silently, she was telling me, "Don't bother trying to find me." But I didn't believe her, so I began reciting the famous opening lines of the poem by T.S. Eliot she was referring to.

"Let us go then, you and I, when the evening is spread out against the sky."

"Like a patient etherized upon a table," Emily continued.

"Is that how you feel?" I asked.

She looked surprised. "Are you my therapist or my lawyer?"

"Both," I said. "We're on a tight budget."

Emily smiled at my joke. "Okay, then, yes."

I nodded. "Well, given the circumstances, that seems like an appropriate reaction."

She smiled again. "So, you've determined that I'm sane and competent to proceed. What else do you want to know?"

Rachel, I told myself, she's as smart as you are. This one's going to hurt if it doesn't come out right. Of course the junkie in me—addicted from day one to the drama of my chosen career—was almost whimpering with joy. Damn the torpedoes, this was the kind of case every public defender was born for: the chance to help, to explain, to protect, to defend, to make right. Hell, the chance to change the course of another person's life. Hubris? You bet.

I picked up my pen and wrote the date, October 15, 1985, on the top of the page. "Usually I start by asking my clients for a little background information, but if you want to tell me what happened, we can start there as well."

She shrugged. "There's not much to tell. He was coming toward me and I happened to have a pair of scissors in my hand, so I stuck them in his gut. Poor Hal, he looked so surprised. He looked as if I'd betrayed him, which I suppose I had."

"How come you happened to have a pair of scissors in your hand?"

She looked blank for a moment. "Oh, because I was in the middle of sewing. I was making a pair of his pants a little longer."

"I see." I wrote down the answers, then waited for her to expound on them. Emily nodded, but remained silent. How odd. Most people, even if they were guilty, would at least try to explain their behavior.

I dropped the pen, signaling that for now our conversation would be more of a discussion than an interview, a chance to explore various possibilities before settling on any particular "truth."

"Well, in cases like this, defendants generally rely on certain defenses such as denial, accident, heat of passion, or self-defense."

"Or I could just plead guilty, right?"

"You could, but I wouldn't recommend it. You're facing a life sentence."

She bit her lip. "I think I should just plead guilty. After all, I'm the one who stabbed him. I'm the one responsible for his death." She paused. "He *is* dead, isn't he?" Suddenly she looked nervous.

"What if he wasn't?" I asked for the hell of it.

"If he wasn't? Well, I guess I'd stop feeling so guilty and start worrying more about retaliation. Hal doesn't like to be opposed." She was watching the door now as if Hal might burst in at any moment, retaliation on his mind.

I shook my head. "I'm sorry, Emily. I didn't mean to confuse you. He's dead."

"Ah." She nodded sadly. "That's what I thought. And so I think I'll go ahead and plead guilty."

As a public defender, I'd interviewed more than a thousand clients, many of whom were mentally ill. Emily wasn't crazy, but she was missing something that most people would agree was essential. During that first interview, I couldn't have said what it was, but I noticed I was beginning to feel alarmed for her. In retrospect, I would say Emily lacked a sense of self-preservation. In a Darwinian universe like ours, without protection, she was doomed.

"Emily, did you think your husband was going to hurt you when he was coming toward you?"

"Of course he was."

"Then why isn't it self-defense?"

Emily looked at me as if she hated to be the bearer of bad news. "Because I was still there after ten years of it, because I never left. For the last three years, I even had a suitcase filled with some of my favorite clothes hidden in the upstairs closet. Hal never found it."

I considered giving her a short lecture on battered women, but she beat me to it.

"Yes," she said, smiling wearily. "I know. I've read a number of books about battered women. I know all about the cycle of violence, the theories of learned helplessness, the analogy between a battered woman and a laboratory rat who keeps pressing the bar and mostly gets shocked, but occasionally gets rewarded with a pellet of food. I know all about it and I'm sure you do, too. But in the end, the jury will still wonder, why didn't she leave?"

I glanced at my watch. I was supposed to be at the Justice Center at one thirty. Judge Solomon would be irritable if I was more than five minutes late. On the other hand, Judge Solomon was often irritable even when I was on time. I looked up again at my new client. "Okay, so why didn't you leave?"

"That's just it," she said, rising from her chair to help me end the interview. "I don't know. It just never seemed like a truly viable option. I could picture myself pulling out the packed suitcase from behind all the boxes in the closet. I could picture myself grabbing my purse and the keys to my car, picking up the suitcase and heading for the front door. But I could never picture myself actually walking through it. I suppose I was like a bird that's been in a cage too long. Even if someone unlocks the cage and swings the door open, it remains on its perch staring at its freedom, but not moving."

I slipped my pen and legal pad into my briefcase, then stood up to face her. "Then that's what we'll tell the jury. I'll be back as soon as I've finished reviewing all the police reports. In the meantime, don't give up."

"Now that I have you, I won't." Suddenly, she swayed a little and I grabbed her arm. "My goodness," she murmured, "Hal's really dead, isn't he? And I'm really here."

"I'm afraid so." I pushed the door open and checked the hallway, which was empty. Normally, Emily would have simply crossed the hall to the women's cellblock, knocked on the thick metal door, and they would have let her in. "Would you like me to call a guard?"

She shook her head. "Oh no. A cup of tea and I'll be fine. Thank you."

***

By the end of the day, I'd skimmed through the initial police reports, which included interviews with the coroner, the emergency room doctor, the emergency medical technicians who'd first responded to the scene, the defendant, two neighbors who hadn't heard or seen anything, and the deceased's elderly mother who lived in a nursing home in Denver. There were no surprises. My client had obviously told the truth about how the victim had died and there was no physical evidence, helpful or otherwise, to suggest what might have precipitated the stabbing.

In the next week, the detectives on the case would interview the rest of the neighbors and any other relatives, but nobody would be working overtime on this one—they didn't have to. They had the 911 tapes in which the defendant repeatedly advised the police dispatcher she'd stabbed her husband and thought he was dead, a crime scene video with plenty of blood, and a good, fairly coherent confession that lacked any mention of self-defense. What more did they need? It was an open-and-shut case. Lady goes berserk, kills husband, feels remorse, calls police, confesses to the murder. The end.

Because the defendant had no prior record and had killed her husband in Boulder (one of the most liberal jurisdictions in Colorado— maybe only Aspen would be better), the prosecution would eventually offer her second-degree murder. She would plead out, spend a couple of decades in prison, and then...who cared?

I did. If this was self-defense, then Emily Watkins would plead guilty over both Hal's and my dead body. She was a battered woman. Somebody had to stick up for her. Who better than Rachel Stein, Public Defender (it's my job, ma'am)? With the help of my talented investigator, Donald Baker, I would figure out how to convince the good citizens of Boulder to acquit her.

In a first-degree murder case, time is of the essence and I was already three days behind the police. If not investigated, evidence disappeared, witnesses forgot helpful facts and possible leads evaporated. While Vickie snored beside me, I read and reread the reports, then considered various strategies. At four in the morning, of course, the case looked grim, but almost every case starts out that way. Criminal defense is like trying to fit your station wagon into an impossibly small parking space—there's no way you'll ever make it. But you position yourself as close as you can and begin inching back and forth, back and forth, creasing a few edges if you must. You tap the car in front, tap the car in back, then bump the car in front, and bump the car in back. And then, after you've created as much room as possible, you take a deep breath, hold it, and with great finesse, you squeeze yourself in. *Voila*!

The next day, I asked Donald to meet with me at noon. Donald was an excellent investigator, but so physically unappealing that none of the lawyers in the office used him unless they had to. As far as anyone knew, Donald lived in a battered VW van, which he parked behind our office. He was somewhere between thirty-five and sixty, with dark ferret eyes, a bad complexion and long greasy hair. His belly strained ominously against the one shirt he always seemed to wear, which was always stained with whatever food he'd eaten in the last month. Worse, he smoked Marlboros nonstop and reeked like an overflowing ashtray.

In a town like Boulder, where everyone jogged, meditated and made their own granola, it was hard to believe a guy like Donald would be successful, but almost everyone he tried to interview was willing to talk to him. They let him into their homes and answered his questions not, as you might think, because they felt sorry for him, but because he made them feel better about themselves; no matter how bad off they were, here was a loser in much worse shape. I imagined potential witnesses thinking, *What harm could there be if I talk to someone like him?*

At exactly noon, Donald clumped into my office without knocking and sat down on one of the two client chairs that faced my desk. Without looking up from my reports, I asked him to put out his cigarette.

"I'm not smoking."

I looked up. He wasn't. He just smelled like he was.

"Oh," I said.

I gave him a copy of the police reports and quickly filled him in on what I knew, then handed him a sheet of paper. "Here's a preliminary list of witnesses I'd like you to start interviewing today."

"This the lady that killed the ex-cop?"

"Her husband was an ex-cop?" Shit. Emily hadn't bothered to tell me. "How did you know?" But Donald always knew things the rest of us didn't.

"A guy I know from Greeley told me. The vic used to be a cop up there about ten years ago, got shot in the leg and had to go on disability. I'm sure the police down here know all about it by now."

"That's a bad fact," I said.

"It ain't good," he agreed. "Accident or self-defense?"

"Self-defense."

Donald nodded. We talked strategy for another thirty minutes, and then he stood up to go. "When you see her," he said, "ask if she's ever gone to the doctor or a hospital. Maybe we can get some records to show he's hurt her in the past."

"I will."

"In the meantime," he said, "I'll nose around, see if anyone in the neighborhood has ever seen her with any bruises."

"Great. I'll get the names and addresses of all her friends, relatives and acquaintances. Let's meet again on Friday."

"Okay," he said. There was a huge red smear across the front of his shirt. Normally, I refrained from commenting on his appearance, but this time I couldn't help it.

"That's not blood, is it?"

Donald had no sense of humor. He looked down at his shirt and considered the stain. "Unlikely. Probably ketchup."

***

The next time I saw Emily Watkins, she had a black eye.

"What happened?" I asked as a female guard was escorting us into another tiny interview room.

The guard grinned and put her hand on Emily's shoulder. "Last night, this one here got in between Alicia and one of the other inmates. The first one who ever stood up to Alicia. If it wasn't for her, that other lady would have been hurting pretty bad before we could have stopped it."

After the guard left, I examined Emily's eye and said, "So now you're Superwoman?"

Emily smiled at me. "Is there only room for one in this relationship?" She had pulled her thick blond hair into a youthful ponytail. Barbie goes to jail and gets a black eye.

I sighed audibly. "Yes, but not because I'm selfish. You're in jail facing first-degree murder charges. I need you to keep a low profile and keep yourself safe."

"No one's safe."

"Okay, you're right, but I'd prefer you don't get a reputation as a fighter. If we're going to rely on self-defense, I want the jury to believe you'd never fought back before, that you were too afraid."

Emily's face grew serious. "That's absolutely true. But now that I've done it, I'm not afraid to do it again. Now, I wish I'd resisted Hal from the very beginning. He either would have killed me right away or he would have respected me."

"Which do you think?" I asked, pulling out my legal pad.

"Oh, he would have killed me. He used to be a sheriff in Weld County. Did you know that?"

"I found out yesterday."

Emily nodded. "Hal was eleven years older than me. He started working for the sheriff's department right after graduating from college. It was his boyhood dream. When I met him, he'd been a sheriff for fifteen years and still loved it. He was tall and lean and incredibly self-confident. We'd been married for only six months when a teenage boy shot him in the knee. He had to go on disability and that's when he started drinking."

"I see." While I wrote down what she'd told me, I asked, "Did he ever hit you before that?"

She hesitated. "Just once, when I asked if he'd like to have children. For some reason, that upset him. Later, after crying and apologizing, he said he wanted it to be just the two of us. I never brought it up again. It was one thing to risk my own safety, but I would have never risked anyone else's." She rubbed her injured eye. "Oh dear, now I have a headache. And I'm feeling so ashamed. Not about Alicia, but about my relationship with Hal. I think I might need to go lie down. Could you possibly come back later?"

"There's a lot more questions I need to ask you."

"I miss him," she confessed. "I'm sorry I killed him. I don't wish we were still married—oh, yes I do—I just wish we were happily married."

"Makes perfect sense."

She shook her head. "I just want to plead guilty and get this over with." She closed her eyes then and sat very still. She was gone for only a minute or two, but her absence was palpable; clearly she'd been practicing this for a long time. The art of vanishing. I watched and waited. According to the police reports, she was thirty-six, only a year older than me, but the skin on her face was prematurely lined and drawn, living proof that a decade of being battered by your loved one isn't good for your complexion. Eventually, she opened her eyes.

"Hey, you promised not to give up," I reminded her.

"Did I?" She sighed, sat up a little straighter. "Besides Frost and Eliot, I've always loved Emily Dickinson's poetry. I was named after her, you know. She was such a brave young woman. Very tender, but saw things clearly. She had a weak constitution and died young. I think I must be like her."

Now it was my turn to shake my head. "I don't think so. You're a fighter. You told me, you're Superwoman."

She laughed, which made her look ten years younger. "Why does that appeal to us?"

"That's easy. Nobody likes to feel helpless. It's a sickening feeling."

"You want to know what's worse?" she asked.

"What?"

"When you get used to it."

***

The preliminary hearing was set for the end of November. During the five and a half weeks leading up to the hearing, I probably visited Emily about ten times. If I had to go to the jail to see another client, I'd drop by the women's section and visit Emily as well. Each time I gleaned a little more information, but after a while, I mostly came to keep her company.

Each week I checked her inmate sheet. No one else ever visited her. We talked poetry, politics, theories about battered women, co-dependency and addiction. One day, I described rock climbing (my other passion besides saving people) and promised to take her up an easy pitch after we won her case.

From those hours we spent together, I learned a few surprising things. Despite never finishing college, my client was fluent in both French and German, she knew how to ride a unicycle, and the only time she'd ever cried was at her mother's funeral. And though I revealed some personal information too—that I wished I were closer to my mother, that I was ethnically Jewish but thought all religions were irrational—I never told her the most important thing: that my partner was a woman and that we'd been together for eight and a half years. I knew it wouldn't matter to her, but keeping it to myself was a way of maintaining the attorney-client relationship with someone I was already beginning to care too much about.

A preliminary hearing is just that, a hearing to determine preliminarily whether there's probable cause to believe a crime has been committed and that the defendant committed it. A few days before Emily's hearing, Jeff Taylor, the prosecutor, called me.

"What do you need on this one, Rachel?" he asked. Jeff had been a prosecutor in the Boulder County District Attorney's office for as long as I'd been a public defender, almost twelve years. We'd actually gone to law school together and even went out a few times during our first year when I was still dating men. We had a good working relationship and generally trusted each other.

"I need you to dismiss it," I said.

"Right," he laughed. "It's fine if you need to do the prelim. I understand. Let me know when you want to talk. This case could be a little sticky, though, because the victim was an ex-cop. His buddies have been calling every week. They want me to hang tough."

"He was an abusive bastard," I said.

"Can you prove it?"

I hesitated. So far, Donald had located a few hospital records that established Emily had sought medical attention for a broken arm, a dislocated shoulder and a torn ligament in her knee. These were significant injuries, but she'd always lied about how they happened. None of the neighbors were helpful. Hal's mother wouldn't rat on her son (she'd seen a number of bruises on her daughter-in-law, but claimed not to know where they'd come from), and none of Emily's acquaintances had suspected a thing. My client's best friend had moved to New York about eight years earlier and had visited only twice. For years, she'd wondered if Hal was an abuser, but Emily would never confirm it.

"There wasn't a scratch on her when she was arrested," Jeff reminded me.

"So what?" I said, a shoo-in for Miss Bravado of 1985. "It doesn't mean she wasn't acting in self-defense."

"You're a great lawyer, Rachel, but I don't think even you can pull this one off. Anyway, you know I'll eventually offer second-degree murder. Maybe we'll find a number she can live with."

"That's not good enough."

"It's the best I can do. See you on Wednesday."

I stared out the window at a bluebird roosting in the branches of a naked tree. The wind was blowing steadily, ruffling his short feathers. He looked cold, but resolute. The rest of his clan had long since headed south. I tapped hard on the windowpane and wondered for a moment if he'd frozen to death, but then saw his head move slightly in my direction.

"Hey," I shouted, "it's almost winter, you idiot. Get the hell out of here."

On Wednesday, I let Donald sit with Emily and me at the preliminary hearing. At trial, however, I would try to hide him in the audience. Donald didn't clean up well, even when he tried. The last time he'd testified at a trial for me, he'd worn a pair of brand-new polyester pants that were at least two sizes too small, the same shirt he always wore, and a brown wrinkled tie with hula girls on it.

At two o'clock, Jeff was calling his last witness, the lead detective on the case. By two thirty, Judge Thomas would find probable cause and bind the case over for trial on first-degree murder. After quizzing the detective about Emily's statements to the police, Jeff looked up from his notes and addressed the court.

"Your Honor, I'd like to ask the detective a few questions about a search of the defendant's house that was conducted early this morning. The defense hasn't been given notice of this because I just found out about it myself."

Judge Thomas said, "Ms. Stein, do you object?"

I thought for a moment. "No, Your Honor." Since the case would be bound over regardless, there was no reason not to learn as much as possible.

"Detective Moorehouse," Jeff began, "could you tell the court what you found at the defendant's home early this morning?"

The detective turned to the judge. "We found some papers in the back of a kitchen drawer. One of them pertained to an insurance policy on the deceased's life."

Oh-oh, I thought, here comes a little surprise. God, I hate surprises.

"How much money was the deceased insured for?" Jeff continued.

The detective spoke in a careful monotone. "The deceased was insured for a quarter of a million dollars."

"And who was the beneficiary on the policy?"

"The defendant."

"Detective Moorehouse, were you able to determine who had taken out the policy on the deceased's life?"

I heard Emily make a small distressed mewing sound.

"Yes," the detective answered, "we called the insurance company. They informed us the defendant had taken out the policy three weeks before her husband died."

"That ain't good," Donald muttered.

"No, it ain't," I agreed.

We both looked at Emily.

"You probably won't believe this," she whispered. "I mean I can hardly believe it myself, but until now it never occurred to me it was even relevant. That's pretty naïve, isn't it?"

"I'll say," Donald muttered.

I gave Donald a dirty look and then turned to Emily. "It's okay, I believe you, but in order for us to help you, you have to start thinking—"

"I understand," she interrupted. "If I don't want to spend the rest of my life in prison, I have to start thinking like a criminal."

Donald and I considered this and then nodded. "Exactly," we said.

CHAPTER TWO

Judge Thomas cleared his throat and everyone in the courtroom immediately stopped talking. "Thank you," he said. "The court will start by calling *People versus Watkins, 85CR1260.*"

I grabbed my file and walked to the podium, signaling Emily to join me. She was seated in the jury box where the prisoners always sat except during jury trials. She was dressed in the usual Boulder County jail uniform: loose cotton navy blue pants and matching pullover blouse. On Emily, somehow it looked more like an outfit than a uniform.

The district attorney stood up from his table and said, "Good morning, Your Honor, Jeff Taylor for the people."

"Good morning, Mr. Taylor. And Ms. Stein, how nice to see you so early in the morning."

I grimaced. "God, I hate these early morning court appearances."

Judge Thomas smiled at me. He was a thin, distinguished looking man with graying hair who looked exactly like what he was: a district court judge. "And yet you were on time. I'm impressed."

"It was an accident, judge. I just didn't sleep well last night."

"Well I'm sorry to hear that, Ms. Stein."

"Thank you, Judge. For the record, Rachel Stein appearing on behalf of Emily Watkins, who is now standing next to me at the podium."

"Your Honor," Jeff said, "the case comes on for arraignment. This court heard the evidence at a preliminary hearing in November and bound the case over on the original charge of first-degree murder."

"I remember," the judge said. "Is the defendant ready to be arraigned?"

"Yes, Your Honor," I said. "The defendant pleads not guilty and asks that her case be set for a jury trial sometime in late April or early May."

"Very well," Judge Thomas said, and then leaned over to confer with his court clerk. "All right, a jury trial will be set for the week of May second. Both sides have thirty days to file any pretrial motions. I'll set a motions hearing for March twenty-sixth. I assume you'll need the entire day. Is there anything else?"

"Nothing from the defendant."

"Nothing from the people," Jeff echoed. "Thank you."

I walked Emily back to the jury box. "I'll come and see you tomorrow or the next day," I told her. "Are you all right?"

She nodded. "I just wish I were here under different circumstances. It's actually quite interesting. If this was a field trip, I'd love it."

A heavyset guard, whose face was pitted with scars, approached us. "Emily," he said. "I'm sorry to interrupt, but I have to take you downstairs and get someone else that I forgot to bring up."

Emily smiled graciously. "Of course." She put her hands out in front of her so that he could refasten her handcuffs.

"Does everyone at the jail know your name?" I asked. The county jail was a busy place where hundreds of inmates came and went every week.

"Larry's niece is one of the women I've started teaching to read," Emily explained. "She's in here for stealing her mother's Vicodin. Listen, try some hot milk with honey and a dash of nutmeg. It's always worked for me."

I had no idea what she was talking about.

"For your sleep," she added.

"Oh, right. Thanks."

I watched her being escorted out of the courtroom. She was doing remarkably well for a middle-class housewife suddenly living among sociopaths, drug addicts and prostitutes. Too well. A jail is one of the strangest, most artificial, almost surreal environments you can imagine. Actually, you can't unless you've been there. Reading about it is like reading about cancer—until you or someone very close to you has been diagnosed, you can't truly comprehend it. And yet my shy, bright, poetry-loving client had quickly adapted to it. I felt my stomach lurch. Emily, I thought, stop worrying about your lawyer's insomnia and wake up. Denial is an excellent short-term coping mechanism, but this is a coma. Don't get used to it.

Of course I knew I had my work cut out for me. Emily had been hibernating for almost ten years—if not longer—and had no real desire to ever wake up. She'd seen what was out there and figured she wasn't missing a thing; the prince had already kissed her and it had been a disaster. The vision I was offering her, of hacking through the forest on her own in a world without princes, wasn't an appealing one. But neither was snoozing on a lumpy cot in a ten-by-twelve foot prison cell for the rest of her life.

I left the courtroom and caught up to Jeff in the hallway.

"Hi Rachel," he said. "You ready to talk?"

"Nice suit," I said, fingering the buttery soft fabric on his sleeve.

"Thanks," he said, looking embarrassed.

"Hey, you can't help it if you were born independently wealthy. It's to your credit that you work when you don't have to."

Now he was actually blushing. Unfortunately for the defense bar, Jeff Taylor was not only rich and handsome he was genuinely nice. A young, self-effacing Cary Grant who'd gone into law instead of acting. Juries invariably loved him. "So what do you want, Rachel?"

"Felony menacing with probation," I said with a straight face. Sometimes the difference between lawyering and acting is too subtle for ordinary laymen to distinguish.

"On the Emily Watkins case? Maybe you haven't noticed, but there's a dead body."

"Oh yeah, that."

"Yeah, that," he said.

"Look, how about reckless manslaughter with community corrections? That's as high as I can go." I stroked the sleeve of his jacket. For my clients, I was shameless.

"You're dreaming, Rachel. I'm offering second-degree murder, but we can talk about the number. I'm thinking somewhere in the thirties, maybe even the low thirties."

"I don't want her to go to prison," I said.

He shook his head. "I know you think she acted in self-defense, but the evidence doesn't support it. She seems like a nice lady, everyone at the jail likes her. If you can come up with anything, you know I'll listen. That's the best I can do." He patted the shoulder of my fifty-dollar blazer.

"I wish you were an asshole," I said.

He looked surprised. "Why?"

"So I could hate you."

He looked incredulous. "Why would you want to do that?"

And there you had it, I thought as I hurried to my next court appearance in division four, the reason it was so difficult to practice law in the 20th Judicial District: everyone was so goddamned nice. The judge, the prosecutor, the guards, the defense attorney, even the client. The tragedy of Emily's life would get lost in all that pleasant backslapping congeniality. It would slip, unnoticed, like a suicide off the side of a ship during a wild and happy party. A quick slight splash, and she'd be gone.

"*Ah, Ms. Stein,*" *Judge Thomas would say at Emily's final hearing.* "*How nice to see you again.*"

"*Nice to see you too, Judge.*"

"*And Mr. Taylor, what a nice suit jacket. Is it cashmere?*"

"*I'm not sure, Judge, but thank you. Your Honor, Ms. Stein's client has agreed to plead guilty to second-degree murder and we'll be stipulating to a sentence of only thirty years in the state penitentiary.*"

"*Well, that sounds like a nice disposition. I will accept it and sentence the defendant to the Department of Corrections for a mere thirty years.*"

"*Thank you, Judge,*" *Emily would say.* "*You've all been very nice to me.*"

"*Well, you've been a very nice defendant. And now, is there anything else?*"

"*Nothing from the defendant, Your Honor. Thank you.*"

"*Nothing from the people either. Thank you.*"

"*Well, thank you all for appearing. The best of luck to you, Ms. Watkins.*"

"*Thank you, Judge.*"

***

I was still thinking about Emily's case as I drove downtown to meet Donald at Tom's Tavern for a working lunch. I was hoping he'd uncovered a few more witnesses to prove Emily's husband had been abusing her for years. It was the kind of testimony that was crucial in a self-defense case.

I found my investigator sitting at the bar, talking to a man I'd represented a few years ago for his eighth DUI. The place stank of hamburger grease and cigarette smoke. It was Donald's favorite restaurant and in another fruitless effort to be nice, I'd stupidly agreed to meet him there.

"Come on," I said to Donald, "let's get a booth."

As we groped our way through the smoke to an empty booth, Donald said, "The guy I was talking to said you used to be his lawyer. Said you couldn't do much for him, and that he had to spend a year in the Boulder County Jail. Seemed like a nice guy."

I glanced back at the bar. "One of these days he's going to get drunk and smash into a car full of unsuspecting people and kill them. But other than that, I guess he's all right." I picked up a sticky menu and began studying it. "Let's order quickly and get to work."

"Well, he seemed like a nice guy," Donald said, pulling out a cigarette.

"Well, he's not. And please don't smoke."

"Okay fine, he's not," Donald said, putting his cigarette away. He muttered something under his breath that I couldn't hear.

Rachel, I warned myself, the man sitting across from you is your only ally in the case. Don't alienate him. It was a sobering thought. "I'm sorry, Donald. I didn't have time for breakfast this morning. I think I just need to eat as soon as possible."

Donald looked around until he spotted our waitress. "She's coming," he assured me, as if I were a two-year-old who'd been separated from my mother and was on the verge of losing it.

The waitress arrived and Donald went first, ordering a hamburger and three glasses of Coke.

"Three?" I asked, attempting at the very last moment to sound curious instead of judgmental. Your only ally, I reminded myself.

"I'm trying to cut down on coffee."

"Oh," I nodded. "Good idea."

"What'll it be, sweetie?" the waitress asked me. She was a scrawny blonde with a tired face and improbably large breasts.

"Could you possibly make me a large garden salad with a few pieces of grilled chicken in it? I didn't see anything like it on the menu."

"That's because this is a hamburger joint," she said. "Nobody orders salad here."

"I see. Well, okay, I'll have a hamburger without the bun and could I have something on the side besides french fries?"

"Not really," she said.

"I'll eat them," Donald offered. Chivalry, I was glad to discover, wasn't dead.

While we waited for our food, Donald summarized his latest interviews. Of all the neighbors he'd contacted, only one had observed any act of violence between Emily and her husband. A few years ago, she'd seen Emily and Hal arguing in a parked car in front of their house. Hal got out of the car first and went around to Emily's side as if to open the door, but Emily was already climbing out. Hal said something and then slammed the door on her foot. At that point, the neighbor said she closed her curtains and stopped watching.

"It might have been an accident," she told Donald. When he asked how it could have been anything but intentional, she said she didn't know.

"Great," I said. "Another lackluster witness for the defense. What else do we have?"

Donald placed his pack of cigarettes on the table. "How about I smoke just one and blow it in the other direction?"

I hesitated. "How about half of one and you blow it in the other direction?"

"Deal," he said, lighting up. Wreathed in smoke, his face looked gray and unhealthy. I hoped he didn't have a heart attack before the case was over. Me and Donald: like my childhood TV heroine, Emma Peel, and her equally dashing compatriot, we had it all—adventure, witty repartee and a strong understated physical attraction for each other. Right.

Miraculously, Donald had found all of the local doctors who'd treated Emily in the last ten years. Each of them was willing to come to court and describe her injuries, but none could say her explanation was implausible. Only one had had any doubt (about a cracked rib), but it was certainly possible she'd fallen on it.

"Well, it's something," I said. "At least they want to help."

Finally our food arrived. After a couple of bites, I asked about Emily's friends.

Donald licked some ketchup off his fingers. "She doesn't have any, just the lady in New York, Alice Timmerman, who says she'll do whatever she can. Problem is, she didn't see anything. A couple of times she called to speak with Emily, Hal hung up on her, but that don't exactly prove he's an abuser."

"No, just an asshole. Did you talk to the officer who busted Hal for domestic violence?"

Donald nodded. "It ain't much. The cop said he mostly took him in 'cause he was drunk. At first, Emily claimed Hal slugged her, then immediately changed her story to a light slap. Later, she tried to recant the whole thing. I subpoenaed him while I was there."

"Brick by brick," I said, finishing my burger. "You might as well start with Hal now, see if you can find anyone who will say anything bad about him, especially about his temper or his drinking."

Donald downed the last of his three Cokes. "Did they find any alcohol in the vic's body?"

"Some," I said. "Over a point one. Legally drunk but just barely."

Donald looked pensive. "It's too bad she didn't wait until he'd hit her at least once."

"I know." I stood up and grabbed the check off the table. "It's on me, Donald. We're never coming here again."

On the way out, I reminded him that we still had Emily as our star witness, and that she was smart, likeable, and attractive, someone the jury would be inclined to acquit if they had any reasonable doubt.

He shook his head. "Yeah, but there's something about her. I don't know what it is. I don't mean she's loony, but she ain't all there."

As we walked to my car, I said, "That's what happens when you're a battered woman. A part of you checks out. It's a survival mechanism."

He shrugged. "Well, you're gonna have to hang on to the rest of her. I once had this helium balloon when I was a kid, but I got distracted. I think some guys were chasing me with switchblades. Anyway, I let go of it for just a second and it was gone."

For a moment, I was dumbstruck. Donald as a little kid? No, I simply couldn't imagine it—nor did I want to—but his analogy was apt and I wondered, not for the first time, whether I'd underestimated him. "Don't worry," I finally said, rummaging through my briefcase for my keys. "No matter how bad it gets, I won't let go."

***

Although I promised Emily I'd see her soon, I had to spend the rest of the week dealing with a rape case where the victim kept waffling about whether she'd originally agreed to have sex with my client and then changed her mind, or been forced from the very beginning. I hated those kinds of cases, but of course I did them.

On Sunday, I drove to the jail and spent the afternoon and evening visiting all the new clients I'd picked up the week before. Finally, at around quarter to nine, I asked to be escorted to the women's module. When I arrived, I looked through the glass and saw Emily seated in the day room addressing a group of women, all of them younger than her. Two were obviously pregnant. Like most inmates, they were hungry for a break in their routine. Any kind of break.

"What's she doing?" I asked the guard.

"Emily? She wants to start a book reading group. This is their first meeting. I'm surprised how many of the inmates were interested."

A book reading group? My stomach lurched again. "Look, tell her I'm here but I'm too tired to wait. Tell her I've only got about twenty lucid minutes left." The guard unlocked the steel door, slid it open, and went inside. A few minutes later, Emily hurried out to meet me.

"I'm sorry," she said, as we sat down in the interview room. "I had no idea you'd come so late. I know your time is extremely valuable."

"A book group?" I said.

Her face lit up. "Why not? Most criminals can read. I used to lead a group at the library. The surroundings here are seedier, but the discussions might turn out to be quite interesting."

I stared at her. "You're scaring me, Emily."

"What? How? Tell me and I'll stop it."

Behind her, I could see various AA slogans taped to the wall: *Easy Does It. One Day At A Time.* Fine, if you were an alcoholic.

"Look, this might sound funny," I said, "but you're adjusting too well to the environment. Either that, or you've convinced yourself that you're here as a social worker, not as an inmate."

Emily understood immediately. "I see. You're worried that if I get too comfortable, too institutionalized, I might not fight as hard to get out."

"Exactly. And you're too smart to spend the rest of your life in prison. It would be a terrible waste."

She shook her head in wonder. "You genuinely care what happens to me, don't you?" As if I were someone who'd been courting her for months but she still couldn't quite believe it.

"I do. And I don't want you thinking this is even tolerable. I want you to claw your way out of here."

Emily gazed down at her hands, and then back up at me, her blue eyes as impenetrable as ever. "What if my nails aren't sharp enough?"

"Uh-uh. You've already done it once, you can do it again."

And then, without any warning, my client disappeared. We were still facing each other, but she wasn't there; it was as if I were sitting across from a hologram. She'd left like this before and I never tried to stop her. After three or four minutes, she always came back looking calm and somewhat resigned, as if she'd considered the possibility of remaining where she was and decided, once again, to return.

"Hey," was all I said when I knew she was back.

We sat quietly for a while, listening to the sounds of the jail, of too many people living against their will in tiny inhospitable quarters originally meant to house less than half of them. Eventually, Emily broke the silence. "You want me to make a decision, don't you?"

It never ceased to amaze me how well she could read my mind. There was no point waffling. "Yes, it's time."

Somewhere outside the room, a female inmate began yelling. A few seconds later, we heard the sound of running feet and a couple of guards ordering her back into the day room.

"No!" the inmate screamed. "I have to see the nurse tonight!"

"About what, Maria?" one of the guards demanded.

"None of your fucking business. Let go of me! Fuck you!"

"Okay, calm down, Maria. You can see a nurse tomorrow."

"No! You're a bunch of fucking liars!"

"All right, Maria, that's it. Let's go."

We heard them dragging her down the hall, still screaming and cursing. When they reached the steel door, it sounded as if she was kicking it. One of the guards yelled at her to cut it out. Finally we heard the door open and then clang shut. After that, it was quiet again.

"So what's it going to be?" I asked.

Emily sighed. "You know, it's not the food or the tedious routine that gets to me. It's not even the violence or the palpable unhappiness of the place. It's the noise." She paused. "What are my chances at trial?"

I looked at her soft, kind face. She was as pale now as all the other inmates. "It'll depend on you. If you do well on the stand, they're better than fifty-fifty."

"And if I don't do well?"

I didn't answer.

"Have you talked to the district attorney?"

I nodded, keeping my face impassive. "He'll offer second-degree murder and he's willing to stipulate to a number in the low thirties."

"What's the range for second?" she asked, sounding like a seasoned pro, which broke my heart. She'd been talking to the other inmates, of course.

"In your case, twenty-four to forty-eight."

Emily stood up and began to pace in front of me. "Will he go below thirty?"

"I don't think so. Not now, anyway."

"How much time would I really do if I was sentenced to thirty years?"

"I'm not going to plead you to thirty years."

"But let's just say I was."

Her pacing was beginning to annoy me. "I don't know exactly," I said. "It's hard to predict. You'd be parole eligible after twelve or thirteen years, but you could do closer to twenty."

She was nodding to herself. "So, worst-case scenario, I'd be fifty-seven when I got out."

I kicked at her empty chair. "Okay, that's it, Emily. Stop pretending to be some kind of gun moll. This isn't a movie. It's your real life. Sit down."

She stopped pacing, put her hands on her hips, and tried to look indignant. "I thought I was being very tough, very...Barbara Stanwyck."

"More like Judy Holliday," I said, patting her chair. "Try to imagine getting out of prison after eighteen years. You think you're institutionalized now?"

Finally she sat down. "Don't worry, Rachel. I'm not going to take the plea agreement. I was just trying it on for size."

"Well it's too big." By then, I had a headache and wanted to leave.

"Okay," Emily said, recognizing as usual when the interview was over, "you're the one with the eye."

I stood up to go. This one has to turn out right, I told myself.

Emily smiled reassuringly. "I have complete confidence in you."

Although I rarely drank, that night I was tempted to stop at one of the liquor stores on 28th Street and buy a bottle of something with a high alcohol content. But then I remembered it was Sunday and decided to go home and eat some leftover tofu and vegetables instead. When I finally crawled into bed, Vickie spooned me until she fell asleep. After that, I was on my own, just me and my worried mind.

***

During the following month, I settled my sexual assault case, tried a hopeless burglary and won it, and thought about various pre-trial motions—all of them losers—that I could file on Emily's behalf. Donald, meanwhile, had located a couple of witnesses who were willing to testify that Hal used excessive force when he'd arrested them. Two more bricks, but still not enough. If Emily was going to risk her life, I needed something more to tip the balance solidly in her favor: a missing witness or some crucial piece of evidence.

I started waking up in the middle of the night imagining the looks on the jurors' faces when they found out Emily hadn't actually been attacked on the night she stabbed her husband. I'd seen those looks when I was a baby lawyer, before I figured out that jurors wouldn't acquit my clients just because I begged them. Reasonable doubt involved crafting a strong understandable defense that would hold up against the worst facts in the case. Without something more, Emily's claim might get overrun. Finally, on a cold February morning, while Vickie and I were making love on our king-sized bed, I found it.

Eureka! I would get an expert who could testify about battered woman syndrome, someone who would educate the jury about the general characteristics common to women who have been psychologically and physically abused over a lengthy period of time. I could then ask my expert a series of questions about Emily's behavior and ask her to explain why Emily may have acted the way she did. If I called the expert before my client took the stand, the jury would be much less skeptical during Emily's testimony. Yes, it would work!

Of course, I still had to find an expert and convince Judge Thomas to let me put her on. It was 1986, about ten years since the first battered women's shelter opened in North America. Although a few states had already recognized battered woman syndrome, Colorado wasn't one of them. But these were merely obstacles. What was the name of the psychologist who wrote the book on battered women? Lenore Walker, that was it. She lived in Denver, didn't she?

"Rachel?"

"Huh?" I said.

Vickie's head was about six inches below my navel. She'd stopped doing what she was doing and was now looking up at me. "Where did you go?" she asked, sounding slightly petulant.

I was so ashamed, I told the truth. "I'm sorry, Vickie. I was thinking about my case."

She slid her strong slender body all the way back up until our faces were only a couple of inches apart. Her eyes were glazed and her lips were the color of pink coral. With her jet-black hair tucked carelessly behind her ears, she looked especially beautiful.

"I'm so sorry," I repeated.

"I want you to come back," she said, brushing her breasts against mine.

"I'm already back."

"Because," she continued, pressing her pelvis into mine and then gently grinding herself against me, "this is the last refuge we have against the world and all its sorrows."

"I understand." I attempted to kiss her, but she averted her face and was biting my ear.

"Once we let it in," she whispered, "there's no place left where there isn't pain and sadness." She pushed my legs apart with her knees.

"No place left where there's only the pure physicality of our love for each other."

"Okay," I said, panting a little as heat rushed to my face.

She slipped a couple of fingers inside me. "This is the only time when I demand your complete attention."

"Not a problem," I gasped, then pulled her down to me and kissed her until the world and all its sorrows was back where it was supposed to be, right outside the door, waiting patiently for us to finish.

CHAPTER THREE

"Remind me again why I love climbing," I told Maggie as I prepared to lead the fourth pitch of a climb on the Redgarden Wall in Eldorado Canyon, a world famous climbing area about ten miles south of Boulder.

"Because you like being scared?" my best friend asked, clipping her belay device (a small metal contraption through which the rope is threaded) into a locking carabiner attached to her harness. "You're on belay."

It was a gorgeous Sunday in March, unseasonably warm and cloudless. According to the almanac, spring was only two or three snowstorms away. Although the motions hearing in Emily's case was coming up fast, requiring considerable preparation, I still had enough time to take an occasional day off to play. I'd been climbing for three years and had just begun leading at the end of last summer.

I loved everything about the sport, even the danger. If I'd been single or in a relationship with someone who shared my passion, I would have climbed every weekend. But Vickie was a hiker and a gardener whose sense of adventure was more than satisfied by a pleasant stroll in the foothills during which she'd have to stop every couple of yards to look at the wildflowers and try to identify them. Because she was also an internist who treated accident victims, including the occasional climber, she thought lead climbing was both crazy and dangerous. For the sake of harmony, we'd agreed to disagree on the subject.

The climb today was six pitches long and we were alternating leads. This would be the hardest pitch I'd ever led, but Maggie thought I was ready. I studied the thirty-foot traverse in front of me. The handholds looked good, but the footholds looked nonexistent. I stared at the smooth granite until I could detect a few tiny bulges along the face that might hold me if I placed the balls of my feet on them and allowed friction to keep me from slipping. Maggie, of course, was tied into three bombproof anchors. If I slipped, I'd swing, but I wouldn't go far and she'd be able to haul me up.

"No, that's not the reason," I said, referring to Maggie's mock serious suggestion. "I actually hate being scared."

Maggie nodded, then played out enough rope so that I could begin climbing. I stepped out onto the rock and stuck a few fingers into the horizontal crack above me. "A bit tenuous," I muttered.

Maggie laughed. "You'll feel better as soon as you get a piece in."

I reached down with my right hand, unhooked a small camming device from my harness, and placed it into the crack. Maggie let out some more rope and I quickly clipped in. For the moment, I was secure.

"Good," she said. "Now, at the risk of offending you, I'm just going to say I know you can do this, but if you don't feel like it for whatever reason, I'm happy to do it instead. The next pitch is easier, but still quite exciting."

"Thanks, but no thanks." I tiptoed my left foot across the face until I found a little nub, then slid both hands to the left. After adjusting my weight, I moved my right foot over as well, a mad little caterpillar inching my way across a large expanse of rock hundreds of feet above the ground. There were three or four black birds flying in circles below my feet.

After clipping into my second piece, I looked back toward Maggie. "The precise reason I love climbing is because I could die at any moment, which makes me feel so alive."

"Makes perfect sense," Maggie said, "but don't try explaining that to a non-climber. Our girlfriends would have us committed."

"Right. So how come we aren't involved with other climbers?"

Maggie shrugged. "I came on to you about ten years ago and you turned me down. Remember?"

"Oh yeah." I slithered another eight feet to the left, found a delicate ledge to stand on, and stopped to put another piece in. "You aren't still holding that against me, are you?"

"No," she called. "In fact, I'm very glad."

"Humph," I said, but we both knew the conversation was merely to keep me company while we were still in sight of each other. As soon as I climbed around the corner, I wouldn't have anyone to talk to and I'd be on my own. Just me and my devilishly inventive mind.

I finished the traverse and was approaching the corner. My left foot slipped a few inches, but then it held. The next move was the crux and then I'd be around. I turned my face toward Maggie. "Once my murder trial is over," I called, "let's climb as much as possible. It's the only way I'll ever improve."

"I'm going to Nicaragua, remember?"

I slid my arm around the corner searching blindly for something to grab onto. "Oh right. Nicaragua. Weren't you supposed to go this winter?"

"Yes, at the beginning of February," she answered, "but we had to postpone it. There was too much fighting."

"What's the name of your group again?" I was still groping for my next hold.

"The Boulder-Jalapa friendship brigade." She paused. "Just make the move, Rachel. It's not as bad as you think."

I hugged the wall and edged around the corner. She was right. After getting another piece in, I stopped to consider the steep vertical crack above me. Maggie had described it as eighty feet of sustained crack climbing.

"Eek," I said out loud, which would have been funny if someone else had been there to hear it. I forced myself to take a deep breath, to look around, and appreciate the spectacular view.

We'd started our approach to the climb at eight thirty when it was still quite chilly in order to get down before dark. I glanced at my watch. It was already a quarter to one. Time flies when you're busy squandering adrenaline.

Okay, baby doll, time to start moving. I shinnied up about eight feet, fumbled around on my harness until I found the piece I wanted, unclipped it with sweaty fingers, and stuck it in the crack. As I clipped in, I rolled my neck, and made the mistake of looking down. Jesus Christ. Maybe I only loved climbing in retrospect, after it was all over and we were safely on the ground. Maybe I only loved the *idea* of climbing. All right, that's enough; best not to think. I nodded (you can do things like that when you're all alone), then hauled myself up the next forty feet without incident, singing an old Pete Seeger tune, "If I Had a Hammer."

I was just pulling up the rope to clip into a small cam when I heard a voice from somewhere above me scream, "Rock!" The climbers ahead of us must have accidentally dislodged it. Immediately, I pressed my body as close to the crack as I could and simultaneously felt a large boulder whiz past my right shoulder. Without thinking, I'd let go of the extra rope and grabbed onto my piece. A second later, I heard the boulder smash into the ledge below me.

"Are you okay?" Maggie yelled.

"Missed me," I yelled back.

"What?"

"I'm fine," I yelled louder.

"All right, good."

My right hand was bleeding—I must have scraped it against the rock—but other than that, I was unscathed. I clipped in and tried to stop myself from imagining what might have happened if I hadn't grabbed the cam, or if the boulder had fallen a few inches to the left. You're fine, I told myself, keep moving, but I couldn't. I was paralyzed, not so much by fear as by a surfeit of imagination. Holy Mother of God, what the hell was I doing here? I remained absolutely still for what seemed like hours but was probably about ten minutes.

"What's happening?" Maggie yelled.

"Nothing. I'm just resting."

There was a pause. "Resting is good. Take your time. I've got you."

When your climbing partner tells you resting is good, it's not. She means it's time to start climbing again, even if every cell in your body begs you to stay put on the side of the mountain, build a cozy little nest full of bird feathers and live there forever.

Climbing was occasionally dangerous, I reminded myself. If I couldn't handle the risks, I had no business being there. Maybe my doctor girlfriend was right—that I spent too much time in the fast lane courting disaster—and my body knew it even if my intellect didn't. Was it trying to warn me? Maybe I was more susceptible than I thought, like my father who died way too young at fifty-six. And just because I couldn't climb didn't mean I couldn't hike or ski. I could still have all kinds of outdoor adventures. Hell, I could make my beloved very happy and join her on her slow meditative walks, learn the names of every wildflower that grew in the region. Who knew, I might even come to like it.

Luckily, that did it. I scrambled up the last thirty feet in less than five minutes, set up my anchors, and yelled a triumphant, "Off belay." About twenty minutes later, Maggie crawled into view.

"God, it took forever to get that small cam out," she said. "It must have been the one you were hanging on. So, other than that, how was the climb?"

"Great," I said, and decided that Vickie, blinded by love or fear, was dead wrong about me. I wasn't particularly sensitive and I didn't need to slow down and smell the flowers. I was my mother's daughter: tough, thick-skinned, indomitable.

The last two pitches went smoothly and despite a long tedious down climb, we managed to get to the car before dark. I was tired, dirty, a little bloody and very happy.

***

The next day, at the jail, Emily asked about all the cuts on my right hand.

"Crack climbing," I explained. "I probably should have taped my hands before we started."

We were sitting in one of the larger group rooms near the women's module. There was an old, beat-up piano in the room, and a blackboard with a number of AA slogans scrawled across it. The table between us was strewn with Christian pamphlets geared toward prisoners who might be tired and desperate enough to let Jesus into their lives.

"You don't read this stuff, do you?" I asked, pointing to one of the pamphlets with a picture of a shepherd surrounded by a flock of obedient-looking sheep.

She glanced at it, then said, "I read everything I can get my hands on."

Immediately, I felt ashamed. "Sorry. I have no idea what it's like to be locked up day after day."

"No, you don't." Even as she reproached me, my client's face remained kind and serene, like Sally Field's in *The Flying Nun*.

I had a feeling she was referring to more than just her incarceration in the Boulder County Jail. I did a quick calculation. Emily had been an inmate for five months. Unlike the majority of my clients, however, she never complained. Was that a good sign, or a bad one? Did it mean she was tough and resilient, or more like one of those sheep on the pamphlet?

"Don't give up, Emily," I warned.

She smiled at me. "Do you know how many times you've said that to me?"

I smiled back. "No, how many?"

She placed her hand lightly on top of mine, the first time she had ever touched me. "At least a hundred times."

I shrugged. "Well, it's very important."

She nodded, and then gently slid her hand away.

"So," I said, "what did you think of Dr. Midman?"

Karen Midman was a psychologist who specialized in treating battered women. She'd come highly recommended by Lenore Walker who wouldn't be available until early summer. I'd sent Dr. Midman to interview Emily a few days earlier and planned to meet with her myself at the end of the week. I was hoping to submit an affidavit signed by her as an offer of proof at the motions hearing and then ask Judge Thomas to allow me to call her as an expert on battered woman syndrome at trial.

"I thought she was a warm, intelligent woman," Emily answered. "I liked her very much. She'll make an excellent witness."

I laughed. "You should have been a lawyer."

Emily stood and walked over to the piano. "I should have been a lot of things, but I chose to be Hal's wife instead and now I have to live with it."

I shook my head. How could anyone be so calm and matter-of-fact about making such a drastic mistake? Because I was speaking to Emily, not some desperate drug addict or three-time felon who wanted some reassuring pap, I chose my words carefully. "Well, you're right. You'll always have to live with it, but hopefully not behind bars. If the judge allows Dr. Midman to educate the jury about battered woman syndrome, we'll have a decent chance to win and then you'll have the rest of your life to make better choices."

"My goodness." She rubbed her face. "I can't imagine that."

"You have to," I said, "or you'll lose."

Suddenly, Emily sat down at the piano and played a couple of chords that sounded sad and bluesy.

I was surprised. "I didn't know you could play the piano."

She glanced over her shoulder at me, but continued playing. "There are still a couple of things about me you don't know." Her expression was one I'd never seen before, proud and aloof.

I thought she was kidding, pretending to be flirtatious. Piano bar patter. "Like what?" I asked.

She played for another few minutes and then stopped. "You know," she said, "it doesn't seem quite fair that I'll get to tell the jury my side of the story, but Hal won't be able to."

We'd been over this before, but she obviously wasn't done with it. "Fair?" I tossed one of the pamphlets across the table. "What's fair about him hitting you whenever he drank too much or got frustrated with his life?"

"He didn't hit me all the time, you know. Sometimes he could be very tender."

"Uh-huh."

"It wasn't a daily thing, or even a weekly one. When I think back about it, we got along fairly well almost all of the time."

"Uh-huh."

She stood up from the piano to face me. "Stop saying 'uh-huh' as if you know something I don't."

"Then stop revising reality."

Someone else might have taken offense at my remark, but not Emily. Everyone has a temper, but for obvious reasons she'd had to send hers far away. Who knew if they even kept in contact?

"I'm not revising anything," Emily said. "Every few months, Hal lost control of himself and hurt me. But did he deserve to die?"

I kept my face impassive. With Emily, I seemed to have infinite patience. "That's not the question you ought to be asking yourself. Would you please sit down?"

She sat. "What's the question then? I've forgotten."

"The question is whether you deserve to spend the rest of your life in prison for defending yourself."

"What if I wasn't?" she asked, and for a moment my heart stopped, not because I thought she was telling the truth, but because she was even capable of asking the question. Which was also why I loved and admired her. Even behind bars she insisted on living the examined life. How wonderful, unless of course you happened to be her defense attorney, in which case it was a nightmare.

"Listen, Emily, the very first time we met, I asked you whether you thought Hal was about to hurt you when you stabbed him. Do you remember?"

She sighed. "I remember."

"And you said, 'of course he was.'"

She spread her hands on the table. "But I could have been wrong. I'd been wrong in the past. For all I know, he might have been planning to kiss me."

We were in dangerous legal territory now, a tricky no-man's land where the right jury instruction could mean the difference between freedom and life in prison. "Okay, Emily, I need you to listen carefully. No matter what Hal's real intentions might have been, based on your past experiences, you thought he was going to hurt you. He'd broken your jaw just six weeks earlier. Right?"

She nodded reluctantly. "Right."

I dug through my briefcase and pulled out a sheaf of papers. "These are all cases that say in self-defense situations like yours, the defendant gets to have an instruction on what's called 'apparent necessity and the right to be wrong.'"

For the first time since we'd started this conversation, I could feel Emily beginning to yield. She was leaning forward, paying close attention now.

"So these cases say," I continued, "that an apparent necessity instruction should be given when the trial court's self-defense instruction doesn't adequately inform the jury of a person's right to act on the appearance of being killed or receiving serious bodily injury. In other words, we can argue that someone who's been subject to the battering and domination of another may have an altered perception and evaluation of a situation, and could, on the surface, appear to overreact to a particular incident. The instruction will tell the jury that it has to consider your prior experiences of helplessness, beatings and threats which may have caused a heightened response at the time Hal came at you."

Emily was staring at me. "Do you think it'll work?"

It has to, I thought, and then stood up to leave. I had five arraignments scheduled for one o'clock at the courthouse. "In conjunction with Dr. Midman's testimony, absolutely."

***

A few days later, I met Donald for another working lunch. Since we couldn't agree on a restaurant we both liked—he couldn't smoke or get a hamburger in the ones I favored, and I couldn't stand the way my hair and clothes smelled after eating in the ones he preferred—we'd settled into bringing our own lunches to the office and working together in the conference room.

After interviewing the staff at both the library and the Humane Society, the two places Emily had worked as a volunteer, Donald had found only one witness at the Humane Society who'd noticed a couple of bruises on Emily's forearms. The woman was unenthusiastic about testifying and told Donald that Emily always acted aloof and seemed to have an attitude problem.

"What kind of an attitude problem?" I asked, nibbling on a carrot stick.

"Couldn't say exactly," Donald replied, tearing into his third Big Mac. "Like she thought Emily read poetry all the time because everyone's conversation bored her."

"Oh." Poor Emily: wrong husband, wrong century, wrong life.

Donald took another huge bite of his hamburger, squirting special sauce on his shirtsleeve. A cigarette was burning in an ashtray next to his plate.

"Why don't you put out that cigarette?" I suggested. "You can't smoke and eat at the same time."

"Sure I can." Donald picked up the cigarette, inhaled deeply, and then bit into his hamburger. Smoke drifted out from between his teeth as he chewed.

"That's really gross, Donald."

He looked pointedly at the open container of hummus next to my carrot sticks. "Talk about gross," he said, burping loudly.

Help, I thought, I'm trapped in a room with a four-year-old. But, I reminded myself, a four-year-old without whom I would not win Emily's case. I picked up my carrots and hummus—they *were* kind of gross—and tossed them in the trash. Donald stared at me as if I were crazy and then laughed. Thank God four-year-olds don't hold grudges. I glanced at my notes.

"What about Louise Watkins, Hal's mother?" I asked.

Donald lit another cigarette, but was careful not to blow any smoke at me. "She lives in some kind of retirement setup in downtown Denver called The Lincoln Suites. I tried calling her again last week and she hung up on me."

"Shit. Louise is probably the only person alive who saw Emily's black eyes and bruises. Not that she ever asked about them of course. And she knew about Emily's broken jaw as well."

Donald flicked his ashes in the general direction of the ashtray. "I'll find the doc who treated her for the jaw," he promised. "He just moved to Utah, but I'll find him."

"Thanks," I said and meant it. I drummed my fingers on the conference table and glanced around me. The room was lined with shelves of forest-colored law books: Colorado statutes, treatises on search and seizure, books about forensic medicine, legal encyclopedias, tomes on blood splatter analysis, ballistics, eyewitness identification and various journals devoted to the so-called science of criminology. There was one cheap print on the wall that our secretary had brought in to liven up the place, a French café scene in which everyone appeared drunk and uproariously happy. The picture always made me feel sad.

"Hey," I said, "why don't we just drop in on Louise and see if she'll talk to us?"

Donald picked something out of his teeth. "That's not a bad idea. It's harder for people to tell you to get lost to your face. Could you go now?"

I nodded. "Let's take my Toyota." I'd once looked inside Donald's van, a horrifying experience I never wanted to repeat. "My car's faster."

The ground floor of The Lincoln Suites looked like a classy hotel with exposed brick walls, oak floors and expensive looking southwestern-style furniture. At first, Donald and I thought we'd come to the wrong place, but a woman dressed in a stylish mauve pantsuit whose nametag identified her as "Barbara" assured us we hadn't. I told her we'd come to visit Louise Watkins.

"Oh yes," Barbara said. "Unfortunately, we're in the middle of switching to a new phone system, so I can't call and announce you beforehand. You'll have to take the elevator to the third floor and knock on three-twelve."

"No problem," Donald said, and then we hurried to the elevator before anyone could stop us. "Pretty ritzy," he mumbled on the ride up.

Any vague hopes I might have had that Mrs. Watkins was a timid old lady were immediately dashed.

"Who are you?" she demanded, peering at us through a peephole in her door.

I pushed Donald to the side. "My name is Rachel Stein. The court appointed me to represent Emily Watkins. I'd like to ask you a few questions about your son, to find out what kind of man he was."

"He was a good man," she said through the door, "and that bitch he married deserves the death penalty."

"Would you be willing to let me in and tell me why you think that?"

"Why should I?" she asked.

I looked at Donald, who shrugged. "Well," I improvised, "how else can I find out what a good man he was? So far, nobody's willing to come forward and talk to me about him."

This was all true. None of Hal's acquaintances (mostly ex-cops) were willing to be interviewed. It had been five months since her son was killed. I was hoping she wanted to talk about him, even to us. I was right.

We heard the door unlock, and then we were face-to-face with a thin, elegant-looking woman in her late seventies. Her hair was stark white and recently permed, not a strand out of place. I'd have bet that none of the lines in her face were from laughing. In fact, she looked like someone who'd been dissatisfied for a very long time, maybe her entire life. I couldn't imagine Emily cooking dinner for this woman and her son every Sunday afternoon. How could she have survived it? Dissociation, I decided, cheaper than booze, easier on the body.

The room matched Mrs. Watkins's hair. Everything in it was white: the carpet, the walls, the loveseat, the two chairs, all perfectly arranged and lacquered into place. Donald looked astonished, as if he'd stumbled into a nightmare landscape. Just don't touch anything, I thought.

"My son's life," Mrs. Watkins said, taking the loveseat and leaving us the two chairs, "was ruined by your client, even before she murdered him. He never should have married her. He'd been engaged for years to a wonderful young lady he'd met in high school, the daughter of a good friend of ours. Janet, however, couldn't bear the idea of Hal going into law enforcement. She thought it was too dangerous. When she broke it off with him, he never recovered."

I couldn't help myself. "So it was Janet that ruined his life?"

Mrs. Watkins looked confused for a moment, and then shook her head. "No. It was Emily that made him so unhappy."

"Which is why Hal drank?" Donald tried.

Mrs. Watkins glanced at Donald as if he were a bug that was unfortunately too big to kill. Donald receded into his chair and I knew he would simply take notes for the rest of the interview.

"Please go on," I urged.

Mrs. Watkins was nodding. "Oh, Hal drank, but only enough to stand his marriage. He'd made a commitment and he intended to honor it. Hal was very much like me. We honor our commitments."

"You and Hal were close?" I asked, already knowing the answer.

"Very."

"Did he confide in you?"

"Always. And I was always there for him." She paused. "But I wouldn't give him money as long as he stayed with her."

"And so," I continued smoothly, "he told you that sometimes he'd lose his temper with Emily and then feel badly about it?"

"Of course," she said, and then thought about her answer. "But he never hurt her. If she said he did, she's lying."

I backed up a little. "He was very lucky to have you as a confidante."

"Yes. He had little in common with his wife."

I decided to take a leap. What the hell, she'd never talk to us again. "He was concerned, wasn't he, that Emily was so accident-prone?"

Donald blinked, but said nothing. Mrs. Watkins looked wary; she was no dope.

"What are you getting at?" she asked.

I shrugged. "Nothing. Just that Emily was obviously very clumsy. All those bruises and black eyes. She must have always been running into things."

Mrs. Watkins hesitated, and then said, "I didn't see anything." The interview would be over in a minute. I had to move fast.

"Well, the last Christmas you all spent together, didn't Emily have a black eye?" Before she could answer, I said, "Didn't Hal tell you she'd run into a door in the middle of the night?" I was totally prevaricating now.

"That sounds familiar," she said cautiously.

"And that Easter Sunday when she was too embarrassed to go to church with you and your son because of the bruises on her face? Surely you remember that?"

"I think so. I'm not a hundred percent sure." She sounded old and tired, and I was beginning to feel sorry for her. But I felt sorrier for Emily.

"One last question. Which car was Emily driving when she got into that accident and broke her jaw? Hal's car or hers?"

Mrs. Watkins shook her head impatiently. "What difference does it make?"

"But didn't Hal tell you?" I pressed.

"Hers, I think. And now I'd like you to go." Donald and I both jumped up as if we'd been ejected from our chairs. Mrs. Watkins escorted us to the door.

"I hope they give your client the death penalty," she said.

"Well, thank you for sharing your thoughts with us."

She shook her head and closed the door. Then locked it.

"What a bitch," Donald said as we headed down the hall. "Poor Hal. I assume you want me to follow up on this Janet lead?"

"I'd appreciate it."

On the drive home, I thought about Hal and Emily's marriage, and how it had been sabotaged from the very beginning. Without his mother's toxic support, Hal might have given Emily a chance and they might have had a normal relationship. But, probably not. Mrs. Watkins didn't make Hal drink, and she didn't make him hit his wife either.

The rush hour traffic finally caught up to us and we had to slow down until we were barely moving. Every once in a while, Donald groaned in frustration, no doubt counting the minutes until he could smoke again. To the west, the foothills were bathed in a soft peaceful glow. It would be dark in less than an hour.

"This is a sad job we have," Donald muttered.

I looked over at him in surprise. "Yes, it is. Nobody ever needs our services for a happy reason." I hesitated. "Okay, you can smoke, but you have to lean as far out of the window as possible."

"Really? Thanks!"

I sighed. "You're welcome."

We drove the rest of the way home in companionable silence.

CHAPTER FOUR

When I was nineteen years old and still suggestible, I allowed my friend Leslie to talk me into dropping acid with her. We were at a party on the bohemian (i.e. seedy) edge of Beacon Hill celebrating the end of our first year at Boston University.

I'd known Leslie since the third grade and whenever I'd gotten into trouble—ditching classes, smoking cigarettes in the park, getting drunk at my sixteenth birthday party, hitchhiking to the Newport Folk Festival—it was always with her. We'd been inseparable all through high school and so far through college.

Although it never occurred to us we ought to be sexual ("alternative lifestyles" weren't quite yet in vogue), it's clear to me now that had one of us been male, he or she would have been my first ex-lover. Instead, we were simply best friends: innocent, sweetly clueless women who dated men but preferred each other's company to anyone else's.

As soon as we arrived at the party, a fashionably gaunt man with long flowing hair handed each of us some blotter acid and advised us to hurry since everyone else had already dropped theirs twenty minutes ago.

"We want everyone to be in sync," he explained.

I looked at Leslie. "I don't know about this."

"Oh come on, Rachel. It'll be a new experience."

It was May 1969 and everyone was being urged to use psychedelic drugs to blow their minds and thus expand their ordinary limited consciousness. And so, before I could stop her, she swallowed her portion. Throughout our years together, it had been Leslie's genius that got us into trouble and mine that got us out—usually at the last possible moment—mainly because I could think faster than almost everyone around me and even more importantly distinguish the truly dangerous people from the merely wacky. But I couldn't help Leslie, I reasoned, if I couldn't understand her and so I swallowed mine as well.

About forty minutes later, I tapped Leslie on the shoulder and informed her I'd figured the whole thing out. We were part of an unorthodox but valid experiment in which some people had been given LSD and others a placebo, the point being to see if those of us who had been given the placebo would begin to imitate the ones who were genuinely under the influence.

"It just stands to reason," I explained, lifting my arms to include, at that moment, the whole gestalt of everything.

Leslie stared at me for a moment, then burst out laughing. "That's brilliant," she said, pulling me down to the floor. For the next hour, we crawled around on our hands and knees trying to guess which people were under the influence and which ones were faking it.

"I bet they're faking it," Leslie would say, pointing at a couple of women who were tossing record albums out the window, or a group of men trying to light their hair on fire.

"I don't know," I'd reply. "It's becoming increasingly difficult to tell." Although I was trying not to notice, it seemed as if I could actually see all the atoms in the air zipping around and colliding with one another like bumper cars in an amusement park. The room felt very crowded.

"What about that cannibal in the corner?" Leslie finally asked.

"What cannibal?"

"The one with the big white bone in his nose."

I stared in the direction she was looking. "I don't see any cannibals, Les. Which makes me think you took the real thing, not the placebo."

She shrugged. "Anything's possible. What do you see?" She pointed across the room at a middle-aged man with short black hair who was wearing a tuxedo.

"Him?" I started to smile. I could feel my face cracking as if it were made out of dried clay. "That's Jerry Lewis, but he's acting genuinely funny which makes me think I took the real thing as well, since Jerry Lewis is never genuinely funny."

Leslie shook her head in awe. "My God, Rachel, you're probably the only person in the world who could have rationally determined you were out of your mind."

If so, it was the last rational thought either one of us had for the next twelve hours. The night is sketchy, but at some point I was sitting cross-legged on the floor watching Leslie press her thumb repeatedly into the carpet attempting to kill thousands of tiny blue insects. After what seemed like hours, I grabbed her arm and told her it was useless, that she'd never get them all. The Doors were singing "Light my Fire," and the next thing I remember we were kissing.

When we finally stopped, Leslie traced a finger down my face and said, "I thought I was kissing myself."

And I said, "I thought I was kissing a tabby cat." Which we thought was hilarious.

I can't recall if we kissed again, but an hour or so before dawn I remember following her down a narrow hallway into an overly bright kitchen. As I stood there shielding my eyes, I saw a table covered with various foods, all of it alive and wriggling. I watched Leslie reach for the chicken wings and stopped her just in time.

"Watch out, Les," I warned, "they're alive!"

She dropped the wing in horror. "Oh my God, you're right," she said. "Let's get out of here."

We stumbled down some streets in the dark and ended up at the Charles River where we bushwhacked for a while until we found a secluded bench overlooking the water. The neon lights from the Cambridge side of the river turned our watery view into a shimmering pink and purple tapestry. We listened to the ancient sound of frogs and to the leaves rustling in the wind.

When we finally woke up, we were lying on the bench with our arms wrapped around each other. Leslie's face was pressed against my neck. The sun was high in the sky and I guessed it was almost noon.

"Wow," Leslie whispered, "wasn't that the most amazing night?"

I thought of all the terrible things that might have befallen us. But hadn't. "We were very lucky."

She nodded happily. "I know. I can't wait to do it again."

My first and only foray into the mind-altering world of hallucinogens. After that, I decided I liked being in control of myself and as much of my environment as possible. And so, unlike Leslie, I passed up spending the next six years doing drugs, continued my education, and became a criminal defense attorney instead. The last time I saw Leslie she was heading off to join a commune somewhere in Tennessee. Although I never tripped again, I still carry a permanent souvenir from the adventure. Whenever I've been under prolonged stress, I suffer flashbacks from the drug: the atoms in the air begin to dance and everything around me seems to be alive and breathing.

"How lucky can you get?" Vickie joked when I first told her about it. "Yogis spend years in silent meditation in order to experience the same thing."

***

The night before the pretrial motions hearing in Emily's case, I lay in bed with Vickie, holding her for a couple of minutes before she went to sleep. Her strong lean body never failed to astonish me.

How could just yoga, walking and gardening make anyone so fit? I was even more fit, of course, but I worked at least ten times harder. Since I was feeling wide-awake and antsy, I figured I would read a few more chapters from *The Golden Notebook* by Doris Lessing (a book I'd started in college and was determined to finish before I died) and then slip into unconsciousness.

Vickie sighed in my arms. "You've been working so hard, sweetheart."

"Doctors and lawyers," I murmured.

"Yes, but I control the number of hours I work and you don't."

My body stiffened slightly. "I try but—unlike you—I don't have the luxury of turning down a client."

"Exactly." But then she sighed again, a lovely sound that meant she didn't want to argue.

Thank God, I thought, then snuggled closer, rubbing my nose against hers the way my parents always used to rub theirs together. Once, when I was seven, I asked what they were doing. "It's an Eskimo kiss," my father explained. I was confused. "But aren't we Jewish?" My father nodded. "This is the special Jewish Eskimo kiss." My mother giggled. "Very rare," she added. And then both of them were laughing. When I told Vickie the story, she clapped her hands delightedly. "Let's be as happy as they were!" I didn't remind her that later on my father died and that after that, my mother was never very happy again.

I brushed my hand across my girlfriend's breasts, considered making love but decided there wasn't enough time. "Go to sleep," I murmured.

Vickie began tracing the worry lines along my forehead. "I just wish you could do your job without it taking so much out of you."

"I can't," I said simply.

"I know." She made a face. "Will it go all right tomorrow?"

"I hope so," I said, ignoring the rest of her concerns. For the past year and a half, she'd worried that the stress of public defending was taking too much of a toll on me. I disagreed but pretended to consider the idea of going into private practice where I'd have a normal caseload, normal hours, and a much less interesting job. You'd think being married to a doctor would be great, but in many ways it wasn't. She was an internist, not an oracle, but try telling her that.

Vickie hesitated. "Is anything in the room moving?"

I knew what she meant. "The drapes are breathing a little."

She looked like she might start lecturing me again but didn't. "When you finish Emily's case, after you've won it, I'll take you on vacation."

"That sounds lovely. I'd like to go somewhere peaceful and quiet where there isn't any crime."

Vickie laughed. "I know it's hard to believe, but the vast majority of people right here in Boulder don't even think of committing crimes."

"Really?" I asked, like a wide-eyed child who's just been told that fairies and elves are always around us ready to help in any way they can.

"Really," she promised, and kissed my forehead like my mother used to when she was young and my father was alive and she was carelessly happy.

"I'm a little tired," I admitted.

"I know." She paused. "You genuinely love this client, don't you?"

I nodded. "I do. And I feel sorry for her as well. I want her to have a life."

"Well I hope you win, for both your sakes."

"Me too." I sensed her next question before she could speak it and shook my head. "Defeat is inconceivable."

"Yes sir," she saluted.

"A little louder please."

"YES SIR."

"Good. Now pass me that thick heavy novel and go to sleep."

"Yes sir."

"You know," I said, "except when we make love, I'd like you to act this way all the time."

She snorted. "In your dreams, baby."

***

Earlier in the week, Donald had located Hal's ex-fiancée, who lived in Littleton, a suburb of Denver only thirty miles away. He'd simply looked through Hal's high school yearbook and found her. In 1956, she'd been Janet Roberts. Now she was Janet Ellers. When Donald told her why he was calling, she asked if she could talk to me in person. I met her the following day at a trendy new vegetarian restaurant in Denver.

When I first saw her in front of the restaurant I was so shocked I stopped walking and simply stared, my jaw dropping open the way an amateur actress might register a bad surprise. That bastard, I thought. Janet lifted a tentative hand to acknowledge me.

"I know," she said as I approached. "I look just like her. I saw her picture in the paper when she was arrested. Let's go inside." She ushered me through the door and found us a table by the window.

"It's uncanny," I said.

"Yes." Even her eyes were a similar blue, but less opaque. It was like looking at the Emily that got away, the one who finished college, pursued a career, got married and had children. The Emily who never learned to flinch. My stomach hurt just looking at her.

A young energetic waitress appeared with a pitcher of water and filled our glasses. Immediately, I drained my glass and asked for more. Janet picked up her menu, dropped it, and picked it up again.

"I felt so bad when I read about the murder," she said. "The reporter quoted you as saying that you would rely on self-defense."

"That's correct," I said, waiting to find out if she was the ally I hoped she was.

"I'd like to meet her."

I blinked in surprise. "Why?"

She took a deep breath and then let it out. "Because I believe she's telling the truth, that she killed him in self-defense."

"Did he hit you, too?" I asked.

She drummed her fingers on the table. "I think I've been waiting thirty years to tell this to someone."

I nodded but said nothing. Every criminal defense lawyer learns how to act like a therapist, or they find another profession.

"Only once," she finally said. "Actually, he just shoved me really hard and I fell against a table. Immediately, he was apologetic and assured me it would never happen again, he was so sorry. I wanted to believe him, but I'd seen something in his eyes just before he pushed me, something cold, almost reptilian, which scared the hell out of me. I knew I had to break it off with him, but I also knew I shouldn't tell him why."

The waitress returned and we ordered a few dishes off the menu. Neither of us was hungry. While we waited for our food, which we wouldn't eat, she told me the rest of her story—how she managed to sidestep Emily's fate. She'd held off for more than three months. Finally, when the Weld County Sheriff's Department hired him, she found her way.

"For as long as I'd known Hal, he'd always wanted to be in law enforcement. While other boys fantasized about becoming an astronaut or a doctor who discovers the cure for cancer, Hal always dreamed about arresting the bad guys and locking them up."

Janet went to her parents and told them she didn't want to spend the rest of her life worrying whether her husband would come home at the end of each day. She asked them to break the news to Hal and his family. Although Hal's mother, Louise, assured her parents that Hal was willing to choose another career, Janet refused to hear of it; her husband, she said, would always hold it against her. And so she managed to extricate herself.

"Did your parents suspect anything?" I asked.

"You know, I think they knew it wasn't the real reason, but they didn't ask. They just supported my decision. I've always been grateful, especially now."

We picked at our food and wondered out loud why Emily hadn't seen the writing on the wall the way Janet had.

"She probably did," I said. "She just didn't run."

Janet pushed her plate away, and then dropped her napkin on top of it. Outside our window, a river of people flowed down Colfax Avenue on their way back to work. "I know this sounds ridiculous," she said, "but I actually feel a little guilty."

I nodded sympathetically. "It sounds ridiculous because it is, but I understand what you're saying. Because you managed to get away, your look-alike had to suffer in your place. Emily on the cross."

She laughed. "Something like that. It truly took my breath away when I saw her picture." She paused. "Do you think it would be too painful for her to meet me?"

"I don't know," I said, giving up on my food as well. "I'll think about it. I wish there were some way you could testify at her trial."

Janet pulled out a twenty-dollar bill and laid it on the table. "Please, let me pay. I'd be happy to testify, but would it be admissible? I'm a paralegal, but I mostly work on civil cases."

I made a face. "No, probably not. It was a minor incident compared to the abuse we're alleging Emily suffered and it happened thirty years ago. I'll file the motion, but I can't imagine Judge Thomas letting it in."

We stood up to go. "Well," she said, "I'm willing to help in whatever way I can. I want to support her."

We hugged and I watched her walk down the avenue, tall and straight, back to the law firm where she worked, the Emily that might have been. And then I thought of my real client snug in her cell at the Boulder County Jail, dreaming her life away.

***

In a murder case, you can't file too many pretrial motions. Twenty-five is good, fifty is better. If nothing else, you might set up some error that could later be appealed if your client gets convicted. Compared to most murder cases, however, Emily's was pretty straightforward. She'd either acted in self-defense or she hadn't. There were no snitches in the case, no codefendant confessions, no critical scientific evidence or procedures to litigate. The blood was Hal's, the confession Emily's. The victim was dead and the only other eyewitness was my client.

Still, I'd managed to draft thirty-seven motions, some of them demanding additional information, some moving to suppress various searches and statements, and the rest requesting the court to rule favorably on the admissibility of "crucial" defense evidence—Dr. Midman's and

Janet's testimony—and unfavorably on the admissibility of "highly inflammatory and prejudicial" prosecution evidence—photos of the autopsy, Hal's life insurance policy, et cetera.

My strategy was to fight hard on every single motion as if any adverse ruling would be a major violation of my client's constitutional rights. Because the judge would rule against me on every substantive motion, I was hoping he'd feel guilty enough to give me what I really needed: Dr. Midman's testimony. If he did, it would be a first. I knew Jeff would strenuously oppose it, but I had the advantage of being in a jurisdiction where it wasn't nice to make the defense lawyer cry. I *needed* my expert. I *had* to have her. If it meant lying down on the courtroom floor, kicking my pumps off and screaming, then so be it. Later, I could always change my name and practice law somewhere else.

There was only one case, a probation revocation hearing, scheduled before ours. Emily and I sat in the jury box and watched Ellen Silver—the new baby lawyer in our office—cross-examine the defendant's probation officer. I tried to pay attention so that I could give Ellen some helpful feedback, but I was feeling too distracted. Dr. Midman hadn't arrived yet and I was getting a little nervous.

Emily patted my hand. "She'll be here, Rachel. She's very reliable."

"How do you know?"

My client smiled. "Because except for my intimate partners, I'm an excellent judge of character."

I turned to look at her. "So Hal wasn't your first lover?"

Emily blushed. I loved that about her. "No, I had one other boyfriend—lover—in college."

"Tell me about him."

She shook her head. "There's nothing to tell. It lasted about nine months and then I received a letter informing me it was over. *C'est la vie.* So, what's the game plan today?"

"Wait a minute. You're changing the subject too fast. Did you love him, and why did he break it off?"

"I don't really want to talk about it." One of the other inmates had trimmed her hair in a very becoming way. Emily was always pretty but unlike most of my long-term clients who typically gained ten to fifteen pounds eating the starchy jail food, Emily was losing weight. I wondered if she was secretly worrying about the case but didn't want to tell me. She hated, as she put it, "to distress" me.

I waited patiently.

"Don't be so nosy. How could this possibly be relevant?"

I shrugged. "I don't know whether it's relevant or not. Maybe I am just being nosy, but I represent you on a charge of first-degree murder. Your life is in my hands."

"Oh, for God's sake. Yes, I loved him and he didn't tell me the reason he wanted to end it. I felt hurt and then I got over it. Satisfied?"

"Thank you," I said. "Speaking of past lovers, I had lunch a few days ago with a woman named Janet Ellers."

Emily nodded. "Yes, Hal's ex."

"Right. How did you know her name?"

Emily smiled mysteriously. "I have my ways. Actually, Hal and I used to talk about her. We didn't keep any secrets."

I wondered if I should tell her what Janet looked like. I doubted he'd told her that. If it helped cut some of Emily's loyalty toward him, I was all for it, but what if it backfired and simply caused more pain, more caving in?

"One day," Emily said, reading my mind as usual, "I was looking through Hal's wallet trying to find a ticket from the dry cleaners, and I found an old photo tucked behind some other pictures. It was Janet's."

"Oh," I said. "So you know what she looked like?"

"She looked like me when I first headed off to college."

"What did you do?"

"What did I do? Oh Rachel, sometimes you're so young and idealistic, so sure of yourself. I put it back in his wallet. I knew how it felt to be rejected."

When would I ever learn? Like all of the favorite people in my life, Emily refused to be pigeonholed. Sometimes she acted according to my invisible script, but just as often, she ignored it. How unfair, I thought: to be the best possible defense attorney I had to be a control freak, and at the same time I had to understand and even anticipate that nothing would ever go the way I expected. No wonder I was confused.

By the middle of the afternoon we'd resolved every motion except the one concerning Dr. Midman, who'd shown up on time looking sleek and elegant (a babe, Vickie would have said). There had been no surprises. As I'd predicted, Judge Thomas granted most of my discovery motions and denied everything else. Janet would not be allowed to testify, whereas the crime scene video, autopsy photos and Hal's insurance policy were all coming in. Since each of the searches in the case as well as Emily's statements to the police passed constitutional muster, they were also admissible.

"All right now," Judge Thomas announced. "Shall we deal with Ms. Stein's final motion concerning Dr. Midman?"

Jeff and I both nodded. I hoped he was as tired as I was.

"I've read your briefs," the judge said, "as well as an offer of proof from the defense. I understand, however, that Ms. Stein would like Dr. Midman to take the stand and summarize her proposed trial testimony. I will allow a short presentation."

I stood up. "Thank you, Judge. As you know, the only issue in this case is self-defense. Without Dr. Midman's expert testimony concerning the battered woman syndrome, a jury can't be expected to understand why my client reacted the way she did. Unless Dr. Midman is allowed to educate them concerning the syndrome and to give her opinion as to whether Ms. Watkins exhibits all of the characteristics of a battered woman, my client won't receive a fair trial. I can't stress how pivotal this testimony is to our case—"

"Ms. Stein," Judge Thomas interrupted, "I understand how important you think this is. Please, why don't we hear directly from Dr. Midman?"

"Thank you, Judge. May I assume you'll accept her as an expert on the psychology of battered women without my having to qualify her?"

"Yes, for the purposes of this hearing only."

Jeff was beginning to feel left out. He jumped up and stated his strong opposition to my motion, reminded the judge that no court in Colorado had ever recognized the syndrome, and how unfair it would be to the prosecution if the defense were allowed to call an expert to give an opinion about whether the defendant acted in self-defense when the defendant was perfectly capable of taking the stand and telling the jury herself.

"It's not rocket science, Judge," Jeff argued. "Despite Ms. Stein's assertions to the contrary, the issue of whether a person acted in self-defense is fairly simple to determine. If you allow Ms. Stein to call Dr. Midman at trial, you'll be allowing her to put her client on twice to say essentially the same thing. It's unfair and it's unnecessary."

The judge nodded. "I understand your position as well, Mr. Taylor. And now, could we put Dr. Midman on the stand?"

I motioned to Karen Midman, who was sitting in the courtroom, to come forward. My proposed expert was indeed lovely, which never hurt. I watched Judge Thomas follow her progress from the back of the room to the witness stand. She was slender, with green eyes, and honey-colored hair that kept falling across her face. Her blue silk pantsuit fit her perfectly. She sat down, smiled at the judge, and then raised her arm for the oath. I glanced over at Jeff and caught his eye. Using standard courtroom telepathy, I told him I was sorry, but that I had to win this issue no matter what. You're not sorry, he shot back, and I hope to God you lose.

After a few preliminary questions, I asked my expert to explain the battered woman syndrome.

She nodded. "Certainly. The syndrome constitutes a series of common characteristics that appear in women who are physically and psychologically abused over an extended period of time by a dominant male figure in their lives. Although in rare circumstances the victim may be a male, the literature suggests that the vast majority of victims are women. Dr. Lenore Walker conceived the phrase, 'battered woman syndrome' in 1979 in her groundbreaking book, *The Battered Woman*. I've included in my affidavit a bibliography of other books and studies on the subject that I'm familiar with as well." She stopped and took a drink of water.

I waited until she put her glass down. "Dr. Midman, are you aware of any cases in this country where the syndrome has been recognized by a district court judge in a criminal case?"

"Yes. It's been recognized in a number of states. Two years ago, for instance, it was recognized in Washington in a case called *State versus Allery*. I was the expert witness in that case. I know it has also been recognized in New Jersey, North Dakota, Missouri and Kansas. There may be other states, but those are the ones that come to mind."

"Thank you. Could you now tell the court why expert testimony is crucial in this particular case?"

"Absolutely. In a battering relationship, violence doesn't occur all the time. Rather, there's a cycle of violence, which has three phases. The first is a tension-building phase, the second is the acute battering stage and the third is a tranquil and loving phase. The cycle is continually repeated until the victim becomes unable to predict her own safety or the effect that her behavior will have on the abuser. As a result, the woman is reduced to a state of learned helplessness and is no longer capable of determining exactly when she is in danger. Because Emily stabbed her husband as he was coming toward her—before he physically touched her—it's essential that a jury understand why she reacted the way she did. In situations such as this one where an uninformed jury would not see any threat or impending danger, an expert can explain how a battering relationship generates different perspectives of danger, imminence, and necessary force."

I nodded in agreement. "Can expert testimony help the jury in other ways as well?"

"Oh sure. Expert testimony can rebut jurors' stereotypic assumptions by explaining why a battered woman like Emily would stay in an abusive relationship, and why she never sought help from the police or from her friends."

I then asked my expert a number of questions about Emily's background and history of violence. I had at least ten more questions, but stopped when I saw Judge Thomas glancing at the clock. I couldn't afford to irritate him. I needed this expert more than I'd ever needed one in any other case I'd tried. If it had been allowed, I would have massaged the judge's back, washed his feet and prostrated myself before him. I might have even promised never to be late for court again.

"Thank you," I said and sat down.

"Mr. Taylor," the judge said, "I will allow a short cross-examination."

Jeff walked to the podium without any papers in his hand. He'd interviewed my expert a few days earlier and—if he lost this hearing—would save his real cross-examination for trial. All he'd do today was try to show how irrelevant and superfluous her testimony would be. I was confident she could hold her own, but I still felt anxious.

"She'll be fine," Emily whispered.

Oh Emily, I thought, I would rather you take care of yourself.

"Good afternoon, Dr. Midman," Jeff said. "Have you ever misdiagnosed a client?"

The witness smiled. "I'm sure I have, at least initially."

"You spent approximately six hours with the defendant?"

"That's correct."

"Would you agree that many clients lie to their therapists?"

"Some do. Some lie because they're not ready to face the truth, because they're in denial."

Jeff nodded. "This defendant, even six months ago, would have told you she wasn't a battered woman. Correct?"

"Objection," I said, "calls for speculation."

Jeff looked at the judge. "Let's see if the witness can answer it."

"I'll allow the question," Judge Thomas said.

"Yes," Dr. Midman said. "In fact, she still denies it." She swept a few strands of hair off her comely face and nodded at the judge who nodded back.

"But," Jeff continued in a louder voice, "now that she's facing a charge of first-degree murder, she's willing to tell you about all those prior instances of violence."

"That's correct, but she still tends to minimize the violence and the effect it's had on her."

"Dr. Midman, isn't it true that if the defendant is lying about those prior instances of violence, then your diagnosis of her would be incorrect?"

My expert leaned forward to emphasize her answer. "Yes, but I don't believe she's lying." Then, she sat back and crossed her legs.

Confident but not arrogant, the kind of expert lawyers dream about but almost never find.

"Well, as far as I know, there are no eyewitnesses to these acts of violence, no witnesses who can even corroborate that they occurred."

Dr. Midman nodded. "Unfortunately, that's often the case. The abuse happens in private and the victim is usually isolated from her friends and family. Many if not most battered women won't reveal the abuse until they feel safe. Although Emily feels terrible about her husband's death, she's now safe from him and can begin to tell the truth about what her life was really like."

Jeff was beginning to look frustrated. "Dr. Midman, since there's no way to verify whether these instances of violence actually occurred, your diagnosis depends entirely on whether the defendant is telling you the truth."

"Yes, but by virtue of my training and experience, I'm confident that I can accurately evaluate the information a client shares with me. And, of course, I didn't base my diagnosis solely on what Emily actually told me or thinks she told me."

Jeff was getting nowhere and he knew it. "Just a few more questions, Dr. Midman. When all is said and done, only the defendant knows for sure whether she acted in self-defense or not."

"I agree."

"And no one, besides the defendant, knows for sure what happened in the seconds before she stabbed her husband."

"I agree with that as well."

When Jeff finally sat down, Judge Thomas declared a recess, promising to return in thirty minutes with a decision. Ellen Silver, our newbie who'd stayed all day to watch the hearing, now came bounding over to the defense table. Her blond bun had come undone and there was a splotch of mascara (which I never wore because it often streaked) above her left cheekbone. She looked about seventeen, but must have been at least twenty-four.

"Rachel, you were wonderful!" Her eyes shone with the excitement and unmistakable hunger every new public defender feels when they first begin to realize that lawyering could get them higher than any recreational drug.

"Thank you," I said. "But it doesn't matter if I don't win."

"Oh you will. You have to!"

Her enthusiasm would be tempered in a year or two, but for now it made me smile and at the same time ache a little, as if I were an accomplished athlete at the top of my game, but for how long?

I left Emily with a sheriff's deputy who was obviously fond of her. I heard them joking about some of the inmates as I walked Karen Midman out of the courtroom.

"That was perfect," I told Karen. "Thank you. I'll call you this evening with the judge's ruling."

Karen took off her jacket and folded it under her arm. "I always forget how tiring it is to testify. You have to really pay attention. Now, all I want to do is curl up with a glass of wine and a Marge Piercy novel. You must be exhausted."

I flashed her my best world-weary smile. "I have miles to go before I sleep, so I can't afford to notice."

She looked concerned. "Don't let yourself get wiped out, Rachel. These are very difficult cases. In my experience, jurors are not particularly sympathetic to this defense. No matter what you tell them, they still think the woman should have left."

During the recess, two more colleagues showed up to root for me. Ray Martinelli, my best friend in the office, really liked Emily and hoped she'd be acquitted, and Larry Hanover, our office head, came to see whether I would make new law. I was surprised how grateful I was for their support. Lately, I realized, I'd been isolating myself in my office thinking I didn't have the time to wander through the halls and joke around with everyone. I'd forgotten how sweet it felt to be a member of the gang, my chosen professional family.

We all stood when Judge Thomas entered the courtroom and took the bench again. After adjusting his black robe, he waved at us to sit down.

"Okay," he said. "I promise to have a written order by next Wednesday, but I'm prepared to rule as follows: I believe the defendant is constitutionally entitled to present a defense and I am convinced that she can't do that without presenting evidence concerning the battered woman syndrome. I will therefore allow the defense to call Dr. Midman as an expert on the psychology of battered women and to opine, if she chooses, on the ultimate issue of whether the defendant acted in self-defense. I will not, however, allow the expert to recite the defendant's statements that were made to her, since I am persuaded that the *Stiles* case, cited by the prosecution, prohibits their introduction into evidence as an exception to the hearsay rule. This means, of course, that I expect the defendant will take the stand and be subjected to cross-examination, which seems only fair. If the defendant, however, chooses not to testify, that is certainly her right, but I will reconsider my ruling and very likely grant the prosecution's motion prohibiting Dr. Midman's testimony. I hope this is clear to both sides. Any further motions based on this ruling should be filed no later than next Friday. Thank you everyone. Court is adjourned."

I'd won. It was going to cost the public defender's office another few thousand dollars, but it would be worth every penny. For a couple of seconds, I allowed myself to sit quietly and bathe in the happy news. If I'd believed in God, I would have thanked her profusely. After my colleagues came up and congratulated me, Jeff walked over and offered us twenty-eight years.

"You did a great job," he said. "Twenty-eight is my final offer, though. You have a week to decide."

"I don't need a week, Jeff. We're going to trial."

He shrugged. "It's your choice. Just because you have an expert doesn't mean a jury will acquit her. A life sentence means forty real years before parole eligibility. Maybe you should think about it."

"There's nothing to think about."

When he left, I turned to my client who hadn't said a word since the ruling.

"We won," I said, smiling. "We now have a decent chance of winning at trial."

"That's wonderful," she said. "You've worked so hard. I hope you can go home now and relax."

I studied her face, which as usual gave nothing away.

"You're not afraid to win, are you?" I asked.

Instead of blurting out something inane, Emily considered the question as if it truly mattered. "Well, I might be—I probably am—but I'm more afraid of losing. I hope that's good enough."

"It's good enough."

As I drove home, I noticed the atoms in the air were dancing all around me, that the stoplights were pulsing rhythmically as if they were alive and breathing. Oh well, at least it was worth it, a small price to pay if it saved my client. I thought about Ray's bleeding ulcer and Larry's high blood pressure and considered myself lucky. If I closed my eyes, I knew I'd see all the colors of the rainbow bursting through my poor tired capillaries. No problem: I kept my eyes open, concentrated on driving.

CHAPTER FIVE

I remember the last time I made love with a man. His name was Michael Burnside, and I'd met him at a wild New Year's Eve party given by one of my classmates. I was twenty-four, in my last semester of law school.

Michael, who was five years older than me, was already a successful personal injury attorney in Denver and was looking to settle down. After just a few months of dating, I could tell he was a man with a plan: work hard, make money, buy things, marry, have children, enjoy life, retire, buy more things, die. Sharing his life sounded like I'd spend it sitting next to him on a train speeding across a big flat state like Kansas and at the end of the ride, I would be old but not in the least amazed. On the other hand, he was handsome in a blond god kind of way and surprisingly sweet, which I valued. He also had the most beautiful white teeth I've ever seen.

Although Michael owned a house in Denver, we spent most of our nights in my tiny studio apartment right off Broadway within trotting distance of the law school. The last time we made love was in May 1974. It was six in the morning and bright sunlight was already pouring in through the one east-facing window in the apartment. We could hear the first batch of traffic rumbling up Broadway, the early birds getting their worms.

After Michael had been on top for a while, I flipped us over so that I could sit up and control the amount of penetration. We were both sweating. I remember gazing down and admiring the muscles in his chest, his biceps, the easy way he held me above him, his beautiful white teeth. I remember checking my alarm clock to make sure I'd have enough time to shower before my eight o'clock seminar. And then, I remember looking down again and seeing Dr. Silber, my childhood dentist, grimacing with pleasure, about to come, and attempting to hold off for as long as possible.

I closed my eyes, but the image of my dentist (a nice pleasant man who gave everyone sugarless chewing gum that had no flavor) persisted. When I'd been his patient, Dr. Silber had never acted inappropriately, never given me any reason to suspect he'd show up unbidden like this fifteen years later. Seeing him again, without an appointment, was a bad surprise, like slamming into a wall at fifty miles an hour. After a few seconds, I gave up and let him finish without me.

I averted my gaze in the shower hoping by the time I'd toweled off, Michael would have pushed Dr. Silber aside, but twenty minutes later my dentist was still there, waving goodbye to me from Michael's BMW. I stood on the porch and watched him drive away.

"See you later, babe," he called, unaware that our days together were seriously numbered.

Dr. Silber wasn't the first kindly man from my childhood to show up and spoil my relationships with the opposite sex. Murray Goldman, the stoop-shouldered rabbi at my Hebrew school, killed any slight attraction I might have had toward a fellow law student who used to rock back and forth while we studied together. And my fifth-grade schoolteacher Mr. Tierney—a short man with a beard and a pronounced goiter—slowly poisoned my relationship with a grad student in my last year of college. To be fair, my boyfriend, who'd stopped shaving and had a wild look in his eyes, had already begun to remind me of Charles Manson before Mr. Tierney took over.

The truth was there was nothing wrong with any of the men I dated. They just weren't women. My mind was simply doing what it could to alert my body that it was barking up the wrong tree. A few months before I ended it with Michael, I'd caught a glimpse of two women kissing passionately on the corner of Pearl and Broadway and felt electrified. Later, when I replayed the kiss in my mind (over and over), I realized I'd never felt riveted to someone the way they seemed to be, that I'd never been in love. I'd always assumed I was too dignified to fling myself at another grownup and possibly lose myself in the act of flinging. Until I came out of the closet, romantic love had always struck me as either frivolous or dangerous. Overblown, like Marilyn Monroe, and ending disastrously the way she did.

Turns out I was just a lesbian. By the time I met Vickie at twenty-seven, I was a seasoned veteran of Sapphic love with the requisite number of medals pinned to my chest and plenty of shrapnel in my arms and legs to prove it. The first time I saw Vickie sitting in a restaurant, I couldn't take my eyes off her. She was dark, handsome, vivacious, possessing that *je ne sais quoi*. After five or six dates, I decided she was the love of my life and that I was finally ready to commit: to fling myself at the same body—which looked remarkably similar to mine—every day forever and ever. Are gays and lesbians more narcissistic than straight people or just more honest about it? But I digress.

***

The night before Emily's trial, I lay as still as I could trying not to wake my beloved who slept soundlessly on the far edge of the bed in order to give me as much psychic space as possible, something she always tried to do when I was in trial. That night, if she'd moved any farther away to give me my space, she'd have fallen onto the floor. Looking back, there were so many ways Vickie tried to give me enough space, but I always wanted more.

At around four in the morning, Vickie asked if I was still awake.

"Yes, but I'm resting," I answered. "It's okay, go back to sleep."

She rolled closer and put her hand on my shoulder, a test. If I shrugged it off, I still needed to suffer by myself; if I allowed it, I was ready to be comforted. I allowed it.

"Is it late?" she asked.

I sighed. "Very." Four a.m. was my least favorite time of night—too early to get up, but too late even if I managed to sleep a few hours to avoid walking around the next day looking as if I'd been punched in the face.

"Is there anything wrong other than that you can't stop thinking?"

"No, I'm just ready for it all to be over."

"Well then," she ran an affectionate finger down the front of my body, "let's do something to make you stop thinking."

I smiled and patted her arm. "I think I might be too tired."

"That's all right," she said, urging me to roll over onto my stomach. "How about I just do you? A freebie."

I resisted rolling all the way over. "That doesn't sound very...equal."

"Fine," she said, pushing me flat on my face. "If you feel like it afterward, you can reciprocate."

I gave up and lay motionless, slightly embarrassed, but not so much that I wanted her to stop. One should always try to be gracious in these kinds of situations.

Suddenly I heard our Hitachi vibrator (the Cadillac of vibrators) start buzzing and imagined the worst: feeling as if without any foreplay or warning I'd stuck my finger into an electrical socket. But Vickie surprised me and began massaging my back and shoulders with the round vibrating knob.

"What a novel idea," I said and we both laughed. The packaging for each new Hitachi—we'd gone through several—always featured a June Cleaver look-alike holding the wand over her left shoulder, ready to massage her tired aching muscles. As if that was what anyone ever bought it for.

After a while, I could feel the muscles in my back starting to relax. Up and down with nice firm pressure, Vickie worked both sides of my back, my shoulders, my lower back and—very matter-of-fact—my butt where I hadn't realized how much tension I'd been holding. Up and down my torso, taking her time, slowly dissolving each successive layer of armor and getting down to the real body inside, to the one that might be willing to open its doors and let the right guest in. *Mi casa es su casa.* During the next ten or fifteen minutes, she allowed the vibrator to occasionally slip down between my legs, then back up again before I could get used to it. By then, my doors were flung wide open and I was feeling quite hospitable. As time went on, the vibrator slipped more often and I started begging her to stay.

Finally, she leaned down and whispered, "Would you like my hand as well?"

"Sweet darling," I breathed, "I thought you'd never ask."

She laughed, tousled my hair, then brushed some languid fingers down the length of my body, stopping for just a moment to pay homage to a small scar on my lower back (a bicycle accident when I was six) and then dropping out of sight.

Within minutes, I came big with a slight otherworldly cry of pleasure. After the contractions died down, I rolled over and gratefully kissed her mouth, face, neck and breasts. "Now it's your turn," I whispered.

"You really don't have to. It's late."

I licked the side of her neck. "Oh, but I want to. I wouldn't feel satisfied if we stopped now."

In the early morning light, she looked shy and innocent but willing to be corrupted. "Well, all right."

I studied her face for perhaps the millionth time. She had a wide generous mouth, cheekbones to die for and a flawless olive complexion. Unlike me, she wasn't vain, but unlike her, I wasn't classically beautiful.

"Something along the same lines?" I suggested, blowing softly in her ear. The pusher man.

She reddened slightly. "Yes, but then I want to do you again."

I shook my head. "Then I'd want to do you again, too. It would be endless. We'd be stuck in lesbian hell."

"Is that what they call it?" she asked, smiling.

I tried to look serious. "Yes, but not only that, we're going to run out of time." I pried the vibrator out of her hand. "And so I propose that after you, we make love together, the old-fashioned way."

"Nothing wrong with being old-fashioned." She rolled onto her stomach.

I gazed down at her and shook my head. "God, you have a lovely ass."

"Don't embarrass me."

We made love until it was time to crawl out of bed and separate once again into two independent beings. In less than thirty minutes, I took a quick shower, got dressed, wolfed down some scrambled eggs and drove to the courthouse. If my face looked a little haggard, at least I'd enjoyed myself. I could have done without the gritty eyes, but as soon as I entered the courtroom, they were of no consequence—I was in trial. Like any good criminal defense attorney, the moment I stepped into my role as someone's advocate, nothing in the world mattered except saving my client. Anything unconnected to that goal was simply extraneous. Tired eyes, civil uprisings, a nuclear explosion: all immaterial.

This trial, however, meant more to me than all the others combined. By then, of course, I knew I'd violated a fundamental rule, one of the Ten Commandments for lawyers—thou shalt not love thy client. Too late, all I could do now was win. During the past twenty-four hours, as part of my preparations, I'd visualized the only acceptable outcome: Emily and I standing shoulder to shoulder as Judge Thomas read the not guilty verdict. For the next couple of weeks, I'd simply have to work backward to make it happen.

Over the weekend, I'd laid out enough outfits to cover the first six days of trial. After that, I'd have to resort to some clever mixing and matching. Jeff, on the other hand, had enough suits to last him through Labor Day. This morning, I'd worn my favorite, the one I almost always wore on the first day of trial, a gray silk suit with matching pumps, a rose-colored blouse and my lucky trial necklace (a gift from my mother that came in the mail without any card or explanation; it took me a week using the process of elimination to figure out who sent it). To be honest, I didn't much care what I wore. Dressing for court was like donning a costume. If my role required me to appear naked, I'd have done it.

At the motions hearing, I'd received permission for Emily to wear her own clothes during the trial. As she was being escorted in by a male guard, also in street clothes, I saw that she'd chosen a green linen suit for the occasion, something she might have worn to an afternoon concert of classical music at the Boulder Public Library. Her blond hair was pulled back as usual, but held in place by a lovely green barrette.

"You look beautiful," I told her as she sat down next to me at the defense table.

"So do you." As if we were sisters at a ball in a Jane Austen novel.

My investigator, however, was not even close to beautiful. He had a large boil on the side of his neck that I could only hope would burst or go away before he had to testify. Maybe I could find him a scarf, some Hollywood-style cravat? To his credit, Donald had bought a brand-new white shirt, which still had the creases in it, but his pants were much too tight, and the hula girls were still gamely swaying across his wide stained tie. I told him to sit in the back of the courtroom and that I'd confer with him later.

Right before we started, Jeff walked over to the defense table with his hand outstretched as if this were a friendly tennis match. But it wasn't and I couldn't force my hand to take his, even for a moment. Although he didn't know it yet, I'd already metamorphosed into the vicious guard dog that had been trained to attack and kill all intruders.

"Well good luck," Jeff said. A true sport, not like me.

I nodded.

He waited a few more seconds and then retreated. Out of the corner of my eye, I saw Emily's little moue of disapproval.

"What?" I asked. "Should Churchill have wished Hitler good luck?"

Emily shook her head and laughed. "I know you won't like the comparison, but sometimes you sound just like Hal. He had a mordant sense of humor, just like yours."

I made a face but didn't say anything. Although she knew perfectly well what I thought of her life with Hal and her lingering feelings of love and loyalty, we both pretended she could always express her true feelings.

"I miss him, Rachel. I'm sorry but I still miss him. I wake up every night at three fifteen, the only time the jail is ever quiet, and for a few blissful seconds I can't remember where I am. And then when I remember, I feel so sad. I can't believe I killed him. I know I did, but I can't believe it."

I finished arranging my files into short neat stacks on the table. "Do you think you ever would have left him?"

She shook her head. "I doubt it. I've never been very good at standing up for myself. When I was seven, I wanted to go to school like all the other girls, but my mother had her mind set on keeping me at home and teaching me herself. I deferred to her until I was sixteen."

"You were brought up to be obedient," I said.

She nodded. "So how come I'm on trial for murder?"

"You defended yourself, Emily. Even good obedient people have the right to defend themselves."

Behind us, the courtroom was packed with at least fifty potential jurors, numerous reporters, a few of Hal's relatives and the usual assortment of spectators who show up at well-publicized jury trials for the free entertainment. There was one row of tough-looking, husky men who I assumed were from the Weld County Sheriff's Department where Hal had once worked. Nobody, I realized, besides my debonair investigator and me, was there for Emily. Alice Timmerman, Emily's best and only friend, wouldn't be flying in until the weekend.

"Maybe I wasn't defending myself," Emily whispered.

I sighed. "Okay, maybe you killed him for the money."

At least that made her laugh. "I'm sorry, Rachel. I think I'm very nervous. Thank God you're my lawyer. No matter what happens, I want you to know how much I've enjoyed getting to know you. You have no idea how much it's meant to me."

"Cut it out, Emily. We're going to win."

Finally, Judge Thomas entered the courtroom and everyone rose to their feet. Emily stared straight ahead as if she were facing a line of soldiers, their guns pointed at her head.

After we sat down, it took everything I had to ask, "Do you want to take the deal, Emily? If you do, you have to tell me now."

My client placed her pale slender hand next to mine on the table. "No thank you. I'm ready."

***

It took a full day to pick the jury, partly because no one under sixty wanted to spend a couple of weeks being a juror, and partly because a number of women, given the choice, wished to speak privately in the judge's chambers about their experiences with domestic violence. This, of course, was a good sign for the defense. In chambers, Jeff tried as hard as he could to convince the judge that all of these women were biased and therefore inappropriate for this kind of case, whereas I did everything possible to rehabilitate them, arguing that they could still be fair to both sides. Unfortunately, Judge Thomas was the kind of man who erred on the side of caution; he'd let in more evidence than many judges, but he'd also dismiss more jurors for cause if they didn't sound completely neutral.

After bumping a particularly sympathetic juror for cause, Jeff said to me, "Gosh, I had no idea how many women—"

"Don't," I said, cutting him off.

Both the judge and the court reporter had left the room and we were alone.

"Don't what?" he asked.

"Don't say another word or I'll have to stab you with my pen." I was only half kidding.

Jeff looked concerned. "I think you're taking this one a little too seriously, Rachel. It's your client who's on trial, not you." He ran a hand through his black wavy hair and then risked an encouraging smile. Christ, he was much too handsome. I needed jurors who could empathize with the defendant but not be swayed by the prosecutor's good looks. Twelve intelligent lesbians would have been perfect.

I took a deep breath. Jeff was right. Not about my taking it too seriously (you can never take a trial too seriously), but that my feelings were too intense. I needed to back off a little. To be effective, I had to project confidence and sincerity, not desperation.

"You're right," I told him. "I guess I've been more hostile than necessary. I'm sorry."

"It's okay. I know you care about her. I think she's guilty, but I certainly don't think she's evil. Did you ever consider any kind of mental state defense?"

I stood up, grabbing my yellow pad off the judge's desk. "Goddamn it, Jeff. She's not guilty and she's not crazy. She's a battered woman who defended herself."

He put his hands up as if fending off a rabid dog. "Look, Rachel, maybe we shouldn't talk until the trial is over."

"Good idea," I said and stormed out.

As is often the case, the jury we ended up with, six men and six women, represented a compromise for both sides. Jeff and I each used up all of our peremptory challenges weeding out the jurors we considered most likely to buy our opponent's arguments. Jeff dumped teachers, social workers and yuppies, the obvious liberals who might be sympathetic or even identify with the defendant. I scratched the accountants, engineers and born-again Christians, the kind of people who tended to discount the mysterious paradoxical aspects of the human psyche, or in the case of the two born-agains, those who might condemn Emily's dissatisfaction with her marriage, never mind the way she'd finally ended it.

In his opening statement, Jeff assumed a low-key, this-is-the-way-it-is-folks tone of voice, saving the prosecutorial passion for his closing argument. Now he was just doing his job upholding the rule of law. For fifteen minutes, he laid out all of the inarguable facts that proved beyond a reasonable doubt that after deliberation Emily had intentionally stabbed her husband.

When Jeff finally sat down, Judge Thomas asked if the defense wished to make an opening statement as well.

"Yes Judge," I said, then stood up and walked to the podium. Sincerity and confidence, I reminded myself, not desperation.

"Ladies and gentlemen," I began, "this case is about the right of a battered woman to defend herself. In order to understand why Emily Watkins stabbed her husband, whom she both loved and feared, you will need to understand a psychological phenomenon that I hope none of you knows anything about firsthand. It's called the battered woman syndrome. Almost a decade ago, in the late seventies, experts in the field of domestic violence began recognizing that women who were physically and psychologically battered over an extended period of time exhibited remarkably similar characteristics. In this case, the evidence will show that Hal Watkins battered his wife Emily over the course of their ten-year relationship and that she, too, exhibits these characteristics.

"During the second half of the trial, an expert, Dr. Karen Midman, will take the stand and explain the syndrome so that those of us who may be unfamiliar with domestic violence will be able to understand it. Ultimately, Dr. Midman will testify that in her opinion Emily Watkins has been suffering from this syndrome for years. Even more importantly, Dr. Midman will testify that in her expert opinion, when Emily Watkins stabbed her husband, she was acting in self-defense."

I paused to let the information sink in, then spent the next ten minutes listing some of the more important witnesses I intended to call, explaining how each person's testimony would help the jury understand how and why my client had acted in self-defense and was therefore not guilty.

"All beings," I concluded, "are entitled to defend themselves when it reasonably seems as if they are in imminent danger of being killed or of receiving great bodily harm. That is certainly the law in Colorado. At the end of this trial, Emily and I will be relying on you to uphold the law, to safeguard her right to defend herself, and to find her not guilty. Thank you for listening and thank you in advance for your patience and attention throughout the trial. It means a great deal to us."

Although it's hard to sit down when you have a jury's complete attention, the last thing you want to do is bore them. They can't walk out on you like an ordinary audience, but they can convict your client. I'd said enough and projected as much sincerity as I could. Any more, and they'd think I was running for office. Reluctantly, I turned and walked back to the defense table.

***

For the rest of the week, Jeff slowly and methodically built his case against Emily. While she sat very still, her hands clasped on the table in front of her, an endless succession of policemen, detectives, emergency medical technicians, doctors and crime scene investigators all testified about the first seventy-two hours of the investigation.

Although I'd memorized everyone's reports and knew what to expect, still there was something about hearing it out loud from real live witnesses. The problem with reading police reports over and over is that inevitably the reader becomes inured to the horrible reality of blood and death being graphically described. By the third or fourth reading, it doesn't sound so bad; it just sounds familiar. The jurors, of course, are hearing this information for the first time and the look on their faces (shock, horror, disgust) is often a wake-up call for the lawyer who's been living with these facts for months—oh right, getting stabbed to death with a pair of scissors is actually pretty gruesome.

Even the fifty-minute crime scene video, which was about forty-seven minutes too long—here we are approaching the Watkins's house, and now we're walking up the steps to the porch, we're crossing the porch, we're studying the front door, we're finally opening the door, now we're entering the house, we're panning the foyer, we're entering the living room, we're panning the walls, we're approaching the body, we're focusing on the feet, the legs, the torso, the arms, the neck, the head, we're examining the wound from a trillion different angles, and now we're panning the blood on the floor, the blood on the walls, the blood on the television, and because there's still some tape left, we're going to enter every other room in the house searching high and low (including under the bed) for any more signs of blood—seemed for the first time grimly fascinating. Every juror watched it with the kind of rapt attention usually reserved for an academy award-winning thriller.

During the following days, I'd occasionally look over to see how my client was doing. Almost invariably she'd vanished, disappeared deep inside herself to that place where nothing could touch her. After a couple of days, I allowed Donald to sit in the front row behind the defense table. By then, I assumed most of the jurors had figured out he was part of the defense team. Who knew, maybe they'd feel sorry for us. But the truth was, since Emily was so checked-out, I was feeling lonely and beleaguered and needed the company.

This was the painful part of criminal defense, the grunt work of sitting through the prosecution's case, springing up after each witness finished testifying, taking a few potshots, and then sinking down again. When the coroner told the jury that the cause of death was internal bleeding as a result of a stab wound to the abdomen, I stood up and asked him, "How do you know that the cause of death wasn't really Mr. Watkins's stubborn refusal to call for help?"

"Well," he scratched his head, trying to look thoughtful, "unless there's some evidence of that, I have to assume Mr. Watkins wasn't capable of calling for help."

I shrugged, trying to look just as thoughtful. "Well, in fact there *is* some evidence of that. In her statement to the police, Emily said her husband wandered around the apartment for over an hour. During that entire time, he never bothered calling anyone."

The coroner pursed his lips. "Well, even if he was stumbling around, he would have been in terrible pain. Why didn't *she* call for help?"

Of course I was supposed to ignore the question; I was the interrogator, not the witness. But I looked at the jury and said, "Because she was hiding in the bathroom and was too terrified to come out."

"Objection," Jeff called. "Ms. Stein is testifying instead of asking questions. And for the record, her client never stated she was in the bathroom because she was terrified."

"Oh for God's sake," I muttered. "Why else would she spend the night in there?"

Jeff was on his feet, looking self-righteously indignant. "Objection! I'd ask the court to admonish Ms. Stein to refrain from testifying and from making any further gratuitous comments."

I raised my hand to ward off the judge's ruling. "I'm sorry, Judge. It just slipped out."

"Oh right," Jeff said.

"That's enough," Judge Thomas interrupted. "You're both even now. For the record, I will sustain the objections. And please, no more gratuitous comments from either side."

As the week wore on, I actually began to find Donald's presence comforting. I'd realized by then he knew the case as well as I did. At the end of each cross-examination, I began checking with him before letting the witness go. The few suggestions he made turned out to be good and his observations were surprisingly insightful. By Friday, his grim deadpan comments were beginning to seem witty and amusing. Two soldiers in a muddy trench cracking jokes while our shell-shocked comrade stared straight ahead waiting for the next attack.

That afternoon, while the autopsy photos were being shown to the jury, Donald leaned over and whispered, "They ain't seen nothing yet. Wait till they hear she was a cold-blooded dame who whacked him for the cash." I had to bite my lip to keep from smiling.

"Very funny," Emily murmured.

"Sorry," Donald said.

"Actually," Emily continued, "it *is* very funny, in a macabre sort of way." She tried to smile. "You two are doing a wonderful job. I'll never forget it."

"It looks bad right now," I admitted, "it often does, but by the middle of next week, it'll start to get better."

"Yeah," Donald said. "Wait till it's our turn."

***

Rule 101 of trial by combat: start out strong and formidable, dance around and catch your breath in the middle, then end with a fury of kicks and punches. On Monday of the second week, Jeff began his final assault by calling a retired deputy sheriff named Dan Ferguson to the stand. Mr. Ferguson had been Hal's partner in the Weld County Sheriff's Department and had witnessed a young wannabe gangster with a .22 shoot Hal in the knee, thus ending Hal's career in law enforcement. He was being called for three main reasons: to explain Hal's disability, to create sympathy for Hal the true victim, and to opine that any able-bodied person (i.e. Emily) could have easily outrun Hal if she'd needed to.

For over an hour, Jeff and Dan had a heart-to-heart talk about Hal and what a great guy he was. They covered all of the important topics in an easy, free flowing exchange that seemed more like a candid conversation between friends than a witness being questioned under oath. It was an effective way to humanize the victim and by the end of their chat, a number of jurors were nodding in sympathy. Jeff was on a roll now. I needed to break his momentum immediately or I might never catch up.

The moment Jeff sat down, I began marching to the podium. "Mr. Ferguson," I said on my way over, "my name is Rachel Stein and I represent Emily Watkins."

"Yes," the witness said, "I know her."

"You're not a neutral witness, though, are you?"

He shook his head. "No, ma'am, I'm not. Hal was my friend, not Emily." He had a pleasant creased face like an old cowboy, and silver-colored hair that he'd probably worn much shorter when he was still working.

"Thank you for your honesty," I said. "In fact, you weren't even willing to speak with my investigator, were you?"

"No, ma'am." He was smart. He wouldn't volunteer anything extra, even if it meant not explaining something.

"Mr. Ferguson, you worked in law enforcement for twenty-five years?"

"Yes, ma'am."

"Ever arrest anyone for domestic violence?"

He nodded. "Yes, ma'am."

"Isn't it true that most domestic violence cases involve alcohol?"

"Yes, ma'am." Interesting, I thought. He's not going to fight me.

"You arrest a defendant for domestic violence, nine times out of ten, he's been drinking?"

"Yes, ma'am."

"Mr. Ferguson, after the deceased was shot and had to retire, he began to drink, didn't he?"

Jeff stood up. "Objection, Your Honor. This is beyond the scope of my direct examination."

"Well that's true, Your Honor," I said. "I can subpoena the witness for the end of the week." I pointed to Donald who stood up holding a subpoena in his hand. "But since Mr. Ferguson lives north of Greeley, I assume he'd prefer not to come back and that he'd rather answer my questions now."

"She's right. I'd rather not come back," the witness said.

Judge Thomas looked at Jeff. "Well, Mr. Taylor?"

Jeff frowned. He hated to appear unreasonable in front of the jury. If I hadn't made my little speech, he'd have forced me to wait until later. "All right. No sense making him come back."

I repeated my last question and the witness agreed that Hal had, indeed, begun to drink.

"And he began to drink so much that you and all of his friends became concerned, correct?"

"Yes, ma'am."

"Drank so much that you and all of his friends suggested he go into treatment?"

The witness sighed. "Yes, ma'am. It really killed him to retire so young."

"But he wouldn't go into treatment, would he?"

"No, ma'am."

I stared at him, daring him to disagree. "Even though he was becoming an alcoholic?"

The witness hesitated, but then nodded. "Yes, ma'am."

"And when Hal drank, he'd often become violent, wouldn't he?"

Jeff stood up, but before he could object, the witness said, "No, ma'am. Not that I ever saw."

I looked over at Jeff, waited pointedly for him to sit down and then turned back to the witness. I wanted to drag this out long enough to erase all of the warm fuzzy feelings the jurors had been left with at the end of Jeff's direct examination. "Mr. Ferguson, you knew, didn't you, that Hal had been arrested for domestic violence, for hitting his wife, Emily?"

"Yes, ma'am, but the case was dismissed."

"But wasn't that because Emily changed her mind about prosecuting him?"

"I have no idea, ma'am."

"And in that case, Hal was accused of punching his wife in the face, wasn't he?"

"I don't know the specifics, ma'am." He raked some fingers through his thick silver hair. Lorne Greene in *Bonanza*.

"But you knew it was a domestic violence case?"

"Yes, ma'am."

I took a chance. "And you knew that Hal had been drinking when he was accused of punching his wife?"

"Yes, ma'am."

I paused to check my notes. The next topic was drunk driving. "In the twenty-five years you worked in law enforcement, did you ever arrest someone for drunk driving?"

"Yes, ma'am."

"If someone has a blood alcohol of more than point oh-five, it's illegal, is it not, for them to be driving?"

"Yes, ma'am."

"That's called driving while ability impaired."

"Correct."

"And if someone's blood alcohol is twice that, in other words over point one, then they're considered to be driving under the influence and a danger to every motorist on the road. Is that correct?"

"Yes, ma'am."

By this point in the cross, we were the only two people in the world. No one else mattered. It would be that way for Jeff when he was cross-examining Emily. "And any motorist caught driving with a blood alcohol of more than point oh-five would be arrested and thrown into jail. True?"

"True," he agreed.

"In this case, on the night Hal Watkins was stabbed, he'd been drinking, wasn't he?"

"I think I heard that, ma'am."

"Didn't the prosecutor tell you that?"

"Yes, ma'am." An honest cop.

"And in fact, when they tested it, Hal's blood alcohol was over point one?"

"That's what I heard." A very honest cop.

I kept on going. "Which means he was legally drunk, doesn't it, and that if he'd been caught driving that night, he would have been considered a danger to everyone on the road and would have been arrested and thrown into jail?"

"I suppose so, ma'am, but he wasn't driving. He wasn't doing anything as far as I know."

Ah, I thought, the witness is finally getting annoyed. Now, what would it take to make him angry? Let's find out. "You've testified on direct that your friend Hal walked with a slight limp and couldn't run anymore?"

"Yes, ma'am."

"But he could still kick with his good leg, couldn't he?"

"I suppose so, ma'am."

The moment he answered one question, I asked the next. "Hal worked out with weights, correct?"

"Yes, ma'am."

"He was quite strong, wasn't he?"

"Yes, ma'am."

"Much stronger than my client?" I wouldn't have asked the question if he'd been a smart aleck, but this cowboy was a straight shooter.

"Yes, ma'am."

"So even if he limped and couldn't run anymore, he could still punch someone?"

"Yes, ma'am."

"He could still slap someone?"

"Objection, Your Honor," Jeff said.

"On what grounds, Mr. Taylor?" the judge asked.

Jeff had to think about it. "Ms. Stein is asking the witness to speculate. There's no foundation for the question."

"Overruled. The witness may answer the question."

"Thank you," I said. I turned to the witness. "So Hal was capable of slapping someone if he wanted to?" I was leaning forward, my hands resting on the lectern.

"Yes, ma'am."

"And shoving someone?"

"Yes, ma'am."

"Of slamming a door into someone?"

"He wouldn't do that, ma'am."

This was almost fun. "Well, if a neighbor saw Hal slam a car door on Emily's foot, you wouldn't say that was impossible, would you?"

"I'd say it wasn't impossible, but I can't imagine Hal doing such a thing."

I pretended to think for a moment. "How about breaking someone's jaw? Was he physically capable of that?"

For a moment, Jeff looked as if he was going to object again, but then decided not to.

"I don't know, ma'am. Again, I can't imagine him doing such a thing."

"You knew, didn't you, about a month and a half before Hal's death, that his wife Emily suffered a broken jaw?"

"She told me she'd been in a car accident."

I nodded. "I see. And you believed her?"

He nodded back. "Yes, ma'am, I did. I had no reason whatsoever to think she was lying."

"Hal was much bigger than his wife, wasn't he?"

The witness sighed. "Yes, ma'am."

"And he drank too much alcohol, didn't he?"

"I think I already acknowledged that."

"And would you also acknowledge that your friend Hal had been abusing his wife for years?"

Jeff jumped to his feet. "Objection! There's absolutely no foundation. Ms. Stein has no basis for asking that kind of question."

"Do you?" Judge Thomas asked. His face was carefully neutral.

Not really, I thought, but what I said was, "Your Honor, I believe I do. May we approach the bench?"

The judge nodded. Jeff and I hurried over to the judge's bench and stood as close as we could. The judge leaned forward and whispered, "Well, Ms. Stein?"

"My client told me that Mr. Ferguson has also seen her with a black eye."

"That's it?" Jeff asked indignantly.

"Shh," the judge cautioned. "That's not exactly the same as knowing the deceased had been abusing his wife for years."

Like a stubborn six-year-old, I held my ground. "It was enough to ask the question," I said.

Judge Thomas shook his head. "You can ask about the black eye, but that's all."

After we returned to our places, I took a quick drink of water.

"Mr. Ferguson, when you visited Hal and Emily's house a few years ago, didn't you see Emily with a black eye?"

He could have easily denied it and I would have been stuck with his answer. But instead he said, "I think it was about four years ago."

I was beginning to admire him. At that point, I might have sat down, but I didn't think I had anything to lose by asking whether Emily had explained this injury as well. What could he say that would hurt me?

"Did you ask her about it?" I crossed my fingers. Again, he could have said no, or that he didn't remember.

"She said she'd walked into the bathroom door in the middle of the night."

Bingo.

"And you believed her?" I asked incredulously.

"Yes, ma'am, I had no reason—"

"Oh please, Mr. Ferguson. If you'd arrested someone for domestic violence and his victim told you she'd run into a door, would you have believed her?"

"Objection!" Jeff yelled.

"I'll withdraw the question," I said. "Thank you for your candor, Mr. Ferguson. No further questions."

"Not bad," Donald whispered when I returned to the defense table.

"Thanks," I said.

"He was the only one of Hal's friends that I really liked," Emily murmured.

"I can see why," I said.

Jeff stood up and asked for a ten-minute recess in order to find his next witness. As soon as the jury was excused, he grabbed his trial notebook and left the room with Detective Moorehouse behind him.

I leaned over toward Donald. "They're trying to decide whether to still put Hal's mother on the stand. Jeff knows we won't call her if he doesn't."

Donald nodded. He was wearing the new blue and red tie I'd bought him over the weekend. "What are you betting on?"

"That he'll call her."

I was right, but the Louise Watkins who took the stand and answered all of Jeff's questions was not the elegant ice queen Donald and I had visited in March. In the two months since we'd seen her, she'd either taken a few acting lessons or Jeff had prepped her well. The witness who was testifying now might have been Louise's much nicer sister, a sad slightly befuddled woman, not the kind of person you'd want to press very hard on cross-examination. As soon as she was sworn in, she asked if she could have a drink of water. Her hands even shook a little as she sipped from her glass. Jeff kept it short and sweet: her son was a good peaceful loving man; he wasn't happy with his wife but took his marriage vows seriously; he treated Emily with respect and never harmed her in any way; he was the best son in the world and she missed him every day. Jeff thanked her and sat down.

Then it was my turn. I didn't realize until it was almost too late that Jeff had set me up. As I approached the podium, I decided that if she was old and pleasant, I'd be kind and solicitous.

"Mrs. Watkins," I said, "I'm sorry, but I have to ask you a couple of questions as well. I hope they won't upset you too much."

"It's all right." She clutched her glass. "It's your job. I understand."

"Thank you, Mrs. Watkins. First of all, you testified on direct that your son was unhappy with his wife."

She nodded. "Yes, that's what he told me."

"And you think he drank because he was unhappy with his wife?"

"Yes, but he didn't drink that much."

This was my chance to discredit her in a kind gentle way. "So you don't think your son was an alcoholic?"

"Oh, not at all. Just the occasional beer or glass of wine at supper."

"I see. Didn't he also drink because of his disability?"

"Oh no, he'd accepted that."

So far, so good. "Sometimes, though," I continued, "because he was so unhappy with his wife, he'd lose his temper with her?"

She sat up a little straighter and I could see the real Louise struggling to stay hidden. "Well, anyone can lose their temper. Haven't you ever lost yours?"

"Mrs. Watkins, I know this must be difficult, but I need you to answer my question. Sometimes, because your son was so unhappy with his wife, he'd lose his temper with her. Is that correct?"

"Oh I suppose so. Once in a while."

"Thank you. The last Christmas you spent together, Emily had a black eye. Is that correct?"

The witness looked down at her lap for a moment, then up again. "There was one Christmas when she had a black eye, but I'm thinking now that it was three or four years ago. I'm sorry, but my memory isn't so good anymore."

Yeah, right. "Has it declined since you spoke with me two months ago?"

"Excuse me?"

"Do you remember speaking with me and my investigator in March?"

"Of course I do."

"And do you remember telling us that Emily had a black eye the last Christmas you spent together, not three or four years ago?"

"No, I remember you asking me whether Emily had a black eye the last Christmas we spent together, and I said I wasn't sure. Since then, I've thought about it and I think perhaps you were trying to put words in my mouth."

Well at least I didn't have to be so kind anymore. "And since then, you've also met with the prosecutor, haven't you?"

"We've spoken a few times."

"And of course you informed him that you'd talked with me and my investigator?"

"I'm not sure. I may have mentioned it."

"And of course you told him what you'd said to us."

"I'm not sure if I did or not."

"That's a very tricky memory you have, Mrs. Watkins. No further questions."

I stared at her for a moment as if I hoped she might change her mind and tell the truth, then turned my back to her and walked away.

"You were lucky to get out alive," Donald whispered when I returned to the defense table. "What a bitch."

"She lost her son," Emily murmured.

The last three witnesses' testimony pertained to the insurance policy. Jeff was enjoying himself now, asking way too many questions, as if he'd never heard this information before and couldn't quite believe it. On cross, I did the best I could, implying that Emily had been concerned about her husband's health—he wouldn't stop drinking—and therefore it made perfect sense to buy an insurance policy on his life, that the timing was unfortunate but meant nothing. I sat down feeling as if I were the only guest left at a party where everyone else had long since gone home and the hosts were snoring in their bedroom.

I closed my eyes and pictured the bay in Zihuatanejo that Vickie and I had visited, one of the most peaceful places in Mexico. At sunset, when the temperature is perfect (about eighty degrees) the townspeople arrive with their families in tow and the adults all sit at the water's edge in their bathing suits or underwear eating chicken and corn on the cob catching up on each other's news, the teenage girls in bikinis laugh and toss their hair, the boys square off for a game of soccer, and the little kids run back and forth in the water shouting excitedly, until at some point everyone stops what they're doing and their collective gaze turns toward the horizon to watch as the orange sun descends into the turquoise colored sea; and then, there's a moment of silence suffused with the kind of happiness that money can't buy because there's nothing at that moment that anyone would wish to be different. I opened my eyes and sighed.

Finally, a few minutes before five, the prosecution rested. The judge glanced at the clock, and then decided to adjourn for the day. As the guard approached to escort Emily back to the jail, she asked if she could speak with me in private. I told Donald I'd catch up to him in the hall. We waited until everyone filed out of the courtroom.

"Okay," I said, "what's up?"

Emily took a deep breath and let it out. "Is there any way we can win the trial if I don't testify?"

I felt my mouth drop open and my head begin to shake from side to side. "No."

She continued as if she hadn't heard me. "Because I'd prefer not to. I've seen what you do on cross-examination and I can just imagine what the prosecutor will do to me. I'm too confused and I'm afraid I won't do a very good job."

My heart thudded in my chest and I felt dizzy, as if I'd drunk too many margaritas under a blazing sun. "You'd be committing suicide if you don't testify."

She smiled as if I were being much too melodramatic. "A trial," she said in her dreamy sounding voice, "is such an odd way to get at the truth, don't you think? It makes simple things sound terribly complex and complex things sound so simple. Innocence and guilt, for instance. Who isn't both innocent and guilty?"

I wanted to shake her, but she'd had enough physical violence to last her a lifetime. "Emily, wake up! Now is the time. Open your goddamned cage—it isn't locked—and fly away."

In a small bewildered voice, she asked, "Where would I go?"

"Anywhere you want to." I knew I sounded desperate, but I couldn't help it. I gestured wildly around the room, at the judge's bench, the court reporter's empty chair, the rows of deserted seats, the soundproof windowless walls. "Anywhere is better than here."

She stared at me, then blinked her eyes and said, "Yes, of course you're right. Oh Rachel, I'm terribly sorry if I scared you."

CHAPTER SIX

The next morning, I arrived at the Justice Center at a quarter to eight and found Donald sitting on one of the narrow wooden benches in the hall outside the courtroom. Since the doors to the courtroom were still locked, I sat down beside him to confer about our witness list.

Besides Dr. Midman, we planned to call Emily's best friend, Alice Timmerman, seven medical doctors, the neighbor who'd seen Hal slam a car door on Emily's foot, a Boulder County policeman who'd arrested Hal six years earlier for domestic violence, two felons willing to testify that Hal had used excessive force on them, and of course,

Emily. Normally, I would have saved my client for last, but Donald and I both agreed we'd better put her on second, as soon as Dr. Midman finished testifying. After that, she'd be free to dissociate for the rest of the trial. Later, after we'd won, I could tell her the conditions were safe now, and like a political refugee hiding in some other country, she could finally return home.

It took almost forty minutes to figure out which witnesses were available that afternoon, and which ones we'd call on Wednesday and Thursday. None of the doctors could testify until Wednesday after lunch and some were asking not to be called until Thursday. The neighbor, who'd screamed at Donald after being subpoenaed, had the busiest schedule of all: bridge, golf, an art appreciation class and lunch with her daughter-in-law. She'd advised us she was only available between ten thirty and eleven fifteen tomorrow morning.

"Is she worth the hassle?" Donald asked. "She's really pissed off at us."

"I know," I said, "but she's a crucial witness, the only person who ever actually saw Hal hurting Emily. We have to put her on."

He grunted. "Okay fine, I'll phone her this afternoon. How much abuse do I have to listen to before I get to hang up?"

I reached over and began adjusting his tie. "We really need her."

He grunted again. "So a lot." He was trying to frown, but I could tell by the flash of pleasure in his eyes that he liked someone touching his clothes, attempting to spruce him up.

The bailiff, a slight, nervous man who always wore a bow tie and matching suspenders, unlocked the courtroom at eight thirty and we marched inside. After arranging my files the way I wanted, we sat at the defense table waiting for Dr. Midman who promised to arrive early. She would be our first witness. The room was beginning to fill, but the trial wouldn't start until nine. True to her word, my expert showed up a few minutes later carrying a briefcase in one hand and a green leather overnight bag in the other. She looked a little out of breath, but otherwise calm and composed.

"I've been subpoenaed to testify tomorrow in another murder case in Massachusetts," she told us. "If I'm done by one thirty, I could catch a plane at three. If not," she made a face, "there's another one at midnight."

"Another battered woman case?" I asked.

She nodded. "And compared to that one, yours is a piece of cake."

"Why is that one so much worse?" Donald asked.

Dr. Midman shrugged. "The woman handcuffed her husband to the bed while he was sleeping and then set him on fire."

"Any insurance policy on the husband's life?" Donald asked.

"No." Dr. Midman laughed. "No insurance policy." She looked around the courtroom. "Where do you want me to sit?"

Donald pointed to the front row right behind us. "You can sit there. Give us something nice to look at."

"Well thank you," Dr. Midman said, placing her bags on the seat beside her.

"You're welcome," Donald said.

"Donald," I murmured, "you old dog."

He blushed. "Did that sound as dumb as I think it did?"

"Not at all," I said, "very Sam Spade."

"Yeah, right."

Since the first day of trial, my investigator's appearance had steadily improved. The huge boil on his neck had finally burst and he was looking almost presentable in a seedy, used-car salesman kind of way. He'd washed his hair and slicked it straight back, had splashed some water on his wrinkled button-down shirt, and had made an effort not to spill any additional food on his tie and pants.

Besides handling witnesses and keeping me company at trial, Donald had made himself invaluable in other ways as well. The night before, he'd offered to pick up Alice Timmerman at the airport and drive her to my office, which gave me enough time to run home, take a shower and scarf down some yogurt before meeting her there.

Although Alice was clearly tired from the trip, she had a million questions and was anxious to help in any way she could. Within minutes, I understood why Emily liked her so much. Originally from Israel, she was a smart, straightforward woman with a dry, self-deprecating sense of humor. After we finished preparing her testimony, I found some Brie and crackers in the kitchen (if you're in trial, there's an unspoken rule you can steal anyone's provisions) and made us a late night snack. Later, I drove her to the Boulderado Hotel on Thirteenth Street where I'd reserved a room for her.

At a quarter to nine, Donald and I finished discussing logistics and were waiting for the guards to bring Emily into the courtroom. Usually they brought her at least ten minutes beforehand so that we could have a little time with her. While we were waiting, Alice arrived looking very chic in a maroon silk dress. She was a tall, heavyset woman with thick curly hair and a ruddy complexion. The night before, I'd learned she was the executive director of a national children's cancer association based in New York City. We introduced her to Dr. Midman, who admired her dress and asked where in the city she'd bought it. Alice named the boutique and Dr. Midman recognized the name. They laughed and then Alice mentioned a different store and Dr. Midman knew that one too.

Donald and I looked at each other and shrugged. It was a sad day in Hicksville when I identified more with Donald than two fashionable women from the big city. I glanced down at myself and wondered if my navy pinstripe suit was a little too subdued, maybe even drab. When the trial was over, I would make Vickie go shopping with me. Or better yet, I'd call Karen Midman and ask her to take me.

At five minutes to nine, the bailiff stepped into the courtroom to check whether everyone was present. There were about twenty spectators in the audience, at least three of them reporters from the *Boulder Daily Camera* and the *Rocky Mountain News*. Louise Watkins was there, of course, flanked by a couple of well-dressed elderly women. I'd hoped that Hal's ex-colleagues from the Weld County Sheriff's Department would get tired of showing up, but they didn't; today, five beefy representatives, who looked like an advertisement for Budweiser Light, were sitting behind Louise. Jeff Taylor and Detective Moorehouse were bent over the prosecution table, thumbing through one of the many thick black notebooks scattered in front of them. I caught the bailiff's eye, and then looked pointedly at the empty seat beside me to indicate I was still waiting for my client. The bailiff nodded and slipped back out again.

A few minutes later, I saw Janet Ellers walking up the aisle and waved her over.

"You came," I said, smiling at her. I'd guessed she would. I'd called her a couple of weeks ago and told her that Emily was fine about her coming to support us.

Janet was wearing a pale yellow sundress and her hair was pulled back in a ponytail, the way Emily often wore hers. It was still hard to look at Janet without a slight pang: the one who got away. She carried an open cloth handbag with a ball of yarn and a pair of plastic knitting needles inside.

"It took a few days to arrange the time off," she explained, "but I can be here until the trial is over. If there's anything I can do, please ask."

"Thank you," I said and introduced her to Alice and Dr. Midman. Alice immediately made room for her to sit down. If they were surprised at Janet's resemblance to my client, they kept it to themselves. I glanced at the three of them. Until today, the rows behind the defense table were always empty, a dead giveaway Emily lacked supporters. At last, she had a decent cheering squad.

By nine twenty, I was beginning to feel queasy. Why hadn't they brought Emily over yet? Had something happened during the night? What if she'd checked out for good? I didn't really think so, but I couldn't dismiss the possibility. Should we have taken the deal? If I'd seriously pushed, Jeff might have come down to twenty-six, maybe even twenty-five. Stop it, I told myself. Finally one of the side doors to the courtroom opened and I saw a redheaded guard named Sunny who often accompanied Emily to court. Thank God. But then I saw he was alone. Sunny hesitated in the doorway, and then hurried over to where I was sitting.

"Oh-oh," Donald said.

"Bad news," Sunny whispered. "She wouldn't come. We all tried talking to her, but she wouldn't come. She told me to give you this." He handed me a folded sheet of paper. "I'm sorry. We really tried."

For a moment, I had the strongest urge to lay my head down on the table and go to sleep. Just for a few minutes, an hour at the most. But of course I didn't.

"What does it say?" Donald asked.

I spread the paper flat on the table so that we could both read it.

Dear Rachel,

Please don't hate me. I'm sorry, but I just can't go through with it. I've been up most of the night debating with myself, but my courage simply fails me. I know this is something you can't understand because you're always so strong and steadfast, so certain of the right course of action. The thought of your disappointment and disapproval pains me, but taking the stand and justifying my life with Hal to twelve incredulous strangers and then being cross-examined by Mr. Taylor is beyond my present capabilities. You'll have to go on without me.

Good luck,

Emily

I blew out a long breath. Shit. Suddenly my mouth felt dry and I poured myself a large glass of water and drank it. Then, I poured myself another.

"What are you going to do?" Donald asked after I drank the second one.

I sat still for a couple of seconds, then folded the paper and stuck it in my briefcase. "Waive her presence, put on Dr. Midman, go to the jail during lunch, and convince my client to come back and take the stand."

Donald looked at me and nodded. "Okay," he said. "It's a plan."

We turned around to the women sitting behind us and explained what was going on. They were worried, of course, but heeded my advice not to show it. As far as the defense was concerned, everything was hunky-dory. I informed the bailiff I was ready and that I would be waiving my client's presence for the morning only. As soon as the judge took the bench and the jury was seated, I stood up and announced that my client had decided to absent herself during Dr. Midman's testimony because she felt it would be too painful to hear. Jeff looked surprised, but didn't object.

My direct examination of Dr. Midman took about two and a half hours and went even better than I'd hoped. She was a true professional and as Emily had predicted, an excellent witness. Through her careful answers, she managed to convey both her competence and experience without ever sounding like an arrogant know-it-all. Because I wanted the jury to trust her judgment, I spent a considerable amount of time discussing the literature on battered women and attempting to portray my expert as a mainstream psychologist with views generally accepted by the vast majority of the profession. I watched a number of the female jurors warming up to her, and a few of the male jurors admiring the way she looked. Hey, whatever worked.

When I returned to the defense table, Donald looked much more optimistic.

"It was good," he said, "real good. Even I understood what she was talking about."

After a short recess, Jeff began his cross-examination. In order to accommodate my expert's schedule, we'd all agreed to go straight through until he finished and then break for lunch. As I'd expected, Jeff spent very little time attempting to discredit my expert's credentials or the literature she relied on. Instead, he focused like a laser beam on the obvious problems in my case: no one had ever witnessed any serious violence between Hal and Emily; Emily hadn't claimed self-defense to the detectives who arrested her; people often lie about their motives for killing others, especially if they're facing imprisonment; if Emily had experienced only a minimal amount of violence in her relationship, then her fear of being hurt wouldn't be legally "reasonable" and she wouldn't be entitled to claim self-defense; and no one but Hal and Emily were present on the night of the killing, and now no one but Emily was available to testify about what really happened. At exactly one thirty, he asked his last question. His blood sugar must have been very low.

"And so, Dr. Midman, if Emily Watkins wasn't really a battered woman and her real motive that night was to collect on her husband's insurance policy, then all of your testimony concerning the battered woman syndrome would be irrelevant, wouldn't it?" It was argumentative and stupid, but I didn't object. I knew my expert could take care of herself.

Dr. Midman turned and looked directly at the jury as she answered. "You're right, Mr. Taylor. If Emily wasn't a battered woman, my testimony would be irrelevant. But I'd stake my reputation on my opinion that she was, and that she was acting in self-defense when she stabbed her husband. Her motive that night wasn't greed. It was far more basic, to protect herself."

Jeff stood still for a moment looking pale and frustrated. And then he sat down. He needed food.

I stood up. "No redirect Your Honor."

Judge Thomas checked the clock, then told everyone to be back at three. Which gave me an hour and a half. As soon as the jurors were gone, I grabbed my briefcase and hurried over to thank my expert. She was stuffing her blazer into her overnight bag.

"You were great," I said. "Now, if I can just get my client to testify, we might even win."

She zipped up the bag. "These are tough cases, Rachel, even when everything goes right. Call me when you get a verdict."

"I will. I hope you make your plane."

"Thanks," she said. "Good luck."

I checked my watch and then began trotting toward the exit. If traffic was light, I could make it to the jail in fifteen minutes. Alice caught up to me outside the courthouse.

"Let me come with you," she said. "Emily might listen to me."

"All right," I said, then noticed her chest was heaving and her face was even redder than usual. "I'll get my car and pick you up right here."

She nodded, too out of breath to say anything else.

We had to wait at least ten minutes before the jail receptionist could find someone to escort us back to the women's module. When we got there, a black deputy named Penny, who loved Emily almost as much as I did, promised to pull her out for us, even if she didn't want to come. We waited in the dayroom, staring at the battered piano, the AA slogans scribbled on a portable blackboard, the Bibles and religious pamphlets strewn across the table. There was a stack of unwashed food trays on the floor that smelled like congealed meatloaf.

Alice took it all in, but didn't say a word.

I pointed to a red plastic pitcher on the table. "Do you want any Kool-Aid?"

She managed a tiny smile. "No thank you."

I hesitated. "It's tough," I said. "Especially if you've never been here before."

"Yes," she said, "it is."

When my client finally walked in, her shoulders slumped at the sight of us. She was wearing her usual navy blue uniform.

"Emily," Alice said, her voice breaking a little.

"Hello, Alice. It's wonderful to see you. I wish it were under better circumstances. This must be very upsetting for you."

Alice shook her head. "I'm fine," she said firmly. "There isn't much time. Your lawyer and I have come to discuss your decision not to testify."

Emily turned to me. "I knew you'd come, but it won't make any difference. I can't do it, Rachel. I just can't."

Alice moved her hand, motioning me to step back a little. "How long have we been friends, Emily?" she asked.

Emily looked surprised. "Almost thirteen years, I think."

"Thirteen years," Alice repeated. "Yes, that's right. And in those thirteen years, I've never asked you to do anything just for me. Especially something you didn't want to do."

Emily stared at her. "Alice, I would do anything in the world for you. You know I would, so please don't ask me to do this."

Alice shrugged, as if she had no choice. "But I am. I'm asking you to please testify, Emily."

I kept my mouth shut and waited. The minutes ticked by. We heard someone shouting an obscenity, a burst of laughter, then the sound of a toilet flushing. In the hallway, a group of inmates were complaining about not getting their full hour in the yard. One of them, a current client with sores all over his face from shooting too much speed, rapped on the glass and grinned at me. A guard knocked on the door and then came in to collect the food trays.

Finally, Emily nodded. "Okay," she said. "I'll testify."

"You will?" I asked.

"Yes," Emily said, looking at Alice.

"Well that's...wonderful," I said. "Are you sure?"

"Yes, I'm sure."

"Great." I looked at my watch. It was almost twenty to three. "You can do this, Emily, and we can win. Dr. Midman did a fabulous job explaining everything. The jury will be much more sympathetic now. Tell Penny you need your court clothes and that you need to get to the courthouse as soon as possible. She'll make it happen. I'll tell the judge you're coming."

On the drive back, Alice and I were both quiet. Whenever I looked over at her, she was staring straight ahead. As I pulled up in front of the courthouse to let her out, she turned to me and said, "She has to testify, right? There's no other way?" As if I were an oncologist and she were asking if her friend really needed chemotherapy.

I nodded. "Yes, she has to testify. You did the right thing."

She let out a deep breath. "All right, then. I'll see you inside."

***

At a quarter past three, Sunny was escorting Emily over to the defense table. My client looked calm and resigned, like a martyr being led toward a bonfire. As soon as she sat down, I put my arm around her and leaned in close.

"It won't be as bad as you think," I whispered. "You can do this, Emily. I know you can."

After a moment she nodded, and I knew she was ready.

Once the jury was seated, I stood up and announced, "The defense will now call Emily Watkins to the stand."

Without any hesitation, my client walked to the witness chair, held up her right hand, and promised to tell the truth, the whole truth, and nothing but the truth. She smiled briefly at the jury, and then turned her attention to me.

I kept my direct examination as short as possible, leaving out any questions that weren't absolutely essential. I began chronologically with her marriage to Hal and ended with the night she stabbed him. I asked simple questions and she gave simple thoughtful answers. It seemed as if the jury was paying close attention and a number of them looked sympathetic. Toward the end of my examination, I asked why she hadn't told anyone about the abuse and she said, "If you'd asked me this question a year ago, I would have said because I was ashamed and because I loved my husband and didn't want to get him in trouble. But the truth is, I didn't tell anyone because saying it out loud to another person would have required me to acknowledge it to myself. As long as I lied about it to others, I could lie about it to myself. Does that answer your question?"

"Yes," I said. "Thank you."

After an hour, her answers began to sound more uncertain, a sure sign she was close to her limit. I smiled at her and said, "Just three more questions, Emily, and we're done. I know how distressing this is and I can assure you that Mr. Taylor is a kind man and won't belabor his cross-examination."

Jeff immediately stood up, shaking his head at my little speech. "Judge, I appreciate Ms. Stein's confidence in me and will do my best not to…belabor my cross-examination. For the record, I intend to only ask questions I consider to be crucial and relevant."

"Thank you, Mr. Taylor," Judge Thomas said, then turned to me. "Ms. Stein, if you would please finish your direct."

"Certainly, Your Honor." I turned back to my client. "All right, Emily, question number one: did you kill your husband for the money?"

She shook her head and smiled. "No, I'm sure I didn't."

"Question number two: at the moment your husband approached you, did you think he was going to hurt you?"

"To the best of my knowledge, I did."

"And finally, question number three: did you kill your husband in self-defense?"

"Yes," she said, "to the best of my knowledge, I did."

I paused for effect. "No further questions," I said, then walked back to the defense table and sat down.

Not bad, I thought. Her answers hadn't been perfect, but she hadn't waffled on anything crucial. I knew from a friend who was a long distance runner, that a marathon was twenty-six miles, three hundred and eighty-five yards. I studied my client's face. She looked tired but determined. If this was a marathon, she was halfway there. Come on Emily, just thirteen miles, one hundred and ninety-three yards to go.

"Mr. Taylor?" Judge Thomas said.

Jeff stood up and sauntered to the podium with a sheaf of papers in his hand. "Ms. Watkins," he said, "if I understood your testimony correctly, you loved your husband, you miss him and you wish you hadn't stabbed him?" His voice sounded gentle, almost sympathetic.

"Yes, that's true." She hesitated. "But I thought I had to stab him."

"Although looking back, you might have been wrong?"

She stared at him. "Yes, in retrospect I might have been wrong."

"But you want the jury to believe that at the time you felt you had no choice?"

She shook her head. "You make it sound as if I had any time to think about it. I didn't think, I just stabbed."

"And so," Jeff continued, sounding as if he were just trying to clear things up, "it's only in retrospect that you determined you had to stab him?"

She looked a little confused. "At the time Hal approached me, I assumed he was going to hurt me. I reached out instinctively and stabbed him. In retrospect, I understand I did that because I thought I had to."

"And you came to this understanding some time after you'd been arrested?"

She thought for a moment, the way I'd coached her: if it sounds as if he's trying to trap you, wait a few seconds before answering. "Well, I didn't have time to understand my actions when it was all happening."

"And so," Jeff repeated patiently, "you came to this understanding some time after you'd been arrested, after you'd spoken with your lawyer."

I jumped up. "Objection, Your Honor. That's privileged and Mr. Taylor knows it. He's implying that I suggested self-defense before my client told me what really happened."

"Your Honor," Jeff said, "I'd ask that counsel for the defendant be admonished for her statements and that the jury be instructed to ignore them."

"Well," I countered, "I'd ask that the prosecutor be admonished for asking inappropriate questions that call for privileged information."

Judge Thomas waved his hand at both of us. "Please, let's try to get through this as civilly as possible. You are both professionals. Please act accordingly. The last objection made by Ms. Stein is sustained. I'd ask that neither counsel make any more speaking objections. Just state the objection and the grounds. Understood?"

"Yes, Your Honor," I said. "Thank you."

Jeff waited for me to sit down, and then began again. "Ms. Watkins," he said, sounding a little less gentle, "you've testified that you wished you'd had the courage to leave your husband?"

Emily nodded. "Yes."

"But you didn't?"

"No, unfortunately I didn't."

"But you didn't really want to leave him either?"

She smiled ruefully. "No, not really."

"And you weren't seriously thinking of leaving him, even if you occasionally wished you'd had the courage."

For a moment, Emily looked defensive, but then she shook her head. "Well, I had that bag packed, but no, I don't think I ever seriously thought I would leave him." She paused. "Unless maybe if things got even worse."

Jeff nodded, but it wasn't a friendly nod. He wanted to win more than he wanted to be nice. "So let me get this straight: sometimes you wished you could leave him, but you really didn't want to?"

"Correct."

"And you really didn't intend to?"

Emily sighed. "No, not really."

Her face was so pale it was hard to imagine she'd ever looked tan and healthy. Picture the finish line, Emily. Picture the sun on your face, your very own garden.

Jeff, meanwhile, kept his eyes on his quarry. "Ms. Watkins, you lived with your husband for ten years?"

"Yes."

"You slept with him every night?"

She blushed a little. "Except when he was sick or intoxicated."

"But almost every night?"

"Yes." She sat very straight with her hands in her lap. She would not equivocate unless there was a reason.

"You could leave the house anytime you wanted?"

"Of course."

"You could have taken that packed bag and left any time you chose."

"Yes," she said, "I could have, but I chose to stay."

The jurors were looking a little less receptive. The high school principal in the back row had his arms crossed in front of him, and a few of the older women were shaking their heads. "That's right," Jeff said. "You chose to stay. Despite the drinking and the occasional meanness, you chose to stay."

"Yes, it was my choice." Emily leaned forward to emphasize the point, as if she wanted everyone to know she was taking full responsibility.

Jeff paused for a moment, pretending to look thoughtful. "And yet, Ms. Watkins, there was a part of you that was tired of living with your husband?"

She sighed again. "Yes, that's true. Part of me was."

"Part of you wanted to leave?"

"Yes."

"That's the part that packed a suitcase and left it hidden in the hall closet?"

"Yes, yes it was." She was nodding at him as if they were old friends having tea. But he's not your friend, Emily. He's the prosecutor.

Jeff continued. "But there was a problem."

She looked confused. "What problem?"

"You didn't have enough money to leave."

She shook her head. "That wasn't the reason."

"Ms. Watkins, you testified on direct that you and Hal had about twenty-five thousand in savings?"

"I think so. I didn't pay much attention to our finances. Hal did."

"And so if you'd divorced him, maybe you'd have ended up with half. Not enough to live on for very long."

Suddenly, she looked offended. "I could have worked, Mr. Taylor."

Jeff smirked a little. "Ms. Watkins, you'd never had a paying job in your life, only volunteer work."

"So what?" She was actually angry. I hoped she'd stay that way. It would give her the energy to stay sharp and keep going. The energy to save her own life.

"You weren't sure you could get a job, were you?" Jeff asked.

"No, I wasn't sure, but I thought maybe at the library or the Humane Society. I also thought about teaching English as a second language."

"But you had no experience at that."

"True."

"And most nonprofits generally rely on volunteers, don't they?"

She hesitated. "Yes, that's also true." She was caving in again.

Jeff looked down at his notes. "You and your husband lived mostly on his pension. Is that correct?"

Emily nodded. "Yes, well we tried to. Sometimes we had to use our savings."

"And Hal's mother owned the house you lived in?"

"Yes, she did."

"So on your own, separate from Hal, you didn't have much?"

"No, that's true."

"Half the savings, at best."

"Yes." She was doing the nodding thing again. Watch out, Emily.

"Maybe about twelve thousand dollars." He paused. "Before the lawyers."

"What lawyers?"

"The divorce lawyers."

She looked at him, straightened up a little. "Mr. Taylor, I never went through these kinds of calculations in my mind. Ever. I wasn't planning to leave my husband. Not seriously."

"Even though you say he was periodically violent?"

It was time to give my client a rest. I stood up and said, "Objection, Your Honor, the question whether my client was going to leave her husband has been asked and answered numerous times."

"Your Honor," Jeff said, trying not to sound as irritated as he felt, "I am trying to do my cross. I'd appreciate being allowed to do it without frivolous objections."

I allowed myself to look indignant. "Your Honor, as this Court knows, I don't make frivolous objections. The question has been asked and answered. If the prosecutor has anything else to ask, I think he ought to get on with it."

The judge looked pointedly at the clock on the wall. It was close to five. "I'll allow the question one more time." He looked over at Emily. "You may answer the question."

"She may not remember it," I said, in case she wanted a few more seconds.

Jeff made an exasperated sound. "I will ask another question instead. Ms. Watkins, you've told the jury that you weren't seriously planning to leave your husband despite about twenty incidents of violence?"

She took a deep breath. "There were more. A lot more. Those were all I could specifically remember."

"You weren't seriously planning to leave even though he supposedly struck you in the face?"

"On numerous occasions."

"And he supposedly kicked you, shoved you, broke your arm and gave you a number of black eyes?"

She gritted her teeth. "Yes, he did." Then she looked down at her lap, clearly ashamed.

"But you weren't seriously planning to leave despite all the incidents you recounted on direct?" By now, a less seasoned prosecutor would have expressed sarcasm or incredulity, but Jeff was too smart; it played best when you let the jurors have their own reactions without any prompting by the lawyers.

Emily slumped in her chair. "No."

"And you never told anyone about these incidents of violence?"

"No."

"Not even the doctors you went to see afterward?"

She shook her head sadly. "No."

"You lied to every one of them?"

"Yes, I'm afraid so." She looked up at him and then around the room, as if she were seeing it for the first time. There was a look of amazement on her face, as if she couldn't believe what she'd just acknowledged.

Jeff smiled with absolutely no warmth. "You never told anyone during the ten years of your marriage that you were a battered woman."

She shrugged. "I didn't think I was."

"Because the violence wasn't that bad?"

"Well," Emily said, "in hindsight, I think it was, but at the time I thought it wasn't."

"You never thought you were a battered woman until after you were charged with first-degree murder?"

She nodded. "Yes. I knew my husband was violent on occasion, that it would probably never stop although I always hoped it would, but I never really believed I was a battered woman."

"Until your lawyer and your hired expert suggested that you were?"

I jumped to my feet. "Objection, Your Honor! That's the second time."

"Sustained. Don't do it again, Mr. Taylor."

Jeff nodded briefly, but he was on a roll and wasn't about to stop. "You still don't really think you were a battered woman, do you?"

Emily tried to smile, but it came out more like a grimace. "I'm beginning to think I was."

"Because you're claiming self-defense?"

"Because I think I really was."

"Although you never acknowledged it before you needed it as a defense?"

Emily shrugged again. "I'd never acted in self-defense before."

She looked exhausted. Jeff was probably three-quarters of the way through his cross. About three more miles to go, Emily. Three lousy little miles and you're done.

Jeff studied his notes, and then nodded to himself. "Ms. Watkins, three weeks before you killed your husband, you took out an insurance policy on his life for a quarter of a million dollars."

Emily's head bobbed up and down like a rag doll. "It was Hal's idea as well as mine. He agreed to it. I was worried about his health. He wouldn't stop drinking. The doctor told me that if he didn't stop drinking, his health would start to deteriorate. That it was just a matter of time."

"Hal passed the physical?"

"Yes, he did. But he was an alcoholic."

"The doctors gave him a clean bill of health?"

Emily sighed impatiently. "They took me aside and told me that if he didn't stop drinking, it was only a matter of time."

"But it didn't happen that way, did it? He died of a stab wound to his abdomen?"

"Yes."

"And you were the beneficiary of that policy."

"Yes," Emily said, "but I didn't kill him for the money. I never thought about the policy once we got it." She was beginning to sound uncertain. She was getting tired of defending herself.

"Well, you knew you had it?"

"Yes, but I didn't think about it."

"You mean consciously?"

I stood up. "Objection, You Honor." The question was improper, but I was too tired to figure out the reason. "The question makes no sense."

"Sustained." The judge was getting tired as well.

Jeff tapped his fingers on the podium. "Ms. Watkins, you'd just taken out a large insurance policy on your husband's life three weeks beforehand. Are you telling this jury that you were unaware of that on the night you killed him?"

"No, I must have been aware of it, but I wasn't thinking about it. I wasn't thinking about anything. I just did it."

She was close to tears, but fighting to keep control. I glanced at the jury. Don't cry now, Emily. It's too late in the cross; it won't help.

"So you weren't thinking about anything at the time you stabbed your husband?"

"Well, some part of me must have been thinking he was going to hurt me."

"Well, isn't it possible that some part of you must have been thinking, 'That's enough, I've had it'?"

"Objection," I said, "calls for speculation."

"Overruled," Judge Thomas said. "You may answer the question if you can."

"Yes, it's possible," Emily said. Her voice was so low it was almost a whisper. A number of the jurors were leaning forward in order to hear her.

"And isn't it possible that some part of you must have been thinking, 'I can't stand this anymore. I've had it with his drinking'?"

"I guess it's possible."

No, it isn't, Emily. Don't let him put words in your mouth.

Jeff had left the podium and taken a couple of steps toward the witness stand. "And finally, Ms. Watkins, isn't it possible that some part of you must have been thinking, 'I'm going to leave him and this is the only way I can do it'?"

Emily put up her hand as if to stop him. "So many things are possible, Mr. Taylor. The mind is extremely complex; it's capable of having all kinds of contradictory thoughts at the same time. It's capable of dissociation. It's capable of denial. It's capable of convincing itself that things are tolerable when they aren't. I'd had all kinds of thoughts about my husband for years. I was capable of great self-deception." She paused. "But I think at the time I stabbed my husband I was defending myself."

Way to go, Emily. The finish line is just a couple of yards away.

"But you're not positive?"

"No, I'm not positive. But I think so." She hesitated. "I hope so."

Jeff swooped down on this like a hawk at dinnertime. "You hope so, Ms. Watkins. Because otherwise you would be a murderer?"

"Yes, otherwise I would be a murderer."

Jeff retreated to the podium and started gathering up his papers. He was done; the ordeal was over. But then, as if the question just occurred to him, Jeff looked up and said, "Ms. Watkins, would you be surprised if the jury convicted you?"

I jumped to my feet. "Objection, Your Honor! The question is irrelevant under Rule 401 and prejudicial under Rule 403."

Judge Thomas hesitated. "It goes to her state of mind, so I'll allow it."

Emily, I thought, all you have to say is, "Yes, I'd be surprised."

But of course my Emily shook her head and said, "No, I wouldn't be surprised, although I don't think I'm legally guilty. But I'm not an innocent person either. I took my husband's life. I should have had the courage to leave him but I didn't. That makes me at least morally guilty. I will accept the jury's verdict, whatever it is."

For a second, Jeff looked almost apologetic. "Thank you, Ms. Watkins. No further questions."

A marathon is exactly twenty-six miles, three hundred and eighty-five yards. My client had run, walked and crawled her way to the finish line. I turned to Donald and said, "She told the truth. Everyone could see that, even Jeff. I think she did all right. What do you think?"

Donald's face looked gray and puffy, as if he'd been deprived of oxygen for a dangerously long time. There were huge dark stains under his armpits. "Yeah, I think so," he said. "Yeah, it could have been a lot worse."

***

Over the next couple of days, I called twelve defense witnesses to the stand. There were no bad surprises. Alice testified concerning her limited observations of Hal and Emily's marriage, how Emily always deferred to her husband, and how on occasion she'd inexplicably refuse to leave the house. The neighbor grudgingly agreed that she'd seen what looked like an act of unprovoked violence on Hal's part. The police officer verified that Hal had once been arrested for domestic violence and that the case had been dismissed because Emily refused to cooperate. The doctors all described the various injuries Emily had suffered and readily acknowledged that people sometimes lied about the source of their injuries, especially if they were battered women. And the two felons (for what it was worth) both described Hal as a brute who used way more force than necessary arresting them.

On Friday morning, I gave the best closing argument of my career. I pulled out all the stops and could hear a number of people in the audience crying as I described the wasted years of Emily's life and pleaded for the jury to finally set her free. Even the judge seemed affected. Jeff waited a full five minutes before giving his second closing argument which was much more subdued than his first.

Once they were excused, the jurors filed quietly out of the courtroom with downcast eyes, as if they were exiting a funeral. Although it was impossible to tell what they were thinking, I imagined they were worried about the length of time it might take to reach a unanimous decision.

As soon as court was adjourned, Alice and Janet both came up and hugged us. They planned to wait in the hallway for the next couple of hours and then go have lunch together. A few moments later, Ellen Silver and Ray Martinelli walked up to the defense table, holding hands. I gave Ray a look and said, "Well, well." Which was public defender code for "I hope you know what you're doing."

"Your closing was terrific!" Ellen exclaimed. "I cried my eyes out."

"Good," I said, and then looked at Ray who nodded in agreement.

"It was very compelling, Rachel. If there's any justice in this world, you'll win."

Which was public defender code for "I wouldn't start celebrating just yet."

CHAPTER SEVEN

In the criminal defense profession, there's a phenomenon known as trial psychosis, a state of mind every good lawyer slips into a few days before trial and doesn't snap out of until the jury delivers its verdict.

Trial psychosis is an essential state of mind without which there would be hesitation, doubt and pessimism. When a lawyer enters this state, she still sees everything clearly, can still interpret data and adjust to the inevitable surprises. She can tell whether things are going well or not, change her strategy, make tactical objections, etcetera. But something perforce is missing: a useless sense of perspective, the ability to stand back and view the case in the worst light possible. The ability to imagine defeat.

If it weren't for trial psychosis, there would be no way to trudge through cases with atrocious facts, to cross-examine grieving widows or adorable children molested by their fathers and then stand up at the end of the trial and deliver a passionate closing argument, and sometimes win. As Emily's defense attorney, I was keenly aware of the obstacles in her case, how difficult they were, how dangerous, but once the prosecution rested and it was our turn, I knew they could all be overcome.

I knew it until the bailiff called my office less than two hours after the jury began deliberating and informed me there was a verdict. Suddenly my head was clear, my psychosis gone. In a complicated self-defense case like Emily's, the longer the jury stayed out, the better. After a couple of days, the defense could begin to expect an acquittal. On the other hand, if the jurors reached a unanimous decision in less than three or four hours, it was almost always for the prosecution. I drove back to the courthouse with little hope, and by the time I reached the entrance and walked inside, I'd lost the rest. With my perspective back in working order, I could see it all. There would be no miracles; it would not come out all right. As soon as the prosecutor returned from his victory mug of beer at the Walrus Saloon, Judge Thomas would emerge from his chambers, take the guilty verdict in open court, and my client's chronically uncertain future would finally be settled.

When I entered the courtroom, Emily was already seated at the defense table working on what appeared to be a crossword puzzle. Sunny was sitting a few rows behind her, a sour expression on his face, as if he had acid indigestion. But I think he was simply worried for Emily. He'd seen enough jury trials to know that a verdict in ninety minutes—barely enough time for everyone to use the bathroom, elect a foreperson, and take a straw poll—meant a life sentence for his favorite inmate. I didn't see Donald but I knew he'd be here soon. In the hallway, I'd passed Janet and Alice standing near a window chatting like old friends and told them to come inside when they were ready, that the jury had reached a verdict. They must have seen something in my face or posture because they didn't ask me any questions.

As I headed up the aisle, I felt light-headed and nauseous. Once, a few years earlier, I'd been telemarking down a steep black-rated slope in Crested Butte and had fallen face forward on my camera, which I'd stupidly left hanging around my neck. The moment I stood up, I knew I'd busted a couple of ribs. I felt faint and was breathing way too fast, taking shallow little breaths that hurt like hell. My lungs begged for oxygen, but every time I tried to take a deeper breath, I thought I'd pass out from the pain. There was no one around me—my friends had taken a different easier route—and so there was nothing to be done except straighten up, ignore the pain, continue down the hill. And hope I didn't fall again. Eventually, I saw my friends waiting near a clump of trees and headed toward them. "Looking good, Rachel," they called. "Looking good!"

I skied down those last few hundred yards like a pro, but oh how I'd wanted to stop and cry out, to let go of my form, to collapse in pain. But of course I hadn't, and I wouldn't do it now. Instead, I walked slowly and deliberately forward. When I reached the defense table, my client was still busy with her crossword puzzle. I nodded to Sunny, surveyed the nearly empty room, placed my black leather briefcase on the floor beside me, and took my seat.

"What's a seven-letter word for frenzied?" Emily asked without looking up from her puzzle. "It starts with a B."

"Berserk?"

Emily bent her head closer to the page, squinting at a row of blank vertical boxes. "That's it. Thanks."

I looked at my watch. Donald hurried in and I could tell by the look on his face that he'd reached the same conclusion I had. He sat down right behind us and I could smell the alcohol on his breath. He reached over to pat my arm.

"It ain't over till it's over," he said.

"Yogi Berra," Emily responded, glancing sideways at us.

Donald grunted in surprise. "You know, I think you might be right."

Emily nodded. "Okay then, would either of you happen to know the capital of Switzerland?"

"I don't even know the capital of Florida and I was born there," Donald said.

Emily turned to me. "What about you, Rachel? Five letters, also starts with a B."

Suddenly, I felt cranky and uncooperative. "The thing is, Emily, I've never liked crossword puzzles."

She waited patiently, a trait she'd obviously perfected.

I sighed. "Berne."

She tried the letters, which of course fit. "Hey, good guess."

I shook my head. "It wasn't a guess." I reached into my briefcase, pulled out my appointment calendar, and then realized the judge would probably sentence her on the spot. No need to set any further dates in the case. I could tell Emily was watching out of the corner of her eye as I put the calendar away. The defense table was clear except for the crossword puzzle.

"Where did you get that anyway?" I asked, pointing to the puzzle.

"Penny gave it to me."

I drummed my fingers on the table. "Well that was nice of her." I hesitated. "Listen, Emily, I think you should put the puzzle away and begin preparing yourself for the worst."

She regarded me with her kind blue eyes, and then patted me on the shoulder as if I were a good dog, but a little slow. "I'm quite prepared," she said. "Sunny warned me, but I'd already figured it out for myself." A moment later, she returned to her puzzle.

Come on, I thought, let's get this over with. I was feeling sicker by the minute as if I were coming down with the flu. No, not the flu; a flu generally lasts seven or eight days. This portended to be much worse. A bleak, no end in sight, dark gray depression, a gravity-less state in which everything that had been painstakingly nailed down in my life would once again be up for grabs. If I'd had a closer relationship with my mother, I might have run out and called her, wailed to her, "Mama!" Instead, I sat still and brooded.

In the end, my client's husband had managed to win the ten-year war that cost his life. In less than a quarter of an hour, his victory would be memorialized and my client would be led out of the courtroom in shackles. A tiny bleat and she'd be history. And as for yours truly? Destined, once again, to play the stunned and helpless spectator, the liberal do-gooder who had done no good.

"I hate my life," I muttered.

"I'm not that crazy about mine either," Emily said, still bent over her crossword puzzle. "You wouldn't happen to know a four-letter word for a French military cap? Starts with a K."

"No, and if I were an abuser, I'd be tempted to punch you."

She smiled benignly. "Then it's lucky for me you're not."

The courtroom door opened and Jeff rushed up the aisle, stopping at our table. He was carrying his tie in one hand and a yellow pad of paper in the other.

"I heard they have a verdict," he said.

"That's the rumor," I replied.

He looked at Emily. "Well, your lawyer tried as hard as she could. No one could have done a better job."

"I know." She nodded. "I'm very satisfied with her."

"Save the kind words, Jeff," I said. "You did an adequate job. My client's life is over. Congratulations."

Jeff took a step back. "Jesus, Rachel, I think you need a vacation."

After he'd walked away, Emily whispered, "That wasn't very nice."

I shrugged like a sullen teenager. "The one great thing about being convicted of first-degree murder: you won't have to worry about being nice to anyone ever again."

"That may be true for me, but you still have to work with him."

"No," I said, folding my arms across my chest. "I've just decided. I'm done."

Less than ten minutes later, the foreman of the jury—the high school principal—handed the verdict to the bailiff, who walked it over to the judge. None of the jurors looked at Emily. Emily and I stood up and faced the judge's bench. The courtroom was as quiet as a mortuary.

I could feel Emily shaking next to me and decided it didn't matter if I let my feelings show a little.

I pulled her close to me and together we listened as the judge intoned, "We the jury find the defendant, Emily Watkins, guilty of murder in the first degree."

A couple of Hal's ex-colleagues began cheering but immediately stopped when they saw the look on the judge's face.

"There will be no more outbursts from the audience," Judge Thomas warned. "None. If I hear one more sound, I will clear the room." He paused. "Ms. Stein, would you like the jurors polled?"

"Yes, please," I said.

Each juror was then asked to acknowledge whether this was indeed his or her verdict. Each juror said it was. Not one of them looked at Emily. The judge then thanked and excused the jury, which stood up en masse and quickly left the room. A few moments later, two guards in uniform emerged from one of the side doors, motioning for Sunny to change places with them. As Sunny walked past the defense table, he whispered, "I'm so sorry, Emily."

"We'll talk later," she said.

The judge cleared his throat. "All right then, since I have no discretion in the matter, I'm inclined to sentence the defendant immediately. Any objection, Ms. Stein?"

"No, Your Honor."

As Emily and I approached the podium, I glanced back at Donald who was sitting with his shoulders slumped like a big sad bear. Alice and Janet sat next to him, holding hands. Their faces were the color of old snow.

When we reached the podium, Judge Thomas turned directly to Emily. There was genuine sorrow in his eyes, not the obligatory sadness when he sentenced most of my clients, but the real thing. "Fix this," I wanted to cry. "Make it right." But of course I said nothing. The jury had found my Emily guilty. The judge was powerless.

"Ms. Watkins," he said, "as I'm sure your attorney has told you, when someone has been convicted of a class one felony in Colorado, the law requires me to sentence that person to life in prison."

"I understand," she said.

The judge nodded. "In which case, I am remanding you to the Department of Corrections to begin serving a sentence of life in prison." He hesitated. "If anyone can make the best of this, I think maybe you can."

"Thank you," she said.

Thank you? No, I thought, and then the two guards materialized behind us and began escorting her out of the courtroom. It was much too fast.

"Wait," I said and followed them into an adjacent hallway. As soon as the door shut behind us, my client turned to me with an unexpected urgency. She didn't care that the guards were standing only a few feet away from us. I'd never seen her look so serious.

"You have to make your peace with this, Rachel."

I shook my head at her. "No, I don't."

"Rachel—" She placed her hands on my shoulders. "You gave it everything you had. We all did."

I was obviously in shock, but a bitter hopelessness was closing in on me. "So what? We lost. That's all that matters."

She looked as if she was about to cry, then pulled herself together. "Rachel, listen. You need to know how much this meant to me. No one has ever stood up for me the way you did." She was staring at me, willing me to understand how important this was to her. "It's enough."

I pursed my lips and shrugged. "I'm glad you feel that way, but I disagree. Nothing except winning is enough. The rest is just New Age bullshit." It was a nasty thing to say, but I wanted to hurt someone and she was the only one around.

"It's not bullshit," she said, but her voice lacked her earlier conviction.

One of the guards stepped forward, looking apologetic. He was holding a pair of handcuffs.

"I'm sorry, Emily," he said, "but we have to get back in time for lockdown."

Emily turned to face him, placing her delicate wrists in front of her. The handcuffs snapped shut with a cold metal finality. The sound of it killed me.

"Can we have one last moment?" I asked. "I need to apologize to my client."

The guards exchanged a look and then nodded. For Emily's sake, though, not mine.

Before I could say a word, Emily shook her head impatiently. "Rachel, I know you didn't mean it. Listen, this is really important, so pay attention. The way I see it, we have two choices. We can either accept this or not. That's it."

She looked so earnest that I had to smile. "That's it?" I asked. "No third choice?"

She was smiling back at me. "No, that's it, only the two. I'm going to choose the first one and I think you should too."

"Why should I?"

She regarded me with those kind blue eyes. "Because you'll suffer less."

The guards stepped forward, signaling the end of our conversation. Emily held up her hands to me, bowing slightly. Then, flanked by the two burly men, she headed down the hallway toward an elevator that would take her to a holding cell in the basement. In a few days, she'd be transferred to the women's correctional facility in southern Colorado. She must have been terrified, but she held her head up and walked quickly to keep up with the men.

"Take care of yourself, Rachel," she called, as if I were the one who had just been convicted.

***

After a quick surreal conference with the judge concerning Emily's pretrial confinement credit and promises to stay in touch with Janet and Alice, I left the courthouse and headed back to the public defender's office. The lilacs were in bloom, tourists strolled along Canyon Boulevard in shorts, and the sky was a deep unconcerned blue. I pulled into the parking lot and sat there watching a couple of kids playing Frisbee. After a while, I thought of a movie I'd once seen about a man who was trapped in an elevator with no hope of being rescued. At first he was calm, but eventually he started going crazy. Hour after hour, he examined his life, but there was no end to it. Finally, in desperation, he climbed through the ceiling, stood on top of it, and managed to cut the cable above him. The movie ended just as the elevator began free falling through a long dark shaft toward the basement. Freedom. A few minutes later, I roused myself to go inside.

I rapped once on Larry Hanover's door, then marched into his office unannounced. I caught him staring at a spider plant that looked as if it hadn't been watered in a year.

"I quit," I told him.

"Hello to you, too." He was a short, bespectacled man in his forties who was always rubbing his forehead as if he had a perpetual headache.

"I'm serious. I quit."

Larry gestured at the empty client chair in front of his desk. "I guess you lost the trial. I'm sorry, Rachel. I know how much it meant to you."

I refused to sit down. "Thanks, but in a way it's a blessing. I needed something as bad as this to dislodge me."

Larry rubbed his forehead and sighed. He was the office head partly because no one else wanted the job, but also because he was better than anyone at not saying what he really felt, an adaptive skill he'd learned from growing up in a tough Chicago neighborhood. "Please sit down, Rachel."

I hesitated, then, feeling childish, sat down and tried to take a deep breath. There was no reason not to end my twelve-year tenure at the public defender's office with a little grace and dignity. I crossed my legs, lowered my voice to a more appropriate level.

"You can't talk me out of this, Larry. I'm cooked."

"Of course you are. You've been working nonstop for months. Why don't you take a few days off? We'll cover your caseload until you get back."

I shook my head. Suddenly, I couldn't stand my pantyhose for another second. They were hot, itchy and confining, a symbol of all the unpleasant compromises I'd had to make in order to work within the system. I wanted to rip them off, ball them up, and throw them in Larry's face. I didn't, not because I was too mature, but because as a trial lawyer I'd learned that grand gestures never went over as well as I imagined.

My silence, however, was having an effect. Larry had removed his glasses, signaling his concern. "I see. Well, I think we can manage for a couple of weeks without you."

"Try for the rest of your lives. I'm out of here. Twelve years is enough."

Larry was beginning to rock back and forth in his chair, which meant he was irritated. "Oh for God's sake, Rachel, you just need a vacation. You're the best trial lawyer in the office. You can't leave."

I stood up. "Watch me," I said, heading for the door.

"I won't accept your resignation, Rachel."

I stopped and turned to face him. "You have to."

"No, I don't. I'm putting you on a three-month sabbatical as of Monday. If you still want to quit in three months, I'll accept your resignation then."

I shrugged. "Fine, but you're just postponing the inevitable."

Larry waved me away with his glasses. "Get some rest, Rachel. We'll miss you."

I had expected Vickie to be working in the garden when I got home, tending the plants, tinkering with the lawnmower that never worked, taking care of everything I couldn't be bothered with. Vickie: my lover, my partner, my best friend. I'd already pictured myself running toward her and being caught in her reassuring arms.

"I did it, baby! I finally quit. But if I'm not a public defender, who am I?"

And Vickie holding me, smoothing my hair, and comforting me. Except she wasn't there.

I wandered into the living room, sat down on the couch, and flipped through a copy of *The Nation* that had been left on the coffee table. I remembered thinking a few weeks ago how much I loved this simple elegant room, how spacious and comfortable it seemed. How it reflected my sense of style as well as my values. And now it felt claustrophobic, a small ordinary box that I'd lovingly decorated without realizing it was just a cage. I stood up and began to pace, then abruptly sat down again. I looked at my watch. I'd been unemployed for less than an hour and already I was losing my mind.

After critiquing each room in the house and eating a pint of coffee ice cream, I called Vickie at the hospital.

"Where are you?" I asked.

She laughed. "I'm obviously here. You called me."

"Why aren't you home? I need you."

"That's a first." She paused. "Are you all right, sweetheart? What's going on? How did the trial go?"

I sat cross-legged on the rug in front of the fireplace. "I lost. And then I quit my job."

"Are you serious, Rachel?"

I nodded. "I did it. I quit."

"Wow, I never thought you'd do it. Congratulations." She hesitated. "I mean I'm sorry you lost the trial and I feel badly for your client, but you may have just saved your own life."

I didn't even try to contain my annoyance. "Gee, Vickie, that's a bit melodramatic, don't you think? In the meantime, my client's so-called life is truly over."

"You're right, sweetheart, and I'm sorry. I know how hard you've worked, how much you wanted to win. This has to be a huge disappointment. But at least you've also done something positive. You've needed to quit for years."

"Yep, that's what you've been telling me." I reached down and ripped a piece of thread off the edge of my pants, then realized too late the entire hem was about to unravel. Well, fuck it; I wouldn't be wearing these stupid court clothes anytime soon.

"Rachel, I've been urging you to quit for years because I've never seen anyone use up as much adrenaline as you have." She was straining to sound reasonable. "It's a miracle you can even get out of bed, never mind function as well as you do. The supply, though, is not unlimited. When it's gone, it's gone. The health consequences can be catastrophic."

I tried to stand up, but my stomach hurt too much. "Great lecture, Doc, but the timing still needs a little work."

After a couple of seconds, Vickie said, "Jesus, Rachel, why are we bickering?"

I rubbed my face. "I'm not sure, but I suppose it has something to do with how freaked out I am." I stared at the empty carton of ice cream in my lap.

"Do you want me to come home?" she asked.

"I just ate a pint of your ice cream."

"Why would you do that? You're lactose intolerant. I'll be there in twenty minutes."

***

We spent the evening reading Dashiell Hammett's *The Thin Man* to each other and then making love. Before I fell asleep, I was thinking maybe this transition wouldn't be so difficult after all. Then I woke up a few hours later, my face stained with tears, and knew I was in for it. Headed, as the Rolling Stones sang, for my nineteenth nervous breakdown.

I spent the next week roaming from one room to another, never stopping for more than a few minutes in any particular place. I thought of the pale restless lions I'd watched at the zoo when I was a child and wondered if they'd actually understood their true situation—that they were in prison—or if they'd simply paced back and forth because it was their nature. I hoped it was the latter, but knew in my heart it wasn't. At the beginning of the week, I stood in front of my bookshelves and pulled out five or six novels I'd always intended to read, but at the end of the week I hadn't done anything more than glance at the covers. I washed the dishes every day, made the bed, vacuumed the rugs and overwatered the plants. I felt like a mechanical doll, a lesbian Stepford wife.

I kept telling myself that my listlessness was only temporary, a kind of postpartum reaction to having made such a huge, long overdue decision. But I was terrified. What if my paralysis was in fact permanent? What if I turned out to be like Vickie's uncle George who retired, moved into a suite at a hotel in downtown New York and never left for twenty years? Even worse, I could already feel the temptation to believe that if I wasn't doing anything of value (like rescuing people) then I didn't really matter.

One of the main problems of being unemployed, of course, was that everyone else was working. If I'd had someone to climb with, for instance, everything might have turned out differently. Vickie, to her credit, made an effort to come home by five o'clock each day, which must have required juggling everyone's schedule at the hospital. She begged me to try a daytime yoga class, but I balked at the idea of spending an hour and a half practicing a series of slow-motion moves and ending up in exactly the same place I'd started. It reminded me too much of my career in which I'd essentially defended the same five people with the same five problems over and over again. Hiking seemed equally futile. If I wasn't risking my life or trying to save someone else's, why bother?

By Friday afternoon, I was almost comatose. As I lay on the rug in the living room, I decided that only a masochist would have lasted at my job as long as I had. Looking back, I saw a long string of heartbreaks interrupted only occasionally by a handful of inconsequential victories. What kind of career choice was that? Would Vickie have remained a doctor if ninety percent of her patients ended up dying in her arms?

For the thousandth time, I thought about Emily, wondering where in the system she was and how she was doing. I pictured her sitting among sly dangerous women, attempting to find common ground. Would she find any allies? Would she make any friends? Although I'd promised myself I'd stop worrying about her, I couldn't. It was pointless, of course, because she was light years away, living in another universe. You can't protect her now, I told myself. You never could.

And another unexpected thought began stalking me as well. That I'd not only failed as a lawyer, but I'd also failed as a Jew. Which was funny because I hardly ever thought about my ethnicity. Like my parents, I was never an observant Jew. We didn't even believe in God. But they'd suggested early on that being Jewish meant being an advocate for social justice. Since we'd been oppressed for centuries, they reasoned, we were experts at noticing and fighting against oppression. Our mission, if we chose to accept it, was to help repair the world. To do something about a few of the myriad injustices that surrounded us. My father was a professor of American History, my mother a newspaper reporter, and I—taking it one step further—had become a criminal defense attorney representing indigent people. But instead of repairing the world, I'd let an innocent woman fall through the cracks, a woman I'd practically promised to save. Bad lawyer. Bad Jew.

Clearly, I was depressed. When Vickie came home that day, she took one look at me and stamped her feet.

"Enough," she said. "Get up." Her tone meant business.

I struggled to a sitting position.

"I know it's been rough," she began. "I know it really killed you to lose Emily's case, but you have to move on. This isn't helping. Fortunately, I have an idea." She sat down across from me on the rug. "Let's go back to Zihuatanejo. We ended up having a wonderful time there. I think I can arrange to take three weeks. Dave and Allison have agreed to cover for me. What do you say?"

I noticed the lines around Vickie's mouth seemed deeper than a week ago, and I reached over to try and smooth them out a little.

"Thanks for the offer, babe. I'd love to go on a vacation with you, but not right now. I have to figure out my life first. The thought of lying on a beach in a foreign country while the poor people who live there trudge back and forth in front of me trying to sell me junky things that I don't want is too much to bear."

Vickie nodded. "Fine. If you don't want to see poor people, let's go somewhere like Aspen and see rich people."

"That would be even worse."

My partner tried to laugh, but she was obviously frustrated. "Rachel, you have to do something."

I looked into her beautiful disapproving eyes. "Why?"

She looked surprised and then confused. "Because this isn't healthy." She paused. "And you're scaring me."

I sighed and lay back down again, gazing up at a couple of interesting cracks in the ceiling. "Let me get this straight. You want me to stop feeling sad and do something so that you won't have to feel scared. Under the circumstances, don't you think that's a little selfish? Besides, what's the difference between lying on a beach or lying on the living room floor?"

Vickie stood up and was now looking down at me. "That's not what I meant, Rachel."

I waved her away, as if she were a bee that wouldn't leave me alone. "Hey, you know what? If you squint your eyes in a particular way, the cracks in the ceiling look just like stallions racing free across an empty prairie."

Vickie tapped her foot a little too close to my head. "What about a few sessions of therapy? It might be really helpful. Allison says Marilyn Samler is great."

"Good idea," I said. "Maybe you could figure out why you're so fearful. Actually, here's an even better idea. Why not take a vacation without me? It'll be a lot more fun that way. For both of us."

I could hear the sharp intake of breath, as if I'd punched or slapped her. "Maybe I will, Rachel. A vacation without you sounds delightful. It's very tiresome being a guest at your self-indulgent little pity party."

I smiled icily. "Well, the party's over. From now on, whenever you're around, I'll just put on a happy face."

There was dead silence and I guessed she'd had enough. Finally I heard her whisper, "Rachel, we've never fought like this before."

I sat up, grabbed her leg, and held onto it. "I know and I'm very sorry."

After a long pause, she asked, "Are we going to be all right?"

I closed my eyes, rested my head against her leg and said, "Of course we are." And hoped it was the truth.

Later when we couldn't sleep, I apologized again and promised to make a genuine effort. We curled up in each other's arms and I wished that love alone could solve all of my life's problems. Christ, even as a kid, I'd known better. I was obviously regressing, but at least I didn't have too far to go. A few more years, and I'd only be a twinkle in my father's eyes. That night, I dreamed Emily stabbed me in the heart with a pair of scissors.

***

Over the weekend, I called Maggie, Ray and our friends Dave and Allison, and told them about my midlife crisis, but saying it out loud only seemed to flesh it out, confirm its solidity. I realized, too late, that no one truly wants to hear about your midlife crisis unless you can make it sound amusing. Even then, in order to punish and deter you from ever mentioning it again, they'll try to help you figure out why it happened and how to avoid it in the future. Maggie's proposed solution was to go climbing, but I decided to wait until I was sure I wanted to live.

The following Monday, Maggie phoned to tell me she'd fallen on the first pitch of the Yellow Spur and broken her ankle. She'd slipped before she could get her first piece in and fallen about fifteen feet. It was every climber's nightmare. I knew she'd been planning a trip to Nicaragua as a member of some kind of brigade, but I hadn't been paying attention to the details. I'd been too obsessed with Emily's murder trial.

"So now I have to try and find someone to take my place," Maggie said. "Shit. I've been looking forward to this for almost a year. I'm so bummed."

"I can imagine. I'm really sorry." I switched the receiver to my other ear, picked up some dirty dishes and carried them to the sink. "What's the purpose of your brigade again? I forgot."

She sighed, clearly annoyed. "To help rebuild a medical clinic that was burned down by the Contras."

"Oh right," I said. "Sounds worthwhile." I plugged the sink, and then turned on the hot water.

"It is."

I examined the sponge and decided it was time for a new one. "Where exactly was the clinic?"

"Where?" She sounded surprised. "In Jalapa, a little town in northern Nicaragua not far from the Honduran border."

I nodded, then bent down and found a package of sponges under the sink. As I straightened up, I said, "Well, maybe I could take your place."

"You?"

"Why not? What else do I have to do? Vickie's going to divorce me if I don't do something soon. It'll be good for me. I can get out of my own head and hopefully be of some use. It's the perfect solution, actually."

"Do you know anything about the situation in Nicaragua?"

I shrugged. "Some. I read *The Nation*."

Maggie started to laugh. "Do you even know who the Contras are?"

"The opposition."

"Good guess. Are they the good guys or the bad guys?"

I thought for a moment. "The bad guys." I paused. "Which means the United States is probably backing them."

She laughed again. "No wonder you were such a good lawyer. Okay, fine. I'll ask my friend Laura to bring over a packet of information later on today. Don't you think you ought to discuss this with Vickie first, though?"

I turned off the water and started washing some plates. "Vickie's my girlfriend, not my mother. She'll support whatever decision I make."

"Are you sure? You're going into a war zone."

"Hey, I've been in a war zone for twelve years. It can't be any worse. Vickie will probably be relieved."

Maggie snorted. "Don't be naïve, Rachel." She was serious now. "This is the real thing. Real guns, real rockets and real people dying. It could be dangerous."

I studied the plate in my hands, realized it was cracked, and tossed it into the wastebasket. "Well, you were willing to risk it. How bad could it be?"

"That's just it," she said. "I don't know."

I hesitated for less than a second. "Okay, I've been duly warned. I'll work it out with Vickie."

The packet of information Laura dropped off a few hours later was thicker than a small book. Since Vickie wouldn't be home until ten, I had most of the evening to skim through the material.

Nicaragua, I learned, had had a long history of struggling against United States domination. In 1927, a local hero named Sandino organized an army of peasants to drive out the US Marines who were then occupying the country. Sandino's army fought the marines for seven years and won strong popular support. When the marines finally withdrew, they left behind the infamous National Guard headed by Anastasio Somoza as a replacement force. One of the Guard's first acts was to murder Sandino. For the next forty-five years, the National Guard, headed by a succession of Somozas (all of them relatives) became notorious throughout the world for its brutality and corruption.

By this point, of course, I was hooked. I'd always been a sucker for the underdog. I grabbed a glass of iced herbal tea, curled up again on the couch, and continued reading. Backed by the National Guard, the Somoza family not only ran the country, but owned much of it as well, amassing a tidy fortune estimated at four hundred and fifty million. In the meantime, the vast majority of Nicaraguans lived in desperate poverty. The United States, unfortunately, supported the dictatorship. President Roosevelt was even quoted as saying, "Somoza may be a son of a bitch, but he's our son of a bitch." Eventually the FSLN (the Sandinista National Liberation Front) organized the Nicaraguan people and they ousted Somoza in 1979.

Bravo, I thought, and rubbed my eyes. It was almost nine o'clock. The artichoke I'd been steaming was finally ready. I mixed some fresh cumin into a bowl of mayonnaise and then carried everything to the kitchen table. The light was better here anyway. I propped my pages against the bowl and resumed where I'd left off, right after the revolution. When the celebrations ended, the Sandinistas began implementing an ambitious program to rebuild the country's infrastructure, which had been neglected or destroyed in the decades leading up to the revolution. After years of exploitation, the country was in terrible shape and the Sandinistas had to make a number of decisions benefiting the majority but alienating a percentage of the middle and upper classes, some of who had already fled to Miami along with the Somozas.

In the meantime, the United States leadership, headed now by Reagan after defeating Carter in 1980, disliked the Sandinistas who were admittedly brash and not respectful enough of their powerful northern neighbor. Worse, if left unchecked, the Sandinistas' idealistic rhetoric might very well inspire other little countries in the region to overthrow their dictatorships as well. And so when a group of the losers—who came to be identified as the Contras—appealed to the United States for money and support, they were rewarded with both. With bases mostly in Honduras, the Contras were surprisingly effective. Increasingly, the Sandinistas were forced to spend the bulk of their time and resources fighting yet another war, necessitating greater and greater sacrifices from the population.

I was back on the couch and just beginning to read how various international brigades were forming to aid the Sandinistas when I heard the front door opening. Suddenly, I knew Vickie wouldn't feel at all relieved that I'd decided to go to Nicaragua, that she'd be extremely upset instead.

"Hi honey," I said, covering my reading material with one of the pillows I'd been lying on.

"Hey sweetie," Vickie replied. "Anything happen today?" She crossed over to the couch and sat down next to me. She was dressed in a beige linen pantsuit that was wrinkled from a long day at work and then dinner with her friends. No matter how tired she was, she was always gorgeous, which mattered more to me than her. Vickie was a grown-up Girl Scout who valued less ephemeral things like integrity, truth, and kindness. So did I, although like most attorneys, the truth for me was much less static.

"Not much," I said.

She shook her beautiful head. "You're so full of shit, Rachel. I already know you've decided to take Maggie's place on the brigade. Her friend told her sister who's a nurse at the hospital. The nurse told Allison who, of course, told me."

I threw my hands up in a gesture of disgust. "I hate living in a small town where everyone knows everyone else's business."

"Go to hell!" And then she started to cry, which unnerved me more than any show of anger.

Immediately, I put my arms around her and pulled her close to me. "Please don't cry," I murmured. "I've been such a mess since losing Emily's trial. No matter how hard I try, I can't stop thinking about it. I'm ninety percent sure that quitting was the right thing to do, but parts of me don't know it yet and they're still freaking out. I'm really sorry, babe."

Vickie wiped her face with the edge of my shirt. "Why didn't you consult with me first?"

When a lawyer doesn't have a good answer, she has to decide on the spot whether any answer is better than none. Vickie, however, put her fingers against my mouth. "We've been together nine years, Rachel. I thought we were partners."

"We are."

"You're not acting like it."

I sighed. "I may be a rat," I said, recalling President Roosevelt's famous quote, "but I'm your rat."

Vickie must have understood what I was trying to say because she didn't pull away. Or maybe she knew these were tricky times that called for tricky measures. Or maybe she just loved me and didn't want to lose me.

Lying in bed that night with the ceiling fan whirring overhead, Vickie asked me a hundred questions about the situation in Nicaragua. I told her as much as I knew.

"And so where did the Contras come from?" she asked.

"They were National Guardsmen who fled the country after the revolution. The CIA trains and funds them to attack the country in an attempt to destabilize the Sandinista government."

Vickie rolled on top of me and kissed me. "It sounds dangerous, Rachel. I'm scared you'll get hurt."

I shook my head and held her against the length of my body. "I'll be fine. The Contras aren't supposed to kill any North Americans. It's bad for publicity. And the Sandinistas won't let us go anywhere that's under active attack."

"Oh great."

"Hey, don't worry. I'll be fine. We'll be fine. Everything's going to be fine." My God, I was a talking Hallmark card and I couldn't stop.

So Vickie kissed me hard and then we held on to each other as tightly as two people can in a world where strong swirling currents are always ripping things apart.

PART II:
UNSENT LETTERS FROM THE EARTHQUAKE CAPITAL OF THE WORLD

CHAPTER EIGHT

A few days before I left Colorado, Maggie warned me that Managua would be hot. When the airplane hatch finally opened, I thought I would be ready, but if this was hot, then a ninety-five degree day in the Rockies was downright chilly. No, the word "hot" (three little letters, barely a syllable) was entirely inadequate to describe how it felt as I stood in line to exit the plane. It was almost six in the afternoon. Within seconds, I was sweating profusely and beginning to feeling trapped, as if I'd stepped into a steaming sauna and someone had locked the door behind me.

As the line moved forward, I watched each passenger in front of me pause in breathless surprise before descending the portable metal staircase to the ground. The low white buildings in the distance looked too far away; we'd die of heat prostration before we got there. Halfway across the tarmac, I wondered whether lobsters really died or lost consciousness after being dropped into a pot of boiling water, or if people just hoped they did. This trip might have been a mistake—okay fine, it probably was—but it was too late now.

For the past couple of weeks, I'd spent most of my time getting ready: booking last-minute flights through Dallas and El Salvador, buying what I hoped would be appropriate clothes and sandals, borrowing a duffel bag from Maggie, getting vaccinated against diseases I'd never heard of, reviewing my high school Spanish textbooks, and reading every article I could find about Nicaragua in back issues of *The Nation*. I was a lawyer; lawyers hate being unprepared.

One of the things I hadn't been able to do was meet the other members of the brigade who would be arriving together a few hours after me. Maggie, however, assured me they were all regular people (with differing levels of political sophistication) and that I would have no trouble relating to them. Over the past six months, there had been only three or four meetings, which a number of people had missed. Eventually, the organizers had assembled a packet of information and sent it to each participant. If I read that, Maggie said, I'd be up to speed.

On the flights from Dallas and El Salvador, I'd sat with a brigade from Seattle, most of them teachers who planned to spend the summer volunteering in the national literacy campaign. They all seemed kind and decent. In El Salvador, we picked up a group of male Cuban doctors who were a bit too flirtatious but still very nice. They'd been sent by Castro to help out in the rural areas where medical personnel were being targeted by the Contras. Mixed in with all us do-gooders were well-dressed Nicaraguans returning from the States, their children lugging huge stuffed animals and various souvenirs from Disneyland. The rowdy drinkers in first-class were all reporters who had obviously been to Nicaragua many times before; as the day wore on, they got louder and more outrageous, sounding just like old-time public defenders slugging shots of tequila at the annual public defender conference. Which was, until recently, how I'd always imagined I would end up.

As soon as they'd heard my plans, everyone at the office, especially Ray and Donald, had tried to convince me to take a vacation instead of joining a brigade to Nicaragua. As I headed for what I hoped was an air-conditioned building, I considered the distinct possibility they'd all been right. But gorging myself on guacamole and chips and then snorkeling around the bay in Zihuatanejo chasing schools of brightly colored fish seemed so purposeless, which I suppose was the point, except I'd already attained that state and was hoping to find another.

By the time I reached the doors to the nearest building, my clothes looked as if I'd worn them in the shower. The sudden air conditioning was almost as shocking as the heat. After a few minutes inside the terminal, I wondered how I'd ever force myself to leave again. Truth is, I'd have to tell my friends, I never made it past the airport; I spent the entire six weeks browsing through magazines and eating pretzels and Hershey bars from the snack machines. Very restful. Speaking of snack machines, however, I didn't see any, just a long, slow-moving line to get through customs.

Two young men in khaki uniforms were painstakingly searching every piece of luggage for contraband and weapons. *Bienvenidos a Nicaragua, Welcome to Nicaragua*, a country the size of Connecticut, at war with the United States. With the barest of sighs, I shouldered my duffel bag and joined the line.

After a couple of minutes, the man standing in front of me asked, "Did you know it would be this hot?" He'd arrived on the same plane as me but hadn't been part of the Seattle group.

I shook my head. "Lucifer mentioned it, but I didn't believe him."

The man stared at me uncomprehending, then burst out laughing. "Me neither." He pulled out a red handkerchief from his bag and wiped the back of his neck. "Oh well, I suppose we'll get used to it." He looked about my age and was wearing brand-new tan-colored pants and a matching vest with dozens of pockets. A week ago, I'd resisted buying the exact same tropical outfit from a yuppie boutique called Travel Incorporated, opting righteously for cheap cotton clothes at K-Mart.

"I'm David Kramer," he said, offering me his hand.

I shook it. "Rachel Stein."

"Where are you from, Rachel?"

"Boulder, Colorado. What about you?"

"Des Moines." He paused. "Are you a sandalista or a journalist? You don't look like the CIA, but maybe they're getting sneakier."

I smiled. "What's a sandalista?"

He looked pleased to know anything in a foreign country that someone else—even if it was only another North American—didn't. "It's what the people here call the internationals who come to support the Sandinistas."

"It sounds faintly derogatory," I said, ever the cautious lawyer.

He looked surprised. "I—I don't think so. I think it's affectionate." But now that I'd planted the seed, he looked a little confused. Here for only ten minutes and already I was making a difference.

"Well," I said, "in any event, since I'm not a journalist and I'm not the CIA in disguise, I must be a sandalista." I lifted one of my feet and showed him my new leather sandal.

He laughed again, deciding to trust me after all. "Me too," he confided. "I'm headed to Esteli to join a coffee harvesting brigade. My wife is very worried. She's a kindergarten teacher. She thinks I'll get shot or kidnapped but I had to come. It makes me so mad what we're doing to this country."

I nodded, wondered again if I'd made a terrible mistake coming here. I was feeling guilty. It wasn't the Nicaraguan people's fault I needed a cause—they had enough problems—why take it out on them? But I didn't really believe that I couldn't be of use, even if my heart was a little opaque around the edges. I could still lift a hammer.

"What about you?" David asked.

I shrugged. "A few weeks ago, I upped and joined the Boulder-Jalapa friendship brigade." Boy did that sound weird. For twelve years, I'd been a stable, middle-class attorney and now I was someone who'd suddenly joined a "brigade."

"Jalapa? Wow, my wife would have had a heart attack if she thought I was going up there. What's your group going to do?"

Christ, was it that dangerous? "Help rebuild a clinic that the Contras burned down last summer."

"That's great." He hesitated. "You're not going up there by yourself, are you?"

I shook my head. His concern was genuine, but it wasn't helpful. "No, I'm supposed to meet everyone here in the next few hours."

He glanced at his watch. "Well I hope they get here soon. I've heard it's dangerous to travel at night up near the border."

"I'm sure it is," I said, "but we're spending the next two weeks attending a language school in Managua before we leave."

"Oh, then you'll be fine." He smiled reassuringly. The line inched forward. "So," he said, "are you ready to answer the one question every Nicaraguan is going to ask you?"

I hated quizzes and was growing tired of my companion, but what the hell. I had a lot to learn here, and not much time. "What's the question?"

Again, that pleased look. "Will the United States invade or not?"

Thank God I'd studied up as much as I had. But even if I hadn't, as a criminal defense attorney I'd been trained to express an opinion whether I knew anything about a subject or not. Standing silent in a courtroom was something you did rarely and always as a tactic, not because you didn't know the answer.

"Well, for what it's worth," I said, "I don't think so. An invasion here wouldn't be as easy as invading Grenada. The people would actually fight back. We might as well just keep squeezing the country economically with the embargo and let the Contras do the rest."

He nodded. "I totally agree."

"On the other hand, I wouldn't put it past us either."

He nodded in agreement with that as well. So there we were, two sandalistas having just arrived in the Augusto C. Sandino International Airport discussing the political situation in Nicaragua. I was doing fine, I told myself, everything would be okay. All I needed was a fan, a good night's sleep and a bathroom. I looked around until I spotted the women's *baño*. David promised to save my place while I hurried over to it.

Thanks to the United States embargo, there was no toilet paper. Instead, I had to use little squares of newspaper that were stacked next to the toilet. Did newsprint run? I stood up, flushed the toilet, and buttoned my shorts. Suddenly, I felt dizzy and had to sit down again. I put my head between my knees and stared intently at the pink and white tiled floor. It was actually pretty clean for a public bathroom in a third world country.

What the hell was I doing here? For a couple of inglorious seconds, I entertained the idea of catching the next plane out. Julius Caesar's ineffectual cousin: I came, I saw, I left. But I wouldn't, because I had glimpsed the possibility of feeling useful here, of getting high, and I was a junkie whose sources had dried up back home.

***

Three and a half hours later, I was boarding an old-fashioned yellow school bus with the rest of my brigade. Our group consisted of six women and four men. Except for two kids who were college students, and a handsome older man who looked extremely fit, everyone was about my age. Not surprisingly, we seemed to be a homogeneous group of white, middle-class Coloradoans; after all, who else could afford to come? I assumed everyone except Tim and Estelle, the two organizers who were obviously fluent, knew enough Spanish to get by, but like me would all benefit from two weeks of intensive language instruction.

As we headed out of the airport, Tim and Estelle remained standing at the front of the bus chatting with the driver and nodding encouragingly at the rest of us. They seemed completely at ease. Both wore white kerchiefs around their necks as if anticipating the possibility of a noxious cloud of smog suddenly engulfing us.

"Well everyone," Estelle said, smiling, "we're on our way. Some of you may be feeling a bit overwhelmed, but that's perfectly normal. There'll be plenty of time for questions later. Right now, just try to get used to the heat and your new surroundings." She checked her watch.

"It's a quarter to ten. The *barrio* is only fifteen miles away. So it won't be long."

We were headed for the community center in *Barrio Maximo Jerez* to meet the various families who would put us up during our two-week stay in Managua. Personally, I would have preferred spending the night in a quiet hotel room and meeting our families the next day, but this was a group enterprise, not a solo journey. I'd traded my independence for something equally precious: the chance to make a difference. Although my judgment was admittedly impaired, it seemed like a reasonable trade with a potentially huge payoff. As I contemplated this, one of our tires blew out and we almost collided with a taxi. It happened so fast no one had time to react. Miraculously, we came to a halt on the shoulder of the road where we wouldn't be impeding traffic. White-faced, everyone quickly filed out of the bus. After swearing and kicking at the tire, our driver apologized for the inconvenience, and then started walking down the highway. He promised to return as soon as possible.

It was much too hot to wait inside the bus. As we stood by the side of the road, everyone tried their best to remain good-natured and philosophical. This was an adventure after all, not a vacation. No one complained, although one of the women—sporting a recent perm that made her look like a poodle—mentioned she was feeling faint. Immediately, Tim and Estelle hurried over and began urging her to drink more water.

"Listen, everyone," Estelle said, "we're going to have to watch out for heat exhaustion." Despite our recent mishap, she and Tim seemed calm and matter-of-fact as if everything were going exactly according to schedule.

Although it was night, the traffic (which was less than three feet away) was bumper to bumper. None of the cars seemed to have working mufflers, but they all had horns. Trucks and buses routinely backfired as they negotiated their way down the street, which was pitted with huge potholes. The smell of burning garbage permeated the air. And something else too, something sickeningly sweet, like overripe melons or gardenias past their prime. Whatever it was, it was all too much, contributing to a feeling that we were under siege and about to be overrun.

After about forty minutes, most of us ended up sprawling in the weeds behind the bus. The light from the full moon was as bright as a prison searchlight. If we'd been convicts attempting to escape, we would have been caught immediately. There was still no sign of the driver. The poodle lady's face was redder than a beet, and I wondered if she would end up needing medical attention. Almost every group has at least one weak link and one pain in the ass. The poodle lady was clearly vying for the weak link and I thought I knew who might turn out to be the pain in the ass, a sharp-faced woman who seemed to have no sense of humor, always a bad sign especially in stressful situations.

After a long period of silence, one of the college students asked if anyone had any more water. The student was at least six feet tall with brown frizzy hair and a sweet mischievous grin. He reminded me of my cousin Robbie, who I'd always liked.

"You should have brought more," the sharp-faced woman replied. "This is a third world country. You can't depend on others to take care of you."

"It's okay," Tim told the student. "I think there's one last bottle on the bus, although it's probably boiling hot." He shrugged. "But that's Nicaragua for you, everything's boiling hot."

The student nodded. "I was thinking maybe we should pour some over her head." He was pointing at the poodle lady who was now lying on the ground and beginning to snore.

"I'm a nurse," the woman sprawled next to me announced. "I think she's okay, but I'm keeping an eye on her." The nurse had a square pleasant face and like most members of her profession, seemed calm and unflappable. Her presence was good news to a brigade headed for a war zone. She had a huge cloth bag in her lap, from which she pulled out a bottle of pills. "Just in case," she added.

The older man in our group, who'd been squatting next to the flat tire, straightened up and said, "You know, I don't think I've ever seen a tire this bald. It's actually amazing."

"Maybe we ought to take a picture," I said. "Our first flat tire."

My cousin Robbie laughed, the nurse smiled, the sharp-faced woman frowned, and the poodle lady snored on.

Eventually, the driver returned with another tire that looked just as bald as the one that had blown. He must have noticed the looks on our faces.

"*Está bien*," he told us, chuckling. *It's okay.*

After helping him change the tire, we were herded back onto the bus and driven through a maze of rubble-strewn streets to the *barrio*.

***

The community center was a large shell with gray cement walls and a dirt floor. Two sets of old-fashioned metal bleachers faced each other on opposite sides of the room. The pale-faced brigade members sat on one side, the coffee-colored prospective families on the other. Zombies vs. Home Team. During the next half hour, a stout Nicaraguan woman holding a clipboard welcomed us and explained something about local neighborhood committees working with the government to foster friendship between the United States and Nicaragua. She was either a teacher, the head of a local neighborhood committee, or had something to do with the government's literacy campaign. My Spanish wasn't good enough to follow much of what she said, and frankly I was too tired to care.

After the clapping ended, each of us was paired with a family. When my name was called, I was surprised to see a lone woman in her late forties or early fifties stand up to claim me. As we approached each other, she smiled shyly and introduced herself as Sonia. She was a few inches taller than me, about five feet seven, plump, with short black curly hair and a round impish face. I thought I would like her.

It was much noisier now with everyone milling around, shaking hands, and inspecting luggage. Two teenage boys in wheelchairs were offering everyone bottles of Coca-Cola and a woman wearing tight red stretchy pants and a matching blouse was handing out homemade tamales. I was starving but the food smelled vaguely like pork and I was afraid to chance it; the last time I'd eaten strange smelling meat (at a restaurant in Puerto Vallarta), I was sick for a week. Although it was past midnight, at least thirty children were running around the room, buzzed on the sugary soda, shouting and squealing with laughter. Every three or four years, I had a moment when I remembered why I never wanted children. This was one of them.

I did my best to keep smiling, but I was beginning to dissociate. Who cared about friendship? I just wanted to lie down. Finally, Sonia motioned me to follow her outside. Gratefully, I picked up my duffel bag and we walked about three blocks in the dark past an empty field and a number of modest one-story homes to a pleasant-looking red brick house with a broken metal gate in front. My shelter for the next two weeks.

Sonia's living room was sparsely furnished, but immaculate. There was a faded pink love seat in one corner that looked as if no one ever sat on it, a small plastic table displaying her favorite knickknacks, a photograph on the wall of two young women laughing and holding hands at the beach, and a plain wooden chair.

That was it. There were no curtains. The floor was covered in smooth red tile. In rapid Spanish, my host welcomed me and then gave me the grand tour. First, her bedroom, then the bathroom, then my bedroom (which didn't have a door, but at least had a sheet tacked over the entrance), then a quaint open-air kitchen and a backyard patio bordered by high cement walls. So far, I thought I understood at least half of what she was saying. Not bad for someone with only four years of high school Spanish.

Out on the patio, the air smelled like a lush decaying jungle dense with too many trees, plants, flowers and bugs, everything multiplying much too fast for its own good. I felt dizzy again and tried to look casual as I leaned against the nearest wall. I'd be fine as soon as I got some sleep.

"Does anyone else live here?" I asked in my halting Spanish, praying for a negative answer.

"No," she replied sadly, "just me."

I tried hard to conceal my delight. I'd worried about living in a one-room shack with a dozen children, hoping only for a private little corner, but this...was paradise. My shoulders dropped a foot. I had clearly lucked out. Decent shelter, my own room, no kids, private patio and a charming open-air kitchen. What more could a privileged North American princess ask for? Only a good night's sleep.

But since I couldn't think of any polite way to go to my room, I followed Sonia into the kitchen where she offered me another bottle of Coca-Cola. We sat down at a table under a makeshift metal awning and between sickeningly sweet gulps, I told her I was a lawyer (no point trying to explain that I had recently quit my job) and that I defended people who broke the law. Sonia nodded and told me she did many things to make a living, including providing room and board for visitors like myself. Then, for the next fifteen minutes, while I forced myself to pay close attention, she told me all about her family. Despite my exhaustion, I was fairly confident I understood the gist of her narrative.

If so, she had either been married and divorced twice, or married only once, but her husband now lived with his second family elsewhere. I was pretty sure she'd had two children who died in infancy and had a nephew who was either in the army or was a participant in the literacy campaign. She also had one sister who lived in Managua and another in Florida, or maybe just one sister who used to live here, but now lived in Florida. Under the circumstances, I thought I was doing well, especially since I hadn't studied the language for almost two decades and in the interim had used it only occasionally to converse with clients before the interpreter arrived, and to order food and ask for directions when Vickie and I traveled in Mexico.

I finished my bottle of Coca-Cola and was about to excuse myself when a visitor arrived, a tall gaunt man in his forties who looked as if he'd drunk too much rum earlier in the evening. Sonia introduced him as Tomas, but I couldn't understand whether he was her neighbor, a relative, or her boyfriend. Tomas took my hand, held it for too long, and then chuckled as if I'd told him a good joke. I wanted to leave, but it seemed that Tomas had specifically come to welcome me. As we sat down to chat, I noticed his shirt was buttoned incorrectly and that he had a spot of dried blood under his nose. All I wanted to do was lie down in my room and close my eyes. Sonia, meanwhile, seemed to have disappeared.

"How are you?" Tomas asked in English.

"I'm fine," I said, also in English, "but I'm very tired."

"*Sí, sí*," he replied, and then launched into a long rambling story in Spanish about his brother who had either recently died in the war or participated in the national vaccination program. He kept pointing to a dog tag that I assumed was his brother's, but he also kept pinching himself on the arm as if he was vaccinating himself. I wanted to tell him I was sorry, but it wouldn't have made sense if his brother was fine.

Finally, Sonia reappeared with two more bottles of Coca-Cola, which she'd obviously unearthed from some secret stash.

"Thank you for everything," I told her, standing up, "but I'm very tired. I have to go to sleep."

With that, I excused myself and escaped to my room which I now wished had a solid door (with a lock) instead of a flimsy curtain. Oh well. I sat down on the cot and felt the springs sag halfway to the floor. It's only for two weeks, I told myself.

Other than the cot, an empty wooden crate on the floor across from me and a cracked mirror hanging above the crate, the room was bare. I unpacked my clothes and stacked them neatly in the crate, then found my bottle of Benadryl and decided to take a couple to help me sleep. It was almost two thirty in the morning. I lay down and pulled the sheet up to my neck and tucked it securely around my body. It was still well over a hundred degrees and I didn't need the sheet, but I was feeling vulnerable. I could hear Sonia and Tomas talking in the kitchen. My cot squeaked noisily every time I shifted position. I tried to ignore something scrabbling across the wall above my head, but my imagination was stronger than my will. I snapped on the light and watched a dark green lizard scamper toward a corner of the room and try to hide. I knew exactly how he felt.

All of a sudden, I remembered I hadn't taken my malaria pill yet. I tried to get up without making any noise, but of course it was impossible. I kept the sheet around me as I knelt in front of my duffel bag searching for my bottle of pink malaria pills. I popped one and decided to take three Advils and another couple of Benadryls while I was at it. You can never take too many pills in the tropics. As I stood up, I felt a hand on my shoulder and almost screamed. It was Tomas, still grinning from that joke I never told him. Before I could say anything, he leaned over and kissed me.

"I love you, baby," he said in broken English.

I was so flustered, I couldn't remember the Spanish word for "go," and my dictionary was still packed in my bag. Tomas leaned over for another kiss.

"Get out of here," I told him in English, then remembered the highway sign on the border between New Mexico and Colorado. *Vaya con Dios. Go with God.* Under the circumstances, however, that seemed a little too kind. I backed up a few steps and pointed at my flimsy curtain. "*Vaya,*" I ordered.

Before Tomas could respond, Sonia entered the room speaking too rapidly for me to understand, but not for Tomas who left immediately.

"*Gracias,*" I said.

Sonia rolled her eyes and smiled apologetically. "He has many problems," she explained, "but he won't bother you again."

"*Está bien.*" What the hell, a little breaking and entering with intent to commit sexual assault—I'd represented a lot worse. "*Está bien,*" I repeated, and she finally left.

I popped two more Benadryls and climbed into my cot, which sank to the floor. Suddenly, I missed Vickie and wondered if she'd forgiven me yet for ignoring her advice and coming here. A rooster crowed loudly. I checked my watch, but it was only a quarter to three. Nobody, not even the animals, paid any attention to the rules here.

Every time I sighed or took a deep breath, the bed squeaked. Why wasn't the Benadryl working? I'd taken enough to knock out an elephant. I considered getting up and taking a few more, but I heard something clicking its way across the tile floor and decided to stay put. I hoped I'd zipped up my duffel bag. A few moments later, I could have sworn something fairly large, a chicken or a small dog, had hopped onto the bed and then off again, but how likely was that? Although I was lying perfectly still, I was sweating profusely. Maybe it was too hot to sleep? Although I knew nothing about science, it seemed plausible that the human body had some kind of built-in survival mechanism that automatically kept it awake when it was in danger of being parboiled.

Since I didn't want to think about my comfortable bedroom in Boulder or why I'd left the public defender's office, I decided to think about rock climbing. Often, when I had trouble falling asleep, I imagined all the moves on a difficult climb, where I'd placed my protection, what kinds of pieces I'd used along the route. If I stayed with it long enough, I could feel the rock against my fingertips, the air on the back of my neck, my hips shifting back and forth as I crawled up hundreds of feet simply for the pleasure of reaching the top. Because Vickie refused to even watch me climb, she couldn't understand when I tried to explain that it was the only activity I'd ever engaged in that absolutely precluded thinking about anything except what I was doing. To me, it was the quintessential moving meditation. The world could be roaring around me, deafeningly loud, but once I'd stepped onto the rock and placed my first piece of protection into a crack and then clipped my rope to it, everything became quiet. And from then on, until I reached my belay point and anchored myself in, it was only me, my body, and my concentration: Where should I step next? Is that a good place to stick a cam? Am I getting too far from my last piece?

I was half asleep now, imagining myself leading a climb in Boulder Canyon, or perhaps I was already dreaming.

I'm moving steadily up the granite face and feeling the sun on the backs of my hands. Looking up, I notice the finger crack I've been following has ended, that there's no place above me to put in any more protection. Maggie is about a hundred feet below, anchored into a sloping ledge high above the canyon.

"Maggie," I shout, "it's run out. I can't protect it."

"Well, you have to do something," Maggie yells. "Look around you."

I try to remain calm. Panic is my worst enemy. I look to my left, to my right, above and below me—nothing but smooth slick granite. My hands are beginning to sweat which makes my hold on the rock more precarious. First one, then both of my legs begin to shake uncontrollably, a phenomenon known as "sewing machine legs" among climbers.

"Shit," I whisper.

"Are you all right?" Maggie yells.

No, but I will have to keep moving anyway.

CHAPTER NINE

My first morning as a *brigadista* in Nicaragua, I woke up with an aching back and a hangover from the six Benadryls I'd ingested during the night. I looked down and noticed the springs of my cot were touching the floor. It was already ten degrees hotter than yesterday and it was only six fifteen. I could hear Sonia humming to herself in the kitchen, and a low buzz of conversation from the house next door. Belatedly, a rooster started to crow and then someone drove down the street broadcasting a loud recorded message that sounded both urgent and colloquial. Although the sound was completely distorted,

I assumed it had something to do with politics. After a single night, I already sensed that in Nicaragua everything was about politics, even the weather. Regardless, any further sleep was out of the question.

Before I could extricate myself from the bed, I noticed a large brown egg nestled in the sheets between my ankles. I picked it up and stared at it. It was smooth and slightly warm. Where the hell had it come from? Was it part of some strange Nicaraguan welcoming ritual? And then I vaguely remembered the chicken hopping on and off my cot during the night and finally squatting on my ankles. I'd assumed I was having some kind of anxiety dream about Central America. Well, better a chicken than some pathetic loser like the burglar I'd represented who'd fallen asleep on his victim's bed. Or Tomas, my new Nicaraguan boyfriend.

After a few minutes, I got dressed and walked out into the kitchen. The early morning light was blinding. I shielded my eyes as if I were being subjected to a painful interrogation lamp. I wished I hadn't lost my sunglasses the day before and made a mental note to buy another pair as soon as possible. And a fan since Sonia didn't seem to have one.

"Look," I said to Sonia, and showed her the egg.

She smiled delightedly. "Ah, for your breakfast."

I handed it over, my first contribution to the household. Not exactly an elk carcass, but it was something. A few minutes later, she served me a plate of rice and beans, and a soft-boiled egg.

As soon as I finished eating, I washed my plate and then checked the time. I had two hours to filter a couple of quarts of water and take a shower. At nine, I was supposed to be in front of the community center where a bus would take us to the language school. I went back to my room, ignored a lizard on the wall, and pulled out my brand-new forty-dollar water filter from my duffel bag.

As I was setting it up in the kitchen, a tiny elf-like woman carrying a heavy sack appeared in the doorway. Sonia immediately rushed over and helped her carry it to the table.

"This is my neighbor Amelia," Sonia told me in Spanish. "And this," she pointed to me, "is Rachel, my new guest from North America."

"*Mucho gusto*," I said, offering her my hand.

Amelia smiled shyly. "*Encantada.*"

Sonia then explained that Amelia had come over to make tortillas. She and Sonia were planning to make a huge batch and then try to sell them downtown. If I understood them correctly, they felt lucky to have scored the ingredients and worried it might never happen again. Amelia was barely five feet tall and extremely thin. Her thick black glasses were too big for her face and by the way she squinted, probably weren't the right prescription either. I wished my Spanish were better and that I didn't have to ask both women to slow down and repeat almost everything they said. I hoped the language school would help.

Amelia, especially, seemed curious about my water filter. As I started to pump, Sonia told her I was about to purify perfectly good drinking water. I was sure Sonia meant well. She just didn't understand a simple but crucial North American concept: what was good for others wasn't necessarily good for us. Later, I found out the water in Managua was chlorinated and quite safe to drink.

Meanwhile, my bottles weren't filling with water. The women hovered near the stove whispering in Spanish. I kept looking at my filter, wondering why it didn't work. Then, I realized I had to remove two tiny stoppers that prevented any water from flowing in or out.

"Ah," I said, and made a big show of removing the stoppers. "Ah," the women repeated.

But still nothing happened. I read and reread the simple instructions. It took another ten minutes to figure out I had it all backward, that the filter went into the empty bottles and the pump went into the bucket of water. Both women smiled politely as I poured myself a glass of purified drinking water. These are kind people, I told myself, and you have no business being here.

My shower didn't go much better. I didn't care about the lack of hot water, but the huge brownish red cockroach resting on the bathroom floor terrified me. It looked almost as big as my foot. I considered squashing it, but worried what might happen if I didn't completely kill it. Finally, it scuttled behind the toilet and I lunged for the shower. I was only half finished when the water suddenly stopped. I waited about five minutes, but it never came on again. Luckily, I'd rinsed most of the shampoo out of my hair.

"What happened to the water?" I asked Sonia when I came back out into the kitchen.

She shrugged. "*Se fue.*" *It went away.* This turned out to be the standard explanation in Nicaragua for everything that ran out, didn't work or broke down.

I noticed on my way to the community center that many of the homes on the block weren't as nice as Sonia's, that some of the roofs had caved in or parts of the houses were missing. As I passed the open field next to the center, acrid gritty smoke from a pile of burning trash filled my nostrils and made my eyes water. I found a spot upwind of the pile and waited for the rest of my brigade.

Within minutes, everyone but the student who reminded me of my cousin Robbie had arrived. Most of the group looked exhausted and grungy as if they hadn't slept or washed for days, although I knew at least some of them had tried taking showers because they still had streaks of shampoo in their hair. At nine fifteen, Tim and Estelle left to check on the bus, which hadn't arrived yet. There was very little small talk. Like me, everyone seemed to be waiting for their psyches to catch up with their somas.

Finally, the other college student cleared her throat. "Excuse me," she said, "but does anyone's bedroom have a roof?" She bit her lip and shrugged. "Mine doesn't." She was slim and cute, with delicate features and a beautiful complexion. I guessed she was about nineteen.

"That's terrible!" the poodle lady exclaimed.

The sharp-faced woman shook her head. "Get used to it. There's no money here to fix things. Everything goes to pay for the war." There was a large gob of shampoo above her left ear. Normally, I tell people if their flies are open or there's lettuce caught between their teeth, but if it isn't fixable I keep my mouth shut.

The student blushed. "I wasn't actually complaining. I was just curious." She was obviously a nice middle-class kid, someone who could have spent her summer gossiping by the side of a pool but chose to come here instead.

"Well it's still a bummer," I said. "I have a large poncho if you need one."

"Oh for God's sake," the sharp-faced woman muttered. "It's not the rainy season."

"Susan, she was just kidding." The mild-mannered man who spoke was obviously Susan's boyfriend or husband. Why was it, I wondered, that women like Susan often ended up with men who were teddy bears? Susan's teddy bear was a heavyset guy with a full reddish beard that he stroked whenever he was about to speak. It sounds affected, but he was actually just a polite thoughtful guy who'd fallen for his opposite. Love is mysterious.

"Hey, you're all still here! Why am I not surprised?" It was my cousin Robbie, who would have missed the bus by at least thirty minutes if it had been on time. He wore a blue and yellow Hawaiian shirt that was still unbuttoned and he looked as if he'd been running. "Sorry. One of the kids was playing with my alarm clock and broke it." He wiped his face with the back of his hand. "God, it's hot! Where's the bus?"

When our two organizers, Tim and Estelle, returned, we learned that our bus had broken down and that it could be another hour before it was fixed.

"I think I might be having an allergic reaction to all this smoke," the poodle lady said. She wasn't exaggerating. Her face looked puffy and her cheeks were dotted with tiny raised bumps.

After a quick vote, we decided to move inside the center, which was empty. Everyone except the poodle lady sat down in a circle on the dirt floor, as if it were our first day of summer camp.

Estelle whistled to get our attention. "Okay everyone, why don't we go around and formally introduce ourselves." She paused, gauging our reaction. "And also, let's say a few words about why we're here." She was wearing a T-shirt commemorating a demonstration in 1983 where 17,000 peace activists, myself included, had encircled the Rocky Flats nuclear weapons facility outside of Denver. I smiled at the memory. We'd sung and chanted for hours, a modern day Ghost Dance that left us feeling wildly hopeful. Although the plant was still making plutonium triggers, the publicity had hurt and the momentum to shut it down continued to build. Who knew, maybe this would turn out to be equally rewarding.

"Oh God," my cousin Robbie muttered. "It's touchy-feely time." He was sitting cross-legged next to me, his shoulder touching mine.

"All right then," Estelle said, "since it was my idea, I'll start." She had short blond hair, clear blue eyes and a lean athletic-looking body. No doubt she exercised regularly and paid attention to what she ate, a classic Boulderite. She introduced herself and told us this was her fourth visit to Nicaragua since the revolution.

"As most of you know, I work for the Peace and Justice Coalition in Boulder." Her calm face reflected strength as well as confidence. I wondered, if I saw her at the courthouse in handcuffs, what kind of crime she might have committed, a game I sometimes played when I first met someone and knew very little about them. Shoplifting? No, not likely. Criminal impersonation? Possibly, but arson was better. Yes, I imagined that she'd torched the dilapidated building where she and her dedicated colleagues had worked for years on peace and justice issues. With the insurance proceeds, they'd purchased a lovely Victorian house, which they'd converted into a shelter for battered women.

"Anyway," she was saying, "I'm excited to be here and looking forward to working with all of you. If you have any questions, don't hesitate to ask either me or Tim."

Tim, the other organizer of the brigade, could have been Estelle's twin brother except they referred to each other as friends and, I guessed by the easy way they touched each other, were probably lovers. Like her, he was tall and blond, with impressive biceps that required at least weekly maintenance. Either that, or he was a climber.

"Hi." He grinned. "I'm Tim and this is my second trip to Nicaragua. Welcome." He looked around the circle, nodding at everyone. "I hope you all have a positive experience here and that when you leave the country, you'll feel proud to have been part of an historic revolution." He paused to take a slug of water from his bottle. "Let's see, at home I'm responsible for quality control at the Celestial Seasonings herbal tea company."

Theft of trade secrets? Bingo. With his guileless blue eyes and innocent face, nobody would have suspected he'd been hired by Lipton to steal trade secrets from the company; even after he confessed, it was difficult for his employers to believe he was guilty.

Next came the handsome older man who told us to call him Lenny. He was a retired architect who lived south of Denver.

"I'm sixty-three," he said. "Hopefully, I won't slow you all down." He was tan and fit and unlikely to slow anyone down. A serial killer, I decided, with the rugged good looks and sexy smile of a Robert Redford; whenever he stopped to pick up a hitchhiker, she never hesitated to climb right in. "I'm just here to help," he added.

Three down, seven more to go. I could feel my cousin Robbie, whose real name I still didn't know, fidgeting beside me. I resisted putting my hand on his knee to calm him down.

"I guess I'm next," the female student said. "My name is Veronica and I'm a sophomore at CU." She blushed. "I guess I'm also the youngest person on this brigade. I heard about Nicaragua in a class and decided to come. My parents are worried about my safety, of course, but mostly they're supportive—they're old lefties. Anyway, I'm looking forward to everything and I'm just open to whatever happens."

"God, she's enthusiastic," my cousin muttered.

I stifled a smile and hoped no one else had heard him. I studied Veronica for a couple of seconds before making up her crime. Okay, I thought, what if her allowance covered her tuition and books, but not her expenses? To make ends meet, she'd started doing nude massages at a small spa on the outskirts of Boulder. One of her clients turned out to be an undercover cop and she was busted for prostitution.

Before anyone else could introduce themselves, a Nicaraguan boy wearing a faded Mickey Mouse T-shirt ran into the room and told us the bus had arrived. We all stood up and stretched. Estelle suggested we continue the conversation on our way to the language school.

The bus was sweltering and many of the windows were stuck in the closed position. I found a seat with some cross ventilation and slid over to the window. My cousin flopped down next me.

"Hi," he said, "my name is Allen and I'm an alcoholic."

"Hi Allen."

He laughed. "I'm not really an alcoholic, but I'll probably become one. I hate Coca-Cola."

"Me too," I said. "I'm Rachel."

"Hi Rachel." He made a rueful face. "I have a confession."

"Oh good." I crossed my arms and waited.

He sighed. "I'm not proud of myself. I was interested in the situation here and I'm definitely sympathetic to the Sandinista cause, but I mostly came to annoy my father. That's really terrible isn't it?"

I nodded. Now he was waiting for my story. Part of me wanted to tell him the truth, and part of me didn't, so I compromised. "I came because I was having a nervous breakdown and wanted to have it in a tropical setting."

Allen laughed for a moment and then stopped, his dark brown eyes wide with concern. "I hope that's not true." What a sweet kid.

"How old are you?" I asked.

"Twenty-four."

"When I was your age, I was a wiseass too."

"I know," he said. "I could tell."

In everyone's heart, there's an inner sanctum, a special place deep in the center where only a handful of people, living or dead, reside. They're the people you not only love, but with whom you resonate on some mysterious level that makes them precious and indispensable, a reason to have lived. When you look across the vast expanse, they're the ones that seem to be moving parallel to you, sprinting through the same perilous minefield. Some of them have already been blown to pieces, others have self-destructed all by themselves, and the rest struggle on, keeping you company.

The inhabitants of my inner sanctum included my father, my childhood friend Leslie, Maggie, Vickie of course, and Emily. And now I could feel this young upstart—this twenty-four-year-old straight boy—knocking on that door, asking to be let in. Of course it was too soon to know whether he would get any farther; people often stormed my heart and never made it past the first barricades. But still, I could hear him knocking and it surprised the hell out of me.

Meanwhile, the driver was trying to start the bus, but nothing was happening.

"Oh-oh," Allen said.

We waited in silence, sweat dripping down our faces. After a few minutes, the driver got out and opened the hood. We could hear banging sounds and curses. My thin cotton shirt was soaked and sticking to the back of the seat.

"I vote we stand outside until he fixes it," I said.

"Good idea," Estelle agreed.

Everyone climbed out and gathered around the driver who was banging on the engine with a small hammer.

"This doesn't bode well," I said to Allen who'd followed me out of the bus.

Eventually, the driver let the hood clang shut and began walking down the street in the opposite direction of the center.

"*Un momento*," he promised, but already we knew better. After less than twenty-four hours in the country, we were savvy veterans and gave the appropriate response. I called it the Nicaraguan shrug, a combination of helplessness and resignation. Tim led us back to the center where we resumed our places on the floor. After everyone settled down, Estelle motioned me to continue our introductions.

On the bus, I'd considered various things I could say when it was my turn, but none seemed to strike the right balance between honesty and discretion. *Hi, my name is Rachel and I have no idea why I'm here, it was a last-minute decision, and I'm just hoping it'll be better than where I've been.*

"Hi," I said, "my name is Rachel and I'm a recovering criminal defense attorney." Everyone laughed. "While I figure out what to do with the rest of my life, I thought I might be of some use here." I turned to Allen, signaling I was finished.

"Lucky you," he said. "Okay, my name is Allen and I'm hoping I'll be kidnapped by the Contras so I won't have to go to law school in the fall." I started to laugh, but nobody else did.

"That's not funny," the sharp-faced woman said. "The Contras have killed and kidnapped thousands of innocent people. They cut the breasts off women and toss grenades at little children. They burn and destroy clinics, schools and cooperatives."

Allen looked stricken. "I'm sorry. It was a joke. As usual, in record time I've managed to alienate everyone around me."

"It's all right, Allen," Estelle assured him. "There's plenty of room for humor in this brigade. That might have been a little over the top, that's all."

Allen nodded. "I think I'll shut up now."

I glanced at my unlikely new friend—quick, bright and Jewish— then decided he'd been busted for selling an ounce of cocaine to an undercover police officer. His father was so pissed off, he was threatening to disown him but Allen knew he'd eventually come around and hire the best lawyer in town to defend him.

Estelle pointed to the sharp-faced woman. "Let's try and finish this. Why don't you go next?"

"Okay fine," the woman said, her cheeks still flushed with indignation. "I'm Susan and this is my husband Richard." She gestured at the teddy bear beside her. "We've been working in the Nicaraguan solidarity movement since 1982. We want to help rebuild the clinic in Jalapa and in that way express our solidarity with the people of Nicaragua." She had light brown hair and might have been pretty if she was someone who delighted in the company of others, not someone who constantly expected to be disappointed. I decided to wait until her husband spoke, but I was leaning toward codefendants in a string of aggravated robberies.

Richard stroked his beard and said, "As you already know, my name is Richard. I'm a third-grade schoolteacher. I love kids and I love helping people. As Susan mentioned, we've been involved with Nicaraguan solidarity work for a number of years." If they were Bonnie and Clyde, Bonnie was definitely the leader of the duo, and poor old Clyde just went along to please her.

Suddenly Veronica—the female student and occasional prostitute— made a noise and jumped up, flapping her arms around her head.

"Ugh," she said, "there's this weird bug that won't leave me alone." I could see something huge, with thin delicate wings, buzzing near her fingertips.

"Ugh, get away." She was beginning to run in circles.

Richard was getting to his feet.

"Where are you going?" Susan asked, reaching out to stop him.

"To help. She's just a kid."

"It's only a bug," Susan said. She shook her head disapprovingly.

Richard hurried over to Veronica and began batting the insect away from her.

"Ugh," he said, "it's so big!"

"I know," Veronica screeched.

He swatted wildly at her hair. "Let's run outside and see if we can lose him."

They were both laughing and shrieking. Everyone in the circle was smiling except Susan.

"Sorry about the Contra joke," Allen whispered to me. "It was definitely in poor taste. But if they ever do attack us, I vote we offer up Susan and see if they'll take her."

I smiled and nodded. He had the makings of a fine lawyer: good sense of humor, the ability to plan for contingencies, and a fresh creative approach to problem solving.

When Richard and Veronica came back, we resumed the introductions. There were only two women left who hadn't spoken, the nurse and the poodle lady. The nurse was a solidly built woman with a square, intelligent face. Despite her salt-and-pepper hair, I guessed she was in her late thirties. She looked around the circle and said, "Well, I'm a nurse and they need nurses here. After the clinic's been rebuilt, I hope to stay on in Jalapa and work there." She paused. "Oh, my name's Liz and I used to live in Denver." My game (Guess My Crime) was getting old, but this one was easy: forgery and illegal use of drugs. She'd started by stealing a few painkillers here and there, became addicted, and eventually began writing false prescriptions for herself.

Finally, the group turned to the poodle lady who was sitting alone in the bleachers. She blew her nose and wiped it. "My name is Tina and I'm thirty-nine years old. My husband's a principal in the Denver Public Schools. I told him I wanted to do something on my own and he suggested this." She gestured at the empty room. "After reading the packet of information, I felt both nervous and excited. I hope it'll be a positive experience." She dabbed at her nose again and smiled anxiously. Wait until her husband found out she'd embezzled thousands from the Denver Public School system.

Allen tapped me on the shoulder. "What packet of information?" he whispered.

"It was everything you needed to know before coming here," I said.

"Shit. I've been in Chicago visiting my family, but Tim knew my address."

I shrugged. "Too late now. Just fake it. It'll be good practice for when you become a lawyer."

"Okay," Estelle said, looking at her watch. "I guess I'll go check on the bus. Tim can answer any questions about our next two weeks in Managua."

Everyone took a swig from their water bottles, and then stood in line for the bathroom. When it was my turn, I peed and wiped myself with a piece of newspaper, hardly noticing it wasn't from a roll of Charmin.

I wandered around the room, ending up at the edge of a conversation between Tim and a few of the women. I learned that because of the water shortage, each *barrio* was officially scheduled to lose their water on different days. Our neighborhood, for instance, had no water on Tuesdays and Fridays from five thirty in the morning until nine at night.

"But today is Monday," I pointed out.

Tim chuckled helplessly. "Yeah, I know."

"How come there's a water shortage?" Veronica asked.

"Because of the huge influx of refugees from the war zone," Tim explained. "Managua's population has doubled in the last six years from 500,000 to a million."

***

At noon, our driver announced he'd fixed the problem and was able to start the bus. Belching black smoke, we headed for the language school. I sat between Allen, who already felt like family, and Liz (the nurse) whom I wasn't sure I liked, mostly because she seemed so clear about her mission here. Compared to her, I couldn't help feeling a wee bit frivolous. Tina a.k.a. the poodle lady sat alone in front of us, still sneezing and blowing her nose.

As we drove down a street filled with potholes, Liz searched through her handbag, and then tapped Tina on the shoulder.

"Try these," she said, handing her a couple of pills. "It should stop your reaction."

"You got anything in there to help me cope with four kids under the age of ten?" Allen asked. "I share a room with them."

"Even morphine wouldn't help," I said. "You need a tent."

Liz smiled at us. "The accommodations here are likely to be much fancier than the ones in Jalapa."

"I share a bed with a two-year-old who wets it," Allen said. "I'd sleep on the floor, but the cockroaches are bigger than the two-year-old. How much worse could Jalapa be?"

"You'd know if you'd read your packet of information," I told him.

As we drove through the city, I was stunned by how flattened it was. I knew, from the reading material, that Managua had suffered a major earthquake in 1972 that destroyed eighty percent of the buildings, but this looked like the aftermath of an atomic bomb. We passed block after block of wasteland before we saw a couple of movie theaters. Then, more vacant lots, a small middle-class neighborhood, a gaping ravine, and then a modern-looking shopping center. After the earthquake, millions in aid had poured into the country, but Somoza pocketed the money and never rebuilt the city. I realized with a rush of shame that Sonia's outdoor kitchen, which I'd thought quaint, had probably been a regular indoor one before 1972.

I stared out the window. What else didn't I know? Actually, what else *did* I know?

"*Bubkes,*" I imagined my mother saying. "You know *bubkes.*"

It had been one of her favorite Yiddish words when I was growing up. Loosely translated, it meant I knew absolutely nothing. And she was right. What the hell was I doing here? But if I left, where would I go? Not back to Boulder, not back to where Emily in handcuffs had tried to wave goodbye as she was being escorted down a hallway by a couple of guards.

As we passed a working-class *barrio* where the houses were constructed of tin and plywood, I decided I might as well stay put. This was a country in dire straits. Maybe I would be of use here, maybe I wouldn't. At least I could try.

"Hey, Rachel." Allen tapped me on the shoulder. "You got any advice about law school?"

I turned to face him. "Sure. Don't go."

He nodded. "I don't want to. My father's a corporate lawyer who expects me to follow in his footsteps. I can't think of anything more dreadful. What about criminal defense? Would you recommend that?"

"No," I said.

The bus had turned into a dirt lane and was heading toward a pink stucco structure that looked dwarfed by the overgrown vegetation surrounding it. The grounds and building reminded me of Sleeping Beauty's palace after she'd been asleep for a hundred years and unable to maintain it.

"I wonder if they'd let me do a little work around here," Lenny said to the group. He was the handsome retired architect from Denver.

"You know, I like him," Allen said, referring to Lenny. Liz and I both agreed we did too.

"Are you married, Liz?" Allen asked. I wondered why he didn't ask me.

"Amicably divorced."

Allen looked thoughtful. "You know, Lenny's in pretty good shape for someone who's sixty-three."

"No thanks," Liz said, shuddering. "That's one area of my life where I've been a complete failure. I never want to get involved again."

At that moment, I decided I liked her after all. As a rule, I'd never liked or trusted anyone who hadn't suffered at some point in his or her life. Even Vickie, who seemed fairly content, had had an unhappy childhood.

As soon as the bus pulled up to the entrance, everyone scrambled to get out. It had been a long uncomfortable ride. Although a pitcher of margaritas in an air-conditioned restaurant would have been perfect, we settled for a drink of water on the grass under a hot sun. When the ants began biting us, we went inside.

There were four classrooms, each outfitted with a blackboard and about twenty wooden chairs. We filed into one of the rooms and learned that our teacher, Mrs. Rodriguez, had suddenly become ill, and would be unavailable until Wednesday or Thursday.

"Which means Saturday or Sunday," Allen murmured. He and Liz were sitting next to me in the back row. Tina had tried to join us, but her chair collapsed and she'd had to move on to find a sturdier one. Two high school students who looked about fourteen had volunteered to help out until Mrs. Rodriguez returned. There were no books in sight.

"This doesn't bode well," I said.

"No," Liz agreed, "it doesn't."

Allen raked both hands through his frizzy hair. "At least both of you know enough to get by. I've watched you. But I'm in deep shit because I don't know any Spanish at all. I'd assumed a lot more of the people down here spoke English."

"Too bad you didn't read your packet of information," I said.

Liz started to laugh. "Okay, enough. I'll lend him mine tonight."

The group voted to eat lunch and then figure out how to utilize our two high school assistants. We ate in the school cafeteria where a man in a wheelchair served us rice and beans. The regular students, we found out, were on vacation. We sat together at a long table, joking about our misadventures. Toward the end of the meal, one of the assistants told Estelle she had a phone call from Jalapa. Both Estelle and Tim left the room.

When they returned, they looked pale and serious. Everyone stopped talking and waited for the news.

"Well," Estelle said, "last night about fifty Contras slipped over the border from Honduras and attacked Jalapa. They killed twelve people, including an infant, and kidnapped a couple of women. Some of the townspeople found one of the women today. She'd been raped repeatedly and her eyes had been cut out."

"Jesus," Tina said.

Tim took a deep breath and sat down at the head of the table. "We're telling you this because we don't want to mislead you. We're going into a war zone and we want everyone to be prepared. So far, no North Americans have been harmed, but we can't guarantee anyone's safety."

"Are we still planning to go in two weeks?" Veronica asked. She was young and game, not scared.

Estelle nodded. "Unless the government won't let us."

"Well, if it isn't safe—" Tina began.

"It's not," Susan interrupted, "but everyone knew that beforehand."

Liz put her hand on Tina's shoulder. "I think we'll be all right," she said. "Witness for Peace volunteers have lived in Jalapa for years. Personally, I can't wait to get up there and start rebuilding the clinic."

"Me too," Richard said, stroking his beard.

I sat quietly at one end of the table, listening to everyone's reactions, and trying to figure out my own. Like the others, the news had hit me like a bucket of ice water, sobering me right up. But now that I was sober, I realized I was beginning to feel excited. This could be the real thing, a chance to participate in something that actually mattered. We could go to Jalapa during a time when they needed us and help rebuild their clinic. The risks seemed small in comparison. On the other hand, I was a burned-out adrenaline junkie, so what did I know?

"Maybe it's just as well I didn't read the packet of information," Allen told me as we left the cafeteria. "If I had, I might not have come."

"Liz thinks we'll be okay," I said.

"Are you afraid?" he asked.

"I probably should be, but I'm not."

We walked silently down the hall, lost in our private imaginations. As we approached the classroom, Tim caught up to us and told me I had an international call from a woman named Vickie. I'd given her the number of the school, and we'd agreed she would try to call me today.

I hurried to an office at the end of the hall where a woman with a baby in her arms handed me the phone.

"Hey Vickie," I said.

"Rachel, it's so good to hear your voice. I've been trying to get through for hours. How are you?"

"Well, I didn't sleep much and I'm in culture shock, but other than that, I think I'm okay. How about you?"

"I'm just missing you. So, what's it like there?"

The woman had left the room. I sat down at her desk and glanced out the window at an overgrown palm tree. A fat green parrot was perched on one of the branches.

"Everything's larger than life," I said.

Vickie laughed. "How about a few details? Tell me about the family you're staying with."

We talked for about ten minutes before she asked about the situation in Jalapa. I hesitated, and then told her it had been mostly peaceful.

"Good. Just be careful. Oh, your client Emily Watkins called. She said to tell you she was being transferred from the Denver facility to the penitentiary in Canon City and wondered if you'd be able to visit her there sometime. I hope you don't mind, but I told her you were in Nicaragua."

"No, that's fine," I said, running my fingers along the edges of the desk, which were smooth from years of use.

"So, do you have a return date yet?"

I didn't answer. I was thinking about the way Emily used to look up legal terms in an old dog-eared dictionary held together with duct tape that Sunny kept in his desk for her. She adored old things: old books, old furniture, old houses. New things, she said, seemed so cold and lonely. They had no history of being loved and cherished.

"Rachel, are you there?"

I stared out the window. "I guess I am."

"So when are you coming back, sweetie?"

I was glad she couldn't see my face; it would have looked confused and guilty. "I'm not sure, babe. Part of it depends on when we actually get to Jalapa. After that, we've made a minimum four-week commitment to work on the clinic."

"Minimum? What are you saying? Are you saying you might stay longer?"

I waved my hand in the air as if it were no big deal. "Well, anything's possible. I just don't know yet."

"So what are we talking about? A week? A month?" She paused. "A year?" She paused again, waiting for reassurance but I couldn't give her any. "Rachel?"

I expected her to start shouting or even worse, crying at any moment. In the meantime, I stared at a row of empty bookshelves lining the opposite wall, wishing the phone would go dead, that something would intervene before the conversation got any worse. "Honey," I said, "I just got here."

The silence lasted so long, I thought maybe the phone had gone dead after all. Finally, my partner said, "Don't lose me, sweetheart. Don't throw your baby out with the bathwater."

I swallowed hard and nodded. "I won't." I had a strong urge to lay my head down on the desk and take a short nap. It was around three in the afternoon, although according to a clock on the wall, it was a quarter past eight. "Everything's broken here," I said.

CHAPTER TEN

June 10, 1986

Dear Vickie,
You asked for the truth, so here it is: I can picture myself calling the airport
and booking a return flight to North America. I can picture myself hugging
everyone goodbye, taking a hot bumpy taxi ride to the airport, and waiting
patiently while children dressed like soldiers search my bags for contraband. I
can even picture myself boarding the plane, but no matter how hard I try, I

can't picture myself arriving in Colorado and settling back into my old life. My imagination stops at the border.

Having said all that, I don't want you to panic. Everything here, including me, is in flux. The whole country's in a state of trauma—it's probably why I feel so at home. But one of these days, the ground beneath my feet will either stop shifting or I'll finally get used to it. All I need is time; I'm lurching as fast as I can. I probably sound like a lecherous teenager who puts a hand on his girlfriend's knee and says, "Trust me," but trust me. It's still you and me, babe.

Your loving rat,

Rachel

At the end of our strained phone conversation, Vickie and I had agreed from then on we would write instead of call, that Vickie would stop pressuring me about returning home, and in exchange I would tell her as much as I knew as soon as I knew it. In theory, it was a good plan. I reread my letter, which fulfilled my obligation to write, then put it with all the others at the bottom of my duffel bag. At the rate I was writing them—one or two a day—I would end up with quite a collection. Someday, I might even let Vickie read them. Unsent letters from the earthquake capital of the world.

So why didn't I just send the letter or any of the others I'd written? The truth is I don't know. All I can say is that for a number of months after losing Emily's trial, I was a stranger to myself. My motives and desires, usually so clear to me, were suddenly inaccessible. I looked like myself, felt like myself, but didn't act like myself. In the legal profession, this is known as a complete loser of a defense.

In the meantime, which didn't help matters, I was suffering from extreme sleep deprivation, the kind that drives a good soldier to divulge critical information about everyone in his squadron and then gratuitously offer more about his wife, relatives, childhood friends and anyone else he can think of. After a week of practically no sleep, I would have traded my entire kingdom for a sleeping pill (Liz had a limited stash but only for emergencies), and if you threw in a small air-conditioner, performed any sexual favors that didn't leave scars.

Each night, I'd wait until it cooled down to around a hundred degrees, dose myself with a handful of useless Benadryls, sink into my cot, and lie there sweating until I finally passed out around two thirty. Each morning, a few minutes before five, the chicken would hop onto the cot and squat on my ankles. If I kicked her off, she'd wait a few minutes and then try again; three times, five times, ten times, it made no difference. It was exactly how I used to wear down the prosecution on most of my cases.

On my fourth or fifth evening, I made a nice cozy nest on the floor using my softest T-shirts, but the chicken wasn't even tempted. I tried blocking the doorway with my orange crate, but after a few minutes of scratching, she figured out how to climb over it and then hopped triumphantly onto my legs. One afternoon, while Sonia took a neighbor to the hospital, I snooped around the house to see if I could figure out how the chicken was getting in. After finding at least five possible ways, I gave up. I considered various "accidents" that might befall my chicken, but I couldn't quite see myself as a cold-blooded murderer.

Living in the tropics, though, it changes you.

Sometime during that first week, I popped open the childproof cap on my bottle of malaria pills and discovered a million tiny insects devouring the contents. There's no privacy in the third world; it costs money to keep things out. Privileged people can barricade themselves against noise, heat, insects, animals, neighbors and invading armies, but in a country like Nicaragua, there's nothing you can do. It's like being pummeled continuously by a relentless bully who never gets tired. Somehow, you have to develop a thick skin and learn to ignore anything less than a fatal blow.

***

One morning during breakfast, Sonia told me that her nephew Jorge, who was only seventeen, was fighting up north near Ocotal. After one of his childhood friends was killed and two others were kidnapped by the Contras, he'd volunteered to go on a dangerous patrol during which his jeep had almost hit a landmine. Every day she prayed for his safety.

"He's my sister's only child," she said. "I remember the day he was born. It was taking too long and we were very worried. When he finally came, everyone started laughing, even the doctor. And that's why Jorge was such a happy baby."

"How can you stand it?" I asked, pushing my plate away.

"The war?"

"The war, the embargo, the threat of a United States invasion, the lack of food and medicine. How can you go on day after day when there's no end in sight?"

"It's hard," she said, rubbing her temples with her fingertips, "but the Nicaraguan people have infinite patience, and so we wait for peace."

"What if you have to wait a very long time?"

"There'll be nothing left. But in the meantime, eat your breakfast before it gets cold."

I picked up my fork. "Yesterday, Amelia mentioned you weren't feeling well."

Sonia drank some water before answering. "Don't worry about me," she said. "Amelia's the one who is sick. If you go to the dollar store, she needs vitamins."

I nodded, unconvinced. "I'll get vitamins for both of you."

"If you insist," she said, then stood up to clear the dishes.

I stood up, too. "Just tell me what kind you need, and anything else. If they have it, I'll get it."

A few minutes later, Tomas—who didn't seem to live anywhere—wandered into the house and she gave him something to eat. He looked disheveled, as if he'd been up all night drinking. There was a fresh bruise on his forehead. As soon as he stumbled out, Sonia turned to me and said, "It helps to have faith."

"In what?" I asked.

She looked astonished, as if I'd suddenly torn my clothes off. "In God, of course."

Ordinarily, I would have argued that even if God existed, He obviously wasn't paying attention to the plight of the Nicaraguan people, but I could already tell how stupid, mean and thoughtless that would sound. It takes less than a week in the third world to understand that faith is a paradox; it may cost nothing, but only rich people can afford not to have it.

Another speedy realization: once I understood that the lights and water were subject to the whims of unseen agencies making unpredictable decisions about who got what, I abandoned all efforts to plan ahead. Like everyone else, I learned to be in the moment. Buddhists in the United States, I decided, should stop trying to explain this concept and simply ship their students to Nicaragua. If the water came on, I took a thirty-second shower or washed my underwear. If the lights went off and it was dark, I lay down and tried to sleep. After a while, it seemed perfectly natural. Forget the caves in India, the forests of Burma—plan your next meditation retreat in the rubble of downtown Managua and camp nearby in sunny *Barrio Maximo Jerez.*

On the other hand, Sonia and her neighbors, fed up with being in the moment, were constantly on the lookout for large plastic containers to fill with extra water. In fact, containers of any kind, not just buckets, were highly prized. One morning at dawn, I wandered into Sonia's kitchen and noticed an empty pill bottle near the sink. Curious, I picked it up and realized it was the bottle of malaria pills I'd tossed in the garbage a few days earlier. Sonia had retrieved it, emptied out the insects, and washed it clean. After that, I threw nothing away without first showing it to my host.

By the end of our first week, it was obvious that the United States's embargo was a rip-roaring success. After Reagan took office in 1981 and declared Nicaragua under the Sandinistas (total population 2.9 million) a communist enemy, an economic embargo was instituted which prevented the country from obtaining food, medical supplies, world loans, machinery and other essential goods from its usual sources. For the vast majority of Nicaraguans, luxury items such as toilet paper, shampoo, sheets, new shoes and denture cleaners were unattainable. Supposedly you could buy these products at the dollar store, but no matter when we showed up with our dollars, the store was always closed. After three unsuccessful attempts, we wondered if it was just an empty storefront stocked with imaginary items that Sonia and her neighbors liked to dream about. Toilet paper, vitamins and sandals: mythical symbols of a better life in the unforeseeable future.

Thanks again to the United States there was very little fuel. Gasoline, especially, seemed to be in great demand; everyone talked about who still had any, where to find it, and how much it cost, like the way we talked about marijuana in the sixties. Most of the trees around Managua had been stripped bare by all the new refugees living in shantytowns who cooked on wood stoves. Anything made out of wood had long since been dismantled and burned up. I was about as likely to find a piece of plywood to shove between the mattress and sagging springs of my cot as I was to find a brand-new Cadillac parked in front of Sonia's house.

The food shortage, however, was the most alarming. Every morning, on the way to the language school, we passed long lines of people waiting outside the supermarkets. Sometimes the lines wound all the way around the block. Sonia told me that many of her friends got up before dawn to stand in line. I told her that teenagers in the United States did that too when tickets went on sale for a rock concert.

***

On Saturday, we were supposed to visit an agricultural cooperative, but the bus wouldn't start and the driver needed a few extra parts to fix it. We could possibly leave by noon, he told us, if the parts weren't too difficult to find. We all nodded and after a quick vote decided to take the rest of the day off. When the others had left, Allen, Liz and I chose to head downtown with no particular destination. We walked for miles—there were no street signs anywhere—eventually ending up at the Plaza de la Revolución in front of the Managua Cathedral. On the way, we passed through the earthquake wreckage of various neighborhoods, gazing at the concrete shells of buildings where dozens of people lived. Ragged clothes hung across formerly ornate entryways. In the center of the city, cows grazed in empty lots between buildings. On a number of street corners, we saw women cooking food over fires, serving the fare on banana leaves. We bought some kind of meat but decided not to eat it.

From a distance, the Managua Cathedral had looked impressive but up close it was obvious we were staring at the ruins of a building that was once a grand 18th century church before it was destroyed by the earthquake. The inside was gutted. Since the revolution, a huge canvas portrait of Sandino—the original Nicaraguan revolutionary who defied the US Marines back in the thirties—had been draped over the entrance, which sounds incongruous but was actually classy, like good modern art.

On our way home, we wandered into a large *supermercado*. By then, the store was empty and there weren't many products left on the shelves. I picked up a can of Del Monte fruit cocktail and checked the expiration date stamped on the bottom: October 1983. I showed it to my friends.

"Isn't that against the law?" Allen asked.

"That's not exactly their biggest problem," I said.

We strolled down a few more aisles and found three cans of black olives, a can of mushroom soup, some Coppertone suntan lotion (SPF 4) and a whole shelf of Purina cat food.

"I guess things could be worse," Allen said, staring at the cat food.

"I suppose so," I said, "although I don't see any dog food."

"It's pretty depressing," Liz agreed. "And next week I heard the government is going to reduce everyone's ration of rice, sugar and beans."

"Jesus," Allen said, looking upset. "That's all my family eats. The four little kids are always hungry. Half the time, I pretend I'm full and give the kids the rest of my meal. But they need milk. Don't little kids need milk? Do you see any milk?" His Hawaiian shirt was soaked with sweat.

Liz put her hand on Allen's arm. "It's good to care," she said, "but don't get too upset. It doesn't help."

"But kids need milk," Allen repeated.

We walked down a few more aisles and found a carton of grapefruit juice (August 1984), a great selection of plastic cups and silverware, and a can of condensed milk tucked behind some TV dinners that had expired before the revolution in 1979. Allen bought the milk and put it in his backpack.

As we were exiting the store, Allen said, "I feel so ashamed."

"Because we're North Americans?" I asked.

He nodded. We turned left, and then began hiking down the hot dusty highway toward *Barrio Maximo Jerez*. In the distance, the Intercontinental Hotel, shaped like a giant beehive, loomed above the flattened city.

"Look, I understand," Liz said, "but it doesn't help. At least you're here, not back there."

Allen shook his head. "I still feel ashamed. My country's funding the war, which is making everyone miserable and all the people I meet are so nice to me. I can barely stand it."

"But it's useless to feel bad," Liz argued. "Once we get up to Jalapa, we can make a real difference. Doesn't that make you feel better?" She stared hopefully at both of us. Somehow, her cotton blouse and matching skirt looked as if she'd just put them on. My clothes, like Allen's, were drenched.

"I guess so," Allen said, and then looked at me. "What about you, Rachel?"

I shrugged. "I agree with Liz. It's self-indulgent to feel ashamed. It's a waste of energy."

"Exactly," Liz said, nodding.

"But I feel ashamed anyway."

Allen grinned at me.

Liz sighed. "You're both too sensitive."

"It's because we're Jewish," Allen said.

"Do you think that's it?" I asked, and decided he might be right.

Liz was walking between us. She put her arms around our shoulders and we continued down the highway. "It's a good thing you both have me."

Allen and I nodded to each other. Without Liz's cheerful pragmatism, her unsentimental determination to make a difference here, we might have both succumbed to the hopelessness and despair that was constantly nipping at our heels.

A bus crammed with over a hundred passengers, many of whom were hanging onto the windows and doors, rumbled past us, leaving a trail of thick black smoke in the air. We coughed for a few seconds, but kept on walking. It takes less than a day in Managua to learn the Nicaraguan shuffle, the most efficient way to walk when it's unbearably hot and you don't want to use up any more energy than necessary. To do it correctly, no part of the body above the knee moves at all; the head, shoulders, arms, trunk, hips and thighs remain relaxed but still, as if you were standing in the same spot and little rollers under your feet were propelling you forward.

"Rachel," Allen said, "tell us a story about being a public defender."

For a moment, I recalled the metallic sound of handcuffs closing over Emily's wrists and shook my head. "To tell you the truth, I'm sort of trying to forget I was a public defender."

"Oh, come on," Allen pleaded. "My feet are killing me. I need a good story to distract me."

I sighed. "Do you want a funny story or a sad one?"

"Funny."

I thought for a moment. "Actually, all the funny stories I know are also sad. Maybe Liz can tell us a funny story about people dying in the emergency room at the hospital."

Liz punched me in the shoulder. "Cut it out, Rachel. Life isn't as grim as you think."

Both Allen and I stopped shuffling and stared at her. Allen's face, and probably mine as well, was streaked with dirt from the bus.

"Okay," Liz relented, "maybe it is, but the world is bigger than that. There's beauty all around us to balance things out." She raised her arms to indicate all the beauty that Allen and I were missing.

We continued to stare, waiting to be convinced.

"Come on, guys. Nature, love, friendship, those are all beautiful things. And there's also laughter, courage and people who want to help out and make a difference in the world. Those are the things that make life worthwhile."

"Will you be my guru?" Allen asked.

I started to laugh, but stopped when I saw her face.

"Knock it off," Liz said, sounding genuinely aggrieved. "Both of you."

"Hey, I'm sorry," Allen apologized. "Really. I was just embarrassed to admit those are the kinds of things that make my life feel worthwhile too. Forgive me."

"Me, too," I said, "although I'm in more of a waiting-to-feel-that-way-again mode."

Liz hesitated, and then put her arms around both our shoulders again. "You are really lucky to have me."

Amen, we thought.

***

For Sunday, Tim and Estelle had set up a visit to the Managua headquarters of AMNLAE, the national women's organization. At noon, our refurbished bus dropped us off at the entrance. A solemn young woman in her early twenties named Scarlet was waiting to take us around and answer any questions. When she stood up from behind her desk, we noticed she was missing part of her left hand.

Over the next few hours with Estelle interpreting, we learned that before the revolution there were no labor codes or civil rights for women, and as bad as it was now, the tradition and culture of machismo had been much worse. Women couldn't ask for a divorce and had no say in their children's futures. In the workplace, women were forced to take pregnancy tests before being hired, and often their wages were paid to their husbands or fathers. Prostitution was big business—Somoza and his thugs ran hugely profitable prostitution rings.

Since the revolution, there had been many gains but, Scarlet emphasized, these were accomplished only because women participated in the revolution and were now helping to draft the constitution. As soon as the constitution was ratified, it would guarantee that men and women were equal, and that women would be paid equal wages for equal work.

We ended up sitting around a small conference table on the third floor of the building. The walls were decorated with various posters depicting women actively involved in the revolution: a female professor lecturing in front of a blackboard, a teenage girl in army fatigues with a rifle slung casually over her shoulder, a nurse holding a needle while her patient rolled up his sleeve. At the end of our visit, Estelle asked Scarlet about her hand.

"I was involved in the takeover of Managua in June 1979," Scarlet said. She sounded both matter of fact and proud, the way everyone in the States sounded who'd been at Woodstock.

Immediately, we did the math. Seven years ago: Scarlet would have been sixteen, maybe seventeen.

"Would you be willing to tell us about it?" Veronica asked, blushing a little.

Scarlet nodded. Instinctively she cradled her injured hand in the crook of her right elbow. "We were fighting the National Guard in a neighborhood close to the one you're all staying in. We built barricades in the street out of furniture and rubble left over from the earthquake. Everyone who lived there was helping us, including grandparents and little children. Even though the Guard had tanks and planes, we knew we would eventually win. In desperation, Somoza ordered the Guard to start dropping bombs on us. About twelve thousand people died in Managua fighting against Somoza. Early one morning, a bomb exploded and I was knocked unconscious. When I woke up, many of my comrades were dead, including my sister and two of my brothers. But I was lucky. I only lost part of my hand."

None of us could think of anything to say. Scarlet's experience was so far out of the realm of anything we'd known, it was hard to comprehend. She could have been telling us the plot of a war movie or about a nightmare she'd once had as a teenager.

Finally, Estelle broke the silence. "That's quite inspiring, but it's also very sad."

"Yes," Scarlet said. "It's very sad how many people we've lost and how many we continue to lose. When you go back to the United States, please tell everyone you meet that in 1984 we had a fair election, and that sixty-seven percent of the people voted for the Sandinistas. Tell them to stop funding the Contras. I only have one brother left and I don't want to lose him."

We filed out in a somber mood. I knew from my reading that Somoza fled the country on July 17, 1979, taking all his possessions, including the coffins of his relatives. He also took the entire national treasury, about one and a half billion dollars. Two days later, the Sandinistas officially entered Managua and the city went crazy with joy. There was a fiesta in the streets for seven days. Everyone was ecstatic; they thought the war was finally over.

I found Liz on the bus and sat down across from her. "Is there anyone in this country who isn't suffering from post-traumatic stress syndrome?" I asked.

"I doubt it," she answered. "Oh, by the way, the talk tonight on land reform has been changed from seven to seven thirty. There's no bus available. A bunch of us are meeting at the community center at seven. If there's enough of us, we might take a taxi."

"Okay," I said, staring out the window.

"Are you all right?" she asked.

"I'm fine, but if I'm not there at seven, don't wait for me. I'll find another way to go." I was feeling guilty because I had no intention of sweltering through a two-hour lecture on land reform. On the way home from the *supermercado* the day before, I'd noticed the Altamira cinema, and Sonia had told me it was one of the few places in Managua that was air-conditioned.

As the sun set over the flattened city, I was standing in line waiting to enter the theater. Eventually, a Nicaraguan woman in a bright orange dress showed up holding a roll of tickets and began selling them. When I reached the head of the line, I asked what was playing, although I really didn't care as long as it was cool inside.

"It's a North American movie," she told me. "*Los Nerds En Vacaciones.*"

"Oh." I paused, imagining a moment in the future when someone in the States questioned me about land reform under the Sandinistas and I would have to admit that instead of attending a lecture on this crucial topic, I'd gone to see a movie entitled *Nerds On Vacation*. Fortunately, the door opened just then and I felt a cold blast of air on my face and arms.

"One ticket, please," I said.

The film was about rival gangs of rich fraternity boys screeching around Palm Springs in their red convertibles, each gang trying to bed as many women as possible. The movie had been dubbed into Spanish, but unfortunately had English subtitles that I couldn't help reading. For a while, I amused myself wondering what the Nicaraguans in the audience could possibly be thinking. Did the film alarm them? Did they think, *My God, there's no point trying to reason with people like this?* Or did they wonder, *Why do these North Americans even care if the Sandinistas are running our country?*

But, of course, most of the Nicaraguans were sitting there for the same reason I was and would have happily watched a movie about Mongolians learning the hokey-pokey as long as the theater's heroic air-conditioner continued to crank out cool air. It would be a sad day in Managua when it finally rattled to a halt.

After an hour, however, I'd pretty much had it. When a few of the fraternity boys, dressed in togas, began barfing over the balcony onto the heads of innocent pedestrians, I stood up to leave.

"Is that you, Rachel?" I heard Allen whisper.

"Where are you?" I asked.

"A few rows back."

"How did you know it was me?" I asked.

"I heard you groaning. Is the seat next to you empty?"

"Yes."

"I'll come and join you."

The theater was a big hall with a single door that opened to the street. It was dark inside except when anyone entered or left, which happened every three or four minutes. For a couple of seconds until the door closed again, the picture was obscured. Ordinarily, it would have been extremely annoying.

After Allen sat down, he whispered, "I saw Lenny and Veronica in the back row."

"Really?" I was feeling better already.

"I've sat through some real losers," Allen whispered, "but this is the worst thing I've ever seen. I'm hoping that maybe the communists made it on purpose to discredit us."

"You're too hopeful," I said. "But you're young."

Allen put his head on my shoulder. "Rachel, I'm not sure I can ever go home."

After a few minutes, I said, "I know what you mean."

***

By the beginning of the second week, we'd basically given up on the language school. The teacher still hadn't showed and the two high school students seemed to have disappeared as well. We decided to continue attending, however, just in case the teacher recovered or the government found someone else to replace her. If not, we were determined to use the time to improve our Spanish as best we could on our own. None of us, though, would be sorry to leave when the two weeks were up. Learning was good, but helping out would be better.

And then, unexpectedly, a government official contacted Estelle and asked if the brigade would be willing to volunteer for a couple of days at a nearby sand quarry. We'd be filling in for a group of workers who'd recently joined the army. Although the work would be hot and tedious—shoveling sand into trucks headed for various construction sites—we were all eager to go.

When we arrived at the quarry, we saw a huge pile of amber-colored sand, a couple of dilapidated buildings in the distance, and about two dozen trucks lined up in front of the sand. Most of the trucks were at least twenty years old and looked as if they were being held together with wire and electrical tape. A couple of shirtless men in tall rubber boots approached us and told us to sit down and wait, that they expected some of the drivers to show up soon. About an hour later, three grumpy looking teenagers drove up in an army jeep and climbed out. After that, we were all issued shovels and told to begin filling up the trucks.

By the middle of the afternoon, we'd managed to fill twenty-two of them. We were tired and filthy. Although we'd brought hard-boiled eggs and tortillas, no one felt like eating. After a short water break, we moved on to the twenty-third. As we began shoveling, a white-haired man with a clipboard and a set of keys hurried over to one of the trucks and tried to start it. The engine made a couple of dry desperate grinding sounds, then quit altogether. The man cursed, and then climbed out and marched back toward the buildings. A few minutes later, the same man and three others showed up, each carrying multiple sets of keys. They were all clearly upset and shouting to one another. Hopping in and out of trucks, they tried them all, but none of the engines would start, each one making the same horrible grinding sound before dying.

"What's going on?" Richard asked Estelle.

"I don't know," she said, "but I'll go find out." Her face was coated with dirt, like a coal miner's after a day inside the tunnels.

The men were now lifting up the hoods of all the trucks and shaking their heads. Estelle and Tim walked over to join them. Finally, after examining a number of the engines, the man with the clipboard determined the trucks had been sabotaged. Estelle came over with the bad news.

"Sabotaged?" Allen asked. "How?"

"No one was here last night," Estelle explained. "There was a fiesta. Usually someone volunteers to stay."

"Shit," Lenny sighed, "they probably just poured sand in all the engines. It would be the easiest way." He was leaning heavily on his shovel looking more like Walter Brennan than Robert Redford.

"Who would do something like that?" Tina asked, patting her eyes with a handkerchief that had once been clean, white and dainty. "Not the Contras?"

"No, of course not," Susan retorted. "It must have been the seven dwarfs." She threw her shovel to the ground.

"Hey," Liz said, "we're all shocked and upset, but sarcasm won't make us feel better."

Susan shrugged. "Well, it made me feel better."

Richard walked over and put a hand on his wife's shoulder. "Please, Susan."

She pushed his hand away. "I thought we agreed not to interfere with each other."

Allen rolled his eyes, and then turned to Estelle. "If most people don't mind, I'd like to go back to the original question. Are the Contras really operating in Managua?"

Estelle nodded. "Absolutely. Since the Contras look like everyone else, they can easily slip into Managua or any of the other cities. There's sabotage going on all over the country."

Meanwhile, the men had begun to argue and were pointing at the buildings, which seemed to shimmer in the distance. Their voices rumbled like distant thunder that might or might not be heading our way. Tim, who was standing in the middle of the group but not saying anything, kept glancing in our direction. After another few minutes, he motioned Estelle to join him.

"What now?" I wondered out loud.

"Nothing good," Liz murmured.

When the argument was over, Tim and Estelle nodded and then walked back to us. From their careful expressions, we guessed there was more bad news, although we had no idea what it could be. In vain, we tried to brace ourselves.

"Listen," Tim said, "I hate to tell you this, but the men think it would be much easier to work on the trucks if they were closer to the buildings. So it would be, you know, much easier for them to push the trucks over there if we unloaded all the sand beforehand."

"What?" Allen exploded.

"You're kidding, right?" Richard asked, his shoulders slumping at the thought.

Tim shook his head. "I'm afraid not."

"Jesus Christ," Liz said.

Veronica looked as if she might start crying. "Wait a minute, don't the trucks have some kind of lever or something that you pull to dump whatever's in them?"

"Not these trucks," Lenny snapped.

"I can't believe it," Allen said. "We've just wasted the entire day."

Susan raised her hand as if she needed permission to speak. "Excuse me, but there's a war going on, remember? People die, bad things happen. What did you expect, Girl Scout camp?"

Although part of me would have loved to hurl a fistful of sand at Susan's face, the more mature, let's-cut-to-the-chase part that had spent the last twelve years convincing thousands of clients to cop a plea when it was in their best interests understood the simple truth: we would all rather tear each other's hair out than start shoveling again. So I picked up my shovel, held it above my head and advanced in Susan's direction. Everyone, including Susan, looked alarmed.

I stopped a couple of inches in front of her and said, "Okay, do you really want to keep pissing everyone off, or do you want to help me start unloading all this sand before it gets too dark?"

No one said a word. After a long moment, Susan had the smarts to pick up her shovel and start marching toward the farthest truck. "Well, what are you waiting for?" she called over her shoulder. "The fucking sand isn't going to get unloaded by itself, is it?"

***

On Thursday, the *cordoba*—Nicaragua's national unit of currency— was devalued to about half of what it had been worth the day before. In 1912, when it was first introduced, the *cordoba* was worth a dollar. Since the revolution, the currency had steadily lost value and now, with this latest move, it would take approximately 10,000 *cordobas* to equal a dollar. Coming from the United States where inflation was relatively slow and predictable, this was mind-boggling.

That evening, I sat alone in Sonia's outdoor kitchen waiting for my usual rice and beans. The air smelled thick and fragrant, like the inside of a hothouse. While I kept an eye on a huge cockroach that was advancing in my general direction, I could hear a couple of iguanas scuttling across the neighbor's roof. I was thinking about Sonia's health, how tired she'd looked when I'd come home a few hours earlier.

Just then, I heard footsteps on the tile patio. "It's like magic," Sonia said, appearing at my elbow with a handful of *cordobas*. "Without doing anything, I have just made half of these disappear. Poof."

I looked at her dark brown face and at the crumpled wad of bills in her hand. Suddenly, because I couldn't think of anything else, I began to applaud. "Bravo," I said.

She looked surprised, and then began to laugh. After a moment, she placed one arm in front of her waist and the other behind her back and bowed. I clapped even harder. She straightened up and with a mischievous gleam in her eyes said, "And soon they'll be completely worthless and we can use them to wipe our behinds."

"Good. Another problem solved."

She smiled, stuffed the bills into her apron, and sat down across from me.

"What are you going to do?" I asked seriously.

As soon as the question was out of my mouth, I realized how stupid it sounded. If you lived in North America where there were options, the question would have made sense. But here, whatever you could do to make ends meet had already been done. In Boulder, you might take a second job, borrow money from a friend, or sell your car. In Managua, you already had four jobs, no one had any money to lend you, and whatever wasn't bolted down had been sold long ago.

Sonia, however, merely shrugged.

I was tempted to offer her some money, but even I knew how insulting that would have been. Besides, there was nothing to buy. But maybe when I left for good, I could hide some dollars in her bureau.

"Don't look so worried," she told me, patting my arm. "It'll make you look old."

During supper, Sonia told me about a trip she'd taken to Panama when she was twenty-three. Apparently Panama was a popular place for Nicaraguans to visit in the early sixties. She and her best friend Miriam had taken a bus to Panama City and then bummed around the country for almost three months living on their savings. At one point, they'd rented rooms in an old hotel on a beach and taught themselves to swim. It was one of the happiest times in her life. After a few weeks, however, a group of men began pestering them for dates and they decided to move on. When the money ran out, they both got jobs in a dance studio teaching elderly couples how to cha-cha.

"You're kidding," I said.

"And the rumba too," she said. Her eyes had a faraway look and for a couple of seconds I could tell she was back being young and healthy, teaching dance steps in a studio somewhere in Panama, her entire adult life still in front of her.

"Why did you come back?" I asked.

She shrugged. "My father left my mother to start another family with a widow up in Matagalpa. My mother was alone with my two younger sisters to take care of. My father didn't send her any money. She needed me and I returned."

I nodded. That's how it happens, I thought. So many women's lives determined by other people's needs and desires. I thought about Emily, who hadn't finished college because her mother was diagnosed with ovarian cancer and her father had begged her to come home. Within a year, her father was drinking full-time and Emily became the primary caregiver for both of them. She'd ended up spending four years tending to her mother before she finally died, then another six months nursing her father before he, too, followed suit. By that time, she told me, she'd lost her taste for "adventure" and when Hal offered her a permanent position as his wife, she decided to take it.

Later that night, as I lay on my cot listening to Sonia's nightly prayer for her nephew's safety, I thought about my own life and how it, too, might have gone more like Emily's or Sonia's. In my first year of law school, my father had died suddenly of a heart attack. I was an only child. If my mother had requested that I move back to Boston, I probably would have, but she was an independent woman with plenty of friends and a good job as a reporter for the *Boston Globe*. As far as I knew, it never even crossed her mind to ask, and I never offered. We agreed, instead, to call each other once a month and to spend two weeks in the summer together, usually on Martha's Vineyard. When she moved a few years ago to Florida, she called afterward to tell me her new address and phone number. She'd been planning to relocate for at least six months, but never told me beforehand. When I asked why not, she sounded puzzled, as if I'd posed a strange metaphysical question. She had no idea why it mattered to me. What difference did it make whether I called her in Boston or in Florida?

I heard Sonia end her prayers that night by asking God to watch out for her North American guest who worried too much. That's me, I thought, aging faster than a speeding bullet. I lay in the dark and sighed, waiting for my chicken.

***

Although we'd originally planned to leave Managua on Saturday, a few days earlier the government had strongly encouraged us not to travel beyond Ocotal without an army escort, which wouldn't be available until the following Tuesday. In the preceding days, the Contras had mined the road from Ocotal to Jalapa and blown up a truck full of soldiers. Three soldiers had died in the explosion, and a fourth (a female) was missing. The dead soldiers were found in a ditch with their eyes cut out, a favorite Contra practice designed to horrify and demoralize the families of the victims.

On Friday afternoon, Estelle and Tim laid out our various options. We were sitting with our chairs in a circle in the cafeteria of the language school, wondering if we'd end up spending the entire six weeks talking about Jalapa, but never getting there. We sounded just like characters in an existentialist play, but I kept the thought to myself. Everyone looked too tired and frustrated to appreciate it. Nothing seemed to be going according to plan, and we were beginning to understand that nothing probably would.

After a short debate, we voted (nine to Susan) to postpone the trip until Monday, drive to Ocotal and spend the night there, and hope for the promised escort on Tuesday. It was the only sensible choice, but it left us feeling restless and crabby. We'd also just found out that Jalapa had been placed on twenty-four hour alert and if we ever managed to get there, we'd be staying at the Witness for Peace house, not with any of the townspeople.

The following day, instead of heading north on the Pan American Highway, we drove back to the language school. As we lurched down the dirt road toward the familiar pink stucco building, we hoped it was for the last time. To celebrate our final day of classes, Estelle and Tim brought mangoes, a large bottle of Coca-Cola, and a plate of cookies that Tim's host had baked for us. After we finished eating, we broke up into our regular study groups where we taught ourselves some new Spanish words that might come in handy, such as landmine, sniper and ambush.

The school had been a bust, but we'd made the best of it. Our teacher, Mrs. Rodriguez, had shown up once, but was clearly too sick to teach. We heard she'd gone to the hospital, which meant she was gravely ill and would probably die. Since we had no books, we spent most mornings reading articles in *La Barricada*, the official Sandinista newspaper, and then tried to discuss them. In the afternoons, we attempted to teach Allen and Tina enough Spanish to get by in Jalapa.

After two weeks, Allen and Tina could greet people in Spanish and ask where they could hide in case of an attack. Both students could also count to a thousand and recite how many teachers had disappeared in the last year, how many schools had been burned, and how many soldiers had been injured or killed. For their last class, we taught them to order fish, chicken, pork, salad, vegetables and dessert in a fictitious restaurant and understand the waiter when he responded after each request, "*No hay.*" *There isn't any.*

By three o'clock, we were ready to leave. One by one, we wandered into the cafeteria and sat down on the rickety wooden chairs and stared at each other. The bus wouldn't come for another couple of hours, but no one wanted to study anymore. We were done. Lenny and I vowed we'd never read another newspaper for as long as we lived, Liz thought her grammar was much worse after spending two weeks talking to the rest of us, and Veronica complained that the bulk of her vocabulary consisted of words having to do with imperialist aggression and covert CIA operations. Even Estelle looked a little glum.

To cheer us up, Tim suggested we plan a going-away party for our hosts the following evening and have it at the community center.

Immediately we all perked up. Estelle pulled out a pad of paper and made a tentative list of tasks that would need to be done. Everyone was smiling now and talking excitedly. After a while, we broke up into committees. Allen, Liz and I decided to be responsible for the music. Allen thought his host knew someone with a record player, and I figured Sonia would probably know where to find some good dance music.

"Rachel," Tim called from the doorway, "you have an international phone call from someone named Vickie."

"Is that your partner?" Liz asked. She and Allen were sitting across from me at one of the long narrow tables in the room.

I nodded. I hadn't bothered coming out yet, so how did she know? But the people who mattered to me somehow always knew. Like many gays comfortable with their sexuality, my lifestyle had ceased to feel remarkable, but to even the most accepting straight people, it was still "interesting."

Regardless, neither she nor Allen looked at all surprised. "How long have you been together?" Liz asked.

"Nine years." As I spoke, I could feel a small knot forming between my shoulder blades.

"Well good for you," Liz said. "Send her our regards. This is probably the last chance you'll have to speak to each other. We won't have access to any phones in Jalapa."

As I entered the same office I'd entered two weeks earlier, the same woman with a baby in her arms handed me the receiver. I held it to my head as if it were an unexploded bomb and said, "Hello?"

"Hey," Vickie answered. Her voice sounded higher than usual, which made her sound young and vulnerable. "I know I promised not to call, but it's been a couple of weeks and I haven't received any letters. Maggie's heard you're heading out soon."

My stomach was beginning to hurt. I felt dizzy and sat down on the floor. "It's the embargo," I said. "Nothing's getting through." It was the new me talking, the stranger who'd run away from home.

My girlfriend was silent.

The old me struggled to the front, elbowing the other one aside. "Vickie, I'm sorry. I'm trying as hard as I can to figure everything out, but it's still too soon. I don't know what I want."

"Do you want me?"

I resisted hitting myself in the head with the receiver. "Of course," I said, wondering for a nasty moment if I really did. No, I did and yet I wasn't acting like it. What the hell was I doing? "Vickie, please, I definitely want you. I don't know anything else, but I know that. Babe, I'm so sorry, I was hoping I could tell you what my plans were but I'm still waiting."

"For what?"

Yeah, for what? "Clarity," I said. Sometimes the truth sounds lamer than a lie.

Again, she was silent. Ugh. I'd subjected my best friend in the world to silence for two weeks, and I couldn't stand two lousy seconds.

"Listen," I said, feeling frantic now, "you've got to hang on. This is just a blip in a long-term relationship. These things happen. Remember when Maggie and Linda were having such a hard time? It probably took them half a year, but eventually they worked it out. We can too."

"I talked to Maggie about the situation up in Jalapa," she said, ignoring everything I'd just said.

"And?"

"Stop being so goddamned cagey. She told me everything. She said there had been lots of fighting recently, that the roads were dangerous, and that you might not even get through."

I rubbed my face and stared at the empty bookshelves. "Are you mad at me?"

"Of course I am. You lied to me."

I sighed. "I'm sorry. I know I keep saying that, but I am. And I love you."

"Love has never been the problem," she replied, and I waited to hear what was. But after another interminable period of silence, she said, "Take care of yourself, okay?" And then she hung up.

On my way back to the cafeteria, I thought of all the things I could have said that might have reassured her. For a nanosecond I considered calling her back and telling her I'd be home in four weeks, no matter what. But the thought of going home was worse than the thought of losing her, so I kept on walking.

***

As it turned out, almost two hundred people attended our party. Earlier in the day, Estelle heard that a literacy brigade of young volunteers from the *barrio* had just returned to the city and she invited them and their families as well. We ended up with four record players, each one playing different music. Nobody seemed to mind. Everyone was dancing, shouting, laughing and eating.

We served beans and cream, fresh tortillas and grape leaves stuffed with yucca, cabbage, green peppers and tomatoes. Bottles of rum appeared as if by magic. At the edges of the party, people discussed the US government's latest appropriations to build roads and military installations on the border of Honduras. Almost every adult was convinced that an invasion was imminent.

The party officially ended at midnight but continued for another couple of hours. When I returned to the house, it was empty. Sonia had gone to another fiesta when ours began winding down. I lay on my cot and watched a couple of geckos scampering along the wall. I could hear roosters crowing and the sound of canned laughter from a neighbor's television set. As usual, someone was burning his garbage.

Eventually, Sonia came home and I listened to her get ready for bed. It was about three in the morning. No matter what time she went to bed, however, my roommate never forgot to pray.

As I listened to her through the thin wall of our adjoining rooms, I knew she was wearing the red satin slip she always wore to bed, and that she was standing in front of a low dresser with Jorge's picture on it. She prayed, as always, as if she truly believed it could make a difference, as if the power of her pleading might influence at least one tiny atom in the universe to bump up against another, which might then start a chain reaction toward something positive. A lovely, if unlikely, idea.

In my small dark room in Managua, I imagined humans thousands of years ago reacting to their first eclipse of the sun by dropping to their knees in awe and praying fervently for their only source of light and heat to reemerge; and then, the sun returning and everyone feeling relieved and grateful. As I thought about it, I realized how satisfying it must have been to pray for something that actually happened. After a few more comparable experiences, it would have made good sense to establish prayer as part of their daily ritual. Of course, there must have been a handful of people on the sidelines who guessed there was no connection between the praying and the thing that happened, rational skeptics who knew nothing about science but nevertheless resisted the easiest and most hopeful explanation. If they were smart, however, they kept their thoughts to themselves and their mouths shut. Why rain on anyone else's parade?

CHAPTER ELEVEN

It was hard to leave Sonia, but I promised I'd see her again before I left the country. The night before, I'd stashed twenty-five dollars in her bureau. Not such a paltry amount that it wouldn't be of use, but not so much that she'd be angry or ashamed when she found it. Or at least that's what I told myself. I knew I shouldn't leave anything—I'd paid for my room and board—but I justified it as a tip for special service. After all, how many innkeepers prayed for the welfare of their guests?

I was packed and ready to leave by seven. Sonia walked me to the community center as if it were my first day of school. But instead of reminding me to play nice with the other children, or to eat my sandwich before my snowball cupcake, she warned me not to take chances, and to hide if I heard any gunfire. I knew that before the Sandinistas triumphed in July 1979, Sonia had hidden in her bathroom for forty days without lights or running water while the National Guard roamed the streets of Managua in a last desperate attempt to squelch the revolution.

"That was the worst time," she'd told me. We were standing side by side on the patio drinking lemonade. It was almost four in the morning, one of the many nights when neither of us had been able to sleep. A million insects were chirping their hearts out. Something—maybe the lateness of the hour and the shared feeling of being the only two people in the city who were still awake—had triggered her memories. When she began recounting them, I mostly just nodded and let her talk.

"One evening," she said, "the Guard broke into my house looking for Sandinista collaborators. I was hiding in the shower but of course they found me. My heart was beating so fast, I thought I'd have a heart attack."

"No wonder," I said.

She sighed and shook her head. "They searched the house and ate the rest of my food. Then they questioned me about my friends and neighbors. They promised if I told them the truth, they wouldn't hurt me."

"What did you do?"

She grinned. "I could tell they were in a hurry, so I told them that everyone I knew, including all my relatives, had died in the earthquake."

I nodded approvingly. "Excellent. Did they believe you?"

She grinned again. "They must have because they left without harming me." She paused. "Before the Sandinistas finally triumphed, I'd lost more than fifteen pounds. I've never looked so good in my life."

We both laughed.

"A lousy way to lose weight, though," I said.

By the time Sonia and I arrived at the center, most of the group was standing outside, their luggage piled next to the curb where the bus should have already been waiting for us.

It was time to say goodbye. Suddenly, I felt shy and awkward. I didn't really know my host, but I knew some important things about her. We'd had a brief but genuine connection, two passengers thrown together for the length of a ride that would be over in a matter of seconds. "Thank you for your kindness and hospitality," I told her. "It was a pleasure to have met you."

"Likewise," she said, her brown eyes twinkling.

"I'm sorry I couldn't find you any vitamins."

She waved my words away. "It's not important. Take care of yourself."

We hugged and she turned to go, then turned back again. "If you see Jorge," she said, "tell him to write."

"I will."

"*Adiós mi amiga*," she said, and started walking back to her house.

"*Adiós.*" For just a moment as I watched her walk away, I felt ridiculously bereft, the way I'd felt when my mother first left me in front of the Charles Logue elementary school in Boston. I'd comforted myself back then by starting up a conversation with another little girl who looked as if she felt even worse than I did. As soon as Sonia disappeared from view, I tapped Tina on the shoulder and asked her where the bus was.

"I have no idea," she replied. "I thought we were supposed to meet at six. When I got here, the center was deserted. I didn't know what to do. I thought the brigade had left without me." Her eyes were still red from the experience.

"That must have been awful," I said, feeling better already.

By nine o'clock, the group was getting worried. Tim and Estelle had left over an hour ago to call the driver. The street seemed strangely deserted. No cars in sight and no one hurrying to get anywhere. Not even a pile of burning garbage.

"This can't be happening," Veronica said. She'd washed her hair and was wearing a pink sleeveless blouse that looked brand new. She was pacing back and forth, occasionally kicking pebbles into the street, a disappointed teenager who'd obviously been stood up.

Lenny, who was standing next to me, shook his head and sighed.

"It is a bit frustrating," Richard acknowledged. Sometime in the last two weeks, he'd stopped stroking his beard and had begun tugging at it instead. It's the stress, Vickie would have whispered if she were standing next to me.

"Then lower your expectations," Susan advised him.

Richard stared at her for a long moment, his face a bit redder than usual. "That's not very helpful," he finally said, then sat down on the sidewalk next to the luggage.

"I've never hit a woman in my life," Lenny whispered in my ear, "but if I was Richard, I would have slugged her."

"And I would have defended you for free," I said.

At ten thirty, Allen announced, "I don't know about the rest of you, but I'd rather be shot at than wait all afternoon for the bus. I'm heading north today, even if I have to walk."

We all nodded. Instantly, I envisioned us marching up the Pan American Highway dragging our suitcases and duffel bags, a line of well-meaning North American refugees fleeing Managua for a chance to be helpful up north.

About an hour later, a large funky pickup with a canvas awning over the bed lumbered up the street and stopped in front of the center. A man we'd never seen before was behind the wheel, smoking a cigar. Tim and Estelle jumped out, looking very pleased with themselves. Finding an available truck in Nicaragua was akin to winning the national spelling bee in the United States, but probably harder. Amazed, we all crowded around them.

"Where did you get it?" Liz asked.

Tim and Estelle exchanged a private look. "Well, it's kind of a long story," Estelle said, "but I once sort of dated this government official. Until I found out he was married. Anyway, I called and told him he owed me a favor." She hesitated. "I may have also agreed to go out with him again, but I guess I'll just deal with that later." She grinned. "So, any other questions? If not, hop in."

We swarmed to the back of the truck and tossed our bags inside. There were two rows of seats facing each other built into the bed. We all squeezed in and a few minutes later, we were heading out of Managua.

Soon, we were climbing into the hills and passing long stretches of empty countryside. The sun was hot, but the awning overhead provided enough shade to keep us comfortable. Now and then, we passed *campesinos* walking along the road carrying heavy-looking sacks slung across their shoulders, or balancing baskets filled with fruit and vegetables on their heads.

"It's just like in the movies," Allen murmured. It sounded idiotic although it was the same thing I'd been thinking but was too smart to say out loud. The difference, I guessed, between being twenty-four and thirty-six.

As we drove steadily north, we saw hillsides planted with coffee and tobacco, as well as smaller plots of land being worked by single families. Men on horseback wearing large sombreros nodded and sometimes waved as we passed them. Every few miles, we'd see a shack made out of tin and plywood, with naked little kids playing outside in the dirt. There were lines of laundry blowing in the wind, and skinny brown dogs dozing under shade trees.

Allen had fallen asleep, lulled by the back-and-forth rhythm, his head resting on my shoulder. Liz, perched on the other side of Allen, looked over and grinned at me. The wind on my face felt wonderful and I grinned back at her. My doubts had miraculously vanished and the world seemed once more navigable. A delicious sense of well-being flooded through me. This is called joy, I told myself. I glanced at the sunburned faces of my colleagues and felt an odd sensation of unconditional love for every one of them, even Susan. I was part of a group, and the group was part of a movement, which was part of something even larger, an international community of like-minded men and women working together to improve conditions for the current and future inhabitants of the planet.

Don't start getting starry-eyed, I warned, but for once, nothing I told myself could chip away at the unfamiliar feeling of happiness that was washing over me. It didn't matter that it wouldn't last, or that I might never be this happy again. For at least ninety minutes on the Pan American Highway, June 1986, sitting among my compatriots in the back of an old pickup driving past acres of unfamiliar countryside, I was content.

***

Since our truck's top speed was only thirty-five miles per hour, it took almost two and a half hours to reach Esteli where Tim and Estelle had arranged for us to have lunch. We parked near the main square in a neighborhood that had been heavily bombed by the National Guard. Most of the houses within a two-block radius had been leveled. On the way to the restaurant, we took a quick tour of the cathedral, which had also sustained heavy damage. Tim told us that one of the last major assaults against the Guard occurred on July 16, 1979 in Esteli, and that on the following day, Somoza and his family fled to Miami.

The restaurant was set up in the front room of a pink adobe house. Other than six mismatched tables and chairs and a large silver cross on one of the walls, the space was empty. There were no other customers. Estelle introduced us to Carlos Jimenez, the owner of the house, who told us to sit wherever we wanted. Allen, Liz and I chose a rickety table in the corner. Everyone ordered beer; after two weeks in Nicaragua, no one could stand the taste of Coca-Cola anymore. Within fifteen minutes, Carlos's wife brought us homemade tortillas, beans and rice, fried cheese and a stew with chunks of pork in it. Everyone looked happy and relaxed. Although we should have known better—this was, after all, Nicaragua—it was impossible to resist feeling hopeful and even optimistic.

Halfway through our meal, two men wearing bright yellow bandanas around their throats entered the restaurant. Each man carried a huge metal canister with a long plunger. The men nodded to us, and then began spraying.

"Jesus," Liz yelled, "cover your food!"

We all dived over our plates, protecting them with our hands and forearms. The spraying lasted at least five seconds and then without a word, the men left. The room stank of chemicals, and a fine mist of whatever they'd sprayed hovered in the air above our heads and shoulders. Tina was already beginning to wheeze.

"You don't think that was DDT, do you?" Allen asked the group.

"I sure hope not," Lenny said.

"Maybe it was some kind of strong mosquito repellent," Estelle suggested.

"It's possible," I said, "although I haven't noticed any mosquitoes around here, have you?"

"Not really," Estelle said.

"You know, I think I'll wait outside," Tina announced, scraping her chair back.

"Good idea," Liz said to Tina. "You're starting to take care of yourself."

"Maybe we should all go?" Allen asked.

Susan snorted. "God, you're acting like a bunch of paranoid North Americans. Get used to it." She shook her head, then picked up her fork and started eating.

Allen and I looked down at our food, trying to decide whether to dig in again like Susan. "What do you think, Liz?" I asked.

Liz hesitated. "I don't know. In a way, Susan's right. We *should* get used to it."

I considered the idea. "Kind of like a smallpox injection or polio vaccine."

"Exactly," Liz said. "It's the principle behind homeopathy. In minute doses, like cures like."

"So we *should* eat this?" Allen asked, looking back and forth at each of us.

"I suppose so," I said, "but I'm not going to."

"Neither am I," Liz said.

Allen laughed and grabbed us both around the shoulders. "God, you guys. What would I do here without you? I'd be a dead duck, that's what."

I squeezed his hand. "You wouldn't be a dead duck. You just wouldn't have as much fun."

Liz looked pensive. "It *is* fun having you both here with me. It'll be different when everyone leaves. I'll have to adjust." She picked up a can of beer and drained it.

Allen looked surprised. "Who said we're leaving?"

"Yeah," I nodded. "Who said we're leaving?"

"Please," Liz said, "neither of you is suited to a long-term commitment here."

"Why not?" Allen asked. "I don't want to live in the United States anymore. I hate my government. Besides, I'd have to go to law school. I don't want to be a lawyer."

"And I've already been one," I said.

Liz shook her head at us as if we were silly children. "Okay, fine. Let's see how you both feel in a month."

As soon as Susan finished eating, we all left the restaurant and walked back to the truck. After everyone climbed in, I noticed we were all sitting exactly where we'd sat before. How funny, I thought, the things we do, consciously or unconsciously, to ward off evil and make ourselves feel safe. In my lawyer days, I'd worn the same necklace (the one my mother sent me) during every trial for twelve years. After a while, it seemed less neurotic to wear it than to try not to.

"Listen, everyone," Estelle said as we lurched into second gear, "from now on, we have to start acting like a team in which every member is valued and respected. We're heading into dangerous territory and we need to be able to depend on each other."

Allen leaned over and whispered, "Does that mean no more Susan jokes?"

"Well, at least less," I whispered back.

"In Ocotal," Tim was saying, "we'll be very close to the border. We'll probably hear some sporadic gunfire throughout the night, which doesn't necessarily mean anything. The Contras keep it up as a form of psychological warfare. The townspeople are used to it, but they're also ready for an attack at any time. Since the revolution, the Contras have made three serious attempts to take Ocotal, establish it as their capital, and then call for international recognition."

"And so it's really important," Estelle continued, "that we stay calm but vigilant, that we look out for one another, and that we're able to reach consensus quickly when necessary. Do you all understand?"

Everyone nodded. Solemn-faced, we drove the next hour and a half in silence, each person lost in the jungle of their private thoughts. Eventually, we turned off the Pan American highway and headed east on a smaller road to Ocotal. At the outskirts of the town, we heard a loud bang and Tina gasped in horror. The truck veered onto the shoulder of the road and then stopped. There were no further bangs.

"I believe our tire just blew out," Lenny said, mostly for Tina's benefit.

We all jumped out of the truck to examine the tire, which was as flat as a tortilla. Naturally, there wasn't a spare. After a few minutes, the driver whose name was Enrique motioned everyone to get back in.

"*Está bien. No problema*," he said, lighting another cigar from the stub of the one he'd been smoking since we left Esteli.

"I think he means to drive on it," Allen said. "Won't that damage the rim?"

"You're thinking like a North American," I told him.

Richard sighed. "We have no way to fix it out here."

"Well, how far is it to the hotel?" Liz asked.

After a brief discussion, we reached consensus. We would leave our luggage on the truck and walk alongside it into town.

Finally, we were beginning to act like a team.

***

I guessed the population of Ocotal was around fifteen thousand and was surprised when Tim said it was at least twice that. Some of the bigger streets were paved, but all of the smaller ones were still dirt. We were clearly in Sandino country now, his silhouette stenciled on houses, stores and restaurants. Pro-revolutionary graffiti declaring allegiance to the Sandinistas and that Nicaragua was not for sale and would not surrender was scrawled across almost every adobe house we passed. On the side streets, many of the buildings were riddled with bullet holes or had large chunks of plaster missing. Red and black FSLN banners were tacked over doorways fluttering defiantly in the breeze. Live free or die, the official motto of New Hampshire, took on a whole new meaning here.

As we crossed the main square, we saw a number of civilians with knives or guns tucked into their waistbands hurrying to their various destinations. No one dawdled in Ocotal. Even the children seemed unnaturally alert, as if they were ready to drop whatever game they were playing to run home and help defend their families. At the edge of the square, a group of impossibly young soldiers in full camouflage were laughing and smoking cigarettes. Tim told us the locals referred to them as *los cachorros*, Sandinista "wolf cubs."

As we drew closer, two soldiers wearing heavy looking ammunition belts across their chests approached Veronica and offered her a cigarette, which she politely declined. As we proceeded past them, they whistled and clapped. Tina stumbled self-consciously and they clapped even harder, grinning without a hint of malevolence. In a country at peace, they would be teenagers hanging on a street corner, sharing a bottle of rum, and whistling at every female no matter how old or young, plain or pretty.

According to Estelle, the last attack on the town had occurred a few months ago, but in the past week the Contras had booby-trapped the door to a kindergarten which exploded when the teacher opened it, killing her and injuring the students who were with her. As I walked along, I thought I knew how someone from Boston or New York might have felt entering a town like Tombstone, Arizona in the mid-1800s: excited, fully alive and a little bit scared. Ocotal was a town where anything could happen at any time. In other words, it was my kind of place.

Our hotel was a large dilapidated house that had once belonged to a Somoza supporter who'd fled the country. There were five bedrooms on the first floor arranged in a semicircle around a crumbling courtyard. The upstairs was empty and unused. The only available bathroom was in a separate outhouse that could, if necessary, seat up to three people at a time.

After a late supper, we returned to the hotel and agreed we'd be ready to leave at six in the morning. We had no idea when our army escort might arrive, but we didn't want to hold them up.

The room I shared with Liz had two sagging cots and a bureau that was missing half its drawers. My cot was even more uncomfortable (if that was possible) than the one I'd slept on at Sonia's. I had no illusions, however, about sleeping on the floor. I'd already seen three scorpions and a tan-colored tarantula the size of my fist in the hallway.

We turned the light off at ten thirty. I flopped around on my cot, trying to find the least unbearable position to sleep in. At midnight, I heard a single gunshot followed by a succession of rapid bursts that sounded like a machine gun. A moment later, I heard three more shots, and then another round of bursts. Both Liz and I sat up in bed.

"Would you characterize that as sporadic?" Liz asked.

"Define sporadic," I said, turning on the light.

"Occasional."

There was another volley of shots followed by a small explosion. We both jumped out of our cots and started getting dressed.

"How far away do you think it is?" I asked.

"I can't tell from here. Let's go out into the courtyard."

"Okay, let me just find my sandals."

When we got outside, most of the group was huddled around the empty fountain, their faces pale and serious. Allen and Lenny were still buttoning their shirts and zipping up their pants. Tina was hunched over, holding her stomach as if she might throw up. Richard was trying to comfort her. I noticed Susan's shirt was inside out and her sandals were on the wrong feet. A few yards behind them, Veronica was walking in a circle, praying quietly.

"Has anyone seen Tim and Estelle?" I asked.

Susan pointed across the courtyard to the front of the house. "They're over there, conferring."

The gunshots sounded louder out here, but I still couldn't tell how close they were. There was another small explosion that lit up the sky, followed by more gunshots. A few townspeople were shouting in the street. Tim and Estelle finished talking and hurried back to us.

"We're going to run over to the mayor's house," Estelle told us, "and see if we can find out what's happening. Everybody needs to stay put until we get back. Okay?" Both she and Tim were dressed in dark green shirts and pants that they must have bought at the army store in Boulder.

"Oh my God," Tina whimpered.

"Do you think we'll have to evacuate?" Lenny asked. His face was lined with worry. All our faces had aged a little in the past few weeks. The day I left Colorado, Vickie warned that I was jumping from the frying pan into the fire. "In which case," I joked, "I'll probably feel right at home." She'd sighed and then wished me good luck, which I now thought for the first time I might need.

"I have no idea," Tim was saying. "Right now, the fighting is at least half a mile away. If it gets any closer, we'll consider it."

"Isn't this close enough?" Tina asked, her voice quivering with fear.

"Jesus, get a grip," Susan muttered.

Richard turned to his wife and said, "Shut up, bunny. I mean it."

"Well she doesn't belong here," Susan said.

"Maybe not," he conceded, "but she's here anyway."

Liz put her arm around Tina's shoulder. "What should we do in the meantime?" she asked Estelle.

There was a long burst of machine-gun fire that seemed to last forever. When it stopped, Estelle suggested we all find hiding places until she and Tim returned.

"But don't leave the grounds," Estelle repeated. "Unless it's an emergency."

Veronica looked pale and scared, but was staying calm. "My bedroom door is so warped, it won't even close."

Richard took her hand. "There are plenty of places to hide upstairs." He turned to the rest of us. "Come on, let's go."

Liz began pushing Tina toward the front of the house. "I need to find my first-aid kit. I think it's in the kitchen. I'll take Tina with me."

There was more shouting in the street and a couple of neighborhood dogs had begun to howl. Estelle and Tim rushed off, and then everyone else ran toward the house. I was standing alone in the middle of the courtyard watching the sky, wondering why I wasn't scared. Maybe it was too unreal, or maybe I'd lost the ability. I knew it wasn't smart to remain outside, but I didn't think I was in any imminent danger. A few minutes later, I heard a couple of sirens going off and wondered if they signaled something new or if they'd suddenly just started working. There was so much noise now that in an odd dissonant way it seemed eerily quiet, almost peaceful. My heart was beating faster than normal, but it wasn't an unpleasant sensation, more like a state of high alert, as if I'd just downed a twenty-ounce cup of coffee.

Then the night lit up with another explosion that sounded closer than the ones before. I thought of Sonia and decided to hide in the outhouse. I crossed the courtyard and tried the outhouse door, which was locked. I knocked and heard Allen ask, "Who's there?"

"Me," I said.

A second later, I heard the door unlock. "What if I'd been a Contra?" I asked, sitting down on a plank of wood between the toilets.

Allen sat down next to me. "You wouldn't have understood my question."

"Right, but then I would have shot you."

Allen thought for a moment. "You're not supposed to shoot North Americans."

"Gee, I'm really sorry."

We heard a large boom, more shouting, and then people running through the courtyard. Allen grabbed my hand as we propped our feet against the outhouse door. We paid close attention, but no one seemed to be lingering. Eventually we relaxed a little, but continued to sit without speaking, listening intently to the erratic sound of gunfire, of rockets exploding in the air, and imagining various scenarios that might or might not be happening. After about forty minutes, the gunfire began to subside.

Allen broke the silence first. "There's a huge hairy spider on the wall across from us." Although it was dark, our eyes had adjusted and we could see more than we wanted to.

"I know," I said. "I've been watching him."

"He's really enormous."

"I know."

"Bigger than a catcher's mitt."

I nodded. "Maybe we should go outside. It's probably safe now."

Allen hesitated. "I think we should wait a little longer, although if he comes any closer, I'll probably change my mind."

"All right," I said, "but don't wait until he's within striking distance."

Allen let go of my hand. "Rachel?" He sounded very young.

"Yeah?"

"I think I might not be suited to a long-term commitment here. I think maybe I'll stay for another month and then go to law school and become a public defender. Like you were."

"It's a plan," I said.

"What about you?"

I shrugged like a native. "*No se.*" *I don't know.*

"Do you think I'd make a good public defender?"

"Yes, but don't stay too long." I paused. "It's amazing, isn't it, how we can choose to come here and put ourselves at risk and how we can decide to leave whenever we've had enough."

Allen blew out a long breath. "Whew, that's pretty privileged, isn't it?"

"Obscenely privileged, but don't waste your time feeling guilty. It doesn't help."

We could hear Estelle calling everyone to come out of hiding. As if we'd been playing an extended game of hide-and-seek and it was late now, time to go home and be somebody's kid again. Time for supper and then a bedtime story with a happy ending. *Come out, come out, wherever you are.*

"How will we get past the spider?" Allen asked.

"I don't know. Let's just make a run for it."

After we were all together again, we learned that the Contras had attacked a farming co-op on the edge of town and destroyed their grain silo. Eight people had been killed, five had been wounded. A woman and her teenaged daughter were missing.

"It was terrible," Tim said, shaking his head, "but as a group we were never in immediate danger." He looked at his watch. "It's almost two. We should all try to get a few hours of shuteye."

Liz and I both fell asleep with our clothes on. When my alarm clock beeped at five thirty, I wanted to smash it against the floor. I felt dangerously tired. My eyes burned as if I'd spent the night in a sandstorm. My limbs refused to obey even the simplest command.

Liz groaned as she sat up. "God, I dreamed I was working at the hospital and everyone on the ward had a heart attack at the same time."

"What did you do?" I asked, my face still pressed against the mattress.

"I think I was running around trying to decide which patient to save first."

"Do you think you could peel me off this mattress?"

Liz helped roll me out of bed, and then we packed up and walked out into the courtyard. The sun was just beginning to rise against a pink and orange sky. Tim and Estelle were sitting cross-legged on the ground, leaning against each other, looking tired but resolute. They'd been holding hands, but stopped when they saw us.

As soon as everyone was present, they shared the bad news: the Contras had taken over a stretch of road between Ocotal and Jalapa. Nobody was allowed to go through until the Contras were driven back into Honduras. The army wanted us to wait at least another week before escorting us to Jalapa. Everyone was silent.

Finally, Estelle stood up and shrugged. "This isn't a vacation," she reminded us. "This isn't a tour. We're here to help in whatever way we can. I'm sorry we can't get to Jalapa right now, but there are plenty of things to do in Managua while we wait. All of our host families can take us back. We've checked."

They must have been up all night.

After another round of silence, Lenny said, "Well, unless you need me somewhere else, I think I'd like to do some carpentry at the language school. Half the chairs are broken and the front porch needs shoring up."

Tim nodded approvingly. "Estelle and I can interpret for some of the newer brigades."

Susan and Richard then expressed interest in a building project in Matagalpa. "We'll come back in a week," Richard promised. Susan nodded and patted Richard's hand. For the first time since they'd stepped off the plane, they looked like a happy couple.

Liz, of course, could work at any of the local hospitals, which desperately needed professional help. "There's actually one within walking distance," she told us. "I visited it last Tuesday. They told me to drop by whenever I had the time."

At that point, Allen stood up and volunteered to do childcare for the mothers who lived in the *barrio*. Veronica immediately offered to assist. They both looked proud of themselves.

"That's a wonderful idea," Estelle said. "I'll find out if you can use the community center."

Which left just Tina and me. After clearing her throat, Tina announced her decision to leave the country as soon as possible. Nobody tried to talk her out of it.

"Thank God," Liz whispered.

Which left just me. I'd spent the last twelve years of my life learning how to cross-examine police officers. What the hell could I do in Managua? I didn't really like children, I knew nothing about carpentry and my Spanish was mediocre at best.

It was a perfect time to leave. I could have flown back to the United States, patched things up with Vickie, then collapsed onto my firm, comfortable mattress and slept for the next three months. After I'd fully recovered from the latest knockout, I could have decided whether I was ready to step back into the ring again or not. In any event, I could have made an informed decision.

Instead, I simply nodded to let everyone know I was still on board. Tomorrow or the day after, I'd figure out something worthwhile to do. In the meantime, I could help Sonia around the house, try the dollar store again. On the way back to Managua, I snoozed for a couple of hours, woke up with a headache and a slight fever, but figured I was basically fine. If the world was still reeling around me, then that's just the way it was. As any battered woman will tell you, a person can get used to anything.

CHAPTER TWELVE

We'd headed back to Managua with no assurance that the road from Ocotal to Jalapa would be open anytime soon. As we drove down out of the mountains and into the capital, it was getting dark and the atmosphere felt thicker and clammier. There was also a scent in the air that reminded me of an overripe fruit salad; inhaling deeply, I could smell mangoes, bananas and papayas, every ingredient a few days past its prime. Or maybe I was just getting hungry. I realized, then, that the tropics no longer alarmed me, that I was beginning to adapt to the too muchness of it all: the noise, the smells, the heat, the vegetation, even the bugs. A few minutes later, as if on cue, hundreds of fireflies suddenly swarmed in front of the truck giving us a great phosphorescent light show.

Liz was bouncing up and down next to me. "A good omen," she said, smiling.

"What, the fireflies?" I asked.

She nodded. "Sure."

I should have left it alone—it was just a careless happy remark—but for some reason it irked me. "Do you really believe that?"

She looked amused. "Why not?"

"Then would you say that the fighting last night was a *bad* omen?"

"Oh, stop being a lawyer. I thought you quit."

I rubbed my eyes. "Well, it bothers me when people assign meaning to random acts of nature." I paused. "Maybe I'm jealous. Maybe I'd like to think the fireflies are a good omen too, but it seems so arbitrary. So fanciful."

She patted my shoulder sympathetically. "It must be tough to be so rational all the time."

I sighed. "It is. And not only that, it makes no sense. Why *not* have faith in things? Why *not* believe in good omens? There's no real downside as far as I can tell."

Liz laughed, then looked at me the way a nurse might if I'd shown up in the emergency room complaining of a headache and racing thoughts. "You need to get more sleep, Rachel."

As we pulled up to the community center, it was hard not to feel sheepish. After all, we'd been gone less than two days. None of our host families, however, seemed at all surprised that we'd been forced to turn back. Making plans that actually worked was a luxury most Nicaraguans hadn't enjoyed for years. Despite how late it was (we'd had more truck problems outside of Esteli), a representative from each of our families was waiting on the sidewalk, ready to welcome us as if we'd just arrived in the country.

I was surprised Sonia hadn't simply waited at the house, but there she was waving as enthusiastically as everyone else. When she caught sight of me, I could see the relief and pleasure in her smile, which touched me more than I would have expected.

"Jeez," Tim said, "I called from Esteli just to give them an idea when we might be rolling in. I didn't expect them to stay up and meet us."

That night, I sank into my cot at Sonia's humming an old Bob Dylan tune about being stuck inside of Mobile with the Memphis blues again. But in fact I wasn't at all unhappy. I actually loved how unstable my life felt. For the first time since entering law school, I had no idea what I'd be doing in the coming days, weeks or months. Finally, I'd managed to escape the ubiquitous rules of both civil and criminal procedure. The dizzy free fall—without an appointment book in sight—was exhilarating. But of course I hadn't landed yet.

***

As it turned out, I spent the next two days picking up garbage and ashes from the field next to the community center. Instead of joining a building brigade in Matagalpa, Richard and Susan had concocted an unlikely plan that involved cleaning up the field and turning it into a playground for all the kids in the *barrio*. After returning to the States, they intended to convince local elementary schools to donate their used playground equipment. Despite the embargo and the prohibitive cost of shipping, they believed that some organization would be willing to take on the project. I wasn't as confident as they were, but what did I know? Maybe I was already too acculturated and my imagination had withered accordingly. At least the field was clean.

On Friday, Susan had wanted me to help move a gigantic pile of rocks from one section of the field to another, but I told her my host needed me, which wasn't a complete lie. While I was in Ocotal, Sonia decided she could make some extra cash giving manicures. She'd done it years ago in Panama and had saved all of the necessary utensils. To build up her confidence, she wanted to practice on me and on some of her neighbors. I couldn't imagine who in Managua would shell out their precious dwindling *cordobas* on a manicure, but Sonia thought there was a market. And so, despite how much fun it would have been to spend the day moving rocks with Susan in one hundred and fifteen degree heat, I had to support my host.

On Friday morning, as soon as I finished breakfast, Sonia plunked down a bowl full of soapy liquid in front of me. She was wearing a light blue, professional-looking smock, like a dental hygienist's, which made me smile. I'd been dawdling over my rice and beans, worrying about her health again. Something was up. For the past couple of days, she'd been more preoccupied than usual, her face looking drawn and set, reminding me of my mother's when she was in pain after my father's death but determined not to show it.

"So, what do I do?" I asked, staring at the bowl.

Sonia looked amazed. "Haven't you ever had a manicure?"

"No, this is my first one."

She clapped her hands together as though wonders never ceased. "Well, then, put your fingers in the bowl and let them soak."

I plunged my hands into the liquid while she busied herself laying out various metal utensils as if she were a nurse in an operating room.

After about five minutes, Sonia determined I was ready. First, she massaged my hands and fingers, kneading them like dough, then cut my fingernails. Finally, she spread my hands on the table to examine the state of my cuticles.

"Horrible!" she exclaimed.

I pretended to look concerned. "It's that bad?" I asked, glancing down at my fingers, which looked much better than usual now that I wasn't climbing.

"Almost beyond repair." She picked up a thin, ominous-looking instrument and began pushing the skin back to where it belonged.

I held still although it hurt a little. "Thank God I got to you in time," I joked.

She didn't respond. After a while, I looked up at her face and noticed a couple of tears rolling down her cheeks. "Sonia, what's wrong?"

"Nothing." She switched to my other hand.

"Yes, there is. You're crying."

She wiped her face, tried to keep going, but I pulled my hand away.

"Please tell me what's making you sad. Whatever it is, I want to know."

Unlike my mother, thank God, she wasn't a true stoic. "It's Jorge," she said. "He's missing."

Oh no. My nagging little headache suddenly felt worse. "For how long?"

She shook her head. "I don't know. I got the letter on Monday saying only that Jorge was missing in action. His whole patrol is missing."

"His whole patrol? Well, maybe they're chasing the Contras back into Honduras?"

She nodded, looking unconvinced.

"Why didn't you tell me sooner?" It wasn't until the words were out of my mouth that I could hear how presumptuous, how classically North American, they sounded. I'd been her guest for all of three weeks. Why in the world should she confide in me?

Sonia, however, took no offense. "I didn't want to worry you," she explained.

No, of course not, I thought, then took her soft, tanned hands in mine. "I'm so sorry, Sonia. Is there anything I can do?"

She hesitated. "Maybe you could pray for Jorge."

"Certainly," I said, although I hadn't prayed for anything since I was twelve, and even then I hadn't believed it would help—it didn't, I still had to go to summer camp. And after that, I gave up even the pretense of praying to an unseen, unproven deity. But so what? It was the least I could do. In the unlikely event some benign force in the universe could hear me, it wouldn't mind that I was another Jewish atheist going through the motions.

By the end of the day, I'd had another manicure which I obviously didn't need, a pedicure that I did, and a neck and scalp massage that was vaguely irritating. Right before bed, I agreed to let Sonia slather my face with a strange-smelling lotion that made me gag. As I turned out the light, I made a mental note to beg Susan to think of another project.

The following morning, Sonia took a bus downtown with her utensils. As I'd feared, no one was interested. In the afternoon, she tried the lobby of the Intercontinental Hotel, but the concierge immediately asked her to leave. From then on, she stuck to her friends and neighbors who occasionally traded food and other goods for her services.

***

Saturday night was the first time since losing Emily's case that I fell asleep before midnight. I'd had a headache for days and wondered if I was fighting the flu. I slept deeply for at least four hours before I heard a voice—mine—ordering me to wake up. I opened my eyes and stared at the ceiling. This is an emergency, the voice said, your primary relationship is in trouble. Stop pretending that doing nothing isn't doing something. I sat up against the wall, turned on the light, and tried to think. How long had it been since the phone call when Vickie hung up on me? What the hell was I waiting for? I scrambled off my cot, grabbed a notebook and a pen, and then sat down on the edge of the bed. I needed a plan. I looked down at the blank page on my lap and began to write.

Plan A: Pull your head out of the sand before you get so comfortable you learn how to breathe down there—it's not your true home.

I stopped. Was I sure about that? No, of course not. I was blind and stupid and unsure about everything. Sometime in the last few months, my intuition had taken a leave of absence, perhaps a permanent one. Consequently, I knew very little. But I knew this: when you're blind and stupid, preserve all options. I would write (and send) my girlfriend a heartfelt letter, not a falsely reassuring one, but nothing suicidal either. I chewed the tip of my pen for inspiration. I was a good writer, but this felt too much like a test. If I failed, I'd flunk my life.

Dear Vickie,

It's three a.m. and I'll probably be awake for the rest of the night. If you were here with me, I could lay my head in the crook of your shoulder and you could smooth my hair and sing me silly songs. I wish I liked the taste of rum; Sonia says a glass always puts her right to sleep. Although it's hard to be back in Managua—I'm sure Maggie's told you all about it—I don't wish I was in some other country. I can't explain it, but the emotional landscape suits me. If it were possible, I'd have our relationship frozen, like we did last summer

*with our membership at the fitness center. And then I'd have the time I need
to think. I'm still waiting for clarity, but as usual she's very late. While I wait
for her, will you wait for me?*

Love, which has never been the problem,

Rachel

Excellent, congratulations. I ripped the letter out of my notebook
and placed it in an envelope with enough stamps to make it to the
United States. Tomorrow, I would ask Sonia how to send it. Before
turning off the light, I stood in the middle of the room and watched
two geckos playing tag on the wall across from me. First, one would
chase the other, both scampering madly as if their lives depended on
it, and then all of a sudden, without any obvious signal, they'd reverse
roles. Over and over, back and forth, chasing and being chased. Unlike
humans, however, the geckos seemed endlessly content with their game.

As I climbed back into bed, I wondered what Vickie would do when
she finished reading my letter. Would she wait like I asked? Sure, and
a man with a big fat belly shouting "Ho, ho, ho," would slide down
my chimney in December, loaded with presents. Sorry, Virginia, but
hot-blooded Italians do not wait. They get mad and call. It was easy to
imagine the conversation.

"Rachel, how can you freeze a relationship?"

"I don't know. I guess it's a lot to ask."

*"Oh, now there's an understatement. How long do you propose we do
this?"*

"I'm not sure, but I'd say three months."

*"I see. And what am I supposed to do during this period of time while you
wait for clarity?"*

"Just live?"

*"Just live. I see. And can you at least promise that at the end of the three
months you'll return to Boulder?"*

"It would be my intention, but I can't promise. I'm really sorry, Vickie."

"Me too, sweetheart. Well, have a nice life, Rachel."

"You too, Vickie."

After about ten minutes, I switched on the light again, grabbed the
notebook, and wrote another sentence.

Plan B: Stick head back in sand and take a deep breath.

Waiting, I told myself, isn't always a passive activity. For instance, sometimes when you're climbing, it looks as if there's no way you can make the next move. You stare at the rock in front of you and wonder why it isn't rated much harder than the guidebook says. Your hands begin to sweat and your breathing gets shallow. You imagine a series of moves that all end in disaster. Better to do nothing at all. While you're waiting, though, you're still looking, but it's different now because the pressure's off. After a while, your eyes focus on a hold that seems almost irrelevant because it won't get you more than an inch or two higher. With nothing to lose, however, you try it and suddenly the landscape is completely different. All kinds of holds emerge that weren't visible before. Right.

Plan C: Cultivate a taste for rum.

I glanced at my watch; it was too late to try any tonight. I turned off the light, attempted to lie still with my eyes closed, gave up and decided to take a shower. In a few more hours, I'd be meeting Allen and Liz at the community center. To celebrate our fourth Sunday in Managua, we'd decided to try the famous buffet brunch at the Intercontinental Hotel. If the dollar store was open—fat chance, it was never open— we'd stop on the way back and buy some vitamins, shampoo and Kotex for our hosts.

***

Every Sunday, the Intercontinental Hotel offered brunch to the public from nine until noon. During that time, for eight dollars, you could eat as much as you wanted. We'd intended to get there by bus, but after three of them passed us by with people hanging off the sides, we broke down and took a cab. We were dressed in our Sunday finest, which meant jeans and a Hawaiian shirt for Allen and loose cotton pants and pastel blouses for Liz and me.

When we arrived at nine thirty, there was a line stretching out the door of the restaurant and into the lobby. The hotel was nondescript but surprisingly modern with floor-to-ceiling windows, white arches and columns and polished marble floors. We could have been in Los Angeles, Mexico City or San Jose. An old Nicaraguan woman with a limp took our money and showed us to the end of the line. The men in front of us were dressed casually in the kind of clothes that are advertised in travel magazines, suits that are always tan or white, never wrinkle, and are equally appropriate for a brunch or an important business meeting. According to Estelle, many of the people staying at the hotel were journalists from the United States and Europe, here to chart the ongoing war between David and Goliath. They'd been waiting off and on since 1979 for either the United States to invade, or for the Sandinista government to collapse from within.

At first, the line didn't move at all. Allen kept shifting his backpack from one arm to the other, tapping his feet, and sighing. Finally, he said, "I feel a little funny being here."

I nodded. "That's because you've stepped out of one milieu where you don't fit in but you wish you did, into another where in fact you do fit in but you wish you didn't."

Allen looked a little confused. "I think I understand what you just said."

Liz laughed. "Do all lawyers think the way you do?"

I shrugged. "If they've been at it long enough."

"Oh boy," Allen muttered, "I can hardly wait."

Liz was surveying the spacious sunlit lobby. After a couple of seconds, she said, "You know, it does feel funny to be here. There's too much dissonance between this world and the *barrio*. I vote we eat quickly and get the hell out of here."

Allen and I both concurred. As the line moved forward, we stepped into the restaurant and caught our first glimpse of the buffet, a huge table heaped with all kinds of fruit, cheese, bread, rolls, salads and desserts.

"Wow," Allen breathed. "I feel like Dorothy standing before the Emerald City."

Immediately, I knew which of Dorothy's two compatriots Vickie would think I was. When the line moved again, I clanked forward to keep up with my friends. *If I only had a heart.* But that was unfair. Just because it was temporarily lost and out of radio contact didn't mean it wasn't there.

The restaurant was packed. I was glad at least some of the diners were Nicaraguan. Everyone was seated around elegant tables with white tablecloths and wineglasses, eating, drinking and chatting. There were huge potted plants everywhere and bright sunlight shining into the air-conditioned room. It was lovely, or it would have been, except for the surrounding circumstances. Context, I decided, was everything. But then, how was this different than anywhere else in the world? In New York City, homeless people rooted around in garbage cans behind restaurants where the customers drank two-hundred-dollar bottles of wine. No, I thought, it's like this everywhere. This is the way the world is.

Finally, we got close enough to grab a plate and begin mentally choosing our food. As anyone experienced at buffet knows, you have to survey the entire table before you make your move. When it was this crowded, there was no going back and forth. At the far end of the table, two men in blue uniforms were lifting metal covers off platters of scrambled eggs and bacon. Suddenly, I was ravenous. My mouth, like Pavlov's apolitical dog, watered involuntarily. As I reached for a hunk of bread, however, my true-blue liberal soul rebelled. Oh, oh, I thought, I might not be able to do this. Out of the corner of my eye, I saw Allen hesitating before a platter of crackers and cheese, his hand wavering in midair. Then, Liz came up behind me.

"I know this sounds ridiculous," she whispered, "but I feel too guilty to eat. Isn't that ridiculous?"

I shook my head. "I can't do it either."

Allen sighed next to us. "I could probably eat half this table, but I keep thinking of my family, especially the kids. How can I gorge myself when they're so hungry?"

Liz nodded in agreement. "Well, shall we get out of here?" She turned to put her plate back.

"No, wait," I said. "We've already paid. Why not stack our plates with as much food as possible, load it all into Allen's backpack, and take it home to our families?"

Allen's face broke into a big smile. "That's a great idea," he said, grabbing a handful of cheese and dropping it onto his plate. Liz was already piling fruit and vegetables onto hers.

"I'll concentrate on this," she told me. "Why don't you go for the bread, rolls and crackers? Nothing perishable. We have a long way to go in the heat."

"Aye, aye, sir," I said.

As we were leaving the restaurant, a Nicaraguan man in a blue uniform stepped out in front of us. In English, he told us he was sorry, but that no one was allowed to take food from the premises. Allen and Liz both looked at me.

I imagined the most pompous lawyer I knew—a guy from Denver who always wore bow ties and sweater vests—and tried to sound just like him.

"Well," I said, "I'm sorry too, but we've paid good money and unless there's a sign posted in some conspicuous place that informs us of your policy, you have no right to stop us." I glanced pointedly at my watch. "Ah, we're late. So, unless you're prepared to refund our money, we must be going."

For a moment, the man looked around for help, but none was available. He checked again, and then dismissed us with a wave. We hurried through the lobby past a group of North American nuns chattering in English and out into the heavy tropical air, which in contrast to the hotel seemed impossibly hot.

"¡Qué calor!" I said, fanning myself the way Sonia did when she uttered the same words every morning, as if the heat that day was something new and entirely unexpected.

On our way home, we decided to stop first at Sonia's, lay out the food on her kitchen table, and then divvy it up from there. Sonia watched as we unpacked item after item and was suitably impressed by how much we'd managed to stuff into Allen's medium-sized backpack.

"Please," Allen told her after we'd spread everything out, "take whatever you'd like."

Sonia leaned over the table, examining the loot. "Could I have a couple of carrots and a radish?" she asked.

"Absolutely," he said. "How about some crackers and cheese to go with them?"

Just then, we heard the front door open and a few moments later, Tomas staggered into the kitchen looking for Sonia. The front of his shirt was torn and he stank of rum. There was a cut over his right eye, which had bled a little.

"*Hola Tomas,*" Sonia said, smiling gently. "*¿Cómo estás?*"

"*Muy bien,*" he replied, but he didn't look it. I think he was surprised to see so many strangers in Sonia's kitchen.

We offered him something to eat, but he just shook his head. At that moment, a truck backfired twice in front of the house, the sound loud and unexpected. Tomas screamed and pushed the table over on its side, scattering food everywhere. Before we had time to react, he'd dropped into a crouch behind the table and was shouting at us. I couldn't understand what he was saying, but it definitely sounded hostile.

For a moment, the four of us simply stood there in the kitchen, looking confused. Then we saw the gun, a large silver and black revolver. It was raised above the rim of the table and was pointed directly at us.

"Oh my God!" Allen squeaked.

We ran to the farthest corner of the patio and huddled in front of the high cement wall. There was no place to hide. We were all bent low but if he'd wanted to shoot us, it wouldn't have been difficult. We were less than thirty-five feet away from him.

"Jesus Christ," Allen said, putting his arms around Liz and Sonia. I was right behind him searching for something to use as a weapon—a rock or a piece of wood—but there was nothing.

"Do you know if the gun is loaded?" Liz asked Sonia in Spanish.

Sonia shook her head. "I'm not sure." She paused to think. "Sometimes it is."

Allen obviously understood her answer. "Sometimes?" he repeated in English.

"*Sí,*" she said, shrugging.

For another couple of minutes, Tomas continued shouting and waving his gun at us. So far, he hadn't moved from behind his barricade.

"What are we going to do?" I asked.

Sonia shook her head again. "He's not here with us."

"I know," I said. "But we have to do something."

"Maybe the gun isn't loaded," Allen said. His shirt was dark with sweat and his shoulders were trembling, but I could hear the anger in his voice.

"But what if it is?" Liz asked. "I've seen dozens of crazy homeless people in the emergency room. You can't predict what they'll do. Some of them can be very dangerous."

Tomas was now shouting political slogans in a singsong voice, repeating the same phrases over and over, his words too slurred to entirely understand, but we got the gist: we were the enemy that had to be defeated.

"Fuck it," Allen said. "Let's call his bluff." He stood up and took a couple of steps forward. Immediately, we heard the unmistakable crack of a gunshot and the high-pitched sound of a bullet smashing into the wall a few yards above our heads.

"Shit!" Allen said, dropping back down again.

"Are you okay?" Liz whispered.

He was crouched a few feet in front of us, his hands covering the top of his head. "I'm great," he muttered.

Liz turned to me. "You're a climber, right?"

I nodded.

"How hard would it be to climb over the wall and get some help?"

I studied the wall behind us. It was less than fifteen feet high with plenty of footholds. I could get over it in five or six quick moves. "No problem at all," I said.

"No way," Allen whispered. "He could get lucky this time and hit you."

"Stop being a guy," I told him, then explained the plan to Sonia.

She thought for a moment, and then nodded. "Find Amelia. He'll listen to her. She was with him during the takeover."

Before Allen could stop me, I turned to the wall, picked out my first couple of footholds and began climbing. I was up and over in a flash. Tomas didn't even try to shoot me.

Luckily, Amelia was at home and after I'd explained the situation, she rushed back to Sonia's with me, entering through the front door. I stayed out of sight in the living room and just listened, hoping she'd be able to reach him.

"Tomas?" Amelia called. "It's me, Amelia."

He didn't answer.

"Tomas?" She took a couple of steps closer. "It's over, Tomas. We won."

This time, he answered. "We won?"

"Yes," she said. "The Guard has fled. We've won. You can come out now."

"Where's my wife?" he called. "Where's Miriam?"

Amelia hesitated. "She's dead, Tomas. She gave her life for the cause. Come on out now."

"She's dead?"

"Yes, but you already knew that, Tomas. It was a long time ago. We buried her in that cemetery in Leon, the one with the beautiful trees. Hundreds of people came to pay their respects. Remember?"

"I don't remember."

"Yes, you do, Tomas." She sounded kind but firm. This was clearly not the first time she'd had to talk him down from a bad trip. "Give me the gun, Tomas. I have a bottle of rum at my house."

"We won," he said.

I heard him slowly standing up and then saw him walking toward Amelia. She took the gun from his hand, emptied a couple of bullets onto the tile floor, and then put her arm around his shoulder and together they left the house.

It took a while to clean up the mess, but most of the food was salvageable. In silence, we laid it all out again, divided it into three piles, and then Liz and Allen prepared to leave. Because they looked so sad, Sonia hugged them and told them not to worry, that Tomas had many friends he could count on.

After they left, she wagged her finger at me and said, "That goes for you too."

I rolled my eyes like a world-weary twelve-year-old. "I know, Sonia. Worrying will only make me look old."

"That's right," she said. "And then I will have to put that lotion on your face."

"No," I said, backing away from her. "Not the lotion."

CHAPTER THIRTEEN

Our month-long stay in purgatory was finally coming to an end. Our souls had apparently undergone the requisite punishment and purification, and we'd been cleared for takeoff. Over the past week, which I'd spent doing whatever cleanup projects Susan and Richard invented, the Contras had been chased back into Honduras and the road to Jalapa was open. On Saturday morning, two weeks later than planned, our funky chariot would be waiting to transport us north toward heaven, or at least as far as Ocotal. And on Sunday, the army promised to escort us the rest of the way.

Most of us decided to spend our last day in Managua with our families. On Friday morning, I woke up with my usual headache, sore throat and slight fever and heard Sonia sweeping the night's leavings off the back patio. She was humming something jazzy with a bossa nova beat. I rolled out of my cot, slipped on a pair of shorts and a T-shirt, and went out to greet her. The early morning light was so bright I almost stumbled. Someday, I told myself, you'll own a dozen pair of sunglasses and you'll never be defenseless again.

"*Buenos días,*" I said.

"*¡Qué calor!*" Sonia replied, fanning her face.

"Oh please, it's the same as it always is."

She smiled mischievously. "No, my friend. Today it's much hotter!"

Sonia's nephew was still missing, but if you didn't know her, you wouldn't guess she was especially worried about anything. It wasn't pure stoicism like my mother's or even fear of looking old, but something more pragmatic: she was a survivor. If she talked about Jorge, it was always in the present tense. Each night, of course, she still stood in front of his photograph and prayed for good news.

In the picture, which I'd studied a few times when Sonia wasn't around, Jorge was sitting on a stone bench, dressed in well-worn army fatigues, a machine gun propped against his left leg, smiling confidently at the camera. He looked young and happy, an adolescent male having the time of his life.

Sometimes Sonia was selfish and prayed only for her nephew, but more often than not, she included all the "wolf cubs" fighting against the Contras. Occasionally, she was very altruistic and prayed for everyone on the planet, including President Reagan who she hoped would find something more important to focus on besides Nicaragua.

That afternoon, Sonia decided to teach me how to cha-cha. I wasn't enthusiastic about the idea (like most gays in North America, the only music I'd ever danced to was disco), but once she'd dragged me to my feet, I decided to be a good sport. At first, she couldn't stop laughing at my self-conscious attempts to mimic the easy way she moved. Finally, she stood behind me with her hands on my hips, swiveling them around as I stepped forward and back chanting, "One, two, cha-cha-cha." After a while, I improved enough and she faced me again, and for more than an hour we danced barefoot without music on the tile floor in her living room. I can still do it now, the footwork smooth and easy, my hips and shoulders moving expertly the way my teacher taught me. Unlike disco, though, you really need two people to cha-cha, which may be one of the reasons ballroom dancing is still popular and disco isn't.

That evening during supper, Estelle dropped by with a letter for me. There was no return address on the envelope, but I recognized the handwriting. Vickie must have given it to Maggie who'd sent it in care of Estelle. I took the letter and stuck it in my pocket. Later, when I was alone in my room, I sat on my cot and stared at the envelope, postponing the inevitable news that Vickie had had enough. Finally, I took a deep breath and ripped it open. Maybe she's not angry, I told myself as I straightened the two pages. Maybe she just misses me.

Dear Rachel,

I just got off the phone with you and I feel sad, angry and confused. I decided to write this letter with no expectation that you'll respond anytime soon. First of all, I think you're a liar (which didn't used to bother me as much as it does now) and that you haven't sent me any letters. If I'm wrong and get one in the next few days, I'll feel embarrassed and happily surprised. But I'm not holding my breath.

What I want to say is how familiar it feels not to expect very much from you. I don't think it's okay anymore. In fact, I don't think it was ever okay. I love you a lot, Rachel. If you came back tomorrow, I'd probably forget everything I'm saying, or at least bury it somewhere deep and never try to find it. But I don't think you're coming home anytime soon. I think you're lost in your grief and that you're having (how can I say this without sounding unkind? I can't) an existential tantrum.

I'm sorry, sweetheart. Maybe I'd feel more empathy if you hadn't left. I know I would. But here it is: I'm tired of waiting for you to figure out how to live in this world. I'm tired of waiting for you to learn the crucial art of balance. Some people can't. Maybe you're one of them.

God, this sounds so bitchy, so unsympathetic, and I'm not. I'm really not. Each time you shut me out because your pain seems unendurable, I'm forced to shut down too. And I'm worried that if I have to shut down too long, I might not be able to come back. This isn't a threat, Rachel—it's actually a love letter although you probably won't perceive it that way. Oh well.

Until whenever,

Vickie

I reread the letter twice, then folded it up, and tucked it carefully into my duffel. The letter wasn't as bad as I'd feared. The relationship wasn't over. All I had to do was learn the crucial art of balance and everything would be all right. I sank down on my cot and tried to imagine what steps I could take short of a lobotomy that might help me learn it in time. There were probably a thousand books on the subject—I imagined some possible titles: *Living La Vida Loca, Say No To Existential Tantrums*—but I wasn't likely to find any of them in the few, poorly stocked bookstores in Managua. Liz might be helpful, though. I could talk to her, see if she had any tips.

A few minutes later, I heard Sonia changing out of her clothes and preparing for bed. I'd promised her more than a week ago I'd pray for Jorge, but so far I hadn't. She would have no way of knowing, of course, but that wasn't the point. Although I'd lied to Vickie more times than I cared to count, for some reason I still didn't think of myself as a liar. I looked up at the ceiling and sighed. What the hell.

I climbed out of bed and tried kneeling on the floor the way children in fairy tales prayed, but it felt so ridiculous I settled for sitting on the edge of my cot. Now what? I clasped my hands together, then immediately unclasped them. In the unlikely event God existed, He, She, or It would surely have a well-developed bullshit detector. All right, just a short prayer for Jorge, for his safe return, and then I could lie down again. So, how did one start? Hell if I knew. Did people take lessons? I'd attended a few Bible classes when I was ten and learned how Noah escaped the flood, something about a burning bush, how the Jews had to bake matzos on their way out of Egypt, but whatever prayers I'd learned had long since disappeared into one of the many Bermuda Triangles in my mind. I would have to improvise.

"Okay God," I whispered, "this is my prayer. First of all, if Jorge isn't dead already, could you please try to save him? Sonia will be devastated if he doesn't come back. And while I'm at it, could you also watch out for her? I think she might be sick. And for Amelia too. Well, for all the people in Nicaragua." I paused. "And hey, if there's any way I could learn the art of balance before Vickie leaves me, I'd appreciate that as well. Thanks. Bye."

I rolled my eyes, climbed back into bed, and tried to sleep. For the first time in a month, my chicken didn't show up at dawn and I feared the worst. I waited an hour just to make sure, but she never came.

***

Our trip north to Ocotal was surprisingly uneventful: no flat tires, no DDT at lunch, no distant gunfire. It made us a little nervous, as if something very bad would now have to happen to make up for it. We stayed at the same hotel as before and prepared for bed with an eye toward being able to jump up at a moment's notice, grab our shoes, and run.

That night, Liz and I shared a room with only one bed in it. Since the bed was shaped like a bowl, there was no way we could stick to our respective sides. Each time we tried to inch our way apart, we'd slide back down into each other. After a while, we gave up and lay still.

"This whole trip is about surrender," I muttered.

"Tell me about it."

We said good night, and then curled up with our knees almost touching our chins and our backs pressed against each other. Miraculously, we managed to doze off and sleep about five hours before a burst of gunfire woke us at four thirty. A few minutes later, we heard a couple of machine guns that seemed a little closer, but after that, nothing. We waited another fifteen minutes but that was it.

"Do you think you can go back to sleep?" Liz asked.

"No way. What about you?"

"Let's go outside and watch the sun come up," she suggested.

"That's a great idea."

We climbed out of bed, padded out into the courtyard, and sat down on the cool pavement. No one else was there. The unexpected silence was exquisite. No barking dogs, no roosters crowing, no people shooting at each other.

I stared at the large empty fountain and imagined how pretty it must have looked when it was full of flowing water and the grounds surrounding it were all kept up. Perhaps the Somoza supporters who'd once lived here weren't bad people, just happily ignorant. Since time immemorial, they might have reasoned, there had always been a division between rich and poor; everyone was entitled to inherit whatever their ancestors chose to leave them, and if the Somozas were corrupt, at least they kept the country running smoothly. As the sky metamorphosed from gray to mauve and then eventually to orange, I considered telling Liz about my relationship with Vickie and the letter I'd just received. But it was so quiet and I didn't think I'd feel any better after I told her. So I didn't. When it finally got too hot, we roused ourselves to go back inside.

As we stood up, my friend put her hand on my shoulder and said, "Rachel, I don't think you should stay here that long."

I was getting a little sick of people telling me what to do and how to live. "Yes I know, Liz, you've told me that before. Why does everyone think I'm so incapable?"

She looked surprised. "I don't think you're incapable. I think you're one of the strongest, most capable women I've ever met."

"Then why shouldn't I stay?"

She hesitated. "Because you're too sad."

I stared at her. "Don't be ridiculous. Everybody's sad here. I'll fit right in." Did I *look* sad? "Besides, it's normal to be sad. Anyone who lives the examined life is sad."

She shook her head. "That's not true, Rachel. I'm not sad. Just because you care about the world doesn't mean you have to be sad." She still had her hand on my shoulder.

"Well, I just lost a big case." And my girlfriend was going to leave me as soon as she realized I couldn't bear the idea of coming home.

Liz kissed my cheek. "And if you take my good advice and leave, which I hope you do, I'll miss you very much." Her face in the early morning light, looked peaceful and rested, as if she'd spent the night in a different hotel than I had.

"Well, don't start grieving," I told her. "I make a point of never taking anyone's good advice."

She sighed. "Okay, I tried. Let's round everyone up and get some breakfast." She looked at her watch. "The army is supposed to be here in a couple of hours."

"Yeah, right," I said and we both snickered.

***

In Nicaragua, nobody intended to lie. When people said they would do something or be somewhere at a certain time, they meant it but because of circumstances beyond their control, it was usually impossible. When the army promised us an escort at eight, they meant it was their *intention* to get there at eight, and if they showed up anytime that day or even the next, we'd be lucky. As it turned out, we were very lucky and they were only six hours late.

Our escort consisted of five Nicaraguan teenagers who looked as if they'd all decided to dress up as soldiers for Halloween. I doubted if any of them were older than eighteen. Two of them were young women. Each one carried the requisite AK-47 slung across their back. The soldiers spoke with Tim and Estelle first, shook their hands, and then Tim introduced them to us: Omar, Francisco, Javier, Miriam and Marta. Omar and Francisco were already grinning at Veronica who was probably two years older than they were.

Ten minutes later, after speaking with someone on their radio, the teenagers hopped into their plain brown jeep and shouted for us to follow. We all cheered, then clambered into our truck and began the last leg of our journey to Jalapa.

"Do you think it really exists?" Allen grinned at me.

"Yes, Dorothy, I think it does."

As we picked up speed, Estelle was trying to look stern. She was leaning forward, her short blond hair blowing in the wind. "Now remember," she warned, "this isn't completely safe. The road is twenty-five miles long, mostly unpaved, full of bumps, potholes and dozens of hairpin turns. We'll be driving parallel to the border, staying just a few kilometers south. As you can already see, the terrain on either side of us is different than what we've been used to. Lots of cliffs and canyons. Stay calm, but stay awake." She paused. "I can't believe it, but we're almost there."

Tim put his arm around her and she allowed herself to lean against him, the only indication that she might have been under any kind of pressure and would have liked, for just a couple of minutes, to let down her guard.

It was immediately apparent we were the only ones on the road. No more *campesinos* in sombreros riding mules or donkeys waving to us, or young women carrying fruit and vegetables glancing shyly as we passed them by. The fields of sugarcane and tobacco had been replaced by ominous-looking cliffs and hundreds of overhanging rocks. If all the bumps and ruts didn't keep us awake, our imaginations would.

After a while, we drove over a bridge that crossed a wide stream and rumbled into the tiny village of San Fernando. We saw a couple of kids fishing in the stream against a mountainous backdrop, but the main street was empty. The small wooden houses looked plain and humble, with only one or two windows to let in the light. Tim told us there was a permanent army garrison here because of all the attacks in the area. Instead of continuing straight through, our escort jeep turned off onto a smaller dirt road and disappeared from view. We had no choice but to follow. We assumed we were heading for the garrison, but a few minutes later, we saw the jeep pull up in front of a gray ramshackle house. We stopped behind the jeep.

"What are we doing here?" Lenny wondered out loud.

"Beats me," Tim said, jumping down from the truck.

Omar, the tallest of the teenagers, stepped inside the house and a couple of seconds later, a woman in her mid-thirties came rushing out, laughing, and calling to the other soldiers.

"Javier! Miriam! Francisco!"

She treated them like beloved errant children, grabbed their ears, smoothed their hair and kissed them. Omar was blushing and I guessed he was her son. The woman was strikingly beautiful, with high cheekbones, and thick dark hair in a braid that reached her waist.

"Come in, come in," she cried, grabbing Miriam's arm and waving at the others. Omar leaned toward her and whispered something. Immediately, she turned to us and shouted that we were all welcome and for everyone to please come in.

We looked uncertainly at Estelle. "Don't be rude," she said, smiling.

We jumped out of the truck and followed the soldiers inside. The house was hot and sparsely furnished, but obviously well cared for. I noticed a simple wooden cross on the wall, and a rifle propped just inside the doorway, like an umbrella you might grab on your way out in case of inclement weather. Our brigade stood in a cluster near the door while Estelle explained to Omar's mother who we were and what we were doing in Nicaragua.

When Estelle finished, Omar's mother approached each of us and shook our hand. Her name, she said, was Sandra and we were very welcome in her home. A moment later, she disappeared into the kitchen. The soldiers gestured toward a wooden bench and three uncomfortable looking chairs, insisting that we sit.

"We are soldiers," Javier laughed. "We aren't used to sitting on furniture. It'll make us weak."

To be polite, a few of us sat down. Francisco had already cornered Veronica near the doorway and was peppering her with questions that she clearly didn't understand although it didn't seem to matter. They were both smiling. Lenny tried one of the rickety chairs, then immediately got up and said something to Omar. Together, they squatted down and Lenny pointed to one of the legs. Omar nodded and then Lenny carefully set the chair on its side and began trying to fix it.

After chatting with Javier for a couple of minutes, Tim and Estelle wandered into the kitchen to help Sandra who was obviously planning to feed everyone before we left.

At one end of the bench, Liz had struck up a conversation with Miriam who was nodding very seriously. Liz's Spanish sounded smooth and confident; she would get along fine in Jalapa.

"Yes, I've often thought of becoming a nurse," Miriam was saying, "but I'm afraid it might be too hard to learn."

"Nonsense," Liz declared. "You have to study, of course, but I'm sure you could do it."

"I'd like to," Miriam said, nodding again. "My country needs nurses badly. The Contras keep killing them. And I don't mind the sight of blood." She blushed. "I mean I don't like it, but as a soldier, I've gotten used to it."

"I'm sorry to hear that," Liz said. "But it will make you a better nurse."

"Yes, that's what I tell myself."

At the other end of the bench, Allen, Richard and Susan were questioning Javier about the situation in Jalapa. Javier was laughing and clearly enjoying the attention. He had the confidence of someone at least ten years older and I imagined if he survived, he would rise quickly through the ranks to become a leader. Richard was translating the conversation for Allen.

"And so in the town itself," Javier concluded, "I think you should be safe." He paused. "Except on Saturday night."

"What happens then?" Allen asked.

"The soldiers all get drunk and then they like to shoot their guns. It's possible to get shot by accident."

"Oh great," Allen said, which made Javier double over with laughter.

"Allen, he's kidding," Richard said, then translated the comment into Spanish for Javier.

"Not really," Javier replied and laughed even harder.

I caught a whiff of fresh homemade tortillas and decided it was the best smell in the world. Lately, I hadn't been feeling well enough to eat much, but suddenly I was ravenous. Vickie was right—in Managua, I'd succumbed to an existential depression that stalked the city, preying on the weak and helpless. I'd been vulnerable and had let it catch me. But up here, I was beginning to feel like my old "can do" self again.

I saw Marta standing by the window and decided my Spanish was good enough to chat with her. She saw me approaching and looked expectant.

"Hello," I said. "My name is Rachel."

She had dark, shoulder-length hair, chocolate-brown eyes, and that beautiful olive skin that every Nicaraguan girl seemed to be blessed with. She looked strong and fit. She smiled and told me her real name was Leida but she didn't like it. Now that she was on her own, she was asking everyone to call her Marta.

I nodded in agreement. "Marta suits you better. Where are you from, Marta?"

"I grew up in Esteli." She pointed at the other soldiers. "The others are all from here. Where are you from?"

I thought for a moment. "Well, I grew up in the eastern part of the United States near the Atlantic Ocean, but for the last fifteen years I've lived in the state of Colorado where there are many high mountains."

Her eyes grew big. "Do you have a lot of snow?"

So I told her about skiing, and then about rock climbing. She had a dozen questions about climbing and how it could be done safely. She was almost eighteen and had been in the army for a year. She and her two older brothers had joined after her father was killed during an attack on an agricultural co-op north of Esteli.

"When they found him," she said, "he'd been shot more than thirty times, and his eyes had been cut out." Her voice sounded matter-of-fact, as if she were reciting a story that had nothing to do with her.

I shook my head. "That's terrible."

"Yes, thousands of people have died in this war."

And the survivors, I thought, had the worst PTSD imaginable. "There are many North Americans," I said, "who don't like our government and want it to stop supporting the Contras."

She looked grave, as if she hoped I was telling her the truth.

"But I don't know if our government will listen," I added.

"Perhaps you should overthrow your government." She wasn't kidding.

I considered telling her how unfeasible that was, but ended up simply nodding as if it were an option, and then changed the subject. "What would you like to do when the war is over?"

Her face softened and she looked like a teenager again. "I would like to go back to school and become a journalist. Then I could travel the world writing about various people and their struggles for freedom." She smiled broadly. "And maybe someday I could fly to Colorado and you could teach me how to climb."

I shrugged and nodded. "Well, if you can spare the time."

A few moments later, Sandra, Tim and Estelle emerged from the kitchen carrying platters piled with cheese, hard-boiled eggs, homemade tortillas and watermelon. I grabbed one of everything and attacked my food like a starving dog. Everything tasted wonderful. As we ate and talked and laughed, I had another perfect moment in Nicaragua, another magical chunk of time when I felt utterly content, as if everything I'd ever done in my life was worth it because it had brought me by some long circuitous route here to this particular time and place. Sometimes, I thought, you have to go a long way from home to find it again.

Finally, Javier looked at his watch and announced it was time to go. We all knew it was dangerous to be on the road after dark. Everyone hugged Sandra goodbye and thanked her. As the soldiers climbed into their jeep, Francisco patted the seat next to him and suggested Veronica switch places with Omar. Omar, he joked, could continue his conversation with the *Yanquis*, and he could continue his with Veronica. Both Javier and Estelle immediately shook their heads.

"It's not safe," they said in unison.

Veronica looked disappointed but joined us in the truck. Within minutes, we were back on the main road and lumbering, once again, toward Jalapa. It was almost six o'clock. The terrain seemed lonelier now and more deserted. Everyone was glad we'd stopped, but we were aware of the time and anxious to arrive before dusk. Because the road had so many curves, we often lost sight of the soldiers, but it was comforting to know they were less than a mile ahead of us. There were a couple of dark gray clouds overhead and I wondered if it was going to rain. It would feel nice, I decided, but would make the road muddy.

"This is such a great little country," Lenny was saying. "I wish I'd tape-recorded all of the conversations I've had with the various people

I've met here. I would force everyone I know back home to listen." He sighed. "But it probably wouldn't make any difference. You have to be here to understand."

At that moment, as we headed around a sharp curve, we heard a loud explosion. Everyone froze. Enrique's cigar fell out of his mouth as he braked to a halt, and then we just sat there looking stunned. Was it a landmine, an ambush, or both? We strained to hear any sounds of gunfire, of people running and shouting, but there was nothing. The silence was enormous. After two or three minutes, Estelle was standing up and shouting, "Go!" It seemed to take forever before the truck started to move. Everyone was leaning forward, looking pale and anxious, their eyes already glassy with anticipation.

Allen had grabbed my hand and was squeezing it much too hard. It hurt, but I didn't pull away. Later, my entire palm would turn purple.

"Allen," I said, "don't panic. They might be fine. Everything might be okay."

He was so upset he could barely speak. "You think so?"

I didn't, but I was a world-class liar, so I nodded and said, "It's possible."

CHAPTER FOURTEEN

We drove as fast as we could around two more curves before we saw a shallow burned-out crater about six feet wide in the middle of the road. A landmine, I thought, buried under a layer of dirt making it undetectable until they'd driven over it and triggered the explosion. We screeched to a halt and frantically craned our necks searching for the soldiers.

"Where the hell are they?" Estelle shouted.

A second later, we spotted the jeep, which had landed on its side halfway down a small hill just below the road. All of its wheels were gone and there was a gaping hole where the seats had been. Thick black smoke was gushing from the engine.

"We have to get them out of there!" Richard screamed.

Like everyone else, I leaped out of the truck and started running down the hill. I was sliding and falling, knocking into whoever was beside me in an effort to reach the soldiers as quickly as possible. The smoke was making me cough and it was getting harder to see. Fear was flowing through my arteries like an electrical current. As I hurried, a terrible knowledge was bearing down on me, probably just a couple of seconds away.

"They're not down there!" Estelle shouted from the road. I looked up and saw her arms waving back and forth like windshield wipers in a blizzard.

"Where are they?" Liz yelled, a few yards above me.

"Over here," Tim shouted from a little farther down the road, and I started scrambling in the direction of his voice.

I'd lost one of my sandals on the way down, but didn't stop to search for it. Go, go, go, I told myself, as I drove my body forward through the underbrush to get back up the hill.

Their bodies were scattered along the shoulder of the road, like bundles that had been tossed off the back of a truck. As I ran forward, I could hear Francisco moaning. He was lying facedown with both legs bent in anatomically impossible positions. Miriam was a few feet away, covered with blood. One of her hands was missing. Liz was on her knees leaning over her. She'd ripped her blouse off and was tearing it up to use as bandages.

Enrique, our driver, was panting right beside me. "Don't move them!" he shouted. "My brother died because they moved him. I know a doctor in town. I will bring him."

"No!" Liz yelled.

Enrique turned and started running toward the truck. As he ran, I heard Liz yell, "I'm a nurse! We have to take them to Jalapa now!" But Enrique had already jumped into the driver's seat and was starting the engine. Tim, who was closest to the truck, hopped in beside him.

"Goddamn it!" Liz yelled, then looked wildly around her, as if searching for something. She'd grabbed her first-aid kit from the truck, so that wasn't it. "I need water," she shouted. "Rachel, get me some water!"

Allen was throwing up on the side of the road. Veronica was trying to get to Francisco, but she kept falling down.

I ran to the truck just as it was pulling away. I jumped into the back, staggered down the aisle and gathered up as many water bottles as I could find. The truck was picking up speed and it was hard to keep my balance. Then I jumped off again, fell down, and lost my other sandal. My shins were bleeding, but I didn't feel any pain.

Estelle and Lenny were shouting that they'd found Omar and Marta. A few seconds later, Richard and Susan yelled that they'd found Javier.

"But he might be dead," Susan yelled.

I hurried back to Liz, gave her three of the bottles, and then ran across the road to where Richard and Susan were crouched next to Javier.

"Here's some water," I said, dropping a couple of bottles on the ground next to them. Their faces looked dazed, as if they'd just woken from a deep sleep. There was blood on their shirts and hands.

"He's not breathing," Richard was saying.

I glanced down at Javier's body and my stomach lurched. His eyes were half open and the expression on his face looked disappointed, as if there were still so many things he'd meant to do. I gazed at his hands, which were curled into useless fists. Perhaps he isn't dead, I thought, but then I noticed the blood behind his left ear and that the back of his skull was crushed. Which was why he wasn't breathing. And never would.

"Where's Lenny?" I asked.

It took Richard a couple of seconds to focus, but then he said, "Up the road with Marta. Across from where we stopped."

"Okay," I said. "And where's Estelle?"

Susan pointed behind us. "Not as far as Lenny, but down a small ravine. She's with Omar. I should go help her." She turned to her husband. "There's nothing we can do for Javier."

"I know," Richard said. "It's just that—"

I couldn't wait any longer. I picked up the water bottles and ran to the edge of the ravine. I could hear Omar moaning in pain.

"Estelle," I called, "here's some water." And then I tossed two of the bottles down to her.

"Thank you," she called back.

"Is he going to be all right?" I asked.

"I think so, but there's a piece of metal sticking in his thigh. He keeps trying to pull it out. I need Liz."

I nodded. "I'll see if she can leave Miriam for a minute."

"All right, thanks."

And then I rushed over to Lenny, who was kneeling over Marta's body, pressing the heels of his hands hard against her chest. She was unconscious and unresponsive, a Sleeping Beauty.

"Is she alive?" I asked.

Lenny made a strange exasperated sound, halfway between a sob and a shout. "How the hell should I know? I doubt it, but I don't want to stop CPR until Liz tells me to." He paused to wipe the sweat out of his eyes, or maybe the tears. "What do you think?"

I didn't have a clue. "I think you're doing the right thing, Lenny. Don't stop. I'll get Liz to come over as soon as possible."

He nodded. "I'll just keep doing this until she gets here."

As I hurried back to Liz, I was figuring first Marta and then Miriam and then Omar and then Francisco. I knew almost nothing about first aid, but from what I'd glimpsed, it seemed like a reasonable triage.

As soon as I told Liz everything I knew, she stood up and rolled her neck. "Okay, I'll be right back. Francisco's in a lot of pain, but he'll make it. I don't know about Miriam, though. She's lost a huge amount of blood. Right now she's stable, but that could change. If the bleeding starts up again, you'll need to tighten the tourniquet."

I tried to imagine the procedure. "Just twist it?"

Liz nodded. "Yes, it's very straightforward."

"All right then, I can do it."

"Are you sure?" She was staring at me.

"I'm positive. Go."

After Liz left, I could hear Francisco crying out and wished we could straighten his legs. I looked over and saw Veronica lying on the ground next to him, weeping softly. Out of the corner of my eye, I saw Allen stumbling up the road in the direction of Lenny and Marta.

I sat down next to Miriam and checked the tourniquet on her wrist. I didn't see any fresh blood oozing from the bandages covering the stump. I felt dizzy for a second, but then it passed. Liz had fashioned the tourniquet out of the strap from her bag and used a pen to tighten it. I couldn't help wondering where Miriam's hand was, if it was still intact, lying in the bushes nearby. I glanced at her face, which was pale and waxy looking, then realized she was shivering. I pulled my T-shirt off and draped it over her chest.

When Liz returned, she told me that Marta was dead.

I rubbed my face and sighed. "I guessed she was, but I still hoped you could save her."

Liz knelt down beside me. "She died before we got here. It was probably instantaneous."

I nodded, and then looked up at the sky, which was cloudless now, a dull monotonous blue. "What do you want me to do next?"

Liz leaned over and placed two of her fingers against the side of Miriam's neck, checking her pulse. "Go help Susan and Estelle. Make sure they keep Omar's hands away from that piece of metal. He's very strong and he really wants to yank it out, but he mustn't." She paused to wipe some tears that had leaked out of the corners of her eyes. "Richard, Lenny and Allen are sitting with Javier and Marta. Just let them be."

"All right," I said, then glanced toward Francisco who was still moaning. "Is there anything we can do for him?"

Liz shook her head. "No, we'd only make things worse. He needs an orthopedic surgeon."

I stood up and nodded. "That's what I thought. Okay then, I'm off."

A few seconds later, I reached the ravine and slid down the short embankment on my butt. Omar was conscious, but no longer struggling. Estelle was sitting on his right arm and Susan was holding his left. The ground around them was stained dark red. Both women looked exhausted, especially Susan.

"Watch that wound on his neck," Estelle was saying, "I don't want it to open up again."

I stared at the piece of metal stuck in Omar's thigh. It was dark silver, about five inches long and almost an inch thick. It must have originally been part of the jeep, maybe the engine. It was impossible to tell how deeply imbedded it was.

I knelt down beside Susan. "Would you like me to hold his arm for a while?"

She nodded gratefully.

As I took his arm, Omar began to whimper and rock from side to side. It was hard to watch.

"Do you know where Richard is?" Susan asked, smoothing Omar's forehead with a wet cloth.

"I think he's still with Javier," I said. "And Lenny and Allen are with Marta." I searched their faces. "She's dead. You know that, right?"

They both nodded.

Suddenly, Omar thrashed wildly and tore his right arm out from under Estelle. In one swift determined motion, he grabbed the end of the metal and pulled it straight out of his thigh. Bright red blood immediately began gushing from the wound.

Estelle ripped off her blouse, balled it up, and began pressing the material against his leg. Susan put her hands on top of Estelle's.

"We can't put enough pressure on this," Estelle cried. "It's bleeding right through."

I scrambled to the top of the ravine and shouted, "Liz! He pulled it out! The leg is gushing like a fountain. I don't think we can stop it."

I waited a second, then ran toward the road and repeated what I'd just said.

"Put a tourniquet above it!" Liz yelled. "Like the one on Miriam's wrist. Tighten it until the bleeding stops."

The sky around me was getting darker. Damn it, why hadn't anyone shown up yet?

"Rachel," Liz yelled. "Are you wearing a belt?"

I looked down at my waist. "Yes."

"Use that. I can't leave Miriam. Can you do it?"

Fuck, of course I could. "Yes, I can do it."

I rushed back to Omar and the two women. As I dropped to the ground, I slid my green canvas belt out of the loops of my shorts. While the women held Omar down, I wrapped the belt around his thigh a few inches above the wound and tried to pull it tight. The bleeding slowed down, but didn't stop.

"Help me pull it tighter," I said.

Both women tugged on the belt and between us, we got it pretty tight. Omar screamed a few times and then passed out from the pain. No matter how tight we pulled, however, there was still a small amount of blood spurting from the wound. Why wasn't it working? I pictured the tourniquet on Miriam's wrist and realized I needed a stick.

"Where's that piece of metal?" I asked.

Estelle began scrounging around until she found it in the dirt and gave it to me. With their help, I managed to tie a knot in the belt and then insert the piece of metal into the middle of the knot. Then, I twisted it just until the bleeding stopped.

We sighed with relief. After a while, Estelle figured out how to secure the metal with strips of cloth and we were finally able to remove our hands from his body.

"Thank God," Estelle breathed. Her face was bathed in sweat and her short blond hair was soaking wet. Susan nodded wordlessly, still trying to catch her breath.

I stood up. "I'll go tell Liz what's happening. And I'll try to get one of the guys over here."

My last assignment was to search for Miriam's hand.

"I know it's a long shot," Liz explained. "But maybe they can re-attach it. We should at least try to find it."

So Allen, Richard and I dutifully wandered up and down the road and then crawled through all the nearby gullies, but we never found her hand. Eventually, we gave up. In the meantime, Lenny went to help with Omar.

I walked back to Liz and dropped to the ground beside her. Together, we watched over Miriam while Richard and Veronica tried to soothe Francisco. Allen left to check on Omar but wasn't needed. When he returned, he lay down with his head in my lap.

A few minutes later, we saw a line of trucks and jeeps clattering toward us. The noise was unexpectedly loud and jarring, like an alarm clock in the middle of the night. We jumped to our feet and waited, suddenly aware that most of us were shirtless and covered in blood. I was shivering, but I couldn't have been cold; it was at least a hundred degrees. Allen grabbed my hand and I winced in pain. My shins were beginning to throb as well.

"It's the good guys, right?" Allen asked.

"Right," Liz assured him. "The bad guys don't announce themselves beforehand."

Allen nodded, but didn't let go of my hand until we saw Tim waving to us from the first truck. There were four more vehicles behind him, each one carrying three or four townspeople. Before the truck had completely stopped, Tim jumped down and ran to us. We put our arms around him, told him who was alive and who wasn't. The other cars pulled up and various people hopped out, some of them carrying rifles.

Estelle quickly stepped forward and explained the situation. In less than a minute, a decision was made to take the three soldiers who were still alive back to a hospital in Ocotal, and transport the other two to Jalapa where the army could arrange for their burial. A very pregnant woman volunteered to contact the families. A few moments later, with Estelle hurrying along beside them, the townspeople carried the soldiers to their vehicles and prepared to take off. And then, a minute or two after that, they were gone. One of the jeeps, with a few older men inside, remained behind to escort us to Jalapa. It was dark out but I had no idea what time it was. Somewhere along the way, I'd lost my watch. A small, pearl-colored moon had risen in the sky behind us and a couple of coyotes had begun to howl.

Tim told us that the Witness for Peace volunteers had been notified and were expecting us. The army, however, had changed its mind and wouldn't allow us to spend more than a night there.

"I'm sorry," Tim said, "but we have to leave by noon tomorrow. Only Liz can stay. They're saying they don't have the resources right now to protect us. I said we didn't care, but they're adamant. We have to go."

"No, that's impossible!" Susan shrieked. "We can't just turn around and leave. Look what it took to get here. I don't care how dangerous it is. I'm not afraid. I came to help and I'm staying."

Richard shook his head. "I'm sorry, bunny, but we can't."

Susan's face was smeared with dirt and blood. She looked half crazy in the moonlight. She shrieked again, then raised her fists and ran toward her husband who calmly stood his ground. She hit him twice in the chest, then collapsed in his arms and cried.

"It's all right, bunny," he crooned. "We'll come back next winter." He smoothed her hair with his free hand.

"But we came to help. I'm so disappointed."

"Me too, bunny. Next winter."

The rest of us trudged back to the truck and climbed in. A few minutes later, Richard and Susan, walking arm in arm, got in behind us. As soon as the engine started, Lenny yelled, "Wait." Enrique looked back at us.

"I don't know," Lenny said, shrugging slightly. "I guess I want to pay my last respects to Marta and Javier. Say goodbye to the others as well. We'll probably never see them again."

"I'd like to do that too," Veronica said.

We all nodded. Estelle motioned Enrique to turn off the engine. The jeep in front of us turned off theirs as well. We sat facing each other in the moonlight, wondering what to do next. I'd only been to one other funeral, my father's, and I realized now I had no memory of what anyone said or did during the entire event. At the time, though, I thought I was fine, that it was my mother who was seriously in shock, not me.

Estelle smiled sadly. "All right then, I'll start." Just like at our first meeting when we sat in a circle on the dirt floor of the community center. Our first morning in Nicaragua, which now seemed like a thousand years ago.

"I'd like to say goodbye to Javier," she said, "whose cockiness and machismo should have turned me off, but somehow didn't—instead, I was charmed. Although I barely knew him, I could tell he would have been a great leader, maybe a government official someday with a loving family and a mistress on the side. *Vaya con Dios,* Javier."

Richard nodded and began to sob. Susan immediately pulled him close to her and began to rock him back and forth.

Veronica wiped a few tears off her face and said, "Goodbye Francisco. It was really fun to flirt with you. I couldn't understand half of what you were saying, but maybe that's just as well. I hope your legs heal and that peace comes before you're tempted to enlist again."

There was another moment of silence and then Lenny spoke.

"Goodbye Omar. I sure hope the doctors can save your leg. I also wish you and your mother the best of luck with that restaurant you told me about. I'd love to come back some day and have a meal there, try some of your mother's famous pork tamales. *Hasta luego.*"

An owl hooted twice, then flapped its wings and took off over our heads. We looked up and watched as the dark heavy form disappeared into the night. No one spoke for a while. Finally, Liz shifted slightly, signaling her intention to go next. She looked down at her hands and sighed.

"What can I say, Miriam? It was such a pleasure talking with you, learning something about your life and aspirations. You would have made a great nurse. Maybe you still will. If I can, I'll get down to Ocotal and visit you. We can talk some more about nursing or about your brother's friend, the one who won't stop teasing you. In the meantime, we'll be praying for you."

Before anyone else could speak, I cleared my throat. "Goodbye Marta." My voice sounded strange. I wanted to say what a terrible shame it was that she wouldn't grow up to become a journalist and climb mountains, but suddenly I was afraid I might cry, and I never cried. It was a decision I'd made a long time ago when I first became a public defender. Criminal defense lawyers didn't cry. If they did, they might never stop. So I shook my head and said nothing.

Allen put his hand on my shoulder. "So long, Marta. You were very beautiful and had the most amazing biceps, much bigger and nicer than mine. I would have really liked spending more time getting to know you." He hesitated. "If your jeep hadn't hit that landmine first, we probably wouldn't be sitting here." He shook his head. "What a terrible day. *Adiós* Marta. *Adiós amigos*."

We sat for a little while longer listening to the coyotes calling to each other, an ancient, oddly reassuring sound. As if they had been in these hills forever and would still be there long after all the stupid humans had come and gone. Amen, I thought, and then as if he'd heard me, Enrique lit the stub of his cigar, puffed to get it going, then started the engine and headed for the Emerald City of Jalapa.

***

It took less than thirty minutes to reach the outskirts, but it wouldn't have mattered if it had taken hours. Time had finally ceased being important. We would get to wherever we were going when we got there. Although the road was pitch-black, no one was scared, or if they were, they didn't care. Fear, too, had become irrelevant. Besides, the worst had pretty much happened.

We drove into town and found the Witness for Peace house on a rutted dirt road a few blocks from the main square. If we looked bizarre, our hosts didn't mention it. They clapped us on the shoulders, offered us food, which we declined (our appetites having gone the way of our fear), and then led us to a small dark room full of cots. Since only two of the cots had mattresses, we took a quick vote and gave those to Lenny and Veronica. I could see a courtyard with trees through the window. We sat down on the beds, considered washing up, and then decided we were too tired.

One by one, fully dressed, we lay down on our metal springs and closed our eyes. Within seconds, everyone seemed to be asleep. After a while, a few of the guys began snoring. Sweet oblivion, but not for me. I lay face up in the darkness, feeling wired and irritable. Liz's cot was less than a foot away.

"Liz," I whispered, "how can you still believe in God?"

I'd assumed she was asleep, but she murmured, "God had nothing to do with it." I made an exasperated sound, but before I could say anything, she reached over and patted me on the shoulder. "It's okay, Rachel, some of my best friends are heathens. Now go to sleep."

CHAPTER FIFTEEN

In the morning, we ate hardboiled eggs and slices of fried cheese, then immediately queued up to take showers. We were all still wearing our clothes from the day before—no sense changing until we'd washed the blood off our bodies. When it was my turn, I didn't care that I had to share the primitive bathroom with a small tarantula. I showered quickly, aware that three people were waiting behind me. It felt wonderful to wash all the dirt and dried blood off my hands and feet. Both shins and an elbow were badly scraped, but other than a few blood blisters on each heel, my feet were miraculously free of injury. As I examined my elbow, I wondered again whether Miriam, Omar and Francisco had survived the night. So far, Estelle hadn't been able to reach the hospital. Patience wasn't just a virtue in Nicaragua, it was a commandment.

When I'd finished toweling off, I stared at myself in the small cracked mirror hanging over the washbasin. There I was, a slim, dark, ethnic-looking woman in her mid-thirties, nice eyebrows, black shoulder-length hair, and a full, slightly crooked mouth. Except for the dark circles under my eyes and a pallid complexion, I wasn't bad looking. Of course my biceps and stomach muscles weren't nearly so impressive after a month of no climbing, hiking or weightlifting, but from past experience, I knew I could get it all back in a couple of weeks (although having a washboard stomach didn't seem quite so important anymore). Actually, considering the events of the past twenty-four hours, I looked remarkably well, remarkably untouched. My headache and slight fever were back, but that was to be expected. In fact, if this was the worst I would feel, I was one lucky lady.

I let my eyes close for a moment. All of a sudden, I was remembering the last conversation I'd had with Emily when she'd begged me to accept her conviction. How impossible it had seemed at the time, how counterintuitive. And now, how simple—at least in theory. As if she'd begged me to accept my age, or the fact that my father was dead. How could I not accept those things? What good would it do? And that's when it hit me, the ineluctable bottom line truth: whether I accepted it or not, my sweet gentle friend was going to spend the rest of her life in prison. I could rage until the cows came home, but in the end, after I'd cursed and shouted, banged my head on the floor, and broken all my toys, my client would still be doing life. So what had I been thinking? I opened my eyes and gazed at myself in the mirror again.

"Those are some pretty dark circles under your eyes, lady," I murmured, then quickly dressed and exited the bathroom.

***

We spent the rest of the morning sitting around the courtyard drinking coffee and watching lizards chase each other up and down the trees. For the first time since we'd come together as a group, no one felt like talking. The only thing that mattered was what had happened the day before and at least for the moment, there wasn't anything more to say about it. To chat about anything else, though, seemed inconceivably crass, like discussing an upcoming ski trip at someone's funeral.

We could have gotten up and explored the town, of course, but no one felt like it. Our curiosity had been extinguished. And so we sat and listened to the sounds made by others, to the birds squawking overhead, to the half-hearted barking of some neighborhood dogs, to the rumble of an occasional truck negotiating its way over and around the least serious ruts in the road. Occasionally someone would sigh or yawn or stand up and then sit down again.

In the meantime, Tim and Estelle disappeared to make phone calls. They hoped to get through to the hospital in Ocotal, contact our host families in Managua, and obtain as much information as they could about flight schedules. A brigade from California was due to arrive tomorrow and its members would be staying with our families. Since there was no time to set up alternative housing, most of the group planned to leave immediately.

Around noon, one of the volunteers who lived in the house, a hearty Texan named Miranda, stuck her head through the doorway.

"*Compañeros*, we have more coffee and one of our neighbors just brought over some homemade tortillas. You're welcome to share them with us."

We all stood up and headed for the kitchen. No one was hungry, but it gave us something to do, something to fill up the time before we had to leave.

A little while later, Tim and Estelle returned with good news: all three of our friends were stable and would probably survive.

"That's wonderful," Liz said, beaming at everyone. "I didn't think Miriam would make it. To tell you the truth, I had my doubts about Omar as well." She looked around the table. "Well, maybe now I can eat something. Are there any tortillas left?"

Liz has the perfect constitution for this place, I thought, as she reached for the basket of tortillas. Like everyone who lived here, she would fuel herself on a diet of anger, determination and hope. She would not succumb to despair. If nothing else, she was too practical. Unless she happened to get shot, blown up or kidnapped, she'd be fine. No, more than fine, fulfilled.

Finally, it was time to leave. Our bags were in the truck and Enrique was motioning for us to climb aboard. We all crowded around Liz to say our last goodbyes. Allen started to cry. Liz and I both put our arms around him.

"Take care of yourselves," Liz said. Her eyes were sparkling with happiness. Unlike us, she was home. "I'll miss you all."

"Promise us you won't get killed," Allen said, wiping the tears off his face.

Liz shrugged helplessly, but I nudged her in the ribs. "How about this," she said. "I'll do everything humanly possible to keep myself safe."

He shook his head. No, not good enough.

She sighed and pulled him close to her. "Okay, fine, I promise not to get killed."

"Good," he said.

One by one, the group hopped into the back of the truck. As I stepped onto the running board, Liz grabbed me around the waist and whispered, "You did good yesterday. You know that, right?"

I nodded. "We all did."

"Every time we act, it makes a difference, Rachel. And every little difference matters."

I thought for a moment. "You might be right."

She laughed and squeezed my arm. "Then there's hope for you yet, my friend. *Hasta luego.*"

As the truck lurched forward, we waved at Liz until she was out of sight, then we swiveled around to catch a quick glimpse of Jalapa. None of the streets were paved. The simple wooden houses had once been painted in assorted shades of blue, pink, white and yellow, but the colors had long since faded. As we rumbled toward the edge of town, I saw groups of women and children walking along the road. No one seemed to be hurrying. There were plenty of trees and even a slight breeze. Ahead of us, a couple of skinny dogs were running around in circles, chasing their tails. In the middle of the day, the place seemed peaceful and idyllic. We lumbered across a rickety wooden bridge, swerved for a couple of pigs, and then headed down the long dirt road toward the capital. In the distance, we heard five or six gunshots, but then nothing more.

As usual, the day was hot and clear. The cliffs on either side of the road seemed less ominous, probably because we were heading away from them. As we approached the spot where the soldiers had been blown up, everyone began to fidget and look uncomfortable. The truck slowed and Enrique mumbled something and then crossed himself. The jeep, of course, was still lying on the side of the hill, but it was already impossible to tell how long it had been there. Now it seemed like part of the landscape, incorporated overnight into the larger ongoing story and later when the war finally ended, into a rusty souvenir of the times. The road curved and in an instant the jeep was out of sight.

After a quick stop in Esteli, we headed straight for the airport to drop off Veronica and Lenny. Estelle had managed to book two seats on a plane leaving for El Salvador at six thirty. Supposedly, there was a connecting flight around midnight from there to the United States. Allen, Susan and Richard were scheduled to depart the next morning. Since I still couldn't decide what to do for the rest of my life, Estelle hadn't booked anything for me. She and Tim planned to stick around Managua for a couple of days, then attempt another trip north to Jalapa.

If possible, I would try to keep my place at Sonia's. I felt safe and comfortable there and needed time to think. Otherwise, I was a girl without a plan. Somehow, I couldn't picture myself booking a room at the Intercontinental, mingling with journalists and spies at the breakfast buffet.

In the old days, I could always see a year or two into my future and eventually I'd rebelled. Now, I could barely imagine the next few hours.

It was harder than I expected to watch Lenny and Veronica vanish into the terminal. From the back, Lenny's hair looked more white than blond. And he was listing slightly, like a tired sailor. Veronica walked close beside him, as if they were related and had always loved each other. I'd miss them both. Right before they disappeared, Veronica held up her fist in a gesture of solidarity.

"Remind me never to care for anyone ever again," Allen muttered. "It's too fucking painful when they go." He was staring at me and I worried he might start crying again.

"I have an idea," I said. "Let's meet for dinner at that restaurant near the Managua Cathedral. Sonia says they have great beans and cream. We can order beer and get tipsy and sentimental."

"I don't think I can get any more sentimental," Allen said. "But I could certainly try."

"Good, I'll meet you there at seven."

At the community center, I said goodbye to the rest of the group and proceeded down the street to Sonia's house. I pushed open the broken gate, knocked on her door, and waited. A second later, she was hugging me.

"I was so worried," she told me as she led me toward the kitchen. "How are you?"

I shrugged. "A little tired, but I'm fine. Did you hear about the soldiers?"

She nodded gravely. "They said that two had died and that the other three will live."

"They were so young, Sonia." I flashed on Marta's lovely animated face as she described her plans to become a journalist and travel around the world. And then, on the way she looked as Lenny tried in vain to save her. The blank expression, her vacant eyes.

"Yes," Sonia said, "our children are fighting the war for us." She sounded unusually sad and I guessed she was thinking about her nephew. I didn't ask if she'd heard from him; she would have shared the news immediately.

We sat down at her kitchen table and ate some pineapple. I told her I hadn't decided what to do next and wondered if I could stay there for a while. She hesitated, and then admitted she was expecting another boarder the next evening. I said I understood. She thought for a moment and then her face lit up. She could borrow a cot from Amelia and then I could share her room for as long as I wanted. Suddenly, I had the decency to feel embarrassed.

"Thank you," I said. "But you'll have enough to do. You don't need two boarders."

She raised her hand to ward off any more halfhearted arguments. "It's not a problem. You're my friend. You're welcome to stay for as long as you wish."

If I'd had any self-respect, which I clearly didn't, I would have stood up and left, but I was simply too tired. "Well, just for a few days then, maybe a week. And I insist on paying you directly since the brigade is no longer responsible."

She clapped her hands together. "Good. With all the money I'll be getting from two boarders instead of one, I can finally buy a car."

I managed to smile a little and said, "I don't know about you, but in this climate I'd look around for a convertible."

***

That evening, I met Allen at the restaurant near the cathedral. He'd showered again and was wearing his prettiest Hawaiian shirt. He looked fresh and neat like a young man out on a date or, considering how old I was, a gigolo. We sat at a table for two near an empty birdcage.

"No more than a couple of beers," I warned. "We'll get too maudlin."

"God forbid," he said, patting my hand.

I picked up the menu and pretended to read it. Sonia had already told me that despite the four-page menu, the choices were severely limited to *pinto gallo* or *frijoles con crema*. "I hear the beans and cream are fantastic here."

"Really? Well then that's what I'm going to order."

"Me too." We both smiled.

When our beers arrived, Allen raised his bottle to me and said, "To friendship."

"To friendship," I repeated. Suddenly, I wished Allen had left that afternoon and that I didn't have to sit across from him all evening contemplating his imminent departure. It was too painful. As I'd suspected, sometime in the last month when I wasn't paying much attention, he'd marched right past the barricades into my inner sanctum, kicked off his shoes, and made himself at home.

"Ask me anything you want about law school," I said. "It's your last chance."

He knew what I meant: keep it light, my friend. And he did his best. For the next hour, I described my experiences in law school, talked about being a public defender, and discussed a few notable cases. Then, I asked Allen to tell me about his father and why he felt such disdain for him.

"That's easy," Allen said. "He treats women like shit and thinks J. Edgar Hoover was a great American hero."

"Well that's somewhat...compelling," I said. And we both laughed.

At the end of the meal, the waiter arrived with our check. We paid the bill, about six dollars, and headed for the door. The air outside was hot and humid.

"Let's walk home," Allen suggested.

"Fine with me." I wasn't looking forward to another restless night on another broken-down cot. Maybe hiking four or five miles would tire me out enough that it finally wouldn't matter. Sure, and maybe the United States would change its mind and stop funding the Contras. Maybe, before I died, there'd be an unprecedented period of world peace.

Allen took my hand and we set off across the plaza. As we made our way through the crowded streets, the city flowed around us, a cacophony of buses honking, mufflers backfiring, roosters crowing and groups of people strolling arm in arm, laughing, shouting and living. At an intersection a few blocks from the community center, a man in a wheelchair was selling the latest issue of *La Barricada*. I bought one for Sonia who probably wouldn't read it, but could at least use it for toilet paper.

"Thanks for your support," the man said.

"No problem," I replied.

Finally, we were standing in front of the center, sweating from the long walk. It was almost eleven o'clock. Allen's face was red, but I didn't think it was from the exercise.

"Rachel, can I ask you one last question? You don't have to answer it if you don't want to."

"Go ahead," I sighed.

He tried to smile. "I can't help it." He looked both awkward and adorable.

"It's okay."

He took my hand in his and kissed it. "So, if I was a woman and you were single, would you be the least bit attracted to me?"

It was such a ridiculous question, but there was no point in stating the obvious. He looked at me with his innocent brown eyes and waited. I grabbed him and pulled him close to me. "If you were a woman and you were at least six years older and I was single, I'd be head over heels in love with you."

"Really?" he whispered.

"Maybe."

He hugged me for as long as he dared, then said, "Goodbye, Rachel. Write me when you can."

It was hard to breathe. He was so dear to me. I wanted to put him in my pocket and carry him around forever. "Goodbye Allen."

He turned and started walking away from me. After a couple of seconds, he began to run.

"I love you," he yelled.

I watched him until he turned the corner. Except for the enormous green iguana on the roof behind me, I was completely alone.

Less than an hour later, I was lying on my cot, wishing I could stop thinking and just sleep for a couple of weeks. I could deal with the headache, sore throat and fever, but I needed some internal silence. As I tossed and turned, I could hear Sonia preparing for bed. When she began praying for Jorge's safe return, I rolled over and pulled the pillow around my ears. I couldn't listen anymore. He wasn't coming home. He was dead, just like Javier and Marta.

But then I rolled back over and sat up, staring into the darkness. Why should I assume the worst? Why not hope for as long as possible? I pulled my sweaty sheet up to cover me. Why should anyone suffer before they absolutely had to? They shouldn't, I decided, and then lay back down again and fell into a fitful sleep.

A few hours before dawn, I woke up shivering and realized my sheet was soaking wet. I waited a few minutes, then sneaked into Sonia's room and pulled out a dry one from the bottom of her dresser.

"How long have you been here?" she asked as I was leaving.

"Not long, Sonia. Go back to sleep. Sorry to have disturbed you."

"Why didn't you contact me?" she asked, sounding pleased and excited, and I realized she was dreaming. I tiptoed out the door.

***

The next morning, I decided to walk to the dollar store, and if by some miracle it was open, buy as many bottles of vitamins as I could carry home. I would give them to Sonia and Amelia and anyone else in the *barrio* that might want them. If there were other things for sale, like toothpaste, toilet paper, Alka-Seltzer, hairbrushes and electric fans, I'd buy them too. If I had enough loot, I'd take a taxi home.

It seemed hotter than usual as I set out along the main cobblestone street toward the highway. At some point, I decided to take a shortcut across a field that would save me at least half a mile. In the distance, I could see a large three-story building that had either been hit by a bomb or destroyed by the earthquake; most of its walls and all of its windows were missing.

I hopped over a ditch full of dirty-looking water and saw a woman about my age washing her family's clothes. As she rinsed each article of clothing, she spread it on the ground to dry. She'd already laid out a pair of men's jeans, a yellow slip, a couple of blouses and some T-shirts.

"*Hola*," I said.

She smiled shyly, and then bent down to wash a faded pink towel. I watched for another few minutes, although there was nothing particularly fascinating about what she was doing. For one odd second, I thought I might be too sick to go on, but then the moment passed.

I reached the highway, and then began hiking toward the center of the city. Where was I going? What was I doing? This was stupid. The dollar store probably didn't even exist. My shirt was drenched and I felt a little faint. The road was long, hot and dusty. I could feel the heat through the soles of the cheap flip-flops Miranda had given me in Jalapa. To take my mind off my various physical discomforts, I counted to a hundred in Spanish, and then like an old Girl Scout began singing, "I've Been Working on the Railroad."

Dinah, won't you blow, Dinah, won't you blow...Suddenly my throat felt too parched to make another sound. Why hadn't I brought any water, and a hat? But I didn't own a hat.

Where was I going? What was I doing? Even if the store was open and they actually had vitamins they'd be so out of date, they'd be useless. But I kept on walking, putting one foot in front of the other.

About twenty minutes later, I caught up to a couple of children dragging a tree limb down the side of the highway. The limb was about ten feet long and must have weighed at least fifty pounds. The older of the two children, a boy, looked about seven; the younger girl was probably his sister. They were both barefoot. I guessed they lived in one of the shanty towns at the edge of the city and that they were hauling the tree home to their parents who would cut it up to use for fuel. The boy was pulling the tree from the front, while his sister was trying to push it from the back and sides. They could only drag it a couple of feet before they had to stop and rest. They looked tired, but determined.

I asked if I could help, but they ignored me. I was a stranger and a *Yanqui*. I took a step toward them, but it only made them work harder to get away from me. I stepped back a few yards into a small gully and let them inch past me. The soles of their feet must have been burning. At the rate they were moving, it would take them all day. I wondered if anyone would come looking for them after dark.

Finally, I had to turn away, but was surprised to find that I was kneeling. What the hell? I tried to stand up, but my legs refused to obey me. I waited a couple of seconds and tried again, but my legs had a mind of their own. The sun was beating down on the top of my head.

Where was I going? Apparently nowhere. What was I doing? Nothing. What a funny place to stop, I thought, and then slumped over until my forehead was touching the ground. From a distance, if you didn't know better, you might have thought I was praying.

CHAPTER SIXTEEN

I was lucid again, lying on my back, and burning up with fever. I had the worst headache, as if my skull were much too small to accommodate the pressure building up inside it. Every joint in my skeleton ached, my neck, shoulders, wrists, knees and ankles. Even my toes hurt. I opened my eyes for a moment, and then closed them when the light became too painful. I was tucked into a narrow gully only a few yards from the highway, but doubted anyone could see me. Although I knew I was sick and that I'd been lying there for hours, I couldn't imagine moving or calling out for help. A few cars drove by, so close I could smell their exhaust.

A voice was urging me to get up before it was too late. For a moment, I thought it was Vickie's and wondered how she'd found me, but then realized it was my own. I rolled to my knees, vomited, and then slowly forced myself to a standing position. When I felt like I wouldn't fall, I took a few baby steps toward the highway. I guessed it was late afternoon. To keep my head from exploding, I pressed the palms of my hands against the sides of my skull. More than anything, I wanted to lie down again and it took every last bit of my will to resist the impulse.

At first, I felt shy waving at the cars, but after twenty or thirty of them roared past me, I got used to it. Finally, I saw a cab that already had some passengers in the backseat. I must have looked pretty bad because the driver stopped anyway and let me get in front. *Muchas gracias*, I told him. As soon as the car accelerated, my body fell sideways until I was resting against his arm and shoulder. I was sweating profusely and smelled like vomit, but the driver was either too polite or embarrassed to push me away. After taking the group where they wanted to go, he drove me to Sonia's and deposited me on the front porch. I thanked him again and tried to give him money, but he wouldn't take it.

Time passed but I couldn't tell how much. One morning, just before dawn, I woke up feeling cool and clearheaded. Sonia was sleeping in her bed a few feet away from me and someone else (the new boarder?) was snoring in the other bedroom. All the feverish agitation—the crazy dreams, the hallucinations—seemed to have abated.

When I opened my eyes again, it was bright outside. Sonia was walking toward me with a bowl of soup in her hands. She looked relieved.

"*Hola*," she said, smiling. "*¿Cómo estás?*"

"*Mucho mejor.*" Much better.

"*Muy bien.*" She put the soup down on the table next to my cot and left to bring me a spoon. The soup smelled delicious although I didn't feel particularly hungry.

When she returned, I asked, "How long have I been sick?"

She counted the days on her fingers and then shrugged. "About four days." As if it were no big deal. And of course it wasn't, at least not here. If you weren't dead or missing, anything less serious was hardly worth mentioning.

I gazed down at myself, at the sheet tucked around my feet, at the unfamiliar slip I was wearing, and suddenly felt ashamed. Was there no limit to how much I could take from these people? Apparently not. "Thank you, Sonia. Thank you for everything. I'm sorry I've been such a burden."

Sonia waved her hand dismissively. "You weren't such a burden. Amelia and some of the other neighbors helped and mostly you just slept. But now you have to eat. You've lost weight and we're all jealous." She was joking of course. She'd lost at least ten pounds since Jorge disappeared.

"It's my new diet plan," I said. "Maybe we can make some money selling it to all the rich overweight people in Managua. You do the manicures, I'll do the counseling."

She grinned and nodded. "And then we can be rich and overweight ourselves. But first," she looked down at the table, "your soup is getting cold."

After I drank the soup, Sonia brought me a plate of rice and beans, which tasted better than any gourmet meal I'd ever had in the States. While I ate as much as I could, Sonia filled me in on the latest news: Tomas, it seemed, had had another "episode" and assaulted an older man, but after things were explained, the victim had forgiven him. A neighbor's husband had left her for a widow who lived around the corner. And there were rumors the *cordoba* might be devalued again.

***

By the end of the week, I felt well enough to get out of bed and take little walks around the neighborhood. As I grew stronger, I begged Sonia to let me do the shopping and whatever errands she wanted to fob off on me. I also tried to clean the house, but she wouldn't allow it. Finally, she agreed to let me do all the dishes.

Edward, the new boarder who lived in my bedroom, was a pleasant man in his fifties, a retired schoolteacher from the Bay Area. He was polite and unobtrusive, but his Spanish was almost nonexistent. Whenever he was around—which wasn't often—I did my best to translate conversations between him and Sonia. When I found out he didn't have a Spanish/English dictionary, I gave him mine. He thanked me profusely and told me he'd been searching all over Managua and hadn't been able to buy one. He was so grateful I thought he was going to cry. From then on, I never saw him without the dictionary. Like a security blanket, he took it with him everywhere, even to the bathroom where I heard him telling imaginary people his name was Edward, that he lived in California, and that he was grateful for the food.

While I convalesced, I made no effort to contact anyone except Vickie. Each time I called, however, the answering machine announced she was out of town on a river trip. A river trip? During our nine years together, she'd never expressed any interest in rafting or canoeing. She didn't really like boats. Sometimes she even got seasick, like the time we took the ferry from Boston to Provincetown. What the hell was she doing on a river trip? And with whom? So much for her sitting around the house pining for her absent lover.

Although I was definitely getting better, I knew I wasn't "well." After walking a couple of blocks, for instance, I'd have to stop and rest awhile. If I didn't, I'd feel dizzy and slightly nauseous. I still had my core strength, but it had dwindled from an ocean to a pond, too precious now to waste on unimportant tasks. And though my mind was clear again, it wasn't quite as nimble; sometimes it stumbled, which scared me more than my newfound fragility. Be patient, I counseled myself, and stay calm. Whatever was wrong with me had burrowed deep into the cells of my body and set up camp. Instinctively, I understood that a direct confrontation would be futile. For the time being, we would have to coexist. In a few months, with a little bit of luck and plenty of rest, I'd be fine.

Despite all of the above, I felt strangely content. When my fever broke for the last time, something else had broken too: my longtime alliance with righteous sadness. I wasn't singing in the rain, but I wasn't railing against it either. Like everyone around me, I didn't approve of the way things were, but I no longer *resisted* them. For one thing, it took too much energy.

For weeks, I'd wondered how Sonia and her fellow Managuans did it, how they persevered. How they walked the line between ridiculous optimism and deadly despair. Now I understood. And—now that I understood—it was simple: hopeful resignation, a state of mind in which you mostly focused on the present and hoped that things might improve sometime in the distant future. In the meantime, you lived, you helped your friends, they helped you, you went to parties, drank rum and danced. And, if you were so inclined, you prayed.

That was it. Eat, drink and be merry, for tomorrow you will die. Until I'd spent six weeks in Nicaragua, it had seemed like the most counterintuitive advice in the history of the world. In fact, though, it was the only sane response to the human condition.

During my seventh week, I left three more messages on Vickie's answering machine, but she was still on her river trip. At some point, I realized I had no idea which river she was even talking about—the Arkansas near Canon City, the Green in Utah, or maybe the Colorado running through Glenwood Springs? Hell, I didn't even know which state she was in. In the old days, this would have been inconceivable. I'd have known the smallest details of her day, how many patients she'd treated, when she'd stopped for lunch, what she'd eaten, when she'd be returning home. But the old days, of course, were over. In the meantime, my girlfriend was floating down a river having fun without me. Which was a good thing, sort of.

Ultimately, it was my father who got me out of the country. If I hadn't started thinking about him, I might have stayed much longer. But one morning while I was lying on my cot waiting for the dawn, I remembered jogging with him along the dunes near Provincetown. It had been warm enough to run without a jacket but still a little foggy, the sun just beginning to break through, a quintessential Cape Cod summer morning. I could smell the ocean and the purple salt spray roses that lined our path. Our feet made soft slippery sounds as we ran along the hard-packed sand, heading for the beach at Herring Cove.

Now and then, we saw men emerging from behind the dunes, a popular place for sex, and every time my father called out, "Good morning!" Although by then he was a full professor at Boston College, he treated everyone the same, whether you were the president of his college or the waitress who poured his coffee. It was in early June, about six months before his heart attack. He'd just turned fifty-six. I recalled how strong he looked that day (those gorgeous calf muscles, his military posture), how hard it was to keep up with him. Although children often think their parents are better looking than they really are, he was truly handsome, a Jewish Robert Mitchum with a wicked grin and a full head of thick black hair.

Suddenly, I realized I was only twenty years younger than my father when he died. And like my father, I'd misjudged my body, had assumed it could withstand whatever stress was heaped upon it. If I didn't start taking better care of myself, I might not last any longer than he did. Convalescing in a country under siege was better than not convalescing at all, but I had options. Unlike everyone around me, I could leave.

I sat up in bed and decided that I needed to get out as soon as possible and spend the next few months in a place where life was easier, where I could truly rest and recover. Someplace not currently at war and where the poverty and suffering was at least partially hidden from the tourists. In short, I needed a vacation.

Although I considered traveling to a country where I'd never been before, like Bali or Australia, I knew I lacked the strength to go anywhere new or exciting. In the past few months, I'd used up the last of my lifetime's allotment of adventure. I was living on credit now and whoever inhabited my body in the next incarnation would probably have to spend her entire life waiting tables in a diner somewhere in Kansas or Oklahoma.

***

The night before I left Managua, Sonia invited a few of her friends and neighbors over for a going-away party. Naturally everyone and their relatives showed up, including Tomas who seemed to have forgotten that he'd ever tried to shoot me. Earlier in the day, Sonia and I set up a dozen borrowed chairs on the patio and strung a few extra lightbulbs along the high cement wall. We made fried potatoes and beans with cream. Amelia volunteered to mix up a batch of lemonade and rum. From eight o'clock until we pushed everyone out at two, we danced, drank and talked passionately about politics.

Edward, the boarder who shared the house with me and Sonia, had invited a few members of his brigade and toward the end of the night, I found myself sitting in a corner of the patio surrounded by a group of earnest, good-hearted North Americans who wanted advice about leaving tips for their hosts and whether they should disassemble the bleachers inside the community center the day before some flooring was supposed to be delivered.

I looked around the group and shrugged. "Well, the official policy on tips is this. You're paying for your room and board so it's an equal exchange. Charity is unnecessary, patronizing and possibly insulting." I paused. "But I think small gifts are acceptable."

One of the women nodded and said, "That makes sense." She'd been introduced as one of Edward's former colleagues who'd taught history and math for over thirty years. "May I ask what you think is an appropriate gift?"

I shook my head. "You should ask someone else. Personally, I'm leaving anything I think Sonia can use, and most of my cash as well."

The group burst out laughing, clearly enjoying my candor. I felt like a celebrity being interviewed by a small gaggle of fans who hung on my every word.

"What about the bleachers?" Edward asked.

I started to chuckle. "You mean taking them apart and hauling the pieces outside before you actually see the promised flooring? I thought you were kidding."

Someone snickered and then they all simply nodded.

I crawled into bed around three, dangerously exhausted, but couldn't fall asleep. I told myself I was just anxious about the taxi that was supposed to pick me up at six, but of course it was much more than that. My life in this dear godforsaken country was coming to an end. Like a bad but totally compelling relationship, I couldn't imagine staying for even one more day, but I couldn't bear the thought of leaving either.

A few hours later, I was standing in the living room with my duffel bag slung across my shoulder. I'd hidden a wad of cash in the drawer where Sonia kept her sheets and towels. She would find it in the next few days but I'd be gone by then. The taxi was honking and Sonia was hugging me goodbye.

"*Gracias por todo,*" I whispered in her ear. *Thank you for everything.*

She nodded and hugged me closer. "*Buena suerte, mi amiga.*" *Good luck, my friend.* As if I were the one staying in the war-torn country and she was the one getting out.

And then I was climbing into the back of the cab and heading for the airport. For the length of the ride, I sat with my face pressed up against the grimy window trying to memorize the way everything looked. An hour later, as I scurried up the rickety metal stairs into the belly of the plane, as I settled into my seat and waited for the doors to close, and as the plane skidded down the bumpy runway and finally lifted off, I knew exactly how that tiny privileged group of survivors felt as they huddled in their lifeboats and watched from a safe distance as the Titanic slowly sank into the dark frigid waters of the North Atlantic ocean. Sickeningly guilty, but so incredibly relieved.

As the plane gained altitude and the land disappeared from view, I couldn't decide which I regretted more: coming or leaving.

***

Twelve hours later, I was wandering like a ghost through the Dallas airport waiting for my next plane, the one that would take me directly to Zihuatanejo. It hadn't occurred to me that the culture shock entering the United States might be worse than what I'd experienced landing in Nicaragua. The minute I stepped off the plane, I was caught up in a stream of busy, self-absorbed, thoughtlessly happy people. Decent folks who knew nothing about what we were doing in Nicaragua and who wouldn't have believed me if I told them. I'd be just another liberal kook, as annoying as the Hare Krishnas buttonholing people on their way in and out of the bathrooms.

As I floated through the crowd, I couldn't get over how well-dressed everyone looked (even the little kids), how casually they slung their two-hundred-dollar leather bags over their shoulders and took a couple of bites out of their expensive sandwiches before dumping the rest into trash cans as they hurried past. In my flip-flops, torn khaki pants and cheap cotton T-shirt, I felt like an intruder from the wrong side of the tracks, that I'd snuck into some high-society ball and it was only a matter of time before the butler noticed and ordered me out.

I tried calling Vickie, but the phone was busy. So she'd finally returned from her trip. I poked my head into a couple of stores, but had to leave almost as soon as I walked in. I couldn't believe all the useless gadgets for sale and how much food there was everywhere. I wanted to yell, "This is obscene!" But I didn't, not because I was afraid to sound crazy, but because I thought no one would agree with me.

Every time I passed a phone, I tried Vickie's (and my) number, but it was always busy. I felt a little feverish and hoped the traveling hadn't set me back too far. Eventually, I ended up in the women's bathroom where I stared at myself in the mirror searching for some changeless quality to hold onto, some familiar steadiness reflected around my eyes or mouth that I could be sure of. I drank endlessly from the water faucet, then sat down in one of the stalls and stared at the door. Someone had scrawled, "My heart belongs to Frank," and underneath that, perhaps as an afterthought, "but my cunt belongs to Darrell." Poor Frank, I thought.

At least it was quiet. After ten or fifteen minutes, the wooziness passed and a feeling of not exactly peace but something distantly related to it, settled over me. I was ready for the next chapter.

I hurried to the nearest phone, dialed the number, and this time Vickie picked up after the first ring. She sounded distracted, as if she were in the middle of something. I almost hung up but instead I said, "Hello."

There was a long silence. "Hey," she finally said.

"Hey yourself." And to think I once made my living using words.

After an even longer period of silence, she cleared her throat and said, "Well first of all, I want to thank you for the phone messages," as if I were a stranger who'd recently contributed to the American Cancer Society. "Maggie told me what happened in Jalapa, but I had no idea where you went afterward. I was pretty worried."

"But not too worried to go on your river trip," I quipped, thinking it would sound like a joke, but realizing too late that it sounded more like an accusation.

Vickie, however, simply chuckled. "No, not too worried to go on my river trip. It was a great trip, really fun. So, how are you?"

I blew out a deep breath. "Overall I'm good. Except right now I'm feeling kind of shy and awkward. It's been too long—my fault of course—since we've heard each other's voices. I'm sorry I didn't send you any letters and that I didn't call you sooner. I don't know how to explain it."

"You don't have to, Rachel. It's okay. I'm not mad." She hesitated. "Well, at first I was. That's when I sent you that letter. But after a few more weeks, I decided it was actually for the best."

I opened my mouth, closed it, and thought for a moment. I was leaning against a beige carpeted wall, which felt odd and wrong, as if I were lying down but didn't know it. Finally I asked, "What do you mean for the best?"

She laughed airily, as if I were being much too serious. "I mean it was good to have some time and space to think."

I forced myself to say it. "About us?"

She cleared her throat again. "About us, about me, about everything."

"Well that's a bit vague."

"Come on, Rachel, we're on the phone. Let's just leave it. When you get home, we'll talk. No rush."

A few feet away from me, an elegantly dressed man was shouting into the phone at his secretary for not packing the right papers into his briefcase before he left the office. What was I doing? If our conversation continued down the same road, in two or three minutes, we'd reach an intersection where my girlfriend might be forced to turn left while I steered straight ahead. "You're right," I said. "Later, when I'm home, we can lie in bed and talk for hours. In the meantime, I'm just calling to apologize and tell you that I love you. That's all."

This time, I could have wandered over to McDonald's, purchased the least bad thing on the menu, and wandered back before she answered.

"Rachel, I'm not so sure about us anymore. I didn't want to say it on the phone, but my silence was beginning to feel deceptive. I haven't decided anything, but you have a right to know that I'm questioning the relationship. We can discuss the reasons when you get here." She paused. "So, are you still at Sonia's and what are you doing?"

Until that moment, I hadn't decided whether to tell her I was still in Nicaragua or en route to Mexico, but suddenly (finally) the idea of lying seemed despicable. "I'm in the Dallas airport," I said.

"Oh." She sounded surprised. "You're actually coming home? I mean I wasn't expecting you for at least another month, maybe longer. Wow, I don't think I'm ready. I can't believe I'm saying this, but is there any way you could postpone it for a while?"

A young female Hare Krishna with long blond hair was approaching me with a pamphlet in her outstretched hands. I shook my head, but she was used to that. So in Spanish, I told her to go away, that I needed to pay attention to my phone call. She looked confused, then turned toward the elegantly dressed businessman who told her to fuck off. She murmured something in Sanskrit, a blessing or a curse, but then she left.

"Sorry about that," I said into the phone. "Listen, in a way this is perfect. You don't have to be ready. I'm definitely coming home, but not right now. First, I'm going to Mexico. I need to rest there for a while. I haven't fully recovered from my illness."

"You're still sick?"

It was the concern in her voice that woke me from my dream. It was as if I'd been hypnotized to think I could put everything in my life on hold while I searched for peace and happiness or at least some equanimity, and then suddenly like the sound of snapping fingers, I heard my lover's voice and I was wide awake. Staring at the enormity of my potential loss.

"A little," I admitted, "but I'm getting better every day." How could I have risked losing the one person who put me before everyone else, who knew me better than I knew myself, who'd hitched her life to mine expecting only that I would love and cherish her the way she'd cherished me?

"What are your symptoms?" she asked.

"Nothing that bad." I was desperate now. "Vickie, listen, you were right about almost everything. I had no business going to Nicaragua, but I was having what you termed in your letter a spiritual tantrum. Anyway, whatever it was, it's over. Ironically, I feel more at peace than I have in years. And I'm thinking much more clearly."

"Have you seen a doctor?"

"Vickie, could you forget about my illness for a second and tell me if anything I've just said makes any difference?"

She made a soft plaintive sound, as if she couldn't bear to hurt me. "I don't know. I'll have to think about it. In the meantime, I have to go to bed. Tomorrow, I have patients scheduled every thirty minutes from eight in the morning until six at night."

"Vickie, wait! No matter what you've been thinking, we're not irrevocably fucked. We can pull this out. The most important thing is that we love each other." Before she could disagree, I told her I was heading to Zihuatanejo. "I'll try to find that little place we rented, the one with the pink balcony overlooking the bay. Come and stay with me. I just want to talk, that's all."

I could almost hear her shaking her head. "I don't think that's a good idea."

"Why not?"

"Because you're a lawyer and lawyers are trained to influence people. I need to think about this on my own. I'm sorry, Rachel, but it's late and I have to go."

"Okay, I'll call you from Mexico."

Vickie sighed. "Do me a favor and wait a month. I need more time to think."

My heart was aching, but I kept it light. "I thought that was my line."

"Things change."

I was beyond exhausted. My brain was shutting down. With my last couple of IQ points, I said, "I'll wait if you promise not to break up with me in your head before we speak."

"Rachel, I have to go." She hesitated. "All right, it's a deal. Take care of yourself." And then she hung up.

I replaced the receiver and then sank to a sitting position with my back against the wall. I had a month to heal and figure out how to make things right with Vickie. At the same time, I'd have to accept the possibility that despite how hard I tried, I might not be successful. A tall order, but I wasn't exactly a novice. I would practice what I'd learned in Nicaragua, the art of hopeful resignation. For the past two months, I'd been training with the pros.

PART III:
LEARNING TO KAYAK

CHAPTER SEVENTEEN

Six weeks ago, when I arrived here in Zihuatanejo, my goals were very modest: Sleep as much as possible, eat well, and try not to panic. My spirits were good, but in my life so far, there had never been a time when all three of what I'd always considered to be the essential ingredients for happiness—good health, a loving relationship and a satisfying career—seemed to be in such short supply. If I could, I would replenish them all and if I couldn't, then at least one or two of them. In the plus column, I'd landed in a safe comfortable place (the same studio apartment overlooking the water that Vickie and I had rented three years earlier), I had resources, and I had time. *Time.* A precious commodity now that I'd slowed down and had nothing to do, and almost irrelevant when I was a public defender juggling more than a hundred felony cases.

Each morning for the first two weeks, I woke up as late as possible, strolled to the nearest market, about a quarter of a mile away, bought the healthiest food I could find, strolled back, rested, and then made a hearty breakfast. After that, I napped a few hours, ate a light lunch, and then went out on my balcony to gaze at the junction of water and sky, contemplating how it was that I'd ended up here. I had no epiphanies, no world-shattering insights, but I didn't really expect any. Like a sensible girl on a blind date, I was satisfied just to be having a pleasant time getting to know someone I might actually want to see again.

During the late afternoons and evenings, I read the five novels I'd bought in the Dallas airport and started writing letters. The first was to Allen, then to Liz, then Sonia, Maggie, a few other friends in Boulder, Donald and Ray at the public defender's office, and finally when I was ready, to Emily.

Emily, I wrote, *I'll tell you all about my experiences in Nicaragua when I see you. Right now, though, I'm living in a small apartment in Zihuatanejo, a fishing town on the west coast of Mexico about one hundred and fifty miles north of Acapulco. My apartment has a bright pink balcony that overlooks the ocean. You would love it, except sometimes, depending on the weather, the sound of the waves crashing against the rocks is so loud it's impossible to sleep. Those are the nights I end up on my balcony marveling at all that roiling wildness and feeling small and vulnerable, an experience I used to find disquieting when I was still planning to save the world, one defendant at a time. Back then, I know you loved and admired me (as I did you), but I think you'd like me better now. As for you, I can't imagine all the changes you've been forced to make, but I suspect you've made them gracefully, the way you always have. Which makes me wonder, between us, who was the dreamer and who was the realist? Actually, I no longer care. As you said, we both did the best we could.*

Please forgive me for being out of contact. I know you understand, but I'm still sorry for the blackout. You'll be glad to know that I've made real progress toward accepting the verdict in your case. You were right; I suffer less, although

I still feel sad. But I can stand it now. So of course I want to hear everything about your life inside "the gray bar motel." As soon as I return to Colorado, I'll get down to see you and from then on, you can count on me to visit regularly. In the meantime, write me care of my landlady.

Your friend,

Rachel

After about a week and a half, when I got tired of reading, writing and napping, I began wandering around the neighborhood. In the three years since I'd been there, nothing much had changed. A couple of buildings were under construction to make fancy condos, but most of the houses were still either rentals like mine, small storefront businesses (food markets, tiny tortilla "factories," one-room restaurants) or plain humble homes where the locals lived. Although there was poverty here, it didn't seem as desperate as Managua's. The markets had plenty of food, the currency was stable and the country wasn't wasting all its resources fighting a civil war.

Tourism, of course, accounted for much of the local prosperity—take away the threat of being shot or kidnapped and tourists will flock anywhere there's a nice beach. I imagined that as soon as the United States stopped trying to destroy Nicaragua, as soon as we'd bent it to our will, developers would begin eyeing the possibilities. After you've finished bicycling through Vietnam (visiting the famous Vietcong war tunnels), relax at one of our new five-star Hiltons on the beautiful rugged coast of Nicaragua. Or better yet, buy your own little island on Lake Nicaragua, the second largest lake in Latin America!

By the beginning of the third week, I was longing to join my fellow tourists at the shore—it was all rocks below my apartment—and decided I was well enough for the two-mile trek to the bay. At first, I packed enough provisions for a walkabout in the desert, but before I got out the door, I realized my bag was much too heavy and that I had to jettison nine-tenths of the contents, retaining only the essentials: food, water, towel, pillow and a Windbreaker in case of a typhoon.

I had to stop and rest a few times before I made it, but when I waded into the warm turquoise water, I felt ecstatic, like a kid from the Midwest who'd only read about the ocean and was now finally able to experience it firsthand. For a while, I simply jumped around like an idiot, whirling in circles, splashing, shouting and laughing. After about ten minutes, I began to swim. When I couldn't lift my arms for one more stroke, I dog paddled to shore, curled up on my towel and went to sleep.

Within a couple of days, I could hike to and from the bay without resting until I'd reached my destination. I wasn't my old Amazon self yet, but I walked with a newfound confidence, no longer scanning ahead for a possible place to stop and wait for the dizziness to pass. Each day, I tried to walk a little faster, never pushing too hard, mindful that in the old days I wouldn't have even considered this to be exercise. By trial and error, though, I'd learned that the path to health was not the steep inviting trail that always beckoned, but the slow meandering one that didn't. I may have been a burned-out adrenaline junkie, but I wasn't suicidal; I could see that getting high and coming down, even one more time, might kill me. Which would have greatly interfered with my current plans to live a long and even life, one that for now seemed a bit murky but would have to include moments of frivolousness along with a sense of purpose.

Often when I walked, I thought about Sonia and her friends, wondering how they were coping and what new schemes they were hatching to make a few extra *cordobas*. And, of course, I hoped that Sonia's nephew was somehow still alive, that he'd managed to escape from the Contra camp in Honduras where he'd been held captive, or that he'd been wounded and had found refuge in some Good Samaritan's hut until he was well enough to travel. I thought of a dozen scenarios, none of them likely, but so what? There's no downside to hope. Bad news hurts just as much whether you wished for a different outcome or not, and if the news is good, well then.

***

One morning when I reached the bay (I always got there early, around seven thirty), I was surprised to see another person sitting at the water's edge. Until then, I'd always had the place to myself, at least for the first few hours. The American and European tourists generally showed up around ten, lugging one or two kids, a few chairs, large woven mats and brightly colored beach umbrellas. The Mexican tourists, on the other hand, preferred the afternoon, arriving around one thirty or two in parties of ten or more and carrying boom boxes and huge Styrofoam coolers. The townspeople, of course, straggled in at the end of the workday and stayed to watch the sun go down, a spectacular show that often elicited applause.

The person was alone and sitting cross-legged on the sand. I watched him for about five minutes, waiting for him to move, to turn slightly and acknowledge me. I stood and waited, but he remained motionless. Curious, I walked a little closer and could see that his eyes were closed and that his hands were resting on his thighs. He was a few years older than me, had obviously once been handsome, but was now a little too soft and pudgy. His clothes were classic—faded tie-dyed T-shirt and khaki pants cut off just below the knees. Although he had long blond hair that he wore in a neat ponytail, something about his bearing suggested he was more than just an old hippie living in a bus nearby. As I edged even closer, I noticed that his face was badly sunburned, especially the top of his forehead where his hairline had receded.

Despite his rigid posture, he looked extremely comfortable as if he could sit like that forever and without any outward sign die in the same position. Nothing seemed to affect him, neither the sun on his sunburn, the wind ruffling his hair, nor the waves crashing irregularly a few feet away. He seemed immoveable, like a rock. I stood on the sand and watched, feeling more than merely curious. I was intrigued. No, I was envious. Whatever he was doing, I wanted it.

Finally, about ten minutes later, he turned his head and nodded. "I thought someone was there."

I took a step backward. "I'm sorry if I disturbed you."

He laughed as if I'd uttered an absurdity. "Not at all. You were very quiet, very respectful. I just felt your energy, that's all. It was nice." He had a lovely speaking voice and I wondered if he was an actor or some kind of professional speaker. I might have guessed a lawyer, but not with that hair.

I walked over to where he was sitting and we introduced ourselves. His name was Daniel Morrison and he'd arrived a few days ago from California where he taught physics at Stanford.

"I get to look like this," he said, smiling, "because I have tenure."

I told him I'd been living here for a couple of weeks, and before that, I'd spent some time in Nicaragua.

He made a sympathetic sound. "That must have been heavy."

"It was," I said.

"Do you meditate?"

I shook my head. "No, but I'd like to. Is it difficult?"

He looked me up and down, assessing me in some way. "What do you do for a living?"

"I used to be a criminal defense attorney."

"Ah." He nodded and then patted the sand beside him, motioning me to sit down. "Now then," he said, clearly in lecture mode, "there are many different meditation techniques, but the one I most often practice is a very simple one. And for people like us with great big unruly minds, the simpler the better. Eh?" He waited until I nodded, and then continued. "So, with this practice, you close your eyes and count your breaths. When you get to ten, just start over again." He smiled and shrugged.

"That's it?" I asked.

"Pretty much. When you become lost in thought, which will happen over and over again, simply note that you've been thinking and then go back to counting." He paused. "Would you like to try it?"

"Sure, how about thirty minutes?"

He hesitated. "Well, it's not quite as easy as it sounds. Let's start conservatively with ten minutes."

"Okay," I said, and copied the position of his body—legs crossed, back straight, hands on thighs. Piece of cake, I thought.

"I'll tell you when the time is up," he murmured.

After a while, I figured he'd changed his mind and decided to go for the full thirty minutes. Later, when my legs were numb and my back was beginning to ache, I figured he was testing me, waiting for me to cry uncle. No way, I thought, and resolved to keep going until I fell over. Eventually, I wondered if he'd fallen asleep and took a quick peek at him. But no, he was still meditating, still oozing that peace and serenity I coveted. I went back to counting my breaths. One, two, three, fourteen…Finally, he tapped my arm.

"Time's up," he said.

"Whew! How long did we sit?"

He looked down at his watch. "Twelve and a half minutes."

"Jesus H. Christ," I said, and we both laughed.

He stood up. "See you tomorrow?" he asked, reaching out a hand to help me to my feet. There was nothing flirtatious in the gesture; he was looking for a friend, not a lover.

"I'll look forward to it."

Since then, we've been meeting every morning at seven thirty. It took me a week to build up to thirty minutes. Lately, we've been sitting about an hour. Occasionally, I'll have a moment, no longer than a couple of seconds, when I feel the kind of peace that I've been chasing. *Gotcha*, I'll think, and then of course I'll lose it. The trick, I'm beginning to understand, is not to hold on to anything, even if it's exactly what I want. Better to just watch it all go by.

Often, after we've finished sitting, Daniel and I will talk about our lives. At first, I told him only general things about Nicaragua, the current situation, the brigade I'd joined, the people I'd met in the *barrio*. He was a good listener, asking questions only for the purpose of clarifying something he didn't understand.

One morning, I ended up telling him about the explosion on the road to Jalapa, what we'd seen, and what we'd done to save the surviving soldiers.

"It's the last thing I think about at night before I fall asleep," I said.

We sat quietly and watched a squadron of brown pelicans diving for their breakfast, their low hoarse squawks as soothing as a lullaby. It was a beautiful peaceful windless morning. After ten or fifteen minutes, Daniel said, "The last thing I think about at night is the first thing I think about in the morning. Gin." He paused, waiting for a reaction. When I simply nodded, he made a face and I guessed he was debating whether to tell me more.

"Hey, you don't have to tell me anything," I assured him. "It's not quid pro quo. But in case you forgot, I was a criminal defense attorney for twelve years. There's nothing I haven't heard. Unless you sawed your wife's head off with a Swiss Army knife in front of the children, I'm unlikely to have a reaction."

Daniel started to laugh. "No, nothing out of the ordinary. Just the usual story you might hear a dozen times at a typical Saturday night AA meeting."

"Well then," I said.

Daniel had been a boy wonder since grade school and had graduated college at nineteen. By the time he was twenty-four, he had his PhD and was teaching physics at the University of California at Davis. By twenty-nine, he had become a full professor at Stanford. A few years later, he published a popular book about spirituality and the new physics and became well known and highly respected as a speaker at both academic as well as New Age conferences. From then on, until he was thirty-six, he wrote a book a year, each one more successful than the last. On his thirty-third birthday, he married a lovely professor of astronomy, who also taught at Stanford. Neither of them wanted children; they had their careers and each other. It was more than enough.

"Things couldn't have been better," he said. "My life was a dream come true." He chuckled. "Except I kept waiting for everything to fall apart, for the whole ball of yarn to unravel. It was simply too perfect. Nothing stays the same although I wanted it to. Oh, how I wanted it to. But I knew it wouldn't, that it was just a matter of time, so I kind of helped it along, gave it a little push, figuring at least I'd have a hand in destroying it. Sounds crazy, doesn't it?"

"Not really," I said.

He eyed me sideways, not sure whether to believe me. "Anyway," he continued, "I started drinking, and slowly but surely managed to lose everything I'd been so afraid of losing. My wife was the hardest; she stuck with me until a few years ago. Finally one Sunday afternoon, we went to a faculty party where I got plastered and dove into the host's swimming pool. Unfortunately, the pool had recently been drained and I ended up in the hospital with two broken arms, a broken ankle and a fractured skull. When I finally returned home, my wife had packed her bags and left. She wrote me a note saying she couldn't stand it anymore, that she hoped—for my sake—that my next suicide attempt would be a hundred percent successful."

"I'm really sorry," I said.

"Yeah well. Anyway, to make a long story short, I drank for another couple of years until one day about four months ago, my colleagues burst into my classroom, ordered the students out, and held an intervention on the spot. As a result, I was sent directly to a ninety-day treatment program and placed on an indefinite leave of absence until I'm able to convince the university I can remain sober for the rest of my life, or at least the rest of my teaching life. So, that's why I'm here meditating. Mind-obedience school in the morning, AA meetings in the afternoon and evening."

I was silent for a while, digesting everything Daniel had told me. Somewhere in the back of my mind, I was aware that my three-month sabbatical from the public defender's office was over and that I needed to call Larry Hanover and tell him officially that I wouldn't be returning. "Do you miss teaching?" I asked.

Daniel shook his head. "Not really. I haven't been very good at it for a long time. Entertaining, perhaps, but not very good. The truth is I'm happier than I've been in years. No, better than happy, content. Happiness is too tricky. The only thing I regret is how much pain I caused my wife. She's about to get remarried and I hope this time it works out for her." He paused. "As for me, I'm no longer waiting for the other shoe to drop. So I guess you could say I'm at peace."

I stood up and shook out my towel. He stood up too, looking hesitant and a little shy, like maybe I wouldn't want to be his friend anymore. I put my arm around his shoulder.

"See you tomorrow?" I asked.

He smiled and nodded. "You got a date, sister."

***

A few days before I intended to call Vickie, I started feeling anxious and told Daniel I was afraid she might have already decided to end the relationship, that I didn't want to talk her into coming here if that was truly the case, but that I also didn't want to give up too easily.

We were sitting in our usual spot at the water's edge and were about to start meditating. Daniel scratched the beard he was trying to grow and looked very uncomfortable, as if he had a crick in his neck.

"Well, since I'm the original nothing-left-to-lose guy, you definitely don't want my advice."

I sighed. "No, I suppose not." Then I stared at him and shook my head. "You know, I've tried to get used to it, but I think you should lose the beard as well, Daniel."

He looked surprised. "Too Robinson Crusoe?"

"Too crazy homeless veteran living in a Dumpster."

"Oh. That's not exactly the look I was after."

I sat up a little straighter and placed my hands on my thighs. "I didn't think so. Well, shall we meditate?"

He nodded. After a couple of minutes, he murmured, "If you do end up losing her, can you let her go?"

I sat quietly and thought about it. Eventually, I whispered, "Yes, I think so."

"That's good. That's very good. Well then, *mi amiga*, see you in an hour."

"*À tout a l'heure.*"

"Ooh, French, very fancy," he whispered.

"Ssh, I'm meditating."

***

For the next couple of days, I tried calling our house in the evenings, but Vickie was never there. I left simple messages saying only that I would try again. I could have paged her at the hospital, but I didn't want to compete for her attention. Then I thought about her schedule and decided the best time to call would be around seven in the morning when she usually ate her breakfast. During the workweek, Vickie had trained herself to wake up every morning at five fifteen. After a quick cup of tea, she practiced yoga, then took a shower and ate a bowl of oatmeal. By seven thirty, she was out the door.

My next task was finding an available phone at that time of day. The only pay phones I'd seen were in the larger markets, none of which opened before eight. It took a while, but I discovered that the proprietor of Reuben's World Famous Hamburgers, a nondescript little hamburger stand down the hill, tucked between two construction sites, owned a phone and for a small fee was happy to let me use it. Since Reuben and his wife Frieda have five little kids all under the age of ten, there's no way they can sleep past dawn. Besides, if the kids don't wake them, the roosters do. Unlike their slipshod cousins in Nicaragua, the roosters here are loud and extremely punctual. No one in the neighborhood needs an alarm clock. The birds start crowing at six and won't stop until everyone is wide-awake.

The first time I tried calling her in the morning, Vickie immediately picked up the phone. My heart was racing, but I willed myself to sound calm and unaffected. Just don't be a lawyer, I told myself.

"Hi babe," I said.

"There you are," she replied. "I was wondering when I'd actually get to speak with you. Sorry I've been gone in the evenings. I've been practicing my Eskimo rolls at the reservoir."

I was standing at the window watching an old VW van narrowly miss two chickens wandering across the road. It took a couple of seconds before her words registered. "Eskimo rolls? Like in kayaking?"

"Exactly. I've got a bombproof roll on my right, but my left side is still hit or miss. It's good enough for class two water, but in a couple of days I'm heading for the Blue which has at least a couple of class three stretches."

I shook my head as if to clear it. "Wow. When did you start kayaking?"

"Oh, I guess I started a few weeks after you left. I'm crazy about it." She laughed. "You know, I think I finally understand why you love climbing. Even though it's a little dangerous, it's just so much fun."

"Wow," I repeated, feeling stunned and slightly queasy. Sometime in the last few months, my careful girlfriend had morphed into a thrill-seeking stranger and was doing things I would never in my most feverish hallucinations have imagined her doing. Sitting on a large poky raft with a pair of binoculars maybe, but kayaking?

"Rachel, are you still there?"

"Yes, I'm—I'm just surprised, that's all. Kayaking? It seems so unlike you."

She was silent for a moment. "Let's see, I wonder if I can say this without sounding petulant. Oh, never mind. Anyway, when you left and I wasn't sure when or if you'd ever return, I decided to try something totally new and different, something that wouldn't remind me of you, or me and you. Does that make sense?"

I nodded. "Yeah," I said, "it makes total sense."

"Huh." As if she'd been expecting a little back talk and I'd curtsied instead. "Well anyway, I'm glad you called because I'm coming in less than a week. I'll be there next Monday around five in the afternoon. Are you staying at that apartment we rented three years ago?"

"You're coming? That's…great! What made you change your mind?" I sank down onto a lumpy purple couch, the only piece of furniture in Reuben and Frieda's living room. Frieda was breastfeeding one of her children a few feet away from me. I nodded to her and she smiled back.

"It was actually my therapist's idea," Vickie explained. "We've been arguing about it for weeks. She thinks that after nine years I owe it to you—to the relationship—to sit down and talk with you in person."

"I see." I closed my eyes, counted three slow breaths, and then opened them. "Don't come," I said.

"What?"

"Cancel your reservation. I don't want you coming here because your therapist is making you. You can only come if you have at least a little hope that we can pull this out. Otherwise, I don't want to see you. I'm not as desperate as I was a month ago." While I spoke, one of Frieda's three-year-old twins climbed onto my lap and smeared what I hoped was orange marmalade across my clean white T-shirt. I shook my head and sighed.

"Okay now wait a minute," Vickie said, sounding flustered. "First of all, my therapist can't make me do anything. Second of all, I happen to agree with her, that I do owe you the courtesy of a face-to-face meeting. Besides, I've kept my promise and haven't completely made up my mind. To be honest, I've tried to, but I couldn't." She paused. "Maybe I made it sound like it was all her idea so you wouldn't expect anything."

I shrugged. "I don't expect anything. I hope, of course, but I don't expect. Daniel says the difference—"

"Who's Daniel?" she interrupted.

"The guy I meditate with every morning. At the bay."

"You meditate?"

"Uh-huh, these days for about an hour, although once in a while we'll go a little longer. It just depends."

"You're kidding, right?"

"No, I'm completely serious." Another of Frieda's children had climbed onto the back of the couch and was trying to braid my hair. I leaned forward in an attempt to discourage her, but she put her arms around my neck and held onto me. Meanwhile, I still had the other kid in my lap and a third one grabbing at my ankles. I looked over at Frieda and saw she was grinning: welcome to my world. Not in a thousand years, I thought.

"So you've really taken up meditation," Vickie was saying. "That's amazing. Well, so what's it like?"

"Hmm, let me think." I pictured Vickie's face—those miraculous cheekbones, her dark brown eyes—but the image was a little blurry, like a photograph of someone in motion. Instead of sitting here covered in children, I wanted to be lying down next to her, our legs intertwined and my head resting on her chest. "Actually, I'd say it's a lot like kayaking."

"Is that right?" I could tell she was smiling in spite of herself. "How so?"

"Well for starters," I was making this up as fast as I could, "each requires the ability to sit still and remain calm while you're going through the rapids."

"That's very creative. How's your Eskimo roll?"

I groaned. "It's hit or miss on both sides."

"Tell me about it."

And we both laughed, a lovely sound that I used to take for granted. I swallowed hard, reminded myself to stay in the present. Before I could say anything else, Vickie asked about Daniel.

"Well," I said, "he used to teach physics at Stanford and has written a number of bestselling books on the subject. Unfortunately, he also had a bad drinking problem. After his life fell apart, he went through rehab and now he's down here for a while. He has a very interesting take on the world. I think you'll like him."

"Does that mean you want me to come?"

"Of course I do. It's—" I paused, the lawyer in me searching for the perfect upbeat ending, the words that might just make a difference.

"Time?" she supplied. "I agree. See you next Monday."

***

On Sunday afternoon, my landlady came by with a letter from Emily. I sat down at the kitchen table and turned the plain white envelope over a few times in my hands. The return address gave no clue as to her true location. All it said was E. Watkins, followed by an innocuous sounding street address in Canon City, and then a series of numbers, Emily's numerical identification in the Colorado Department of Corrections. Finally I opened it. The letter was written on lined paper that had been carefully torn out of a notebook.

Dear Rachel,

Greetings from the Gray Bar Motel! I can't tell you how delighted I was to receive your letter. To tell you the truth, when I saw your handwriting on the envelope, I burst out crying. I'd readily accepted that I would be here for the rest of my life, but still hadn't reconciled myself to never hearing from you again. Thank God I don't have to. But please don't feel compelled to write more often than is comfortable. A single letter goes a long way here at the Gray Bar. I'm just grateful that you wrote.

First of all, I'm so relieved that you're safe and well. Someday, I'd like to hear what happened in Nicaragua. It obviously affected you. After Vickie told me when I'd called that you'd gone down there, I started reading everything I could find about the history of Central America, but as you can imagine, the library here is quite limited. In fact, I've been wondering if there's any way to advocate for better funding without getting myself in trouble—always the bottom line here.

Yes, I've been forced to make a few changes, none of which (at least so far) have altered the core of who I am. Ultimately, in order to survive, I will have to learn a whole new language and culture. Luckily, my cellmate, Linda Sue, has taken me under her wing. She just turned thirty, but has been a resident since she was twenty-four. Like me, she's a lifer—her boyfriend shot a gas station attendant during a robbery, which netted them thirty-seven dollars and an armload of Hershey bars. Thanks to her sound advice, I've managed to avoid most of the pitfalls that await newly incarcerated "girls." (Rachel, please tell me if you want more details. The last thing I want to do is bore you. Some pen pals, like my friend Alice, have expressed a predilection for long monologues describing who, what, when and where, which I'm happy to write. But I'm guessing that like me, you'd prefer a shorter, more "poetic" letter. Let me know. In the meantime, I'll trust my instincts and err on the side of brevity.)

I've already begun to think about a potential long-range project here, a hospice program for dying inmates. Since I started working in the infirmary, I've met three young women who have AIDS. What a nightmare! Although more and more inmates are likely to be affected, no one seems to be planning for it. I know this sounds altruistic, but it really isn't. My greatest fear since arriving is not that I'll be attacked or hurt in any way, but rather that I'll end up having lived a life that had no purpose. Which means, for very selfish reasons, I need to find one. Until then, in the immortal words of Robert Crumb, I'll keep on truckin'.

Your friend,

Emily

After reading the letter twice, I placed it on the kitchen table next to a beautiful abalone shell I'd found the day before. Although the room was much too warm, I didn't move to turn on the overhead fan. Instead, I closed my eyes and marveled at Emily's extraordinary ability to adapt and, given her sheltered existence, her surprising wealth of knowledge. For instance, how the hell had she known about Robert Crumb? I shook my head and smiled. My Emily, still full of surprises. If anyone could flourish in a women's penitentiary, it would be her. At the very least, with a little help from her friends, she would endure.

Which reminded me. I glanced at the little Mexican calendar I'd taped to my refrigerator and realized it was time to send another installment of money to Sonia.

"It's called *tsedaka*," Daniel said, when I told him I'd decided to send my Nicaraguan host twenty dollars a month for as long as I was able.

Daniel, who isn't Jewish but has studied many of the world's religions, says that the Hebrew word *tsedaka* refers to the Jewish religious principle of charity, but its root word is the same as in the Hebrew term designating justice. In fact, he says, the term is generally understood to mean an obligation.

"Think of it," he said, "as an obligation you owe as a member of the human race. These days, I give money to the local AA chapter, which needs better coffee and more comfortable chairs." He paused. "I think it's okay that the giver benefits too."

But it's really not *tsedaka*. Well, maybe it is, but to me it's much simpler. Sonia is a friend of mine. She allowed me to stay in her home for as long as I wished; she took care of me when I was ill; she has less means to make a living than I do. Ergo, I will send her money (but not too much or she'll return it) to ease her life a little and, if I know Sonia, the lives of those around her.

***

When it was time, I took a cab to the airport and waited in the terminal for Vickie's plane to arrive. Half an hour later, I watched through a huge spotless window as her tiny commuter plane landed and taxied to a stop in front of me. Within minutes, passengers began emerging from a door next to the cockpit. Vickie was the fourth one out. She was wearing a white sleeveless blouse and matching cotton pants. Even from a distance, I could see the muscles on her arms from kayaking. Her jet-black hair shone in the brilliant sunlight.

I took a deep breath. Well, let's give it a go, I thought.

We hugged for a long time.

"You look terrific," I whispered.

"So do you," she answered, and then stepped back for a more serious appraisal. "You're too thin, but your eyes are clear and your color is good."

"So is yours," I joked, embarrassed by her obvious albeit professional concern.

After dropping her suitcase off at the apartment, we hiked to the bay and waited for the sun to begin its celebrated descent into the Pacific Ocean. We sat facing the horizon, glad to have such an easy excuse to postpone the inevitable, the moment when we looked into each other's eyes and possibly saw the opposite of what we felt. Later, tomorrow or the next day, we would do it. Right now, though, how pleasant to be sitting with our shoulders not quite touching, lobbing safe and noncommittal words back and forth across the net.

As the sun slowly set in front of us, we talked about our friends in Boulder, the heat in Nicaragua, the gear you need to kayak, my current diet, etcetera. When the sunset show was over, we applauded with the rest of the audience, brushed the sand off our clothes, and started walking back. We took our time, stopping at a little market to look for oatmeal which they didn't have, and settling on a ripe papaya, some apples and a couple of bananas. As soon as we walked through the door, I could see Vickie eyeing the double bed with suspicion.

I shrugged. "I'm sorry. There's no room for another bed. Even if my landlady had one."

She pretended it was no big deal. "It's fine, Rachel. We're adults."

She wandered around the room, picking things up and putting them down. I had to resist the urge to stop her. After her fourth or fifth circuit, I began to miss my solitary life.

"Would you like some juice or water?" I asked.

She shook her head. "No thank you."

I showed her the letter I'd received from Emily and the books I'd bought in the Dallas airport. We were running out of neutral topics. Finally, although it was barely nine o'clock, we both said we were tired. A few minutes later, wearing our T-shirts and panties, we crawled into bed and lay face up staring at the ceiling. It wasn't really even dark yet.

"Dear God," I muttered, "please, please, please let us sleep."

Vickie started to laugh and then so did I, which cut some of the awkward tension. After a while, I heard her breathing change, and sometime after that, I fell asleep as well.

At around one in the morning, Vickie bolted straight up, pulling the sheet away from me.

"What the hell is that?" she asked.

"What?" I mumbled, trying to pull a little of the sheet back.

"That loud crashing sound. My God!"

I listened for a moment. "Oh, I guess I've gotten used to it. It's just the waves crashing on the rocks below us. Mother Nature on a well-deserved rampage. She waits until the summer when there aren't so many tourists." I put my hand on Vickie's shoulder. "Come on, let me spoon you."

Vickie sat there for a moment, shaking her head, but finally she nodded.

When she'd settled back down on her side, I slid my body next to hers and pulled her gently toward me. After a couple of seconds, she stopped resisting and even scooted back an inch until her body was pressed snugly into mine. It felt so right, which of course didn't mean a thing.

A few minutes later she whispered, "This isn't a done deal, Rachel."

I inhaled the smell of her hair, the sweet familiar scent of her skin. "I know."

"You risked us."

"I know." Another apology would be useless, possibly even counterproductive. "The defendant pleads not guilty by reason of insanity."

She'd obviously expected something more contrite. "Hah! That's so pathetic, Rachel. Jurors hate that defense."

I shrugged. "Well, if that's all you've got…"

She struggled half-heartedly to twist away from me. "Oh please. How many cases have you ever won using that defense?"

"None, but there's always a first."

"Give me a break." She shook her head and sighed, then settled back against me. "You lawyers never give up, do you?"

I considered the last three months, where I'd been and where I'd ended up.

Sometimes we do, I thought, but not for very long.

ACKNOWLEDGMENTS

Thank you, first of all, to Allen Rinzler, who edited my novel through four drafts. You made the book at least fifty percent better. Thanks also to Katherine V. Forrest, my editor at Bella Books, who helped me add the last important touches to the novel. Thank you also to Bella Books for loving my novel and wanting to publish it.

Thanks to Ellen Klaver, who spoke to me about her time in Nicaragua and who loaned me her book about Ben Linder (*The Death of Ben Linder* by Joan Kruckewitt). I'm ashamed to say that I still haven't returned the book. Sorry. Thanks also to Ruth and Moises Rodriguez who also spoke with me about their life in Nicaragua during the eighties.

Thank you to THE BOULDER-JALAPA FRIENDSHIP CITY PROJECT, which gave me my first opportunity in 1985 to experience Nicaragua, especially Jalapa and its surrounding areas.

I want to acknowledge Peter Davis's wonderful book, *Where is Nicaragua?* The book helped me to remember and understand my experiences in Nicaragua. I also want to acknowledge Susan Meiselas's gorgeous book of photographs, entitled *Nicaragua*, which contains the most amazing, moving, painful, graphic images of Nicaragua shot right before, during, and immediately after the triumph in July 1979. I referred to these pictures over and over again to stimulate my memory and to inspire me.

I also want to acknowledge an article about Nicaragua in the *Boulder Sunday Camera Magazine* written by Julia McCray-Goldsmith—I stole the chicken story from her.

Thank you, Miryam Obando, for being my host in Managua for six weeks in 1987. I don't know where you are now, or whether you're still alive. I hope you are well. I'm sorry I didn't stay in touch, but I was very sick for a number of years after returning to the United States.

Special thanks to Jamie Ash and Kat Duff for letting me read each chapter to you out loud. Thanks to all the extraordinary women in Taos who supported, encouraged and cheered me on, especially April Werner and Jean Thompson.

Thank you, Daniela Kuper, my dear friend who believes in this book and who continually tells me how good it is. Thank you for being such a great supportive friend. It means the world to me.

Thanks also to Natalie Goldberg who, by example, encouraged me to finally quit my job and write full time.

Thanks to Susie Schneider, Curtis Ramsay, Sawnie Morris, Brian Shields, Deborah Winer, Jude Kaftan, Bernice Winer, Kristin Marra, Bert Nieslanik and Leslie Haase who read various drafts of my novel and gave me feedback and encouragement. Your positive comments kept me going more than you'll ever know.

Thank you, Sue Larson, for housesitting for me in Boulder so that I could get away to New Mexico to write.

A huge sad thanks to Molly Gierasch who tried so hard to pick up the pieces when I returned home sick from Nicaragua in 1987. Thank you for everything, Molly.

And finally, my heartfelt thanks to Leslie Haase, who loves and supports me, and understands more than I could have ever hoped what writing means to me.